Also by

EIREANN CORRIGAN

Splintering

You Remind Me of You

EIREANN CORRIGAN

SCHOLASTIC PRESS

N E W   Y O R K

CIP Data Available

ISBN-13: 978-0-439-83243-4

ISBN-10: 0-439-83243-8

12 11 10 9 8 7 6 5 4 3 2 1   7 8 9 10 11/0

Printed in the United States of America   40

First printing, April 2007

The text type was set in 12-pt. Apollo regular

Book design by Richard Amari

for JT Hardaway-McMillen and Aletheia Watts,
who will inherit keys to the kingdom

ACKNOWLEDGEMENTS

This book is built on pure fiction and a little bit of local legend. Still, I am tremendously grateful for the support and thoughtfulness of the faculty, staff, students, and parents at Rutgers Preparatory School.

For the past year, I've spent hours each week with a unique and delinquent collection of writers. Michael Abreu, Sasha Bharrat, Matt Chapman, Katie Clark, Joanna Harmonosky, Shikirra Hines, Jordan Hollander, Caron Johnson, Jess Leeds, Jimit Patel, Halcyon Person, Soma Plotnikov, Nishil Raval, Joe Sancio, and Arielle Sobov all helped shape this book.

Thanks to Anne Glennon, Steve Loy, Pat Neary, and my enormous and amazing family — they have helped shape me.

David Levithan has guided me through the treacherous road of paragraphs without line breaks. As usual, I've leaned on his professional expertise and great faith in my writing.

And thanks to my arsenal of book experts: Christine Corrigan, John Kendall, and Kimberly Paone.

All my love to everyone who happily haunts my little world, especially: Sara Belyea, Win Butler, Daniel Cantor, Ann Kansfield, Eli Kaufman, Sarah Kendall, Stacy McMillen, Meadow Sakovics, Nina Stotler, Brian Pearl, Josh and Morgan Powell, Diane Salzberger, Chris Steib, Shawn Watts, and Bev Weshnak. Also: Shanky Cedarbottom and Sumo Pandabandit.

Finally my whole heart to Jeff Salzberger — my description of the world, my direction home.

CHAPTER 1

Understand I didn't earn the key. I wouldn't have even been considered. That key is something a guy like me would only hear about twenty years later, at some craptastic reunion, long after the secret currents running under the surface of Caramoor Academy stopped dragging past me. We'd all be back, hunched over the same pocked tables in the dining hall, cutting boiled chicken with plastic knives, and someone would start asking, "Who held the key our year? Who was it?" The way we interrogate each other now: "Who did Mr. Kirkman catch jerking off in the music building bathroom?" "Isaiah did how many hits?" Mischievously. Or sinisterly. I've rarely been close enough to tell.

But this year, it's me. I have the key. A junior. And I hadn't even heard of it — didn't know what it was until last July when I held it in my hand, after Ethan had kicked me toward his room to grab quarters for the meters downtown. Ethan used to keep his spare change in a pewter stein on top of his dresser. The stein says, *Greetings from Mount Rushmore*, but my brother's never been to Mount Rushmore. As far as I know, I mean. He could be there now. Beneath the heavy rattle of coins, Ethan hid his stash of condoms, so first I pocketed one of those. Just in case, you know, a girl looked at me over the course of the next decade. Since the top of the key is round and silver, I thought it was a quarter. When I realized it wasn't, I stuck it in the toy car parked next to the stein. That way I could find it again later. I figured the key would open up something.

1

You know how people talk about their worlds? Like: "Baby, you rock my world." Or: "Once I lost my arm in an autoerotic noose mishap, my world was never the same." I try to pinpoint the moment my world tilted. It stopped turning for a second when my mom died. And then stalled out when Ethan left a postcard on the kitchen table with just the word *Later* written across it. I get out of the shower and sink a Pop-Tart into the toaster. Turn to get dressed and instead choke on Ethan's latest poignant communication. This one is caught up in some ass-tastic catalog our mom used to get — the kind that sells vests with cats embroidered on it and umbrellas that you wear on your head. A postcard — two whole sentences — *Wondering? Wandering.* I see his serial-killer handwriting and everything goes still. Then it restarts.

You know that Tom Waits song — "The World Keeps Turning"? Well, it does. Last winter it slowed way the fuck down, though. Picture it. Now it's January and the planet is practically crawling.

This is the first we've heard from Ethan since he left in the middle of November but I go to school without saying anything to Dad and take my exam, barely considering the fact that my older brother has hauled ass without even teaching me how to drive stick. There are really two tests I have to pass: the exam and the acting somewhat normal that goes along with it.

Section 3 — Multiple choice. You're sixteen, with a dead mom, brother gone, and a hard-ass dad who's not exactly capable of comforting you. Do you A) go to the school counselor, famous for his ability to turn every problem you face into proof that you have ADD? B) cry through the exams and hope the science teacher with a nice rack notices and tries to comfort you?

C) find one of the three assholes who you call assholes because actually they're the closest thing you have to brothers, except your brother; but of course your brother isn't around anymore, so this moves the assholes up in rank? Or D) none of the above?

Damn right I choose D. I take the test and then hover around the Ping-Pong table like I care and then, when even eye contact feels like too much effort, I stand around the library. No one is going to interrupt Ethan Simon's little brother's existential quandary in the corner. Most of the assholes at Caramoor don't even know my first name. I'm Little Simon or Simon the II. In Modern Euro, Mr. Phillips told us about the British royalty's two-son policy, how it didn't count as enough to have one son to inherit the throne, because that kid could die and then what? So the goal was to have two sons — the heir and the spare. I'm the spare. Except not so much now. Now I'm the one who's left.

Classes halt for exams, so it feels like a sequel to the winter break, even though the tests themselves eat up the mornings. Campus feels like the waiting area of an emergency room during those afternoons — you see everyone's personality amplified in the stress of testing. The kids who usually hang out at the library stay in the library, but they look like they're drowning in looseleaf paper instead of just swimming in it.

Everyone seems sharper; most of us stop smoking weed a week before exams. Instead, the ADD kids are losing it because they've sold most of their Ritalin. By the time we jerk our way into Friday, all of us are ready to drink or sleep or just disappear. And we have all of one day to do it. There's no restorative three-day weekend for the valiant young men of Caramoor. After they march us through an entire week sweating through exams, they haul us back up the hill that Sunday. We get about an hour of academic counseling in advisory. And then we suffer through six hours of chapel. It's just like school, except on Chapel Day, your ass gets sore from the wooden benches. So Friday night's the one night to seek any kind of chemical comfort, and of course, I spend it at Soma's.

Stick Soma in the asshole-I-pretend-not-to-care-about category. And in true surrogate-brother fashion, Soma asks me how Ethan is doing, and when I say he's still AWOL, he exhales slowly, says, "Blows, man." And then shows me the wonders of whippets.

I let myself into my house at two in the morning. I could try to tell you I'm so fucked up that I go and sleep in Ethan's bed by accident. Except clearly I'd be lying. I pass out right after two and wake right after four and realize I've been dreaming about riding shotgun with Ethan, the summer on my face, asking him what the key I found on his dresser opened. But this is less of a dream than a memory I haven't let myself think about while I'm awake. I know that if my brother was dead, that would make a better story. Me lying on top of the quilt my mom made Ethan out of his old T-shirts and hearing him guide me toward the key I'd set in the passenger seat of the model DeLorean on top of his dresser. It's less thrilling than that. I wake up, remember the two of us in my dad's truck, and then remember the silver of the key glinting against the car's silver seat.

That day, back when he told me about it, I'd thought Ethan was just fucking with me, like when he buried a turkey carcass in the backyard after Thanksgiving and told me he'd found dinosaur bones. This was another homegrown pterodactyl — an ordinary thing that my brother could turn into an amazing story.

4

He said he didn't even know when it started. Apparently, years and years back, when one of the younger maintenance guys held the lofty position of campus pharmacist, he gave the kid who helped him sell weed a copy of one of the staff keys to make accessing the product easier. A master key. When Captain Suds 'n' Buds was inevitably caught with fifty dime bags in his mopping bucket, the local police chief shuttled him off campus in the back of a squad car. But the delivery boy kept the key and while we might have had a dry spell for pot and ecstasy that year, the students added their own tradition to the endless inherited rituals inflicted on us by the administration. Except this one wasn't lame.

Only one kid gets the key every year, and no one is supposed to ever know for sure who has it. That way, no one can rat him out. Whoever holds the key is responsible for passing it along, making that decision based on potential and demonstrated acts.

"Like what?" I'd asked Ethan. All this was news to me.

"Remember the trophy case full of Jell-O?"

"Yeah." It was red Jell-O, in the glass case that lined the whole main wall of the auditorium.

"That was a demonstrated act — a bid for key status."

"Yeah? That kid got the key?"

"Nah. It was given to some guy who rewired the campus golf carts to only go in reverse when Mr. Rollins was on crutches."

Mr. Rollins is our principal. At Caramoor, if you run into academic difficulty, if your kid sister gets cancer, or your parents split up and shit hits the gossip circuit, you go to the headmaster. Dr. Watkins's office has intimidating décor and he is a stern guy you sort of feel compelled to call sir, but at least you know where you stand with him. You have trouble. But you're not in trouble.

It's Mr. Rollins's office that inspires dry mouth and dread. The infraction? You forgot your tie or your blazer was wrinkled. You chewed gum. Late to class or marked as cutting. Foul language, visible piercings. Generally disrespectful or vaguely disinterested. Mr. Rollins isn't known for his tact, or his caring nature, or his understanding. So when he slipped on some ice in the faculty parking lot, he didn't get much from the student body, either. For three months, some poor janitor guy had to drive him around campus in one of the golf carts that the gardeners and coaches use to get around campus. The idea of Mr. Rollins lurching backward uncontrollably despite the driving finesse of whatever lumberjack dude was charged with chauffeuring him was particularly satisfying.

"Jesus Christ, Ethan. What do you know about wiring cars?"

"Absolutely nothing. I cannot claim responsibility for that campaign of hilarity."

"Well — how did you get it, then? What did you do?"

But Ethan only said, "Nothing," and shrugged in his usual I-am-a-man-of-mystery-and-could-play-a-song-about-you-girl-if-only-I-wasn't-so-busy-thinking-about-Kerouac way.

"Nothing. Someone just gave you the key?"

"Yeah."

"No Jell-O trophies or pot brownies in the faculty lounge? Someone just decided you were cool enough for the key and gave it to you."

"Yeah." Ethan seemed baffled that I would press the issue.

"Why?"

"Because I am."

And the thing is, that's probably how it happened. It might be one of the greatest mysteries of my world. I swear to God, Ethan could be sitting at the goddamn Last Supper and Jesus himself would get up and say, "Dude, why don't you go on and take my seat? Nice hair." You'd think I would have been used to it. The way Ethan just rounded up devoted fans, effortlessly. And without caring.

Ethan is elsewhere. I mean now, these days, he's really elsewhere. But even when he was sleeping in the room across the hall from me, he operated in another orbit. Not mine — I'm nothing like my brother, which became obvious as soon as I got through the iron gates of Caramoor Academy. People looked twice at me, but not like they did with Ethan. "No way." I got that a lot when I first got there. "No way. You're Little Simon?"

"Yeah, I'm Emil."

"No shit — Little Simon. Dude, can you believe this is Simon's brother? I mean, come on."

And that's how it is, even after Ethan packed a duffel bag and set out his dumb-ass Post-it and joined a circus or a militant vegetarian commune or a gay outreach program, which is my aunt Judy's latest theory. Love that. Our father hasn't filed a missing persons report or asked me if Ethan ever mentioned where he was going. And my aunts just ask me if he's gay, as if there's a state out west where gay kids feel compelled to migrate.

I don't think he's gay, but I know he's gone. That day, when I asked him if I could have the key, I tried to play it like it didn't mean anything to me, either. No big deal. A sliver of metal that could unlock every single door at a school that had, for two years, seemed completely closed off to me. Part of me wants to think that I was believable, that it was my careful indifference that made Ethan shrug and say, "Yeah sure, whatever, Emo," because he thought I deserved it. And the other half of me wants to believe he gave it to me because he knew exactly how much I wanted it and wanted to give me something, anything that would help keep things bearable after he took off.

Because it was a matter of months. Dad and I woke up that morning that November and Ethan was gone. I don't even know if Ethan ever used the key. Had I not found it, that chapter of Caramoor mythology would have sat in the stupid Mount Rushmore mug for years. So maybe I didn't earn the key, but no one else even had a shot.

CHAPTER 2

So this is how I spent my Saturday morning: in our cellar, digging out my old Cub Scout crap — sleeping bag, plastic tarp, canteen, sterno stove. Then it takes me an hour to walk to the Stop & Shop to buy a flashlight and batteries and stuff I can cook for myself — you know, like granola bars, string cheese. I know Dad's out golfing or logging extra hours in at the office. He will be bringing home subs or Chinese and we'll have a sullen dinner eating off wrappers or out of cartons so no one has to wash up afterward. I know then he'll go and turn on *This Old House* or *The New Yankee Workshop* or some other hypermasculine show that is really just some asshole in a plaid shirt sanding a piece of wood in front of a camera. I know that he'll have a beer with dinner and then a glass of scotch in front of the TV and then another and by the time he is considering calling me downstairs to either pour him another drink or change the channel, he'll be drunk enough for stumbling and will most likely then nod off into sleep. Ethan and I used to time it — countdown to softcore on Cinemax. I'm looking forward to leaving just as much as I'd look forward to porn, though. When I grab my bag I wonder if this is how Ethan felt the morning he left, like Santa all ass-backward, creeping out of the house instead of sneaking in. Ethan is the only reason I stop to leave a note — all I write is *Left early, weightlifting before chapel.* And not because I imagine that my dad will actually worry for a full minute about me.

But because I'm not going to let Ethan handle leaving better than me.

Honestly, I don't even have a plan. I want to see if the key works. And if it does, I've sort of dared myself to spend the night there. One night to dig around and explore on my own. And if it doesn't work . . . well, I haven't really thought that far in advance. I'm all packed. I can just keep going.

I don't take my bike, just my backpack. I bundle up in two coats and set the note in the kitchen where we Simon boys leave our skipping-town announcements. It takes me about forty minutes to walk to Caramoor, mostly because it's almost all uphill. I don't know why I've always assumed the school would be lit up all night. I pass the main street in town and New Market Pond, I pass the post office on Courtlidge and Mr. Canasink's ancient gas station. I keep trudging, head down, the whole time expecting to look up and see Caramoor standing brightly at attention like the Capitol in D.C. But it doesn't. It's just a series of darker shadows rising up into the night. I don't have to climb the iron fence — that might have been exciting. Instead I just find the gate and unlatch it.

I keep ducking down, waiting for floodlights or guard dogs or even a family of rabid raccoons to chase me away. Nothing. It's dark and then less dark beneath the doorways and eaves, where small lightbulbs give off low light. I figure I have a few hours and one key in my pocket and should start with the fortress itself — if the key can open every single door on campus then it's better to face the big guns first. So I walk up to the main entrance of Ainsley House like I'm strolling into my own home. Drop my pack down on the top of the marble steps and dig into my jeans for Ethan's key and check behind me. I let myself spend a moment hoping before I slip the nickel key into the door's ornate lock.

It slips right in and turns.

If I were in a movie or an old Scooby-Doo cartoon, then the ancient, heavy door of Caramoor's main building would let out a long creak — the kind that makes you instantly uneasy and suggests inevitable doom. But God. My life is never cinematic. I cannot get the fucker open, have to bear down and shove it with my shoulder. And then the key sticks in the lock and so it takes a full minute of grimacing and jiggling the knob for me to get in. This gives the ghosts of the old Ainsley House a chance to get their shit organized. They could be lining up in phalanx formation at the top of the staircase.

The presence of ghosts at the old Ainsley homestead is established fact. During the September of my freshman year, *Unsolved Mysteries* filmed a whole episode showcasing the creepy happenings on campus. That was reassuring. New school. Strange kids. Fervent belief that every other male in my gym class had more pubic hair than me. Those things were intimidating. And then a camera crew showed up and some dude wearing makeup asked me had I ever witnessed any paranormal activity outside the principal's office.

I have not, sir, but I've heard about it. Desk chairs rolling on their own on windless days. Lights that seem to randomly flicker on after dusk, while the varsity teams unload off of buses returning from away games. The head of maintenance on the property is this giant former linebacker. Dude is bearlike. And I got to see him say to the reporter, in all seriousness, "I believe one of the spirits is called Ruby. At least I call her Ruby, and this has never seemed to offend her. When I need to enter the building after dark, I just take a minute to honor her presence, you know? I announce myself and say, 'Ruby, it's Al Romano here. I'm just here to do my job.' And I believe that Ruby responds well to this courtesy. I believe she looks out for my welfare."

So Al Romano, who appears to knock down trees with his forearms on his off-hours, needs Ruby to look out for his welfare. What the hell am I supposed to do? I stand there in the doorway like a little kid trick-or-treating for the first time, calling out, "Uhhhhh, Ruby. My name is Emil. Uhhhhh. You don't know me. Mostly because you're dead. Or you know, passed on? But I really need a place to stay. And would really appreciate your help with that."

If it were Ethan, there would be no asking for permission. Ethan would waltz in and call, "Honey, I'm home!"

As for me, shuffling into the darkness pooled in the doorway uses up every cell in my balls. The heavy wood of the door is just as heavy as I close it. I have to lean with my back to it and push.

You always picture haunted houses a certain way. You know — with the white sheets draped over every piece of abandoned furniture. And then, when you creep to the staircase, you half-expect one of the white sheets to rise off some dusty divan, moaning, "Whooooooooo, whoooooooooooooooooo." Which seems to be the universal ghost translation for "Dude in the tweed blazer: Get the Fuck Out of My Home."

So Ainsley House? Not your typical ghost locale. For one thing, people work in the building every weekday, so it's not like I'm the first to invade the space. During the day it's mostly moms of former students who answer phones, issue staggering tuition bills, or organize the vast collection of Caramoor historical documents from the past two hundred years. Because of these ladies, it might be my favorite building on campus. These are not the kind of women who raise cokeheads. They probably organized Cub Scout can drives and sat through about a hundred Caramoor baseball games each. They are the kind of ladies who keep those foam cushions in the car, so that their butts don't fall asleep on the bleachers. They always have an extra pencil if you need one for math class. Sometimes I borrow one just to lean into Mrs. Miano, who smells like the inside of those tins of butter cookies.

It's ridiculous what the motherless will do for the tiniest bit of mothering. It gives me a certain sympathy for Hansel and Gretel. Maybe it wasn't the house built of candy that drew them in, but the fact that the witch leaned over her oven in a way that reminded them of their dead mom.

Ainsley House looks like it could have been made of licorice. All this fancy woodwork around the windows. Peaked eaves and precise shingles. Its doorways hang low because the people who first lived there — you know, the Ainsleys — stood shorter. They probably also wore a lot of knickers and whittled their own spoons. It doesn't look like a home anymore, but it feels like one. Sort of the opposite of my house. Standing there in the darkness, I try to imagine what it could have been like two centuries ago, when the servants rowed canoes up the river to the markets and the girl we call Ruby might have crouched in the hallway throwing jacks on the floor. And I stop being afraid so much. If there's a little girl ghost in the house, she can probably smell the homesickness on me.

*   *   *

Until deciding to add trespassing to my list of student activities, I never considered whether or not Caramoor had any kind of security detail. Standing in the school lobby with a packed duffel bag and a flashlight sort of sparks my curiosity, though. The key in my hand is sweaty from how tightly I've been clutching it. In the seconds between each of the clock's twelve chimes, I assemble an impressive collection of relevant thoughts and facts:

A) Probably all the buildings on campus are rigged with electronic alarm systems. Especially the main administrative building, which houses certain offices like, say, that of the headmaster or the financial records.

B) Probably being caught in said building (or any building for that matter) after hours, in the dark, with luggage, counts as grounds for dismissal.

C) Dismissal for disciplinary purposes is not covered in tuition insurance. If you go on the ski trip and accidentally collide with a snow-covered plow and end up in a coma (yes, this has actually happened), then your parents get some of their money back. If you are tossed out for programming all the school's home pages to constantly return to a site called poopsex.com, your parents' check has already been cashed, thank you very much. We wish you all the luck in your future endeavors.

D) My father? Is a big man. Is an increasingly bitter man. With not much else to lose at this point. Who already resents the money spent on my tuition to this venerable institution. Do you see where I'm headed with this one?

E) Probably I'd be asked how I'd gained entrance to said building. I'd go down in history as the kid who ruined our most valuable tradition. Or probably Ethan would go down in history as the kid whose little brother lost the key. Because the former possibility would require more than five of my classmates to learn my fucking name.

Clearly, Letter E is not so bad as Letter D. Except E goes hand in hand with D, so not only would I go down as the kid whose father reached down his throat and pulled out his lung and beat him to death with it, no one would even feel sorry about it. I'd be the dead kid who lost the key, that's all. This I can do without.

So when the grandfather clock begins its hourly announcements, I bolt up the steps like a greyhound after an electric hare. I don't care what I'm running up into. Blood could be cascading down the walls and the snakes could be writhing across the staircase's wooden banister, I still take them two at a time. Past the second floor with the headmaster's headquarters stretching from one side of the staircase and the Japanese and Latin classrooms on the other. Up to the third floor with its maze of tiny offices.

All I keep thinking is that there has to be a nook in this place that school bureaucrats haven't taken over, a corner waiting to be staked out. I stand at the top of the steps on the third floor and make myself listen for a solid seven minutes. Nothing. Nothing. Nothing. No sirens or footsteps or jangling of keys or, you know, the shocking discharge of a shotgun. So then I lower my duffel bag and let it rest on the top step. I allow myself to flick on the flashlight for a few seconds to keep my bearings, but I try to keep it away from the windows, so that it won't shine out like a beacon across campus. Instead I point it straight up to the ceiling. And that's when I see the door to the attic. A rectangular panel in the ceiling, about the size of the cooler our family used to pack with lunch and lemonade for trips to the beach. The door has a loop of rope to tug down, just like our attic door at home. I climb onto the banister and tug the loop down and discover that the Ainsley attic is just like mine at home — attached to the door's other side is the first rung of a ladder. I'm not a retard. I jump down and stand on the first couple of rungs, sort of bounce on them to make sure they are not eaten through with rot. And then I practically run up them.

I try not to waste a lot of time looking around before I solve the problem of my flashlight beam announcing my presence. It's hard to see through the fog of dust, but an oval window winks from the north end of the long narrow room that was once the Ainsleys' attic. There's an enormous, old headboard for a bed bigger than I can imagine. It takes me a good twenty minutes to drag it over to the window and shove it as close to the window as possible, so that the room won't leak any light.

The whole time, I'm talking to Ethan. Insane, I know. But I've been doing it, like, constantly. When I'm alone in a room or on a bus or walking down along the curving curb to school or home or wherever, it's hard to stop myself from keeping this running dialogue going with him. Okay, not exactly dialogue. Because I'm not insane enough to believe that he talks back.

I find myself brushing the thick coat of dust off my hands, saying "Done" out loud, and glancing sideways as if Ethan's hand is going to clap down on my shoulder. Brotherly. When we were real little, we played like we were soldiers all the time. The two of us were obsessed with Vietnam. Maybe it was the Marine insignia on my dad's arm. Or the other ways we knew the war had marked him. Ethan said it was why he always ate tuna straight from the can. We knew not to mention our game in front of him —that he would clamp his hand around the scruff of one of our necks and seethe, instructing us that war was no game. I can picture him shaking Ethan by the shoulders and saying that grimly. I can picture that so clearly that I think it must have happened.

Still, we played all the time. And we'd narrate firefights even as we were tearing through all the weeds and nettles in our backyard that stretched up to our knees. We'd crouch in the sinking stones of the old barbecue pit and pretend we were in a foxhole, that the settling dusk was actually the thick dark of a hot night. We'd stare out into our own backyard for hours, conjuring up a jungle in between the bordering hedges. Tripped mines and sniper fire. Burning jeeps and crashing copters. All so we could act out the same thing over and over again — the bleeding kid saying, "Go on — just go on without me."

And other brother bent over swearing, "Never, man. I'm not leaving you behind."

Up at the very top of Ainsley House, I drag the door with its built-in steps back up to its rightful place, just in case some boozy faculty member actually does nightly security rounds or something. I survey the room's wooden beams and the trunks and broken chairs and chatter on to Ethan in my toughest voice. "We can work with this. I can bed down here and use it as my center of operations. The rest of campus radiates out and I'll just search it one building, one night at a time. I'll check in at home every once in a while, so that Dad heads out to the Atlanta convention next week without a worry." No one answers. I must sound crazy, like I'm hallucinating.

This may or may not have been part of why my brother took off: lots of drugs. Maybe that's how he got the key, but I don't think so. Ethan was never the dude who sells weed out of his backpack just so that he has some kind of power walking through the school's halls. He was never one of those dudes who wears clothes woven from hemp, for christsakes, or fires homemade bongs in the ceramics studio. And he didn't deal and he didn't talk about drugs all the time, the way some cokeheads will always find some way to joke about it. Not so much because the joke is so fucking hilarious, but because they can't let a full minute pass without the synapse that screams BLOW in their brains firing. Ethan was never a fiend.

But he did them. More than I'd say would be the federally recommended dose if the federal government approved of such things. When I was younger, before I'd really tried anything myself, it was easy to think of Ethan as some wizard mixing all these potions into his life. When our aunts used to grill Mom about what she put in her stuffing at Thanksgiving, she'd say, "A little bit of this, a little bit of that." That's how Ethan seemed to handle the stash he kept taped inside his old Dallas Cowboys helmet. I never knew, even after we started smoking weed together, where he got all of it. Once in a while, we'd drive to downtown Hartford and I'd sit in the car, just about shitting my pants waiting for Ethan to trot on out. And he'd just come sauntering down, as if he belonged in the Hartford projects with his blue button-down shirt and his pansy-ass flowered tie.

18

Ethan was sort of like a mad scientist, experimenting on himself. A little of this, a little of that. And most conversations with his drug-addled self focused on how isolated parts of his body were feeling at whatever given moment. My door would suddenly slam open, Ethan would stride in, announcing, "Is this paranoia? I think this is paranoia." He'd do acid and write in his journal the whole time, utterly convinced of the need to record whatever wise epiphany he arrived at when he hit the peak of the ride. I honestly thought that was a pretty cool way to handle one's narcotic supply. Ethan was like an athlete, testing his body to see how far he could push it. But maybe we should have worried about how seldom he wanted to be himself, free and clear of any extra chemistry.

Standing at the top of Ainsley House, I feel like I'm the fucking lord of the manor. No one can touch me. I have my pick of a dozen roofs to sleep under each night. Just like Ethan has the whole world wide open now. It has to be his greatest experiment to date.

CHAPTER 3

So the goal is to prove I can sleep over in Ainsley House. That is supposed to be my rite of passage. Some Native American kids have to smoke peyote and kill an elk. This is similar. Except I spend all night rearranging my small corner in the eaves. Moving clouds of dust from one side of the room to the other with my hands. Talking to my brother who is probably halfway across the country by now and clearly isn't listening. Talking to some weird ghost child who I hope isn't listening, either. Pretending that Ethan and I are playing war games and that in a few weeks, he'll come back and I'll wait until he's just stoned enough to be charmed by make-believe shit again and I'll say, "You've got to go out with me tonight and see my bunker. It's a top-notch work of military precision." And it is. I unroll my sleeping bag beneath that north window, leave a spare flashlight and an extra set of batteries there in case of emergency. Set up the sterno cans, the mess kit, and the cans of food in the corner farthest to the back on top of a cracked oval mirror that I've laid across two trunks. Then I cover this makeshift kitchen and my sleeping quarters with the tarp, just because it feels right to sort of close up shop before retreating back downstairs.

The rest of the world begins rolling over into morning, stretching and waking up. I make it home in good time without a pack on my back and going mostly downhill. It's funny but as much as I always think I hate it, walking away from Caramoor as the sun rises makes me love it a little. It feels more mine than anything else.

I get home early enough to snag the note I left Dad on the table. No sense using up an excuse that might come in handy later on. You'd think the night would have wasted me, but when the shower's surge hits me, it feels like I'm waking up after the best sleep in months. Dressing for Chapel Day is the same old pain in the ass so it's not like life has gone all Disney or something. I don't glance out the window and see robins draping the pine tree with ribbons, for christsakes. Instead of ironing my shirt, I use Ethan's old trick of tossing it in the dryer with a wet washcloth to get some of the wrinkles out. Pick out a tie that doesn't have any crap spilled down the front, tuck my blue shirt into dark gray pants that are a little short but seemed to go with the rest of the outfit. True or false: The suddenly delinquent juvenile dons the costume of the model student in order to blend in with those who abide by the rule. True, sort of. Partly, I figure why bother drawing attention to myself and earn a demerit for being out of dress code. But it's more than that. I'm in a good mood. I feel like fucking whistling. And something else: It's easier to follow their minor, meaningless rules when you're breaking a major one.

I even eat a wholesome breakfast. Granola bar, orange juice. Fill up one of Dad's travel mugs with coffee just in case I crash in a couple of hours. By the time he comes downstairs dressed and squinting in the kitchen's fluorescent lights, I'm ready to go, with a good forty minutes to spare. Clearly, Dad is not up for this kind of major shift in our morning routine.

"What the hell is going on?"

"Morning. I figured I'd get the second semester off to a good start, right?"

"What is this? Are they starting this crap even earlier this year?" Dad is not exactly a fan of this particular Caramoor Sunday tradition.

"Nope. Just woke up early for some reason and figured I might as well get up."

"Uh-huh. And nothing's going on?"

"Nope."

"You're dressed up." This is not technically true. I am wearing the same basic kind of clothing I wear once a week every week. Only this morning they're mostly unwrinkled and I didn't have to spray deodorant on the outside of them in order to get rid of my own reek.

"Not really. In dress code."

"You look like you're going to a goddamn funeral." And I realize it as soon as he says it. And I see him realize it, too, because he's reaching for the pot of coffee and holds it just a second longer than he normally would before pouring it into his cup. This was the shirt and tie I wore to my mother's funeral or memorial service or whatever. One of the aunts brought a bag over with a bunch of classy shit for me and Ethan to wear. Probably so that he wouldn't show up to the service wearing one of the ties he'd spray-painted with Elliott Smith lyrics.

For the record, we didn't actually bury my mother. She'd requested that her body be donated to scientific research. And at the service and afterward when everyone came back to the house to eat casseroles and crap, all her old lady friends from work yammered on and on about how that just exemplified her.

"That's just like Jane, thinking about others right up until the end." I'd like to point out that it's only a generous move in theory. In reality, it left us with nothing. No coffin to close or headstone to visit. No ashes in an urn on top of the fireplace. At the memorial service, people lined up to kneel in front of an eight-by-ten picture of my mother in a fancy frame. Which seems even more pointless than kneeling in front of a dead body in a box. And for what? So that some med student somewhere could move her head around and make some lame-ass joke right before he used a scalpel for the first time.

"If you think you bombed any of those exams, you better clue me in now," Dad goes on. "Don't think that playing boy genius now is going to save your ass if I see anything lower than a C+ on your report card."

Ah, my father. Ever the optimist. "I had those exams covered," I tell him. This is clearly a lie. But it's one he wants. We've already almost actually talked about my dead mother. An honest discussion of my academic troubles is probably a little more than Dad can stomach at 6:45 in the morning.

"You know I have that sales conference this week. From that, I have to travel on to corporate headquarters in Atlanta." Ah. The return to safe ground: work schedule. In this house every man is an island. Especially now that there's only two of us. I'm sniffing sandwich meat. Dad's on the other side of the open fridge door, using a Sharpie to X off dates on the calendar. It's taking him a long time. When I lean over the door to see, he speeds up. Now look who's playing defense.

Almost the whole first two rows of February are crossed off. I toss the lunch meat back in the fridge.

"Listen, Bear. I know this might feel like a raw deal. But this past year and a half has been an ordeal and we have been well supported by some real men of honor. They toughed it out with us, but I'm going to have to start pulling my weight again. No one wants to pay a salary to a liability."

It takes me some seconds to realize that my dad feels guilty about this. That he is sort of pleading with me to let him off the hook for this one. My father. Is explaining himself to me. "Whatever," I say. But that comes out wrong. It sounds like something a kid would say if he gave a shit and didn't want to admit it. And what I mean is: "Whatever." It's not like my dad stands as this stunning source of emotional support. I mean, it's a struggle for us to make conversation over dinner most nights. Mom established the rule that we all sat around the table each night for supper; the two of us still obey without question. If there's a big game on, Dad will turn on the little FM radio that's mounted above the microwave, but even that we do almost surreptitiously, like we're sure we're going to have to run over and switch it off if a real grown-up enters the room.

I know he'll leave me lots of cash for takeout and even cab fare if it's this cold and it looks like I might run into trouble setting up a ride. And that's when it hits me. Caramoor. A ride back and forth isn't even really necessary. I mean, I could just stay there, if I wanted. I have a room at the inn, after all.

"Hey, Bear? You know you're going to be on your own in college soon enough, anyway."

"Where did you get the new calendar?"

"What?" It'd been bothering me every time I opened the fridge. Every year, at least since I've been tall enough to see it, the same calendar has hung on our refrigerator. This plain, black-and-white thing. No pictures, just a strip of magnet that you have to take off in order to switch the months. Every time I tried to change it, I always made a mess of it and got the months all out of order and crap. It was a stupid calendar, especially back when Ethan and I played sports, and our schedules changed each week. But it was a fund raiser for some school for autistic kids in Hartford and Mom was a sucker for that kind of crap. So every year we had the least colorful, most complicated contraption ever.

"Where did you get the new calendar?" I ask again, because I can't picture my dad ordering it from the weird kid who calls every year. The one who freaks out if you say our zip code is Oh, eight, eight, five, oh. He corrects you: "ZERO, eight, eight, five, ZERO." Not really crap my father would abide.

"Emil, what is this now? I'm talking to you as a man. To a man. And you're what? Fascinated about this goddamn calendar?"

"I just want to know — how did you know where she got it every year?"

"I know that report card's going to get here while I'm away. And I'll tell you one thing — it better be right up there on that fridge door next to that calendar that's so goddamn fascinating. I'll tell you that much."

"Dad —"

"'Dad,' nothing — that is me instructing you on what I expect to see on that refrigerator."

"Yes, sir."

"And I expect that if you had those exams covered, then that report card that I will see next to that calendar is going to positively radiate your brilliance."

"I told you —"

"I remember what you told me. And I think you might have a little more to worry about than which Staples I got the goddamn family calendar at." Nine days without any of this. Nine nights at Caramoor, with only the sounds of my own footsteps and the echoes of my own voice in the corridors. Nine days and nights to find some way to prove I would have deserved the key even if I weren't Ethan Simon's little brother.

Dad and I get in the car in silence, back down the driveway the same way. It's not until my father pulls up to the iron tines of the fence surrounding school that the Staples comment sinks in. True or false? My father purchased the stupid calendar. He might not consider that debate crucial or revelatory. But I think about my mother on the phone with the weirdo autistic kid, reciting our zip code for the Lone Defender of the Word Zero. Pronouncing the numbers on her credit card so carefully for him, ordering up a record of days she would never see. I don't know which of them had it worse, really. My mother trying to get the whole damn house in order beforehand. Or my father finding this year's calendar in a thick manila envelope in the mailbox, realizing that he would have to find a way to replace her.

"We'll talk more at supper."

"It's nine days, Dad," I say like it's nothing, like I'm not already trying to calculate the hours. From the hilly driveway that circles campus, I can see the shingled roofs that cap all the buildings left to explore on the property.

"You know what?" This is where you just nod and say, *Yessir*. I swing open the car door, lean forward to haul my backpack off the floor. "Emil Andrew!" my dad barks.

"Yessir." But I'm not even facing him. I'm surveying the land like this was some gold rush. And it is. The bell at the top of Winslow Chapel tolls. There are hundreds of us falling into place now, streaming through the gates. I get that feeling again. Like I own this place more than the rest of them. Like it owns me, too.

CHAPTER 4

Each homeroom chose a name for itself back on the wilderness expedition the administration sent us out on in the second week of our freshman year. As tempting as it is to sit here and bitch and moan about how I had to dig a hole to shit in and sleep under a lousy tarp during rain, the fact of the matter is that the trip kicked ass. I got to play soldier boy on actual terrain. I don't remember why we chose the name "Good Shepherd Advisory" any more than I remember why Soma stabbed Craig Markson in the arm with his Swiss Army knife. But three years later we're still the Good Shepherds and Soma is the only kid I'd bleed for at Caramoor. He likes to say, "I'd take a bullet for Emil — I mean a small caliber, of course." But the truth is either of us would face a rocket launcher for the other.

You know how adults get a little sloppy with the wine and cheese on holidays and invariably the wife starts going all wet-eyed, talking about when she knew the poor slob beside her was the poor slob who'd be beside her for the rest of her days? Mom used to talk about seeing Dad around campus and how they met up at some rooftop party and she thought she was all that and then some, dressed in this white halter dress. She'd been ticked off that her date hadn't said anything about how she looked that night. And she glanced up and my dad emptied a bottle of Miller Lite in one gulp. He looked past her date, straight into her eyes, and said, "Sweetheart, I think you wore that dress for me." And she thought two things — she thought that Miller Lite was crap beer and that she'd be with him for the rest of her life. Such as it was. When Dad does the story, he makes sure to add that he took her home that night, but Mom at least showed a little mercy in the telling.

Yeah, yeah. I'm not saying Soma and I had this heart-splitting moment. As inept as I might be with women, I'm no gay. But usually I'm inept at all of it — once friendship stopped being about who had the best snacks in his lunchbox, I got shuffled in the retard pile. I have Ethan. Every memory I have until now, I've had Ethan. But we didn't really choose each other. I showed up when he was three, and for whatever reason, he decided not to kill me. And with Ethan, you always knew it was temporary. You always knew he was on his way someplace else and you were barely interesting enough to hold his attention while he was here. You always knew you watched him harder.

So Soma showed up for this three-day wilderness trip wearing head-to-toe camo. Christ, he had packed a ski mask. We all had to meet outside the north entrance by the van that Miss Gabaldon had to load us up in and navigate to some state park. And she? Is not cut out to teach high school. I don't care if we're supposed to be the Future Gentlemen of America or what. The administration who hired her might as well have tied steaks to her body and thrown her into a den of lions. Our homeroom has some big cats. And she teaches bio. This perhaps doesn't seem so whacked out, but she's young. I mean there's no way she's older than twenty-five, which means that when she got here, she was twenty-two. Standing outside this van in these tiny little cargo shorts and hiking boots, with her hair in this optimistic ponytail that should have wilted as soon as she saw the legion of doom assembling before her with duffel bags and hard-ons.

So maybe she was just relieved that she wasn't going to have to spend the day teaching hornball fourteen-year-olds about reproductive systems. Instead she got to shit in the woods with them. Climb on rope courses and rappel off cliffs. Okay, my all-time favorite moment of the Freshman Wilderness Wilding might have been when our guide — some hippie kid with a JewFro and a fucking Phish logo tattooed on his bicep — was hooking Miss Gabaldon up in her harness on top of the cliff she's supposed to rappel off of. And, IN FRONT OF HER TWELVE ADOLESCENT MALE STUDENTS, he murmurs real low, "I bet I'm not the first man to ever tie you up." And she giggled. Come. On. I couldn't get that giggle out of my head for two years.

Sometime on that trip the foreign kid, the one who came from Switzerland or Norway or someplace where kids hunted and people considered "Jan" a male's name, that kid started mumbling some crap to Miss Gabaldon about how he could hunt her down a hare if she got hungry and pulled out a fully loaded, professional crossbow to prove it. Sometime after she shakily confiscated the crossbow and drove Markson to the nearest local hospital to get stitches, Soma and I recognized in each other some similar thirst for blood. I remember sitting around a campfire, listening to Miss Gabaldon explain that at Caramoor, we didn't have homeroom. We had advisory. And she would be advising us for the next four years and she was just so pleased to be beginning this journey right along with us. And I looked over at Soma and saw him mouth something that looked like *meow* and thought, *Dude, this kid's a fucking freak.* Until I realized it wasn't *meow*. It was a word he'd mouth for the next few years anytime he got ready to embrace trouble and delinquency. It was the word *mayhem,* and I was all in.

We might call it advisory, but very little advising goes on at eight o'clock on a Sunday morning in room 105. Sometimes Miss Gabaldon brings in doughnuts. Sometimes she sits at her desk, reading aloud the headlines to us and asking us how we feel about current events. She doesn't teach bio anymore. Someone figured out that in an all-boys prep school, it was probably not so wise to enlist the one female teacher under thirty to teach reproductive sciences. So now she teaches chemistry and walks around wearing a white lab coat and slays me all the same. She usually wears her hair up so that, when she's leaning over whatever's simmering on the Bunsen burner, you start to imagine giving the band that holds her hair back a tug, watching it cascade over her shoulders. And then you start to imagine it cascading over her bare shoulders. See how that works? Soma says it's the only real science she's ever taught him.

Which is mean, but fairly accurate. At Caramoor, there seem to be two squads of faculty. There's the crowd who clearly would rather be teaching at some hotshot university, but for whatever reason landed here. They take the college preparatory part of our name seriously. No one gets an A the first semester. That kind of thing. I have some trouble taking those cats seriously. Last year, I took Advanced Placement Modern European History and Mr. Phillips insisted we read half the crap from primary sources. Which would have been fascinating, but not when it was in fucking Polish. Who the hell reads Polish? And Bolus Liscinski got his half-dead grandmother to translate half of it for him and he got the only A in two sections of the class for that quarter. Thanks to Grandma. But Phillips didn't see that as totally arbitrary. He saw it as dedication to scholarship or whatever new phrase he was using as a euphemism for ass-kissing.

Do I have to broadcast that Miss "Oh no, Mr. Wilderness Guide, no one's ever tied me up before" Gabaldon does not play for that team? She does not even cheer for that squad. She's part of the collection of teachers who seem to wish they were guidance counselors. The kind who give out extensions like extra pencils. So yeah, chem has been a breeze for the kid whose mom died last October and brother went missing in November. I know that's awful. Terrible to feel even the slightest pang of gratitude for the whole grim year just because it's gotten me out of turning in a single lab on time. Or because all I have to do is slump in a rest-my-head-on-my-books way and the hazel pools of Miss Gabaldon's eyes shimmer with pity.

Soma's got another racket working with her. As carefully calculated as everything else he does. His most successful persona is the tough kid who's befriended me, Kid Tragedy. It used to piss me off, but now we have an agreement. He buys me lunch every time he hangs back after class and claims to be concerned about my grieving process. "Emil and I were online most of the night, Miss Gabaldon. I know I've got to start making studying chemistry a priority, but he doesn't seem to feel comfortable reaching out to anyone else yet. I can't sign off just when he's started to open up." Shameless. But brilliant.

It doesn't really make sense to me why I'm so adamant about keeping the key from him. I mean, dude knows just about everything else. And doesn't give up any of it. Soma's the only kid who's seen me cry since the time Ethan witnessed it after he nailed me right across the nose with a Frisbee down the shore. And yes, it was the morning of my mother's funeral or memorial service or life celebration or whatever she instructed us to call it. We were all late, Soma's mom had shown up to check on things, and I was stuck upstairs, freaking out because I couldn't find any matching socks. Mom had planned everything else out — you would've thought she would've laid our clothes out like she used to for the first day of school. Anyway, I'd started pulling out the drawers in my dresser, when Soma suddenly showed up in the bedroom doorway. I was in full pussy mode by this time, heaving sobs, snot running down my face and hanging from the sleeves I'd tried to wipe with. Ranting about how I couldn't find any goddamn matching socks and Soma kicked off his shoes and handed his pair over. When people call him a freak, when he takes the paramilitary shit a little too far, or shows up in a full flight suit to class like that's the most normal thing in the world, I remember Soma's bare ankles. Talk smack about that kid and I'll cut your face.

This morning, though, I sort of want to cut him. He's reached peak maniac status right now, whispering in this hushed pervy tone about how Ben Hendrikson casually mentioned to Jason Hendrikson that Miss Gabaldon wore a garter belt on their second date. "Can you believe that shit? Garters. She wears garters. She's got garters under those Girl Scout skirts." He is panting.

"Ben Hendrikson is scum and so is his little brother," I remind him.

"Whatever, he's scum who has his hand up her skirt on a daily basis. This has been documented."

And it has. More proof that Caramoor's own Madame Curie is not the brightest bulb. She's dating Jason Hendrikson's older brother. Some douche bag who comes home from New Haven every weekend to bang his little brother's chemistry teacher. Jason's always bringing it up in class and pulling that New Haven shit, too. (Why can't those douche bags just say Yale, anyway?) He raises his hand in class to ask, "Miss Gabaldon, I keep forgetting — is Ben coming back from New Haven this weekend or not?" And she gets all flustered, stuttering that she'll speak to him after class.

When he first started pulling this crap, I'd actually feel bad for her. Standing in the front of the room, with chalk dusting the dark sleeve of her turtleneck sweater. Trying to pretend the whole room wasn't picturing her boning Jason Hendrikson's older brother. But come on. What is she thinking? Yale med school or not, Ben Hendrikson is just an overgrown version of us. The kind of guy who drops her off and gets his little brother to smell his fingers when he gets home.

Open-ended essay #1: Construct an argument highlighting the pros and cons of telling your best friend that you have possession of a key that can access pretty much every door on campus. Let me just sum it up with symbols. Dress socks and garter belts. Soma is a minor genius. If there was a kid on campus who deserves the key through sheer continual manipulation of the system combined with bizarre fashion blunders, it's him. But he's also easily led astray. I don't want to do something lame-ass, like leave sex toys in desk drawers all over campus.

Even sitting there in homeroom, listening to Miss Gabaldon murmur breathlessly about how she expects us to sit through the day's inspirational lectures like the gentlemen she knows we are, with Soma panting in my ear about what she might have strapped around her thighs. Even listening to the rest of the Good Shepherds bitch and moan about how no one goes to school on Sundays — not even in North Korea. Even then, I remember the room at the top of Ainsley House that I've laid claim on. It's nothing really — a stupid sleeping bag and a pile of junk from our basement. But it is mine only. More than anything, that's why I keep my mouth shut about it to Soma.

The way the day goes by, it's not exactly a breeze. We sit through one alumnus talking about his inspirational career as a golf instructor in Key West. Another alumnus rants about his inspirational career in social services. An admissions guy from Colby College tries to inspire us to apply to his school. Someone's dad tells us inspiring stories about practicing emergency medicine but ends up telling us a bunch of lame-ass jokes about resuscitating our GPAs. And then the headmaster gives a quick, inspirational speech and commands us back to our advisories. There, Miss Gabaldon hands back all of our exams. And the academic outlook? Is fairly grim. It seems that leaving whole pages blank is not the best way to go, but I'm hoping I can stop by the therapeutic center office and sniffle myself a couple of makeups. Trot out the dead mom again and hope for the best. And yeah, that sounds terrible, but I also feel I'm owed that. A little bit. Every morning, Dad either drops me off or I trudge up the hill on my own and see the SUVs lined up with the tiny women inside, each of whom is someone's mother. The fact that a douche bag like Jason Hendrikson has a mom who throws back her head and laughs at his ricockulous stories pisses me off. There's that. But there's less obvious stuff that's even worse. The covert kind of suck that creeps up on you. Parent-teacher conferences and Dad clueless to how they worked. Basketball practice during Thanksgiving break, with all the guys talking about what incredible cooks their mothers are. The worst is just the totally casual moments, like when regular old screwing around stoops to *your mama* jokes. One kid will say something. And then another kid will elbow that kid or all the faces around the table will go still. And then you have to drink in all the pity along with your stupid carton of milk. All because some dumb-ass decided to tell a *your mama* joke.

If my dad wasn't such a hard-ass, the exams would not require the manipulation of Mr. Verlando, the poor sap who runs the "therapeutic center" at Caramoor. With Ethan AWOL, I'm the only kid who gives Dad a chance at a fancy college sticker on the back window of the car. I can say that the last day of exams is some kind of anniversary or something. Verlando will lean forward and put on his best Gaze of Concern, make a few phone calls, and then I'll schedule a makeup. And let's face it — it's easy as hell to cheat during a makeup session. Makeups are always proctored by some recent hire who has no clue about whatever subject you're taking. The guy's bored out of his mind, probably IMing his frat brothers on his school-issued laptop, seriously debating whether or not he could earn his measly private-school-teacher salary by playing high-stakes professional poker online.

I don't think I've ever gotten less than a B on a makeup test and that B was on purpose, because it was trigonometry and there was no way I could earn higher in any sort of believable fashion. So I begin to exhale a little bit — formulate a plan. I'll sign out to the therapy center during study hall and come up with something to say when he asks about the chem and computer science exams. My dad is leaving on Tuesday — so I really only have to get through tonight and tomorrow without getting him riled up enough to pull one of his call-school-to-check-on-your-progress moves. After Tuesday, I have nine days to explore campus. Ten days and already I've got this list scrolling down in my head. Things I want to see. Possible covert operations.

For the first time in months, I walk through Caramoor without looking for Ethan's back among all the other backs striding through the halls. In Wilson House, there are these student lounges, basically carpeted pits with beanbags and sofas where you're supposed to achieve the valuable male bonding and sense of community that the brochures tout on every page. The walls are covered with framed group shots of each graduating class and Ethan's is right at the top of the steps. For two and a half months or so, I've been using his face in that blurred mass of faces as this weird kind of touchstone. Not like I hang out in front of it lighting votive candles — it's just reassuring. He hasn't disappeared from everywhere.

Today is the first day I don't need that.

CHAPTER 5

By the time I get home, the conclusion has been made: I can't let myself into Caramoor tonight. Not on a Sunday night. Not after the sort of conversations Dad and I had this morning. Not when he's mixing his afternoon martini with a splash of guilt about leaving me on my own for nine days. He's going to want to spend some quality time with the kid.

And that's exactly what happens. I get home and set myself up at the dining room table. Three different books open so that when he gets in the door, Dad will really believe I've been studying for hours. He opens the freezer like he's actually considering cooking something, then tosses me my jacket, asking, "Steak or sushi?"

"Sushi is for pussies," I answer.

"That's my boy."

I'd actually prefer sushi, but there is a routine being played here and we are, apparently, in cowboy mode. We're going to mosey on out to the world of man-to-man talks and maybe even a beer with dinner so Dad can feel okay about leaving me to run the ranch while he's gone. Or the saloon. Depending on whether or not I let Soma come over.

We go to the Home on the Ranch steakhouse. It's the kind of place that has crushed peanut shells on the floor and TVs everywhere you swivel your head. I can watch the Lakers game over his head. He can watch a fight over mine. But what I love the most is watching the bar. It's a happy-hour kind of joint —

the sort of place where even on the weekends the girls from the office meet up to drink margaritas and giggle across the room at the bankers and legal guys hooting and hollering in the booths. The sort of place where Ben Hendrikson might have picked up Miss Gabaldon. You can sort of tell that most of the chicks are paralegals or secretaries and this is their rowdy place. My favorite part is watching them take the peanuts out of the buckets, shell them, and then sort of throw the husks down on the floor with this hesitant defiance. It's sort of sweet and sad, really. Like they're saying, "Hell, yes, I'm wild like that — I can throw my nuts on the floor."

"You see something over there you like?" For a second, I almost point out the peanut thing, but I don't think my dad would get it. He'd rather think I was checking out their racks than falling in love with the way they handle the bar snacks. And it feels weird talking about women with him now. Not that it would ever feel natural. But sometimes I wonder what he thinks about all that, if it hurts to make his own bed, to sleep alone there. Not that I'm ready to wake up to some executive assistant making pancakes in one of his shirts or something.

I mean I know he thinks about it some, because I see him checking out the waitress's ass when she sidles over to snap up his credit card. Classy. He sees me see him and clears his throat. "What do you say we stop at the driving range?"

"Dad, it's dark." God. How much togetherness do we need?

"So what — it's not like we're aiming for a hole. Humor your old man."

"Yes, sir. And thanks for dinner."

"That's more like it, Private." Now I realize he has to be a little drunk. He only busts out the soldier talk when he's drunk.

So, whatever, we hit a couple baskets of balls into the great wide open. I can handle that. In the car, I realize he's even more than a little drunk. Like had-I-not-been-there-he-might-have-actually-reached-out-and-grabbed-at-that-waitress drunk. When Dad drinks and gets behind the wheel, he gets this whole *Top Gun* thing going on. Like the car has transformed into a jet and he's going to hotdog it all the way. Speeding and weaving in and out of lanes. You know, it's a tremendously reassuring combination. Especially when it's just him and me sitting down for the portraits lately. I try to keep it light.

"Hey there, Maverick — how about we slow down a little?"

"I didn't raise you to be afraid of the power of a V-8 engine." This feels like one of those role-playing exercises we do in our Dangerous Decisions unit of health class.

"Yeah, yeah. Consider it proof of my healthy respect for your car."

"Respect for your father is better for your health in the long run." If this was a school role play, I'd have to parrot some crap like, "Hey, buddy, how about you pull into that gas station and take a break? Although I'm too young to legally drive, my dad will give us a lift." Except we never rehearsed the exercise with Dad as the lush with peanut shells in the treads of his shoes and his foot heavy on the gas pedal. Probably because the health teacher knew he'd get an insane amount of parent complaints. So I remain silent, even as Dad parks the car so that it diagonally overlaps the space beside us, making us look like two of those suckwits who think their car is too unbearably kick-ass to risk getting scratched by the minivan beside it.

It actually shocks me how many cars are in the lot, how many men are out here in the dead of winter. Don't these men have families? Hearths to sit beside or something? When Dad pops the trunk to take out his clubs, I start to wonder if this is a daily routine or something. "You keep your clubs in the car?"

"Of course I do. I golf. I golf well."

"It's February."

He hands me a twenty. "Just go get us two baskets. Don't be such a smart-ass." I buy the balls from some kid shivering in front of a kerosene heater in this shack thing. He has trouble making change because he's wearing two pairs of gloves.

"Sucks, huh?"

The kid shrugs. "It'll be warmer up there, under the lights."

"Yeah? Thanks. Stay warm."

"I get all the hot cocoa I can drink." I start to wonder if the kid is sort of slow.

"Oh yeah?" Now I'm using that real bright voice.

"Yeah, when I get home, I'll piss hot okay. I mean hot cocoa. I'll piss hot cocoa."

Now I start to think that dude's just stoned. I mean, "hot okay"?

"Yeah? That's . . . sweet. I mean, like, that's awesome."

"Yeah, I find it interesting."

So, yeah. He's stoned. I try to gather both wire baskets of golf balls and the change as quickly as possible and make a hasty exit.

When I get back to my father, he's shooting the shit with some guy named Chuck. He introduces me as his younger son and Chuck claps him on the back as he leaves. I see my dad nodding here and there at other men as they're teeing up. "You come here a lot, don't you?" I ask.

"That kid behind the counter a friend from school?"

"Him? No. You know he gets all the hot cocoa he wants?"

"That I did not know." My father sets up a ball and knocks it out into the darkness.

"Yeah. He says that it makes him pee hot cocoa."

My father hits another ball, turns to look me in the eye. "Are you stoned?"

"What?"

"Don't take anything that kid gives you."

"What? No. Dad. I don't —"

"Oh, I don't want to hear it. Just don't buy anything off that freak."

"Yeah, well, I wouldn't." After that he just grunts, and we fall into a silent rhythm — bending and swinging that's punctuated by the thwack of the club against the ball. Stonerboy was right, though — it isn't so cold beneath the bright lights. I can't see jack, though. And by the sixth ball, my hands are opening up some ripe blisters. This is the thing: I don't find golf very exciting. My freshman year, I played varsity because the coach just dropped us off at the crappy township course with a score pad and our clubs and some vague instructions on technique. Ted Dougherty and I would get stoned and walk around in the sunshine like we were princes touring our palace gardens. We made up what seemed like reasonable scores and then on match day went out and made asses of ourselves. The only time I actually enjoyed myself was when we played Saint Joe's and they had to call off the tournament because some kid went after a sliced ball and found a body in the woods. And that was it for golf, because the corpse proved to my mother that golf was a dangerous sport.

"Hey, remember when Mom made me quit the golf team?"

"Like most women, your mother could be irrational."

"I never understood that. It's not like golf killed that guy, right?"

"Maybe he got hit in the head."

"No, the papers said he was shot. Didn't they?"

"Maybe he got hit very hard with the ball."

"Dad —"

"Yeah, I don't know. She was worried about a criminal element."

"Because of the dead guy or Ted Dougherty?"

"What?"

"Nothing. Mine keep jutting to the right." I watch my dad sail the next ball in a perfect arc into the field in front of us. "So wait — Mom was concerned about the criminals who frequent golf courses?"

"Emil, don't ask me to explain your mother's occasional lunacy. She was concerned about the idea of you being so close to a corpse. It was a big deal for her. She felt terrible about that other boy, the one who actually found the body. She said he'd be traumatized for years, and that a parent's job was to protect her children from events that would later require future therapy. Your mother was ferocious about that."

I can't help it — I snort, and Dad turns around to glare, warning me. Even still, he lines up a perfect drive. Message received. I bend down to position the ball on the tee. Tug the tee up, as if that's clearly been the problem all along. Dad reaches down and I think he's going to swat at my head or something, but instead he takes a bunch of balls from my basket and drops them into his own.

"You're too slow. The whole point is to hit them as quickly as possible, so that your body practices the same range of motion again and again."

"You really do this a lot, don't you?"

"Ah, but I'm just capitalizing. Driving things away." And coming out of left field . . . all I can think of is that he has to be hammered. My father simply doesn't talk this way. If I'd said that, he would have made me drop and give him thirty push-ups or something. When I force myself to look up at him, he's gazing pretty steadily at me, though.

"Emil. I've been meaning to talk to you about Ethan." Silence except for the thudding of clubs up and down the rows, the balls whistling through the air. I'm looking at the row of men, standing on their little turf islands. I'm wondering what each is thinking about, looking so intently into the dark. And I don't know what my problem is. This is what I've been waiting for. My father talking about something actually important. Acknowledging the new quiet that's settled over our house. All I know is I can't do it. I don't want to know what he's decided about Ethan on the nights he's stood out here. I know my brother. I don't want to hear Dad talk crap about Ethan making his own way in the world or Ethan pussying out and running away or Ethan dousing his brain with drugs like the kid in the shack. It's nice, it's reassuring to know that Dad actually has his theories. I just don't want to hear them.

"I actually have a lot of homework to do." It sounds lame. I try to meet his eyes to make up for it, but that just makes it daringly lame. Dad's not just looking at me. He's *regarding* me. When I see him arrive at some conclusion, I wonder what it is that he's decided. There is an almost imperceptible nod that means, *Yep. My son's a tool.* Or it might mean, *Yep, I should have stopped at the second martini.* Or, *Yep. It's true. Each of us is utterly and completely alone in the world.* But all he actually says is "Yeah." Then, "Let me just knock off these last few balls."

I stand back and watch as he bends and thwacks in fast-forward. He's not even looking at where they are going. Just lining them up and letting them fly. He moves stiffly all the way back to the car, definitely sobering up.

I know what he's thinking. I know he's looking over at me and thinking, *Useless kid. Here I am trying to have an actual discussion with him. An important conversation and all he has to say is that he has homework.* Well, he can think that. I've been thinking that about him every day for months.

When I try to think like Ethan and figure out where he might have gone, I think he would have wanted to travel west. The pioneer spirit and all that crap or maybe up north, maybe he went up to Maine, where we used to spend summers when we were little. I think he would have gotten on a bus or a train and just stopped at a town that looked like a town in a movie about a kid starting over. He would have found work, rented a room, and probably read a lot at night. When Ethan talks about being a man, he's never really outgrown John Wayne movies or Bob Dylan lyrics. He's in some small town living quietly, sweet-talking the waitress into an extra slice of pie.

I know that's the best-case scenario. And people do that kind of thing all the time. You know, somewhere in the Midwest, that might be what growing up means. Moving on and making your own way and all that. But listen, we live in Connecticut. If we were Eskimos and Ethan had to leave to go hunt polar bears or something, I wouldn't whine so much, but he's not. He's supposed to go to Trinity or Tufts and carry his laundry home in a cab from the train station. Like every other goddamn big brother.

As soon as I think of the best-case scenario, I get scared it might be wrong. That one night we're going to get a phone call. Or maybe he's been hurt somehow and doesn't remember enough to come home. He wrote the word *Later* on the postcard because he meant he'd come home after ten minutes, not after months. Truthfully, no matter where he is or how he is, I'd be pissed. Say someone asked for change at the train station and Ethan said, "No" the way he always did — with no hint of apology, just a sneering, punkass "No." Even if some crazy homeless dude stabbed him in the belly, he could still drag himself to a phone booth and call home. Just once in the past three months.

We're home by ten o'clock and I'm actually exhausted. I go straight to my room and Dad stays to putter downstairs. I can hear him in the kitchen. For a second I think about going down there and letting him say what he needs to. He'd be setting up the coffeepot for tomorrow and sort of sigh and talk with this "This is how things are" tone, though. He'll talk about personal responsibility and moving on as best we can and sound so goddamn certain about everything. And I will barely be able to stand there without screaming. So I turn off the light and strip off my clothes. Crawl into bed and lay there until I hear my father's footsteps. I watch the slice of hall light under the door until he lumbers past. Then it's gone.

CHAPTER 6

Monday morning, I hit the snooze button enough times that I have to dive in and out of the shower, use mouthwash because it's quicker than brushing my teeth, tie my shoes on my way out the door, and then flip through the novel we're slated to start in English class.

"You're sure doing a lot of homework for a kid who found last semester to be such a walk in the park," Dad observes.

"Yessir." I didn't grab any breakfast. I'm not at all hungry until I realize that, and then I'm starving.

"I want to see those exams when you get home today."

I start to nod before I realize what he's asking and then say, "No, Dad, they don't let us bring home those exams. They don't leave the classroom."

"Why the hell not?"

I shrug my shoulders. It's a stupid rule, but it's not going to help anything to let him feel even more right. "I don't know. Probably so the teachers can use the same tests every year."

"Why does that matter? You're not going to be taking those exams twice."

That's what he thinks. "No, it's more about kids copying them and selling them to lowerclassmen."

"Why would someone do that?"

"Well, I would assume for profit."

"You'd think you kids would have more respect for your-selves than that. And you'd think that with the tuition I pay, your goddamn teachers might expend the effort it takes to write a new exam every year."

"Yessir." We're now five minutes from school. I can hang on for five minutes.

"'Yessir,' what?"

"Sir?" Honestly, at this point, I have no idea what he wants from me. I'd give anything to crawl back into the hot shower. Just camp out for a while under the water. It's freezing. I swear to God, I'm going to get out of this car and my hair is going to freeze at the ends.

"Emil, I'm not playing games here. I want to see some evidence of your performance on these exams before I leave."

"Yessir." I'd worry about this more if I weren't so concerned that my testicles have crawled up to my lungs. It's that cold out. I move to turn up the heat on the dash and he slaps my hand away.

"You need to wear a hat. And get a haircut. Did you arrange a ride to school for yourself while I'm away?"

"Yeah."

"Yeah, who?"

"Soma will swing by in the mornings. I'll buy him breakfast or something."

"Soma has his license?"

"Yes. Do you suddenly feel less safe on the road?"

"Hell, yes."

"Well, he rarely drinks martinis." At first I think maybe I've pushed it too far. But Dad sort of snorts a little, shakes his head, and goes on to mumble some warning about how Soma better not be drinking any martinis, since he knows exactly how full all the bottles in the liquor cabinet are.

"When I was your age . . ." And I know this story, too. When he was in high school, his father would mark all the levels of his bottles with a black marker. So all Dad would do to outsmart him was fill the bottle back up with water. He figured his dad was so drunk he'd never notice. But then Grandad was no sucker, either. He drew the line way above the level and then whupped Dad's ass for leaving him with a bottle more full than he'd left it.

Dad gets to the ass-whupping part and I'm thinking about how he handled it when Ethan and I sneaked some of his cigarettes from the pack. When he caught us doing that, he sat us down and made us sit there until between the two of us we'd smoked the whole pack. I was, like, eight. I don't think I've ever felt so sick, can remember sliding off the chair, clutching at the floorboards, moaning, "Ethan, make it stop." And Ethan just sat there choking down the rest of the cigarettes.

We're just about at school. "How come you never had us drink an entire bottle of vodka, like with the cigarettes?" Dad pulls the car into the drop-off lane, slows to a stop.

"Didn't want you to get a taste for vodka. Besides, your mother gave me hell for the cigarettes."

"Neither of us ever smoked again, though. See you later."

"I want those exams."

I wasn't bullshitting him, either. I never tried cigarettes after that. Neither did Ethan. It always made me laugh a little bit — my brother would pretty much load anything up into a bong, but he was going to stay as far away from nicotine as humanly possible. Heroin and nicotine — my brother's only rejected vices.

At this point, I'm floating on one of those hunger highs. I'm already late for advisory with no study hall today, so I won't have a break until lunch. It occurs to me that it's going to absolutely torture me to sit through the two morning classes I have in Ainsley House and know that I have a box of Pop-Tarts stashed directly above me.

I recognize the clomp of Soma's army boots as they fall in line beside me.

"You're going to get nailed for dress code because of those boots," I tell him. Caramoor used to be a freaking citadel, with cadets running around all over the place, but army boots and work boots have been recently declared off-limits by whoever decides on the dress code. We are, after all, the future of America. Boots might make us look too working class.

Soma snaps his gum in my face. "Dress code is for fascists," he says, almost automatically. "Hey, you know how slick you looked yesterday?"

"Yeah." I'm wary at this point. This is going nowhere good.

"Yeah, you look the inverse of that today," Soma announces. "What happened?"

"What happened is I realized there weren't any chicks at our school."

"Yeah? Three years — you've just noticed that, huh? What does that tell us about you, my disheveled friend?"

"I don't know. Maybe that I just started paying attention after I stopped doing your mother?"

Soma cackles a little bit, backs his way into the door. "No way, my orphaned friend. Your dead mama precludes you from any mama jokes — it's like you're automatically disqualified." Miss Gabaldon gives a little squeak and I have to laugh at Soma's ability to make a whole room uncomfortable with the truth. You know, except us.

Plus that gives me the perfect opportunity to sulk a little bit through advisory and then ask Miss Gabaldon for a pass to the therapeutic center. Rest my head on my desk for all of three minutes. And then she beckons, "Emil, may I see you up front for a sec?" When Miss Gabaldon used to call guys up to her desk, the rest of the class would whistle and clap. I suppose it's to her credit that these days they just look up and grin.

"You okay, Emil?" It occurs to me that Miss Gabaldon was probably once an excellent babysitter. Like seriously. The kind who would play games and stuff and make instant pudding with you and not just sit on the sofa and watch TV and talk on the phone. This doesn't stop me from lying to her, though.

"Yeah." I say it like I'm trying to convince myself it's true. "I'm fine, really. It's okay. I should probably just suck it up and go to class —"

"Maybe, but maybe not, Emil. What's wrong?"

"Nothing." I drop my voice, mostly because if he overhears me, Soma's steel-toed boots will discipline my ass. "I know Soma was just teasing and all. He's my friend — he'd never say something to hurt my feelings." This is where silence gets important. I bite my lip, dart my eyes away, like I'm trying not to let her see me cry. Wait. One second. Two seconds.

"I know exactly what you mean."

Score. "You do?"

"It must make things even more difficult when your friends are dismissive of your emotions." I'm looking down now, focusing on the pink ovals of her painted fingernails, wondering how far I want to press this.

"It helps to know you understand, Miss Gabaldon." She covers one of my hands with her own and I have to say, my knees get a little shaky. Mostly it's because she's one of the few women I have any regular contact with. There's the middle-aged house-keeper who comes by once a week, the ladies in the office, the cafeteria ladies, and Miss Gabaldon. And clearly if we were running a beauty pageant, there wouldn't be any kind of tearful suspense about the winner. So there's that and there's also Hendrikson's stupid garter story. It's hard to see her hands and not think of them unfastening the little clips, sliding something lacy down her thigh.

But I digress. And I can tell my face is crimson with embarrassment. Hopefully she thinks I'm still just ashamed of my tearfulness. She awkwardly pats my hand, then writes out a pass. It's adorable. I have to stop myself from smiling at her when she hands it over. "Thanks for making that so easy on me," I say instead. Then gulp and look downward, like I'm afraid to meet her eyes.

"Don't you worry about a thing," she says patting again. "I'll duck in and let Mr. Choudry know you had a personal matter that needed your attention."

"Thank you, Miss Gabaldon."

"You can call me Tamara," she says, tearing open her shirt, so that its buttons scatter across the desk. That's what she'll say later on, when I'm repeatedly replaying this exchange in my head. For right now, all she says is, "Don't you worry, Emil." But you know, she says it tenderly. I'm almost out in the hall when I hear her voice shift gears into strict teacher dialect. "Soma. Those boots are out of dress code."

The hallways are empty since the bell hasn't rung and I think of how empty they'll be tomorrow night, when I get the run of the place. I let myself out of the building and cross the grass to Ainsley House, wink at Mrs. Schecter at the front desk, then trot up the stairs to the therapeutic center. Ethan used to say that the trick to staying free and clear at Caramoor was to remember that everyone took his job seriously here. It wasn't until this past year that I understood what he meant. Not that I've aimed to take advantage of anyone's good intentions, exactly. But if you just let them feel like they're helping you survive high school, well, most of the faculty will help you survive high school. They'll be looking hard for you to show gratitude for it, but they'll help you all the same.

It's barely eight thirty in the morning — Verlando already looks like he's sweat right through his shirt. His hair is sticking out in crazy tufts all over his head and when he waves me into his office, I see why. One hand crams the telephone receiver to his ear and the other, the one that was just waving at me, is tugging wildly at sections of his own hair. He's screeching into the phone something about some kid who needs a test to show he needs extra time on tests, and from what I understand, the mom doesn't want to make the kid take the diagnostic test, because he gets so nervous about testing.

"Mrs. Barnes, I understand the nature of Jesse's nervousness. But the first step we need to take to tackle that problem is to get him a diagnosis!" Verlando is practically hyperventilating into the phone at this point. "OF COURSE, any diagnosis would be strictly confidential. OF COURSE, we wouldn't put that on his college transcript. But frankly, Mrs. Barnes, we need to solve this terror of tests thing before we start filling out applications . . . OF COURSE, I'm not making light of your son's academic difficulties."

Verlando spends the next few minutes talking crap about educational trends and diverse learning styles. When he manages to get poor Jesse's mom off the phone, he lets out a long exhale. It sounds like a bike tire going flat.

"You were totally making light of that kid's academic difficulties," I say.

"Well, let's see, Mr. Simon — what academic difficulties do you have, of which I might make light?"

This is the thing about the therapeutic center: It's not really designed for kids who have actual problems. Unless those problems are adversely affecting your academic performance. I mean, you could cut yourself through the SATs and fill in the answer keys using only your own blood. You'd end up in Verlando's office and he'd just be asking, "What? Did you not have a number two pencil? OF COURSE, we can provide you with a number two pencil."

It's not that he doesn't care that you just sliced up your arm. But he figures, fix the test scores first. Get him into a good liberal arts school and make sure THEY have a strong counseling center. Kids talk about Verlando like he's another cog in the machine and, okay, clearly he is. But I sort of like that he knows he's a cog. And if the only way he's actually able to make our lives a little easier is to make sure we get to retake the math exam we scored a thirty-two percent on or fix it so the ADD kids get to take their tests in double the time, then he's going to do that. And he's not willing to pretend it's anything more profound than that.

When I start to feel bad, a little guilty for manipulating the man, I realize: Verlando's met my father. He knows what I'm up against. So I give it to him as straight as I can and still get what I need. "It's not really my academic difficulties that are the problem, really."

"Mmmmmm-hmmmmmmm," he says, even as he's typing into his computer, bringing up my most recent collection of scores.

I try again. "I've dipped in some subjects, but I think there's a reason for that."

"Mmmmmmmm-hmmmmm."

"I know I messed up. Especially on my math and French exams. I should have stayed home from school that day. My dad kept saying that, but I worried about taking makeups. Now I think that might have been the thing to do."

"Were you ill that day, Ethan?"

"Emil."

"I beg your pardon?"

"My name is Emil. Ethan is my big brother."

"I'm so sorry." He looks over at me. We both know I'm going to milk that misstep for all that it's worth.

"It's okay. The thing about Ethan . . ."

"Yes?" I'm chickening out. This feels like betraying someone. I'm still not sure who. But I don't know what saying this out loud will set in motion. Can you get arrested for letting your kid disappear? I think about my dad, how bewildered he seemed last night at the range. Then I picture how he'd look if he saw a thirty-two percent on a science exam. Not even an honors science exam.

"Ethan's missing." Once I say it, the room looks a little different to me. I start to realize why they say blue is a calming color. The walls of the therapeutic center are painted blue and they feel as if they are closing in around me. But in a good way. Sort of like an insistent hug.

"I know." Now I feel knocked down by something soft. The way a wave knocks you off a sandbar in the ocean.

"How do you —"

"Your father called a couple of weeks ago, thought maybe Ethan had checked in with college guidance about student travel opportunities or alternative educational options."

"What, like camping?"

"Well, yeah. Or something like Semester at Sea."

"My father thinks Ethan's *out at sea*?"

"No, we checked on that and made sure that Ethan hadn't registered for that program. He acknowledged that the traditional college experience might not hold much allure for your brother. He thought perhaps Ethan looked elsewhere."

"That's retarded." And it was. I could have told him that Ethan would never have bought into that crap. Some kind of manufactured coming-of-age. He never would have gone for that.

"Emil, your father was just checking up on some ideas. Really, neither of us wished to concern you with the matter. He's of the opinion that your job right now is to focus on your schoolwork, and I have to say, I agree."

Unbelievable. "Well, last week, after we found this new postcard from Ethan, it was difficult to focus on my schoolwork."

"And this fell on the day of the science and languages exams?"

"Yes, sir."

"Well, that's perfectly understandable, and I'm sure we can arrange for you to take the tests again in the near future. Things have settled down some. Let's have another stab at it, shall we?"

I sort of can't believe this. "He's not at Semester at Sea."

"Let me talk to your teachers about next Tuesday. That gives you a weekend to review and Monday to ask any necessary questions. I don't think I need to tell you how important junior year is, Emil. Let's give you the best chance possible with college admissions by shoring up this transcript."

"He's my brother, Mr. Verlando." What I mean is: How can I not be concerned about him? Ethan might have decided it doesn't count for anything, but I haven't.

Verlando leans back in his chair, stops tugging at his hair, and plants the palms of his hands down on his desk. Moves them back and forth like he's smoothing out the wooden surface. "You know," he says, "in my day it was the Peace Corps. People wanted to find the meaning of life . . . stall some big decisions . . . make a difference. God, people were so in love with Kennedy back then. He could have set up a program called Volunteers on Mars and we would have strapped on jet packs to be a part of that man's legacy."

"Ethan's not interested in helping people. He likes to get high and record whether or not he can still recite the whole alphabet."

Verlando grimaces. "All I'm saying is that sometimes when the world makes you feel small, it helps to take on something gigantic just to prove you can make it. Even as an inconsequential speck."

"Whatever." I'm done here. Got what I came for. Verlando doesn't press it, writes me out a pass to second period.

"Let's kick some butt next Tuesday!" he says brightly, and is back on the phone before I'm even all the way out the door. I spend the rest of my class period making lists about why the therapeutic center is useless. About why Ethan would never sign up for Semester at Sea.

I actually have this thing. Mom used to call it a tic. But I'd argue that's inaccurate. Not now. I mean, we don't argue with dead women. My list thing, though — it's more like advanced planning. Generally, my first response to worry or fear or general rootless anxiety is to make lists. Sometimes ones that only vaguely have to do with the situation at hand. For instance, right now I'm feeling slightly self-conscious about my method for dealing with stress. So in my head, I'm listing some of the lists I've made.

1) First day of school at Caramoor: list of all the ties I had in my closet. I'd never worn a tie to school. It helped to know I had plenty.
2) Once, shortly after starting school: a list of all the things I'd like to do to Miss Gabaldon. Or with Miss Gabaldon. I eventually burned that list.
3) When my mom got sick: list of things I could do around the house to make things a little easier. Weirdly enough, I burned that list, too.
4) When my mother died: I stood at the freezer and wrote down every single casserole some lady in the neighborhood had made. This was shockingly easy. Most ladies in the situation, I've learned, label the Tupperware with the name of the dish and the name of the lady who made it. Presumably so we could eventually return the dish. Which we haven't. Most of those dishes are still in the freezer.
5) When Ethan first started really going all Belushi with the drugs. When it started to seem like he was high all the

time: talented people who'd died from ODs. Or just ruined themselves. For instance, Doc Gooden counted.

6) Ethan left: I made a list of all the places he might be. Historical monuments. Lame bands he might have wanted to trail after. Bonnaroo, for christsakes. Scientology.

So that's the general idea. That's how I keep my world in some recognizable shape. As it is now, it's almost impossible to concentrate on anything for the rest of the day. All of a sudden, I'm just tired of hearing about stuff, the Pythagorean theorum, the periodic table, verb agreement. I'm tired of hearing about the best place for paintball and who aced the SAT or got a blow job at the last Saint Bernadette's dance. Yeah, there's a whole other list: things I couldn't care less about. But that wasn't going to calm me down.

I figured it this way: At the absolute very least, I had nine nights. Alone. On campus. As far as I knew, the key opened everything. I started listing, then, the doors that I had to unlock. Doors it would be unforgivable to walk past without looking in. Verlando's office. Faculty lounge. Library. Headmaster's office. Ainsley House. Arts Studio. College guidance. Miss Gabaldon's lab.

And then I made another list of things I wanted to do, anything that came to mind, regardless of possible outcome: find any files people might have on me and Ethan, adjust transcripts, figure out the damn ghost thing, sniff things, execute a respectable key prank. Figure things out. I don't know why I felt like Caramoor held all the answers. Like when the sun sank down and the buses pulled out, the place got to be some kind of hallowed ground. But the other night, when I was here by myself, it felt like it did. Like maybe so many people had filed through there, the place had to have the spirit of some kind of self-revelation. Ethan went off to discover something; that seems as true to me as anything else. He wasn't the only one who needed answers, though. I had a list of questions I wanted to ask.

CHAPTER 7

You'd figure Dad would make this big deal about eating dinner together, but I guess he decided last night backfired. By the time the final bell rang, he'd already left a voice mail saying he'd be late and I should pick up a pizza or some subs. Dude, if you know at three that you're going to come home past seven, that's some calculated lateness. It unnerved me a little to consider that he might not want to see me any more than I wanted to see him. Maybe Mr. Verlando called him.

I do something then that I'm not sure is so cool, but honestly I'm still so angry, I feel sort of owed. Over the course of the two and a half months that Ethan has been gone, I'd maybe gone in his room less than ten times. Mostly when I got drunk and prissy — li'l brother missing ye olde role model. I've taken a total of three things from Ethan's room: the key, obviously, one condom, and a thesaurus that came in handy while writing my Huck Finn paper. But it occurred to me on the frozen trek home that if Ethan took the time to leave a note, he also packed. He must have stood in the center of the room and picked out the things he considered important to bring along.

So I go to his dresser drawers, crammed with all his hipster clothes and vintage shirts. Open season. His guitar. Mine to borrow. And I'm just getting started. I don't pack anything up, just make a bunch of small trips from his room to mine, in case Dad breezes in and decides to act fatherly. The man who has left his dead wife's slippers peeking out from underneath the family-room sofa would probably object to the spare's raiding the heir's closet. I take piles of his CDs and notice that his iPod is missing. Good to know that Ethan's got an expansive soundtrack to accompany his missing status. I dig around in his desk drawers for his porn, grab a fresh set of charcoal pencils. In the top drawer I find a book of stamps with a sheet of almost forty tabs of acid. Then there's a Ziploc bag pretty much brimming with weed in the hull of one of the stupid model ships we used to build together. I trot all of it across to my room. I find new hiding places.

The whole thing weirds me out even more than breaking into Ainsley House. For one thing, Dad will kill me if he finds out, going all apeshit about how in this house, we respect each other's privacy. Everybody has his own personal space. And normally I would have called bullshit on that. Thought he was bluffing. But it starts to make me really uneasy. I mean, if your kid were missing . . . okay, your nineteen-year-old kid, true, but he's still living under your roof and all that crap. If he were missing, wouldn't you go through his things? Even if you sort of think he's run away, wouldn't you want to know what he counted as crucial enough to bring with him? You'd check his desk for his passport, right? If you weren't blind and had actually met my brother, you would have looked around for drugs. What the hell is wrong with my father? What the hell is wrong with me that this is the first time all of this has occurred to me? I cannot begin to list all of it. So you know, I do the next sensible thing, knowing my dad will be home in an hour and I have to sit through a total of maybe three more hours with him before he's halfway across the country for nine straight days.

I take out Ethan's stamp collection. Tear off two tabs and let the acid dissolve on my tongue.

I have this to say for myself: As soon as I do it, I realize it's a mistake. Of epic proportions. My father is not the kind of man who puts up with any bullshit. It's not like he's amused by goofiness. So you can't pass off any drug-addled behavior that way. And out of all the possibilities for narcotic rebellion, acid is the one that would most piss him off. For as long as I can remember, Ethan and I have heard him rant about how LSD was invented by the government to initiate psychosis, how any moron who willingly dosed himself deserved to wind up mumbling to park pigeons for decades.

By the time his car pulls in the driveway, I'm officially tripping balls. Decide that the best thing to do is to hop in the shower, that spending a half hour locked in the bathroom will at least subtract from the time he and I sit across from each other downstairs. In theory, this sounds like a reasonable idea. He'll come in the house, hear the water running, figure out I'm in the shower, and start packing or sit down in front of the news. Maybe he'll have his first drink. That might help, too.

In actuality, I don't know how long I'm in the bathroom. I can't stop myself from looking in the mirror, so you know there's probably at least a half hour spent watching my face slide down to my collarbone. At one point, I look down at my bare feet on the stall's tile, feeling triumphant about the fact that I've remembered to take off my socks. That feels like proof of my genius. And then I just sort of end up hypnotized by the drumming of the water against my skin.

I almost drop to the ground when Dad pounds on the door,

asking what I've picked up for dinner. Manage to yelp out that I've forgotten before becoming really fascinated with the drain in the tub. Then the back door slams again and this time I hear the car back out. I use the time he's out to get myself dressed, to make a list of safe things we can talk about at dinner: hockey and my belief that we should get a dog.

He brings home a rotisserie chicken and some kind of potato salad. At one point, it really upsets me to pick the chicken flesh off the carcass in the center of the dining room table. That makes me think of vultures, of Dad and me being like vultures, and I almost tearfully confess my raid of Ethan's room.

At one point, he tears off a breast and sets it on my plate. And then the chicken starts breathing. It looks like an organ inflating and deflating on my plate. I don't think I will ever eat meat again.

He asks me about the exams, hears that Mr. Verlando has promised to call him with results. "I'm sure he'll get to it tomorrow as soon as he gets to it." I say something brilliant like that. This is before I blurt out that there is no way in hell that Ethan would have signed up to go to sea. At this point, he starts clearing the table. We've eaten off paper plates and I almost put them in the dishwasher. He gets his suitcases out of the hall closet and starts packing, calls up to me as I go upstairs that he's put some extra money in my account for food, transportation, and emergencies. He'll make sure to e-mail me a travel itinerary before he leaves the office the next morning. It turns out that I'm a pretty agreeable son when I'm on acid.

"Better get started on that homework," one of us says to the other. Probably me. I put on an old Galaxy 500 CD of Ethan's and play their cover of "Don't Let Our Youth Go to Waste."

Probably about sixty times. Then I lie down on my bed, above the blankets, and stare at my ceiling until I finally feel myself coming down. At one point, at maybe the third hour of staring at the ceiling, I have completely convinced myself that he's checked Ethan into rehab and just neglected to tell me out of fear that I will tell kids at school.

I wake up at three in the morning, sneak down to the kitchen, and eat three bowls of cereal. After the first two, I decide the milk has gone sour, so I eat the third bowl with Cool Whip. This had less to do with acid, though, and more with my ravenous hunger. It's hard to fall back asleep afterward. Start thinking that maybe it's what I was aiming for, taking it in the first place, but it makes me wonder how often Ethan had sat there at the table with us, playing that game of keeping a stupid secret. I knew about a couple of times. Once I didn't speak to him for a week and a half after I came home from school and found him tripping balls, sitting on the living room floor with Mom lying behind him on the sofa. She was sort of absentmindedly rubbing his hair and he was staring at some game show without blinking. Ethan told me to grow up, that she was so doped up on pain meds that she wouldn't have known, anyway. He said it was like meeting her on a plane that was much more pleasant for both of them. Maybe that's why Dad and I haven't questioned his leaving as much as we should have. Already we were the only mostly sober ones in the house. Both of them sort of faded out even before they left.

I try to make the previous night up to my dad in the car ride to school, but he's distracted. He's doing my trick, listing all the crap I need to remember to do while he's away. Trash day's on

Tuesday. Recycling is Thursday. Money's in the bank. He'll keep his cell phone on from 7:00 PM to 7:00 AM. He already paid the cleaning lady for next week — I shouldn't let her bilk me out of a second envelope of cash.

If I throw a party, he'll know about it. He actually says, making the turn up toward Caramoor, that since Ethan hadn't gotten away with throwing a party, I better not even make an attempt. My parents always made a point not to compare the two of us outright, so this actually makes me laugh. I guess he thinks it was okay to point out that I'm no delinquent in comparison. On another day I might take it as a challenge. Part of me wants to blurt out right there, "Last night I ate chicken on acid with you." The insane part of me. Instead I just sit there, flexing my jaw, picturing the key zipped up in the tiny pocket in my backpack. He doesn't know me as well as he thinks.

I remember when Ethan threw the party. Probably the entire student body and alumni association of Caramoor Academy remembers or has heard about it. It was insane. Dad had taken Mom to Barcelona for their twentieth wedding anniversary. This was right before she got sick. Maybe she was already sick and what they thought was jet lag or too much champagne was actually its first, ugly start. But as far as we knew, we were coasting. Ethan had just gotten his license. He knew some guy who'd been kicked out of Caramoor and sent up to boarding school in Vermont. That guy would drive down and set us up. I say "us," but honestly? I was in the ninth grade. This meant that my job was to ride my bike to Krauzer's Market and buy a crapload of Cheez Doodles.

It was the kind of party that you imagine when you first go

to high school. Even our high school. I mean, somehow there were girls there. One of whom was going at it with Ethan in our parents' bedroom. Someone had set up turntables and was pretending to spin, but really they were just playing songs from Quentin Tarantino soundtracks. I was still Little Simon and the only action I got was from some shrieky chick who clearly had a thing for Ethan. She was not the one he led to our parents' bedroom. She just tousled my hair every time I walked by and told me I had potential.

This was the first night I'd seen Ethan do blow and it sort of shocked me to see him cut lines on my parents' coffee table. But there were a lot of them doing it and no one else seemed particularly fazed. People danced until the floor shook. At one point, my mother's hutch, the one she'd filled with all these carved wooden animals, tipped over, but it's not like she collected spun glass or anything. We got it back upright and tried to set back all the animals as best we could.

Someone called the police. Honestly, I don't know what Ethan had been thinking. My parents had never gone away and left us alone before. Of course, Dad was going to stop by the neighbors, ask them to keep an eye on his young men. At first we thought the sirens were a part of the song and then someone was sober enough to turn down the stereo. Ethan freaked out, then herded everyone out the back door. We turned off the lights, locked the door, and Ethan told me to pretend I was sleeping on the sofa. He wrapped the tray of cocaine with Saran Wrap like it was a plate of cookies.

When the police started banging on the door, Ethan motioned for me to stay still. We heard yelling in the back, where some of the more drunk kids had gotten lost in the jungle of our yard. So then, Ethan looked around and very calmly went outside to talk to the police officers.

I don't know how he did it. He worked the earnest charm, I guess. "Officer, I'm so grateful you've arrived. Our parents — they've gone to Europe and told us we could invite a few friends over. But wouldn't you know it! Those friends brought along guests, and someone (gasp) brought along alcoholic beverages and the situation quickly escalated out of our control." That's how Ethan auditioned for the part of the good kid whose parents don't need to be called, no sir, no way.

And so nothing happened. Now looking back, I think the cops had to have known he was bullshitting. They must have been so impressed at the elaborate efforts that they cut him a break. The drunk kids they'd chased down in cruisers were driven home. Only the ones who were older and belligerent were given summonses for drunk and disorderly conduct. And Ethan and I shut off the front porch light and locked both the door lock and the deadbolt.

We spent that entire Sunday cleaning. One of Mom's mallard ducks had lost his beak in the fall and we glued that. We vacuumed, picked crushed corn chips out of the carpets, and then vacuumed again. We drove to the dump so that Dad wouldn't see the beer cans overwhelming the recycling bins. We dusted, fluffed pillows. And when Mom and Dad got home as scheduled, they walked in to find us watching a movie in the den with homework stretched out in front of us both.

I remember that I could hardly look up. Concentrated on the equations and proof in my algebra book because otherwise one of them would have known exactly everything as soon as I raised my eyes for contact. If I'd been an only child, that would have been it. Nervous kid plus pristine house equals party thrown the night before. But Ethan wasn't about to let my pansy-ass spoil it. He took their suitcases, piled them on the second-floor landing, and started up the charm factory. He hugged my mom and made her giggle with some bizarre story about burning spaghetti the night before and having to order in Chinese food. That was the extent of the mayhem we described: pasta stuck to the bottom of a pot.

For that whole first week after they got back, my heart skidded every time the stupid phone rang. I convinced myself that each call was a parent of one of the arrested kids, a lawyer, or some concerned teacher who'd overheard an account of the party at school. I pictured how my mother would answer the phone as eagerly as she answered every phone call, how she'd have on her chatty, friendly face until the voice on the line kept going. Then her expression would steel itself in grimness. I didn't allow myself to imagine how she'd sit at the desk in my father's study, dialing him at his office.

When it didn't happen the first week, I let myself breathe a little easier. When the second and third week went by, I even let myself forget a little.

In fact, in the time that I let our night of teenage debauchery and the subsequent sirens drift out of my mind, the baseball field thawed. The morning announcements about how our basketball team tried really hard but lost, anyway, morphed into announcements that our baseball team tried really hard but lost, anyway. Welcome to Caramoor Academy, where our athletes valiantly withstand their pitiful records with ironclad self-esteem.

I don't think Mom ever missed one of Ethan's baseball games. She wasn't one of those moms who were all flashy about it — she didn't bake cookies for the team or get her nails done in team colors or anything. Our mother had a little dignity, for christsakes. I didn't even mind sitting next to her at the games. Once in a while, she asked me to explain a decision one of the coaches had made or she leaned over whatever book I had open to see what I was taking notes on. So that's where I was, crouched over my Western Civ book, on the bleachers with my mom at Ethan's ball game. The two mothers in front of us were talking about it for a good while before it dawned on me that they were about to ruin my life. I think Ethan had done something typically miraculous, bobbled an easy hop and managed to still make the third out of the eighth inning. One of the mothers sighed with relief all dramatically, as if her measly life hung in the balance or something. And the mom next to her said, "Talk about cutting it close."

The other one said, "Well, that's Ethan Simon for you. That's who that is, right? The one who threw that party."

"What party?"

"You know — the one I told you about. Alan had to pick up Edward at the police station, can you imagine? It was devastating. Alan and I were beside ourselves. And then that Simon boy told the police the kids were trespassing. There are two of them. There's a younger one. The parents were in Europe. Can you imagine leaving two teenage boys alone in the house? What were they thinking? Alan handled things, thank God."

"Well, did anyone call the parents?"

"The Simons? And say what? 'Obviously, you have no

reservations about letting your boys run wild, but we thought we'd let you know that —' "

"Well, surely they'd want to know."

"Well, all I know is that now Edward knows to steer clear of Ethan Simon. I thought Alan was going to have a coronary."

At that moment, Alan had nothing on my mother, who had gone very still, looking at her hands in her lap as if she didn't recognize how they could be useful. By this time the two brides of Satan in front of us had moved on to the subject of cholesterol medication. Tommy Phelps was swinging away our last shot at bringing the score to a somewhat respectable showing. Ethan had walked and stood coiled at first base as if he believed he could steal every base to home. Tommy swung on, and the umpire called him out. Ethan looked up toward us in the bleachers and blazed a grin out from under the batting helmet. My telepathic messages did not reach their target. Mom eased herself out of the stands and headed toward the car, with me shoving my books into my backpack and bounding after her like one of those yappy dogs that follows the striding tough dogs in the kibble commercials. I don't remember what I tried to talk about, just that it seemed like if I could distract her somehow, we still had a shot at free and clear.

She didn't even bother faking it, wasn't interested in my desperate attempts at entertainment. I climbed in the back of the car, thinking Ethan would want shotgun, then remembering that actually Ethan probably would want the back. Or the trunk. By the time we saw him trot down the field house steps with his cleats in his hand and wearing his dress shoes like some weird nameless guy, my mom had basically, for the first time in my life, told me to shut up. Of course she was classier about it. She said, "Emil, you've done a very good job of keeping quiet for weeks now. Why stop now?" That was all she had to say. I don't think I spoke again the whole night.

I stood there, sure. Ethan and I stood in front of my father and watched his mouth move and his fingers point and his face redden. Ethan had this trick of watching Dad's Adam's apple bob in his throat — that's how he stopped himself from laughing. My father's hands kept fluttering to his belt buckle and you could tell he was wishing he was raising boys in a less enlightened time — had my mother let him, he would have whipped us. Instead we stood there until it was over.

And for the next three days we sat silently through meals. We nodded at each other a lot. We said "Excuse me" when we passed each other in the upstairs hall. The phone rang a lot and my mother and father spoke in hushed voices. I remember noticing how my mother started wringing her hands, how she suddenly looked so much older. I dismissed her, thinking, *Jesus. She is so concerned with what the neighbors think.*

When they sat us down in the living room, I figured they'd finally figured out what to do with us. If Dad had his way, we'd be splitting firewood. Knowing Mom, it would be shifts served at the downtown Hartford soup kitchen. Ethan already had his eyes steeled and I remember trying to send him a telepathic message, *Just nod at whatever they say.*

That's all both Ethan and I ended up doing. Nodding. It wasn't that kind of punishment, that conversation. That was the night they told us Mom was sick. Dad told us and she sat next to him with her hands in her lap. She sort of gave this apologetic smile. You know — like she was embarrassed she'd let someone down. Nobody said anything about the party after that.

But it's the one piece of Caramoor social lore that I can claim involvement in. So far. Walking down the school corridors now, I feel a little different. Eager. Ready. I have a secret. Honestly, a little bit like I felt at the dinner table last night. Seeing the world a little differently and knowing no one knows why. I shift from desk to desk throughout the day, and the whole time I'm imagining the fluorescent lights turned off. Remembering how the hedges look like crouched animals in the dark and the specific shadows that the chair backs throw against the classroom walls.

CHAPTER 8

The idea of my house sitting empty for nine straight days has Soma frothing at the mouth. At the end of the eighth period, he's hovering at my locker. "Get a move on, Simon," he says.

"What?"

"The bus pulls out at three-fifteen."

"What?"

"I gotta get home." Soma says this like it matters to me, and it takes me awhile to understand why. Ride home. My father. Paying him. Ride home.

"Yeah, yeah. I'm ready to go."

"You're holding an open carton of yogurt."

"Yeah?"

"No spoon. And no books."

"Whatever. I'll drink the yogurt."

"All right, Kid Zombie, I don't know who cut your lines of Xanax this afternoon, but think trig test. Think U.S. History quiz. Hello?"

My mouth moves like Mr. Rhodes's does when he's writing notes on the blackboard. Damn. Damn. I didn't pack books. Figured I'd be right back here in a few hours. And then I realize: It's Soma. I let my eyes glaze over.

"God," he says. "If you're snorting your mom's old cancer meds without me, you suck."

And that's the extent of it. He opens my locker. Sorts through my books. Loads up my backpack. I drink the raspberry yogurt and let some of it collect on my lower lip. I lean against the locker like a smackhead at the bus station. For the four hundredth time this week, I realize how much easier it must have been to be Ethan. To just let a haze of some kind of smoke roll over me and cushion me from the rest of the world. So that's what I do. I pretend to be so stoned I can't even talk to Soma.

It's less pretending than just letting the day roll along. Soma drives me through the school lot and through town and I let my hand loll out the window.

"Haven't you seen those bus safety videos?"

I dip my head toward Soma's moving mouth. It's shocking to me how quickly and thoroughly acting stoned begins to equal being stoned.

"You know the ones where the kids lose the limbs they stick out the bus window?"

Lick my lips and look up.

"Get it together, Emil. I know that Sergeant Hard-ass has left the premises, but that doesn't mean that you have to party this hard. On a Tuesday." By the time we hit my driveway, Soma's pissed. "Can you make it inside on your own, Lou Reed? Or do you need me to tuck you in?"

"You've always been my Laurie Anderson."

"Get out."

It takes me awhile to shake loose from the manufactured stupor. By "awhile" I mean "a nap." I set the alarm on my cell phone and put it next to the bed in case my dad calls. I sleep the way maybe men do in shifts during battle, like I'm storing it up so I don't have to slow down later on. This would be a workable plan except Soma calls three times, and each time I sit straight up and alert, thinking the phone's ring is the alarm going off.

When it finally rings for real, I almost shut it off blindly out of habit. I get up and think about men across the country, getting up for night shifts. I think I could work a job like that, the kind where you pack a sandwich and an apple in a metal lunchbox with two thermoses. One with soup. One with coffee. It's the kind of thing that would just about hypnotize Ethan. He'd write a crappy song about it. And waking up and walking through the empty house, I realize that I can set the clocks however I want. It's whatever time of day I say it is.

I get to campus by 10:30. Carry in a sack of nonperishables to deposit in my sleeping quarters. I crack myself up turning down a corner of my sleeping bag and leaving a Baby Ruth near the pillow. Turndown service in Ainsley House. Then I hit the archives.

Whatever part of me that was still scared isn't scared anymore. I practically thunder down the steps. No worries. No way. In the archives, I flip on the light switch and haul out boxes as if I'm sorting through my own dusty attic. Find scrapbooks and old ledgers dated from the 1800s — some with grades, some with tuition payments. I find one slim, black book bound in pebbled leather that lists all the food purchased for the dining hall for the year 1943. It even has ration coupons for meat and milk tucked between two back pages.

I find framed photographs. In one picture, a gym teacher stands on a dock, holding a hula hoop while a kid leaps through it into the river. In another, two young kids — they look like freshmen — bend over stacks of books in a tiny room. Boarders. I find old issues of our school newspaper and volumes of the yearbook back when it was in soft cover. Decades of haircuts. Invitations to proms and, before that, balls. Jesus. I can't imagine the douche bags I go to school with going to a ball.

Then I find photographs that look like they're from the fifties. Kids in cuffed blue jeans and girls in dark lipstick sitting on bales of hay and smoking cigarettes. Not a safety hazard or anything, no way. The girls look tough. Like diner waitresses. The boys look uncertain.

It makes me wonder where they got the girls for these things. It makes the most sense to think they trucked them in from some nearby girls' academy. Like they just tossed two stuffy schools together and some of the kids ran off to a barn to smoke cigarettes. But the girls in the pictures look so much more aware of themselves. They are the ones looking into the camera.

There's a scrapbook about the land the old citadel had been built on, when it was called Wells Farm and stretched from the edges of Hartford and up the valley. Pictures of Ainsley House, labeled, "the Wells Homestead," and rows of stables. There is one picture of a little girl sitting on a set of steps with her hands clasped around her knees. She has a bowl haircut and either her cheek was dirty or there's a smudge on the photograph. I put a fingertip on her face and say, "Ruby," half-expecting the lights to flicker, to hear footsteps scamper down the length of carpeted corridor. Apparently, Ruby has not seen the same horror movies.

She's looking straight into the camera, too. What is it with girls? It's like they're born comfortable with being looked at. The date on the photograph says 1888 and I realize that this girl must have lived here before Caramoor was a school. Otherwise I'd think she was the daughter of a teacher or a caretaker. The scabby-kneed orphan who helped out the cook in the kitchen.

I find a scrapbook with layers to it, like an onion. It's got about fifteen pages, but those pages have about four to five layers of news clippings, photographs, or little scraps of lined paper with shaky ink fading into it. It takes me about two minutes to start seeing the archives as my own library and decide to check this one out.

So that goes up in the attic, tucked into my sleeping bag like I'm trying to keep it warm.

"Ruby." I say it toward the eaves, standing as tall as the attic ceiling will let me. "Ruby — I'm just doing my job." Ruby does not suddenly appear with fangs or a vapory death grip around my throat, so I interpret that as her approval.

Once library hour's over, I think about the locks I have to try my key in. It's a little sad that this isn't a euphemism, but still. Possibilities abound. Verlando's office seems most pressing, but also the most depressing, so I make a decision to wait on that. I think about jerking off in the chem lab. I think about jerking off in the student lounge. I think about jerking off in the sleeping bag and then I decide I can do that at home, later on. By this time it's almost midnight. I've gotten sleepy and restless and when I step down the marble steps and into the cold night every skin cell crackles a little. Walking through the paths between buildings, I feel like Thomas Ainsley Wells surveying my land. I wish I had a pipe to hold between my teeth. Or a cane to tap against the pavement in front of me.

It's easy to pretend I own Caramoor right now. For a second, I allow for the fact that I could have sat at home pretending to own our three-story colonial. Could have sat in Dad's recliner with a brandy snifter and a well-packed bowl. But this is more impressive. And honestly, despite any on-campus urban legends, it feels less haunted to me. It's like a U.S. history hike — I am Jefferson, striding around Monticello. Washington at Mount Vernon. And then I am Emil Simon walking toward the tiny stucco building that is our Arts Studio. The lights are on. At first I think someone's in there singing and playing the guitar but then I recognize that the voice is Elliott Smith's, and unless the spiritual world really is active in a different way here on campus, probably that's a radio.

I do what makes the most sense to me in that moment, which is to barrel into the room where the music blares loudest. I stop at the shelf where Mrs. Larson, the ceramics teacher, keeps the stereo, and I shut it off.

Maybe Soma's right and I'm losing it. Because there are a number of possibilities that I don't even stop to consider here. That it could be Mrs. Larson rocking out to Elliott Smith at 11:30 PM on a Tuesday night. Or, you know, another member of our esteemed faculty. It could be a burly man who's broken onto campus to throw some pots. Some kind of clay burglar.

It happens that it's a hot girl. Well, she's hot from behind. She's washing her hands in the sink, and we have one of those utility sinks in the ceramics studio so she has to lean over and yeah, okay — she has a nice ass. And wavy dark hair that she's got tied back with some weird headband. For a minute, I think this is just a scene I've conjured up. Like maybe I've confused myself and I'm actually jerking off in the chem lab or something. Maybe this is just an echo of last night's acid.

I yell at her in the same voice Al Romano uses to announce his presence to Ruby when he steps through the doors of Ainsley House. "I don't know who you are." Aiming for a firm and gruff tone. The kind my dad would use if he heard scuffling noises outside our house on mischief night. "I don't know who you are," I repeat, "but this is private property. And you should just pack up and leave." This is where I falter a little. "You know — when you're done washing your hands." Okay. That could pass as a kindly security guard who understands the importance of hygiene.

So she doesn't only have a nice ass. And her hair is streaked with red and she has it tied back with what now looks like a necktie. She's wearing a clay-spattered smock and still manages to achieve the kind of hotness that dries up my mouth and makes me move two steps back. Ethan has this thing where he won't buy real porn. He special-orders this skin magazine called *American Connoisseur* and it advertises itself for showing real women — no implants or airbrushing and the girls are always doing something a little more dignified than just spreading their asscheeks or something. Like they're sitting in leather easy chairs sipping tea or something. Or instead of straddling a motorcycle, it's a Vespa. I don't why he bothers with this. He spouts this whole theory about how he won't participate in the degradation of women and whatnot but doesn't seem to understand that just because the naked chick is posing with a calculator or something doesn't mean you're looking at her and thinking she's so . . . smart. Whatever. The point is this girl could have stepped out of one of *American Connoisseur*'s Art School Sweetheart spreads or something. She has clay smudged on her cheek, for christsakes. And a man's shirt that's sort of buttoned weirdly over some kind of tight leggings. She's pretty. Like shame-on-Miss-Gabaldon pretty.

She doesn't shriek like you'd expect a beautiful girl to shriek when confronted by a stranger with a flashlight at almost midnight in a completely isolated location. Which deepens my confusion and lends further credence to my theory that I am in the locker room or on the library sofa with a bottle of lotion. None of this could possibly be real.

"Is this your tie?" She points to the thing in her hair.

"I beg your pardon?" I am sputtering. I am a friggin' teapot.

"Did you leave your tie here? I'm sorry — I'll get it cleaned. You don't want it back now — there's clay on it."

She's brushing her hands on her shirt, and it's getting a little transparent as the water from her hands dampens it. I am insane. I am a pervert.

"That's not my tie." I say this triumphantly. Like it's the most brilliant thing since naked girls on Vespas. Then I remember my security-guard persona. I call her Miss. I say, "Miss, this is private property — I think it would be best if you just moved right along."

We are both puzzled by this. We just stand there on either side of the glazing table. Her head's tilted to the side like she's trying to make sense of me, and I am trying not to look at the way her shirt is buttoned wrong.

"Are you one of my mom's kids?"

This doesn't help me. It's like I'm in a foreign country. On a different planet. By this point I really *am* stuttering. I'm like a waiter in a play where the waiter falls in love as soon as the pretty girl looks up from the menu. He goes to offer, "Water?" But when the word finally comes out, it comes out, "Waiter?"

I'm even worse off than that guy. Because here's what I come up with:

"Mom?"

Thankfully, the Goddess of Clay skims right past that gem.

"Are you in my mom's class?" By now she's talking slow and loud, like I'm foreign. Or retarded.

"Last year." It's like I'm speaking in telegrams. Take a deep breath. "Last year, I took Mrs. Larson's class."

"Oh, well, then you were in her class. Past tense." At this point, the girl in front of me settles down on one of the stools and dips a brush into a little pot of glaze. Delicately.

"Mrs. Larson?"

"Is my mom."

"Mrs. Larson is a lesbian." I say it because I am sure of it. We are all sure of it. Here she is throwing her pots, her hands in wet clay, in a sea of maleness. And she never seems sexy. And it's not because she's older, because she still looks pretty good. It's more this vibe she has. And she wears men's overalls. Every day. With flannel shirts. And sandals with socks. Her voice is as low as most of ours. Ethan told me. And it shocked me in that whole *Wow, a real live unicorn* kind of way. But honestly it wasn't something I took time to reflect on. She was just another woman with whom I didn't have a shot.

"Are you foreign? Or retarded?"

Shockingly, that was not the voice in my head.

"What?"

"You just called my mother 'Mrs. Larson.'"

"I don't know her first name. Listen — are you supposed to be here?"

"You called her 'MRS. Larson.' You know — using the formal title we use in this society to indicate marriage. She's married. To my father. Why would you say she's a lesbian?"

"Everybody knows she's a lesbian."

"Well, then. That's settled. That totally drowns out the wife-and-mother argument I was about to present. Good job there, Sporto." She puts down one little paintbrush, picks up a slim etching tool, and starts scratching into the edges of the clay.

"On your way out the door, could you please turn the stereo back on? My hands are all sticky."

Oh, the thousands of times I will hear that voice repeat the words: *My hands are all sticky*. It's enough to propel me backward out the door, past the stereo that I don't even attempt to touch.

I don't even turn back on the flashlight. Charge blindly almost the whole way up the hill to the administrative buildings before I even notice how fast I'm going. Make myself stop and feel my heart slow down, make my knees slow down. List the things I know that are in my backpack: batteries, granola bars, cell phone charger, long underwear, magazines. List the cities my dad's flying over: Newark, Wilmington, Richmond, Charlotte. List the ways I just acted like a pansy who'd never spoken to a girl before: I cannot even begin.

Try to talk myself down the way Ethan might. He'd say, "Whatever. You didn't expect anyone to be there. She freaked you out." Or, "Whatever. I thought Mrs. Larson was a lesbian." He'd say, "She was probably just as freaked out to see you there." And in that, he'd be inaccurate. I mean, she didn't even flinch. What kind of girl sits alone in the middle of nowhere, in the middle of a boys' school past midnight, and doesn't even react when a stranger stops in? Fine. I might not be a particularly threatening male specimen, but I still count as a stranger. Looming in the middle of the night. Most people would have screamed just out of shock. Let alone awe.

I stomp up the steps at Ainsley and just about splinter the rungs of the attic ladder on my way up. The bed I made feels lumpy and the late-night Pop-Tart tastes like brown-sugar ash in my mouth. I don't even know her first name, this spawn of Larson. She could ruin everything. Okay, probably not ruin as in natural disaster, outbreak of bird flu proportions, but she could, to put it mildly, interfere with serious shit. I try to rehash our whole conversation, trying to figure out if I gave up any clue about who I was, but honestly? It wasn't really a conversation, and rehashing it is just painful. I didn't introduce myself. That would have required balls.

What would she tell her mother? That some weird kid came through the Arts Studio long after school hours. And called her a lesbian. Oh, good God. But the Arts Studio door was already unlocked so she wouldn't necessarily know that I have a key to the buildings. But Mrs. Larson would probably mention something to the headmaster or even just the maintenance staff. They'd do extra rounds at night or check the locks more thoroughly. People will be watching more closely.

Or she could be one of those girls who doesn't talk to her mother. The kind who gets in screaming matches at the mall and breaks into tears after she hangs up the cell phone. She didn't seem like a mall girl, though. And she's here doing ceramics. So they have that in common. She probably admires her mother's skills and stuff. And she was definitely defensive enough about her mother's sexuality. I'm no scientist, but probably not estranged, those two. I cannot believe this. On my back, staring up at the eaves, I notice how industrious spiders have been up above me in the attic. It hasn't even been a week since I dusted out every corner and already it's less a web than a cloak of lace draped from the ceiling.

It doesn't make sense to stay the night at Caramoor. It might be highly unlikely that the young Miss Larson comes snooping up the hill, but I can't shake the thought out of my mind, either. Hell, I can't shake the thought of a brigade of maintenance men storming through the attic.

So that's it. Operations are shut down. Undone by some arty chick who can't even button her shirt right.

CHAPTER 9

I lock up the attic steps, make sure to check all the doors behind me. When I turn the key in the door's lock, its click sounds disapproving. Walking home, it's cold enough that I can see my breath spell out *Loser* in the air in front of me.

At least I don't have to sneak in the back door at home. I sort of pretend I'm Dad striding through the door. Toss my backpack onto the green easy chair. Survey the bottles on the bar, then go straight upstairs to pack a bowl. It's almost one thirty. I may be exiled from the kingdom of Caramoor but I get to smoke weed in front of the television in the middle of the night with no worries. That's something.

It's a miracle that I wake in time to shower before Soma swings by at seven thirty the next morning. Even still, I don't wash my hair. I just wet it. The tie I put on is literally crusty. It takes hot water hitting my face before I remember last night's crash and burn. There's nothing really to do. That's all I come up with. On my way downstairs, I stop into my parents' room. My dad's room. Whatever. For a second, standing over their dresser I see in the mirror exactly what this looks like: kid in filthy necktie, standing over his dead mother's jewelry box. Wonder briefly if Ethan wondered, if he was at all tempted as he headed out the last time. Doubt it. That seems too pedestrian for my brother, the noble nomad. Soma's leaning on the horn just as I'm reminding myself that it's not like I'm hawking my mother's gems at a downtown Hartford pawnshop. I'm borrowing a chain so I can hang the key from my neck. And I don't even take a good chain. I take the one that goes with this magnifying glass thing. I don't even think it's real silver. But I still feel like a burglar, raiding valuables — there's no way I'd touch any of this stuff if there were anyone else in the house.

Clasps pose challenges. Clasps pose impossibilities if you're a dumb-ass kid hurtling down the steps to try to silence your dumb-ass friend who hasn't let up on the car horn since he pulled up the drive a good eight minutes ago. But I get the damn thing on and even though it shouldn't calm me down so much, it does. I like the weight of it. Resting right on my chest. And even though I cannot possibly imagine my mother ever wearing a magnifying glass on a silver chain, I like that it was hers. She was a much classier lady than that necklace. Which means she must have tried it on for whatever crazy person gave it to her and said thank-you over and over, pretending like it was just what she'd been hoping for.

There's a slick of ice on the walk from the side door to the driveway and as I'm sliding around, it's actually Dad I miss. He would have salted the driveway. I go to open the door and nothing. The handle moves, it doesn't give. I look into the car at Soma, but he's not laughing maniacally as usual. He sort of shrugs and mouths, "Pull." Genius. I pull. Still nothing. Soma's window creaks down. "Get in the car."

"Unlock the door." He answers me with a series of clicks that accomplish nothing.

"What is your problem?"

"The door won't open." Between the two of us, we figure out

that it's frozen shut. Not the window, the entire door. So Soma gets out of the driver's side and I have to scoot over and sort of boost my ass over the console.

"People are going to think I'm getting some." Soma smirks and climbs after me.

"No one would ever think you'd be getting some."

"We're going to be late. You didn't call back last night. I left voice mails. I thought you'd choked on your own vomit."

"Let's take two steps back in the conversation. To the part where we talked about you not getting any."

"What?"

"I'm not your girlfriend."

"Yeah, well — this morning you're being a bitch." And he's right. I know it, but can't make myself cop to it. It feels like riding in a car I can't get out of. So we head into the student lot in silence. I grab my bag and go to push open the door before Soma even shuts off the stereo. Don't I feel dickless when I realize it hasn't thawed yet and I'm still stuck. He just looks sideways at me, opens his door, and slides out. Then he keeps walking toward school. I don't try to catch up with him.

If there is any way that she could possibly know it was me who bumbled while meeting her daughter the night before, I figure Mrs. Larson would sic school security for me in the periods right before lunch. Nothing. No school announcements warning us to clear out after school at the end of the day. During lit class, we are supposed to be doing some kind of group work crap where we have to prepare for a trial of this old lady in a story who killed her boyfriend and then slept with the dead body for decades. The story is Faulkner and therefore important and at first I think the trial idea is just another idiotic excuse for

Mr. Cavanaugh to surf the Net instead of lecturing. But then again, looking around the room, I realize half these douche bags are probably going to end up in law school some day.

I let the princes of the debate handle our insanity defense and instead embark on an elaborate fantasy of being finger-printed in the vice-principal's office. That doesn't happen, either. After lunch, we have chapel, which is just a Caramoor way of saying an assembly. It's an unscheduled chapel, so I think we'll hear about the key for sure. But that isn't it. A kid from Knotley Academy was hit hard during a football game with Saint Benedict's over the weekend. He died and the headmaster wanted to tell us himself.

It's weird — I really do go to school with a bunch of douche bags. We only get somber when someone tells us to get somber. After chapel, some homeroom teachers pass some cards around and everybody signs them for the kid's parents. Like that's going to be at all comforting. Nothing like getting a card signed by a hundred living teenage boys to drive home the fact your own son is dead.

It's not that I don't understand what the headmaster was say-ing. Ethan used to say that if Dr. Watkins became a minister, he'd convert to join that religion. And I understand that, too. It's like the aftershave that Watkins puts on is distilled wisdom. So he was up at the podium telling us about this kid Andrew Swenson and how bad things happened and we couldn't stop them. And I thought, *Yeah, yeah*. We have that motto practically embroidered on a pillow in our living room. But then he went on to say that because bad things happened so randomly, we had a responsibility to the people who loved us not to skew the odds. Meaning that we have to be careful with ourselves. We have to be careful not to invite trouble. We have to look out for each other.

And that piece makes sense to me. It's part of why I can't get my head around Ethan just taking off. I mean, hadn't enough happened? Didn't it hurt him to lose more of us? I wondered if this Andrew Swenson's parents had other kids and whether they would love them more now or less. More because losing one kid makes the others more precious? Or less because — whatever.

So the sermon part I understood. What baffles me were the greeting cards being passed around afterward. Guys my age writing things like, "I'm sure Andrew will now be watching over his loved ones." And, "We all respect and miss him so much." Why? I mean, I don't begrudge the kid a few compliments — he's going to miss so much of everything else. But at Caramoor, all we know about him is that he didn't flinch. And as far as the dead-person-becoming-guardian-angel theory, I don't buy it. That's the same crap that all the neighborhood ladies tried to feed me along with their casseroles last year. My mom was amazing. But she wasn't the kind of person who other people noticed like that. Besides us. And I certainly hope she has better to do in the afterlife than watch over my ass.

Miss Gabaldon gets all bent out of shape because I won't sign one of the cards. She does a lot of sighing and finally trots out, "Emil, I would think you'd understand how comforting kind words might be at a time like this."

She is not so cute. Or smart. I tell her that my mother never played football. And then it gets weirder because after chapel, we usually blow off steam running around the greens, tossing around a football, but clearly that isn't going to happen. Guys stand around in nervous circles, as if they're all wondering if it would be insensitive to hacky-sack.

When Soma comes by and gives a nod toward the parking lot, I'm relieved to get out of there and that he's still willing to haul my ass home. "Pizza on Pops?" is my version of a peace offering.

"And beer?"

"You don't want to see me choke on my own vomit, remember."

We pick up a pie. I can tell Soma's restless. He wants to get into everything. I remind him three times not to touch my dad's bar and still catch him gravitating there on my way back from taking a piss.

"Ethan should have left you his fake ID."

"Ethan still needs his fake ID."

"Whatever, dude's on his own now."

"Yeah, but he's not suddenly three years older. Or dead." This stops Soma's foot from jiggling for a second.

"Yeah. I know. Jesus, Emil — that's not what I mean."

"'Course not. I'm just saying."

"'Cause you don't think . . ."

"What? No. No, I don't think my brother's dead. What's going on with you?" I don't need this. It's like breaking some kind of code. Soma and I don't ask each other about crap like this. We exist beside each other and that's reassurance enough. But now he's toeing the carpet like a little girl before a freaking dance recital.

"I've just been thinking some since Watkins's speech."

"That was forty-five minutes ago."

"And it didn't get to you?"

"No. Ethan's not dead."

"Yeah, I know that." He's about as convincing with this as he was about a lack of interest in my father's liquor. And I just don't have any time for it. Not with nine days left on my own and certain obstacles possible in the path. I'm not about to sit here with Soma pasting pictures of Ethan onto milk cartons.

"So I've got a bunch of makeups still," I say.

"Yeah, I can't believe they still let you get away with that." And that's exactly what I don't understand. Which is it? My brother's in some shallow grave somewhere and the world should stop? Or I should buck up and take tests with everyone else? I just want him out of here. I want to sleep some more and then head over to someplace that doesn't feel like the set of a bad buddy movie.

"Yeah, they let me work the system." Groundwork laid. "So the least I can do is actually study." It takes Soma a minute or two to get it. I actually have to stand up like how my mom used to when company stayed too long.

"Dude — are you serious? You've got this place to yourself for nine days and you're tossing me out so that you can Cram For the Big Test."

"Have you met my father?"

"He's a little less of a stranger than you are, these days. I don't know what your problem is. Where are you?"

"I'll call you later."

"Yeah. Sure. Call me on your study break." And then he's out the door. I get in the shower again. This time I use soap and try to clear my head. I set my cell phone to ring at ten o'clock. Tonight I'm going to be through those gates as soon as I see the maintenance trucks pull out. I don't care if I walk in on a whole art school sorority. Having some kind of wet-clay fight. Nakedly.

Of course by the time I get myself up and over there, it's eleven. First of all, it's gotten so freaking cold again that I have to make bargains to get myself out the door. This turns out to be a promise to my penis. I will let myself jerk off on campus. Somewhere good.

Somewhere good turns out to be the faculty ladies' room at Ainsley House. I don't know if all girls' bathrooms are like this or if our female faculty just has to work hard to create some kind of girly island in the sea of testosterone that is Caramoor Academy, but it smells like a perfume store in there. Or the feminine products aisle at ShopRite. It's a private bathroom — just one stall and with a sink next to it. Like in a house. There is a little dish of dead rose petals on the top of the toilet and a basket of magazines and a smaller basket full of lotions. A variety of lotions. What do they do with all of it? I mean, I know what we'd do with it, but this is different. And they have quilted toilet paper. No abrasive, industrial stuff for our ladies at Caramoor. I flush Kleenex into the toilet and half-expect chimes to ring or something instead of a rush of water.

I'm not a pervert. I'm not sitting on the can picturing Miss Gabaldon crapping or something. Just sniffing her lotion. Totally aboveboard.

And I'm not thinking about the girl who may or may not currently be in the Arts Studio, either. I drop off my stuff in the attic and hit the archives. I don't know why this room is my favorite so far, how it could possibly beat out the ladies' lavatory. Maybe I'm inadvertently getting high off of the old glue fumes.

Biggest discovery tonight is these files with candid photographs from old yearbooks. Each labeled with the years and so I look through the years that Ethan would have been a freshman or sophomore — before I got here. There's a couple group shots. He doesn't look so bad-ass in these. He's all rosy-cheeked and doughy. And he looks skittish, like the kind of kid who always looks both ways before crossing the street. Not like the kid who decides to, I don't know, *live* on the street.

I warm up a can of ravioli and decide that I'm not going to let some chick limit tonight's exploits to Ainsley House. Tonight I'm going to branch out. If it's going to cost a shitstorm with Soma and spending most of tomorrow agonizing over getting caught, I'm going to make it worth my while.

CHAPTER 10

The lock in the library doors must be an old one because it takes me a couple minutes to work the key into it and get it to turn. Sometimes I argue with myself about the level of my own geekiness, but then I realize that the feeling shooting through my gut is actually a thrill at the prospect of being able to take books without signing them out. And it becomes clear that this internal debate will never again rage.

It's not just the idea of a borrowing spree, though. Part of it has to do with suddenly having time to really look around. It's weird how we use the library at Caramoor — like the books are just decorations to make it look more studious. People go there for computers or to sit at the wide, wooden tables and study. Teachers bring classes there sometimes but mostly for group work. There are sofas to sit on. And there's one corner of the room surrounded by three walls of windows. But no one really ever actually reads there. So we've got shelves and shelves of books that nobody ever browses through.

But I have all the time in the world right now. It turns out we have an extensive collection of presidential biographies. And one of the librarians is apparently a Cormac McCarthy fan. I find this enormous old book with the art books that has a bunch of William Blake's etchings in them. Blake was a poet and a heroin addict so Ethan was a fan. He could recite the one about the tiger.

I've never seen anything like these before. They are pictures of the circles of hell and all of them are now probably embroidered on the insides of my eyelids. They are that spooky, especially lit up by a flashlight in the darkened library. And then I find a really slim, green leather book that looks and smells moldy. It's called *The Ghost of Wells Farm* and appears to be typed out, like an original manuscript.

The little green book's pages are weirdly thin and the ink looks like it's fading in places. I almost tuck it into the back of my pants but it seems too fragile. I put it in between the covers of a *Scientific American*. So it still feels like sneaking it out. After I lock up the library, I trek across campus to the gym and fuss around with the weights a little.

You can come to campus early to lift with a group of the fat-necked coaches, but that sucks balls, really. There are always lines around everything and it's not like you can try anything new or risky with the fatnecks standing around sizing you up like they're about to eat your weight in protein powder.

I guess what I mean to say is that just like the library, the gym has a culture and it's not conducive to actually getting things done. And I don't have a clue about how to use anything in it. I sort of lift a series of dumbbells until they get too heavy and then work my way back down the row with the other arm. I do some chin-ups and see how fast I can run on the treadmill before my legs just about give out from under me.

Most of the time in there, I'm just looking around. No windows, so it's nice to be able to have lights on without worrying. I keep doing laps around the thought that I have to pull off some major key stunt at some point. Might as well stick it to the fat-neck freaks if I can help it. But nothing brilliant or even halfway decent comes to mind. I could grease the handgrips of all the barbells. Or replace their caffeinated steroids with decaffeinated steroids. None of this seems particularly riveting.

So it's almost one in the morning. I know, logically, that it makes no sense to stop by the Arts Studio. There are, after all, about two hundred other doors that I could practice unlocking.

I don't even bother trying to talk myself out of it, really. I can pretty much tell she's in there as soon as I look out from on top of the hill. The campus is entirely dark, like it's cloaked in shadow and serene silence. Except for the Arts Studio, which is fluorescent with light and practically vibrating with some terrible bass line.

I have the whole walk to formulate my plan. I'll tell her I'm Jason Hendrikson if she asks, and that I have special permission from the music department to record my jazz interpretations of Disney soundtracks in the sound studio. Worse comes to worst, Jason gets called in to answer some difficult questions. Best-case scenario: Girls love Disney.

So Miss Larson is not in an introspective acoustic guitar mood tonight. I can feel the bass line thrumming under the wooden planks of the walkway to the studio. This confuses me at first, because I've seen the Arts Studio stereo. It seems incapable of this kind of environmental shift. And then I get a peek in the window and see that the Iron Maiden has rigged up a system to rival some nightclubs. It's like she's built a wall of speakers. And hidden behind it.

I walk in shouting, but even that's ridiculous. Helen Keller would hear me first. But she's got her back to me and I don't want to just tap her shoulder. Even though, judging from last night's lack of fazing, she probably wouldn't do more than exhale suddenly. I walk around the circular room, putting all the pottery wheels between us. Just in case she's some judo prodigy or something.

"HI," I say again. Shout again. She's got a wheel going and she's elbow deep in clay. She's even messier tonight — it's smeared on her face and up her arms. Her hair's not so ricockulous, though; she's got it twisted back somehow. Honestly, she looks sexy as all hell. As if she's been mud-wrestling with a large piece of machinery. She looks up at me and cocks her head to the side for a second and starts pointing her chin toward the floor. I go to sit down and get a vigorously shaken head. But since I'm halfway down to floor level, it's not so difficult to see the remote control there. I hit mute and for a second think I hear crickets chirping. But it's just the pedal of the wheel, squeaking under her foot.

"Hey." I manage to muster something that sounds vaguely casual. And aim for a look of calm disinterest.

"Hey, Retard," she answers. And so this is already going really well. I go to correct her and tell her my name is Jason. This is the first girl I've spoken to in months who isn't returning my change or something and I really don't want to be anyone other than myself with her here. But I'm also the only white Emil at Caramoor, so there's that concern. Dilemmas, dilemmas.

"Retard's an old family name, you know. They actually named the condition after my great-grandfather."

And she laughs. It's like an electrical surge to my testicles. But without any kind of singeing. I mean, it's somewhat pleasurable.

"So, what's your real name, Retard?"

"Jason. And my last name's Foreigner. After the band."

Another laugh. Hot dog. On a roll. Push my luck. "And you would be?"

"My name is Jade." She even holds out her hand, and I'm so eager to touch her I almost take it, but then the clay registers with both of us and we sort of wave at each other instead.

"Jade?"

"Larson. Remember? Larson."

"No, I knew that part. It's just that Jade's a pretty unusual name. I mean pretty and unusual. I mean, I get that it's a precious stone so that's meaningful and —"

"My mom's an art teacher. I feel like I got off easy." She's laughing again as she cuts me off. "What are you doing here?"

"Well, I could ask you the same thing." Deftly he sideswipes the interrogation with a query of his own.

"I'm just being my mother's daughter. Who are you being?"

Here it goes: "Oh — sometimes I just stay late around campus. To work on my music." I sound like a douche bag.

"Oh yeah? Your parents don't have a problem with you staying at school so late? Or are you a boarder?"

This is perfect. She doesn't know we don't have boarders anymore. But this poses a decision. Am I a boarder? All it would take would be a casual comment to her mother to torpedo both my plan for social dominance and my academic career. I decide not to be a boarder. "No." That's what I say.

"No?"

"No, but my mom and dad are really chill about me coming and going. They understand about the whole artistic lifestyle and how crucial it is to just ride out inspiration." I sound like a used douche bag.

"Yeah. That's great." I'm losing her.

"Do you go to school around here?" Last ditch. Fall back on the kind of thing I'd ask the girl who tears my movie ticket. God.

"No." And that appears to be all I'm going to get about that.

"So you're home from break?"

"No." Score again.

"Okay, so you're Mrs. Larson's thirty-year-old daughter who moved back home after her third divorce and lives with her collection of hairless cats in the refurbished basement." This time I get a laugh *and* a snort. Shockingly, the snort is sort of adorable.

"I should be getting enough alimony then to live on my own, with three ex-husbands."

"Well, it's unfortunate you have such a taste for deadbeats." Another snort. Another jolt to my . . . spine.

"Do I really look thirty?"

"No, you look about thirteen." Which she does — she's tiny and wearing these pigtail braids and what might best be called "play clothes." Except for her sizable rack, she's pretty much prepubescent. God doesn't hate me today, though. And so I don't actually say that.

"Thirteen is a good age."

"So are you going to be here a lot? It's just that I'm working on a project so I'll be around late for the next week or so." This is what Ethan would call "setting the stage."

"Probably. The hairless cats sleep at night. So I try to find ways to occupy my time." Now I laugh. It echoes and sounds too loud, now that she's stopped working the potter's wheel. But it also feels good, like it's the first nonhollow laugh that's risen from my throat in weeks.

When Jade smiles, it reminds me of how the building itself glows against the dark background of campus. She says, "I'll be around here for a little while, too. For the next few weeks, anyway."

"Yeah, well, you probably don't know where the music center is, so I'll just stop by, maybe tomorrow — same time? If you feel like taking a break then?" I sound like a kid trying to sell candy bars outside the supermarket. Pathetic. Desperately pathetic.

But she says, "Yeah." Then she starts up the pedal. So I might be dismissed but I'm dismissed with a date. A date. It definitely counts — plans were offered and established. A connection was forged. Ethan probably wouldn't have called it well-played, but he wouldn't have ruled it a foul, either. So Wednesday night has more to show for it. Improved muscle tone, the little book wrapped in the *Scientific American* magazine that I somehow managed to keep out of sight from Jade. And Jade and the fact that she's named Jade and might have clay on the edges of all her clothes.

I'm not ready to fall back into real life. Everything inside me feels warm and I don't want to walk back through town to the house and let it all freeze up. So I pull my mother's chain over my head and feel around on the wood on the chapel door for the lock. At Caramoor we have chapel in the chapel. Shocking, I know. But the school is also pretty firm about our lack of religious affiliation so it's sort of weird that we call the building that. There's no cross in sight. I mean, it's not like Ethan and I were the only kids here who weren't any set kind of religion. And there are plenty of full members of the Tribe around. We have Sikh kids who wear turbans every day. Nobody blinks about that stuff around here. I have this theory that we name the buildings according to the instructions of whoever donated the money. So the guy who wanted the chapel was clearly a Christian and therefore we don't have a temple or a Wiccan house of Fern Light or something.

It's really just a domed little building with a podium and rows and rows of benches. There's no steeple or stained glass or Jesus around. I still expect there to be candles lit down the aisle or something. But when I swing open the door, it just feels like open air above me, around me. I could be stepping into a cathedral. It's like peace sort of feels massive above me. It makes me want to put away the flashlight, but that's going to end disastrously, so I wrap the top of my scarf over the bulb to make it dimmer. It's strange that just because you give something a name, it carries a feeling.

The building's closer to a library than a chapel. Instead of windows, the chapel has these paneled walls, and hanging against each panel is a different flag representing the ethnicity of someone in the community. For a school that makes us all dress the same and aims to send most of us to the same college, Caramoor harps a whole lot on its diversity. Tonight the number of flags actually impresses me.

We meet in here as a school and listen to lectures or have forums where we're the ones who are supposed to do the talking. In the weeks before graduation, each senior is supposed to get up and give a five-minute talk called "This I believe." Each kid invites his family and it's supposed to be this rite of passage, some stepping up as a man in the hallowed halls of Caramoor.

When Ethan gave his "This I believe" speech, he did it in sign language. He'd taken a deaf girl to the Winter Formal and I think that convinced the administration that he was just demonstrating his profound emotional attachment to her. Which he was not. He spent weeks with sign language books, really poring over them. And honestly the first part of his speech, the actual spoken part, wasn't half-bad. Ethan could have been one of those preachers in the South that charmed snakes and stuff or made people speak in tongues. I mean, if not for the Jewish side of our family and all.

I think most people expected him to talk about our mom. Because she'd just been diagnosed and when the kid with the cancer mom gets up, you assume he's going to talk about her. He talked a little about finding ways of sharing peace with the world. And how sometimes the bonds you formed with people had more to do with caring about them enough to let go of them. I could tell that he wanted people to see that he was talking about graduation, but I doubt if anyone in that room got there. It's weird because everyone loved my brother. He charmed everyone. Ethan wasn't the kind of kid who sat alone at lunch. But he was the kind of kid who always seemed to wish he were sitting alone. He had this distance around him and I don't think I'm seeing that just in retrospect. I mean, no one seems really surprised that he took off. It's like we all sort of expected him to leave. So how do you feel close to someone like that? I don't mean if you're related, but like his friends. I don't think any of Ethan's friends actually felt close to him, not take-a-bullet close, anyway.

So, anyway, Ethan spoke that part of his chapel speech and then he started signing. When he was practicing, he'd say words out loud — I know my parents and I assumed that's how he would do the speech. And that was a little weird. It's not like he dated the deaf chick past February or anything. She wasn't there. So who the hell was he talking to? Basically, Ethan was just fluttering his hands in the air. And the most hilarious part was that he was signing directly in front of the microphone. At one point, he even tapped the mic and asked, "Is this thing on?" And he managed to do that totally stone-faced. He finished up by flipping us the bird. Two of them, actually. Both hands with a flourish.

So that was Ethan's chapel. My dad was pissed, mostly because he was embarrassed. His sisters and their husbands had driven out from Jersey. My aunt Judy just followed him out to the parking lot, pecking him — "Phil, you have to do something about him. That boy is totally out of control." My mom just went to sit in the car right away, like the idea of standing around watching people watch her sip cider exhausted her. It wasn't like Ethan had brought down the house, either. Kids weren't holding back laughter — they just weren't laughing. I remember feeling pretty distinctly that Ethan probably had more to say, that part of the stunt was about him not believing any of us would actually listen, but that's probably hindsight. I'm sure at the time I thought he was supercool.

He didn't really get in trouble. No one could prove that the entire sign language thing was a farce and so Ethan just said that he got overwhelmed with frustration of the plight of the deaf. Dad gave him a lecture about respecting himself and the solemnity of traditions, but in the end, Dad thinks most of the Caramoor culture is sort of a sham so Ethan appealed to that philosophy. Ethan had to write notes apologizing to Aunt Judy and Aunt Leslie. But Mom and Dad didn't make him return the aunts' checks.

I still have a year and a half to figure out what to say at my chapel. Maybe by then I'll be ready to come clean about the key. But that would stop the whole tradition and I can't picture wanting to be responsible for that. You're supposed to start the whole speech, "This I believe . . ." And I don't know what I'd say. Maybe that's part of why Ethan pulled the whole sign language stunt — he didn't know what to say. Or he only had a minute of material and the rest he still needed to figure out. Five minutes is a long time to spend stating things that you're sure about.

The chapel feels a lot bigger when it's empty. But it's still comforting. It's probably not that kid Andrew from Knotley Academy or my mom but it feels like someone's looking out for me in that room. I wonder if when they put up buildings like chapels, even nondenominational ones, they bless them. Like douse it with holy water or something. Or maybe a whole bunch of different kind of holy folks parade through. Like how my parents got married by both a priest and a rabbi.

In any case, I feel better than I have for a while. And it's not just the key or Jade, although those don't hurt matters. It's two thirty in the morning and by the time I get back to the house, it'll be three and my eyes will probably be frozen open . . . but for right now, things seem more possible in general. Hopeful, even.

CHAPTER 11

Soma's half an hour late the next morning. At least this is what I think until I actually call him. And then his voice mail picks up. We all turn off our phones on our way into school. It just makes sense that way. You keep it on when you're driving. But if it rings in class, that's an automatic detention so you turn it off right before you hit homeroom. Where Soma apparently is right now. Awesome. I leave him a message: "Thanks for the heads-up. Asswipe."

I call in to the office and let the secretary know I'm going to be late. She reminds me to bring a note from a parent and I explain that my dad's away on business for the next week. There's a silence in which I know she's remembering about my mom. She asks why I'm late and I tell her that my ride fell through.

"Well, sugar, how are you going to get here, then?"

"I'm going to leave right now, Mrs. Emerson. I should be there in a half an hour."

"You mean to tell me you're going to walk here, Emil Simon? Are you aware that's it less than twenty degrees out, child?"

"I won't forget my parka, Mrs. Emerson."

"Why don't you just sit tight and I'll find someone to buzz over and pick you up in his car. Or I'll have maintenance send over a truck?"

"No, Mrs. Emerson. It's really fine. I'll be in by the end of first period. I'm so sorry to be late."

Sucks. Sucks. Sucks. Back out on the same roads I walked down less than six hours ago. If it's possible, it's even colder out. I get it. And I might be cursing him with every frozen step, but Soma's not so out of line. I should have at least called to apologize, made up some kind of excuse for how I've been acting. Or even just texted him.

So I miss first period. It's no tragedy. It takes me until third period to thaw. Soma is a different story. At this point, I could keep a wooly mammoth in the ice that floats between us.

I don't try to fix things. First of all, we're at school and I don't really feel like getting voted Prom King and King by our classmates. And then what would I say? It's going to take a lot to make this up to him. It would take me admitting I've been an ass and then asking him to stay at my house until Dad comes home. Unveiling the pharmacy that Ethan left behind and sharing. And I just don't have time for that crap right now. Or room for it.

So I don't try to talk to Soma for the whole day. At first it feels weird. We're in four of seven classes together. Sit next to each other. At first I can't even relax my shoulders. It's that tense. But I'm too tired to keep caring through four forty-five-minute periods. You know how people who are in comas sometimes wake up and they're like, "Oh, yeah — I remember when the ER doctor cracked open my chest — I was floating above all you guys. At like ceiling level." That's how lately I've felt at school — during the day, anyway. Completely disengaged. Just suspended above everyone else. I can hear everything and it all sounds so familiar. But I can't really make myself care about any of it. It makes sense to me now, how in the movies as someone's dying, someone else is usually right there, screaming at them not to. If it's a comedy or love story, the hurt person springs her eyes back open. But if it's a drama or real life, the person screaming just eventually stops screaming. I never got that — how you could know you'd be missed and still go. But I guess that's what happens — as you move farther and farther away, you care less and less.

Anyway, that's another reason not to talk to Soma right now — because all I'm thinking about is demented, depressing crap like that. He expects me to bridge some kind of peace with him before the last bell and I don't. So that means another long walk home.

Or not. It occurs to me that I don't have to go all the way home. Right after school, I play dutiful son and call my dad's cell phone. It goes to voice mail, which is what I was hoping for. I tell him everything's fine, last night's party was insane, and tonight I'll work on getting all the vomit out of the living room curtains. I tell him the spew splatter is peacock-shaped.

Then I consider my options. No one's going to raise eyebrows if I'm studying in the library. I can stay on campus until around six or so without getting quizzed or hassled. Then I don't have to walk all the way home — I can just stop in town and eat at the diner. Maybe hit our craptastic theater for a movie, but it's only got two screens.

My socks are matching, my hair's reasonably tamed down, I don't reek — so that's a bonus. I'll look a little too prep school when I meet Jade, but I'll probably just get wet clay all over me when she leaps into my arms and straddles me on the Arts Studio floor. I mean, that's the plan, anyway.

So first stop is the library where I can camp out in the sunny corner on one of the itchy sofas. I wonder if the school buys furniture upholstered like this so that we don't fall asleep on it. I could fall asleep on anything, right now. Get through three whole paragraphs of *The Ghost of Wells Farm* before the bright sun warms my eyes shut. Libraries are so quiet. There's whispering and typing and the occasional hum and whir of the printers. And that's it. I doze and wake up when one of the librarians laughs like an injured terrier.

I think the author of my current light-reading material was a kid, because I find typos all through it. He was clearly a geeky kid, though, because the language is pretty pseudoscientific and there's even a Library of Congress copyright in it and everything. And the author's name is Cecil. I check the publication date and it's 1953, but I think Cecil was probably a geeky name even then. Cecil van Gunder. Jesus. Poor kid.

The first three chapters of Cecil's research seems to focus around an unsolved murder on Wells Farm in 1929. A milkman making morning deliveries found the bodies of the local parish's deacon and the choir mistress in the woods on the outskirts of the old farm. Both had been shot in the head. They'd been rumored to be having an affair and the fact that their bodies were left arranged in a bloody embrace led authorities to point to those rumors as motive. Naturally, suspicion fell on both their respective spouses. But the minister's wife was hosting a church tea and the choir mistress's husband was working the night shift at an iron factory. So the case went unsolved. According to good old Cecil, phantom gunshots can occasionally be heard in the southeast corner of campus, where the bodies of the lovers were found. And classmates that boarded with Cecil at Caramoor contributed their own accounts — four sightings of two figures rising out of the mists on foggy nights and rushing toward each other. Ghostly singing of church hymns in the predawn hours.

Very romantic stuff, Cecil. Maybe I can trot it out later on tonight and talk Jade into a romantic . . . séance. I don't know. That would at least give me an excuse to light some candles. The vacuum cleaners are my cue to move on before the kindly receptionist insists on driving me home herself. I'm still sleepy as all hell and if I were the kind of kid who would have been chosen to hold the key I would have just casually walked up the third flight of stairs in Ainsley House and climbed up to the attic. I could have curled up in my makeshift bed and kept reading.

Yeah, so I haul ass off campus and check movie times on the marquee at New Market Cinemas. Cartoon about ponies or a comedy about triplets. Those are my choices. And although they both might sound vaguely pornographic, it's not that kind of establishment. It's really the kind of place where moms park strollers in the aisles or where you might walk with the kid you're babysitting. I don't choose the pony movie, figuring it would be more crowded, and it turns out that I'm brilliant. The movie *Three on a Spree* is almost completely empty of any kind of audience. As it should be. It's about these two brothers who talk their other brother into participating in a bank robbery. Things go terribly wrong and then pandemonium ensues. The brothers go on the run and resettle in a western town where all three of them live under the same fake identity. I close my eyes shortly after they drive up to a saloon in Amarillo, Texas, and doubt I'll miss anything.

It's warm in the theater and the seat pushes back and it's just me in here and two couples who probably just don't have any other place to make out. They're all about my age except one of the girls looks about twelve. And I don't mean like how Jade looks twelve in her own adorable and messy way. This kid is tiny. She keeps giggling and asking her boyfriend, "Really?" and "Are you serious?" I end up rooting for the boyfriend to get a blow job just so she stops talking.

At the diner down the street, I order a full breakfast for dinner and build egg sandwiches with my toast. Drink about three cups of coffee. I'm pretending to be on the night shift again. I eat like my dad, scooping up the food that falls back to my plate with the crusts of my bread. I think about calling Soma and then don't. When Ethan first left, we called his cell phone like fifty or sixty times. At least I did. I don't know how often Dad called. Usually he'd watch me wait through the ringing and look at me like I was insane to think Ethan would pick up. And I guess I was. It took four days, and then the phone was disconnected.

I don't call Soma and I know that if I call Ethan, some old guy who sounds like a plumber will pick up. We've already met. His granddaughter gave him a cell phone for his birthday and he doesn't know how to work the damn thing. He told me this right after bellowing out, "Ethan? Who?" as if he were yelling up through a pipe.

It feels weird to be eating out alone. The waitress looks vaguely like Aunt Judy, if Aunt Judy was still perming her hair. She's nice to me, because she's a middle-aged woman and they're all nice to me. It's like I put on cologne called Motherless Child every morning. If only that worked with college girls. I sit there, sipping my third refill of coffee and pretending I'm a man who doesn't want to go home to my wife.

It's only 9:15, so I pull Cecil's book out of my backpack. Figure I can read at the table for a little while as long as I leave a really good tip. This time I look at chapter headings: "The Underground Railroad," "The Revolutionary War Soldier," "The Young Spirit on the Steps." The last one sounds like Ruby. Sounds of scampering feet. Eerie laughter late at night, cold breeze. That's my girl.

If it's her, her name is actually Fredericka Cornell Wells. And she had a lousy enough life that I'll never begrudge her a few giggles in the afterlife. Fredericka was the only daughter of one of the first families to settle in the area. When her parents both died of a mysterious fever, she was six years old and their will left her in the care of their neighbor and friend, Jacob Wells. Wells took over the little girl's care and moved her into his home. Yeah, so far this sounds like the plot of a heartwarming musical. Until Cecil gets to the part where Fredericka turns twelve. And Jacob Wells marries her.

Apparently, Fredericka is buried in the Revolutionary War cemetery that's outside our library's window. She lived until she was thirty-two years old. She bore Jacob Wells six children. Cecil acknowledges an alternate theory that the little girl ghost in Ainsley House is actually Fredericka and Jacob's youngest daughter, who supposedly drowned in a bathtub. But he points out that there's no grave for this daughter in the family plot on the grounds. Cecil's own theory is actually pretty compelling. He says that the ghost is Fredericka and that it makes sense that she'd haunt Wells Farm in the form of a little girl. He points out that her sixth year might have been her last one of happiness.

It's an interesting idea — that when you die, you stay put at the happiest time of your life. That Ruby doesn't actually mean to scare anyone — she's just enjoying an eternity of the childhood she never got to finish living out in real life. I sort of like it. I'm also going to keep calling her Ruby. Fredericka sounds like the name of a woman who sits at a third-floor window, staring toward a house she used to live in.

The house she used to live in is still standing. I think it has to, like Ainsley does. They're both historic monuments or something. The Daughters of the American Revolution run the Cornell House as a museum and host community events there. They have caroling there at the holidays and ladies' book clubs, crap like that. There's a dirt path that runs between the two properties. On the way back to campus, I walk down the path, but it's too dark to see much more than a shadowed roof rising through evergreens.

It spooks me a little. For some reason, I feel safer as soon as I fight my way through the thick trees. Sort of the opposite of how Ruby must have felt. Maybe the key is some kind of amulet around my neck. It keeps me safe from the ghosts on campus.

And right now, I'm more curious about the living than the undead. Specifically, the maintenance crew, who it might be better to avoid at this point. It's not ten yet. The cleanup crew's white pickup trucks are parked all around campus and men are loading the backs with bags of trash. That has to be the last stop of the night, I figure — hauling all our crap to the Dumpster at the bottom of the hill. They've got three truckfuls. I'm freezing and my knees are starting to creak in the crouched position. I think about the chapter in Cecil's book titled "The Underground Railroad" and make a mental note to check that one out.

The fact that I almost crap my pants when I hear rustling beside me almost tanks my seduction plans for later on in the evening. I hold back a completely unmasculine scream and manage to control my bowels at the same time. Talent. That's true talent.

But it's not the ghost of Harriet Tubman who emerges from the bushes and almost pokes one of my eyes out with one of its antlers. It's the biggest stag I've ever seen. And it's close enough to me that I can reach out my arm and pet it. Its nose looks wet like a dog's. I'm trying to stay still, to avoid even blinking. It's weird to be scared, I know, but usually you just get a glimpse of a deer. But this guy isn't running. He's just standing there. Regarding me.

So I have a moment with the deer. It's unnerving and it makes me realize that no matter how much camo Soma and I buy at the army-navy store in Westport, I'm never going hunting. I could never fire a gun at an animal now.

So as soon as we come to that understanding, the stag turns slowly and disappears down the path toward the Cornell House. He doesn't dart; he saunters. And I look back to see the maintenance trucks have pulled out. Campus is still. The sun has only been down for five hours or so, but already the grass crackles under my feet. That's the only sound I hear walking — my shoes sinking into the frosted field.

The Arts Studio is still dark and that's okay. I didn't want to stop in to see Jade right away, anyway. I'm already wearing a tie — I don't want to blow it by looking even more eager. For a second I let myself have this dream catcher moment and imagine that I'm some kind of Cherokee warrior or something. I looked into the eyes of the great stag and he passed some of his resilience on to me. Maybe that's the kind of theory that's bred by too much weed. And part of it has to be that walking across the wide, dark field and seeing only my frosted breath and the sky lit with stars makes me feel powerful in an ancient way. It makes me want to do the hardest thing. Open the door that I don't think I can handle.

So clearly that's not the faculty ladies' room. I let myself into Ainsley House and don't even stop to drop off my backpack before unlocking Dr. Watkins's office. This is the scariest knob turn since the first time I let myself in the main door. The Headmaster's Room. It's our version of the Oval Office. I figured alarms would blare as soon as I step onto Watkins's tacky carpet. The carpet is actually legendary on campus. It's got ducks embroidered into it. The whole room is ducks. It's got this wood paneling with mallard ducks and deer hidden among the knots in the fake grain. It's an insane room — like L.L.Bean on acid.

The ducks on the rug don't quack when I step on them. The chair creaks a little when I sit down. Creaks more when I sit back. I feel like I did yesterday standing over my mother's jewelry box. If someone walked in on me right now, if they forgot an important file or showed up to write some late reports, there's no chance I could explain this in any kind of reasonable way. They'd see what they wanted to see.

I don't even really know what Dr. Watkins would have in here that I'd want. I get that he's more of a figurehead — he stands for the school. He's wise like we're supposed to want to be wise. And when he walks through the hallway, he shakes our hands and claps us on the shoulders in the way we all know we're meant to grow up to be experts in. Dr. Watkins is supposed to be the finished product, I think — the man we're all supposed to grow up to be.

He knows all of our names. He's got a shelfful of yearbooks next to the desk — maybe that's how he learns them. He knows me. And if he were to walk in and see me sitting at his desk, he'd say, "Emil," in a shocked voice that had nothing to do with trying to remember my vital stats. When Mom died, the school sent flowers to the house. And Dr. Watkins and his wife sent a little tree. Like the kind of Christmas tree you'd put in a tiny apartment. Or, like Dad said, in a hospital room.

I liked it, though — the idea of an evergreen tree instead of flowers that were going to die off. Ethan and I planted it in the back of the yard where seeing it wouldn't piss Dad off. If Watkins knows us all so well, he must keep files or something and so I start opening desk drawers. I find a row of labeled files in one drawer, but the names on those are actually faculty. Okay, so clearly that holds promise. But it's a little more than I'm up for tonight, communal moment with the deer god aside. There's a small metal box that looks like the kind my mother used to keep recipes in. Flip through it and see that we're all in there. Every kid I go to school with has an index card with our name typed up top. There's one for me, but not for Ethan. So it must just be current students.

Each of our names is up on the top line of the card. Then below that is our address with a note on who we live with. My card lists my father as Philip with *Phil* written beside it in parentheses. My mom is listed as Jane and her name is carefully crossed through with a thick, black pen. In the margin, someone wrote in *deceased*. So they must give each of us a card when we first enroll and then just change up the card when needed. Except a lot can happen in four years. Don't they ever retype the cards? I mean if parents get divorced or switch jobs or, you know, die?

It's weird to think that I thought Dr. Watkins totally understood what it meant to lose my mom, but it didn't even rate a new index card in his world. It makes me want to go home and take an ax to that tree out back. I feel like unraveling some ducks in the rug.

Instead, I sit back in the massive leather chair and fold my hands on the desk blotter in front of me. It has a Caramoor Academy crest on it. Our crest looks pretty vicious — it's these two falcons. Birds of prey. And each of them has his beak sealed around the same snake, like they're wrestling over it. Almost everything in Dr. Watkins's office has either a duck or the crest on it.

When the big talks happen, Watkins sits where I sit and some poor, deflated douche bag sits in the smaller wooden chair on the other side of the desk. I look at my clasped hands and practice saying, "Young man, it's time for us all to part ways" in a stern but caring voice. I bet Watkins soaks with that kind of crap when he tosses kids out of Caramoor. We don't even call it getting kicked out here. We call it "counseled out," because of course it's really for the booted kid's own good. I like it because it sounds like "canceled out." Very sci-fi. You no longer exist.

So that's the seat no kid wants to lay his ass down on. I bet when they found Jackson Young's Web site, they put him there and explained that posting the pictures and addresses of faculty members wasn't good for the community. Neither was listing an award for assassination. And maybe even this is where faculty members sit to get fired. It's where I sat when he told me Mom died. His secretary had called me out of French class. I remember listening to him and not being able to keep up, because I'd been speaking French for forty minutes. I was stoned and switching gears was hard. It took me awhile. And then I kept asking about Ethan — I mean, why wouldn't they tell the two of us together? But Watkins fed me some line about my dad having to deal with Ethan and that I should sit with him until my father could come and get me.

So that's what I did, and I don't know who it was more awful for. Sure, obviously my mom died. But Watkins had to sit there with me for almost two hours. You could tell he had stuff to do — the phone kept ringing and his secretary kept buzzing in on the intercom and he'd answer one of those and say something like, "I'm going to have to get back to you on this later on," in his calm and quiet voice. Then he'd turn to me and offer me water or a soda or something. "Can I get you anything, Emil?" As if we were on a plane and I was flying first-class. It was funny because his voice never took on any kind of edge, he didn't really fidget, or pace, but his eyes darted around a lot. That was the only thing that gave him away.

Now I'm wondering if Dr. Watkins is as wise as we all believe. Maybe he was just born with a soothing voice. Soma thinks he's God. And I get that. I've always liked listening to him make sense of the world. But that afternoon, he had nothing for me except soda.

When the two of us were sitting there, I remember wondering why they'd ever tell me before they at least knew Dad was on his way over to campus. What was the rush, anyway? For the rest of my life, I was going to be some guy with a dead mom. I could have sat in for the rest of French. Soma and I could have sat at lunch and fought over a plate of fries. I could have had one last round of *your mama* jokes before being forever banned. You know — crap like that.

Dr. Watkins does not keep a diary. The spy boy in me was hoping for that, wildly, but no. There wasn't really anything of interest in the hallowed corner of campus. No books of magic, no secret files, no encyclopedia of wisdom that I could flip through and take in. He keeps a pyramid of Diet Coke cans under one side of his desk. Mints in his top desk drawer. Besides the ducks and the crests, it looks like Watkins had browsed through the archives on interior decorating day. His walls are a gallery of framed black-and-white photos of kids with crew cuts, newer versions of our older buildings, even a shot of horses lined up in their stalls.

I thought about what I'd say to me, if somehow I were in charge of counseling a different version of myself out of Caramoor. "Emil," I'd say, "let's discuss your attitude and your progress. Let's discuss the direction of your future." Watkins has these words he leans on. Like Soma says "mayhem" all the time or Miss Gabaldon can't seem to stop herself from ending half her sentences with "Are you following?" Watkins uses the word *fortunate* that way. We are fortunate sons of Caramoor. And usually the word *accountable* follows shortly after. So "Emil," I'd say to myself, "our good fortune requires us to hold ourselves to a higher standard in life. We are accountable for our own progress." Or I'd ask me in Watkins's own lofty way, "Who are you other than fortunate?"

But tonight I'm not even Emil. My name is Jason and I am the prodigy of the electronic music department. I have parents who love me enough to understand the complexities of my artistic genius. They know I need my freedom. They give me no curfew. I am the Super Seducer. Heading out of the office, I check my tie in the mirrored coatrack nailed to the wall beside Watkins's office door. Shake out my hair a little. Lock the door, check the lock, and head out toward the north end of campus.

CHAPTER 12

Ethan and I used to be able to figure out what kind of mood Dad was in when he came home from work by how hard he slammed his car door. It mattered that much. Otherwise it didn't make a difference what Mom set out on the table, how brightly she asked about his day. I can tell Jade's on campus when I'm about five steps out of Ainsley House. I can see the lights on in the Arts Studio and hear the strumming on someone's earnest guitar.

I tell myself that it's the cold wind that has me rushing toward the building, but even my frozen hands in my pockets don't believe me. I have to stop myself from running toward her. You know how when you're a little kid and the teacher tells you not to run to the water fountain so you do that scurrying half-jog, half-hop thing? I'm doing that boogie walk all the way to the Arts Studio.

The first thing I notice is that Jade isn't wearing any shoes. She's got those black legging things on and what looks like four tank tops and then the same striped button-down shirt. She must use that as a smock or something. Her hair's in braids again and she's crouched in front of the glazing station with a paintbrush in her hand. I realize that I'm a little sad that she's not smeared in clay. Soma might be rubbing off on me more than I want to admit.

Hey. The first time I say it, nothing happens in the room and I realize that I didn't really say it out loud. "Hey." I try it again.

Jade doesn't even turn around. "Hey, Rock Star." This could rate as good or bad. Good = She knows it's me. Bad = I don't rate eye contact. Probably she hasn't been counting down the minutes until the opportunity to gaze into my eyes. I go with the good news.

"Hey." I make a mental note to try to say a different word. At least a different syllable. "Is that tonight's masterpiece?" This at least gives me an excuse to move closer to where she's working. On the wooden counter of the workstation she has a circular vase braced in some kind of vice. It looks like it's sinking into layers of greens. Moss and pine and then at the top the green gets brighter. "Jade." I mean the color, but it also comes out like I'm nicknaming her with her actual name.

She gets it, though, and laughs. "Yep. Degrees of me." Swivels on the stool to face me and I feel a little blinded. Like if I look straight into her eyes, my retinas will melt or something. But if I look down, it'll seem like I'm just staring at her rack so I end up looking past her a little, at a framed print of some little troll-like figure that's hanging above the workstation sink. Weird to be in front of the hottest girl I've pretty much ever actually spoken to and still I'm more comfortable looking at a troll.

"So did you bring a soundtrack?" Jade asks me while she's brushing a clear shellac over her entire vase.

Is this a new requirement? "Um, no. I mean, I like your music. You have —"

Jade laughs. "No, I meant the stuff you're working on. In the electronic music lab." For a second I forget to be Jason the genius. I am momentarily mystified. But I save myself just in time to shrug.

"I'd have to check with my agent." Where is this stuff coming from? It's like someone implanted a chip in me. A mediocre conversation chip, but it's still a chip instead of the usual dumb lump in my throat.

"So you're a senior here? At the esteemed Caramoor?"

This doesn't feel as safe to lie about for a number of reasons. She might expect me to drive somewhere if I'm a senior. Her mom might know senior teachers and I'll just look like a moron stuck in remedial classes. And it's one more thing to keep straight. I'm stupid around this girl. It's hard enough to remember that my name is Jason. Plus I still have no idea how old Jade is. For all I know, she's fourteen. And eighteen would make me too old for her.

All of this ticks through my head and then I realize that Jade is still standing there, waiting for me to answer her completely rudimentary, somewhat expected question. "I'm a junior." Congratulations, Me. This clearly mattered more to me than her because she's already moved on. She's bent over in front of me and I have no idea how she got there or what she's doing. Honestly, there can't be a protocol for this.

She backs up almost into me and then stands up. She's plugged in a hair dryer and by the time she gets that it might help to explain all of this, I can't hear her over the blow dryer. I just stand there watching her blow-dry her vase.

She shuts it off and says, "I like how the hair dryer warms up the glaze. It makes it all glossy." Jade shoots me half a grin out from under the wisps of hair that have loosened out from under her brain. "That's my own technique and everything. My mother's an amateur when it comes to incorporating hair-styling appliances into her artistic process."

"I've heard that's where the real cutting edge is. That blurred line between hair care and vase making."

"That's right. I am a pioneer."

I have to stop myself from saying that Jade is a true pioneer. That I am completely undiscovered country. This whole encounter gives me a weird sensation in my chest, like something's scurrying around in there, trying to keep up. For so long it's felt like I've been avoiding actually talking to people and now I'm trying to think of anything at all that would keep this conversation going.

I wish she knew my name because it would be good to hear her say it. Reassuring somehow, like I actually exist in her world. It jars me to hear her say "Jason." I even look behind me and she laughs at that. "What? Are you composing some kind of song in your head?"

"A whole series called the Jade Melodies."

"Very nice. I hope it's something you can dance to."

"Are you a dancer?" This is a sensible question in my head. She mentioned dancing. She's wearing lots of spandex. She looks like she's ready to leap all over the place. But my train of thought is traveling a lonely track lately. And Jade is not onboard.

"In college, that's the kind of thing pre-law perverts ask." She's scolding me, but not really. "They're really just trying to figure out how flexible you are." My face feels hot and I swallow, trying to stop myself from blushing.

"So you're in college, then. Home for break."

Jade's face freezes for a second, like I said something wrong. She answers really abruptly and I can hear the punctuation at the end of her sentence. "No," she says, "I'm not in college."

And before I can ask anything else she turns the hair dryer back on again and returns her attention to the piece on the table in front of her.

So that was like a whole seven minutes. An actual conversation. It gives me more questions than answers, really, but at least I have something to talk about if I ever see Jade again. Or avoid talking about, judging from her reaction.

And she's still reacting, bent over the green vase in front of her. I don't see how it's possible to be that focused on an inanimate object, so I get that it's probably just her way of dismissing me again.

"I saw this huge deer in the woods out there." This is what I blurt out, standing in the middle of the ceramics studio. Not just in my own head. I actually say it. I've never felt so grateful for the sound of a hair dryer. Maybe if I woke up one random morning and heard the sounds of my mom getting ready in my parents' bathroom again — that would top it, but just barely. Jade doesn't react at all. Her back doesn't stiffen or shudder at my supreme dorkiness. So I think she really missed it. It got lost in the wall of sound she's built around her.

I'm not going to risk another possible disaster. I make sure to cross the room in front of her, so that she has to see me head toward the door. She looks up to watch me lean against it and push it open. Sees me lift one hand in a wave that I hope expresses the casual way I'm cruising out the door.

"You're heading out." She's not really asking this. She's announcing it, and I don't know what I'm supposed to say back.

My last-ditch effort is polite. "I don't want to disturb your work." It's sort of funny because it's not bullshit at all. I think about how guarded I am about my secret hours at Caramoor and wonder if they're the same thing for Jade, if they matter the same way.

"No." I don't what she's saying no to. She's a girl, though, and it occurs to me that I might as well get used to hearing that. But she keeps going and this time sounds almost as uncool as me. "I mean. You didn't disturb me. I mean —" She blows her hair out off her forehead. "I'm sorry. I'll see you around."

Which is way better than just being waved off with a hair dryer. So I can summon up a sort of genuine smile. "Maybe tomorrow?" And Jade nods like she might actually be nervous, which counts as an official milestone for me: the first hot girl I've made nervous. And not the clearly-worried-that-I-might-have-a-scrapbook-of-telephoto-snapshots-of-her-somewhere kind of nervous. The please-don't-let-him-touch-my-hair kind of nervous. I think maybe I saunter away from the Arts Studio, almost feel like stopping by the chapel and thanking someone that Jade missed my announcement about the deer.

But when I get to Ainsley House, it hits me exactly how tired I am. Bone-tired. So weary that my knees creak along with the stairs I'm climbing up. It's cold on the first floor, but gets warmer with each flight up. At first I just mean to check on my attic room, but once I sit down in the plaid flannel of the sleeping bag, I'm done for. So the plan is to sleep for a few hours and wake up to hike back home where I can shower and change. Either Soma will be struck by the spirit of forgiveness or I'll have to haul ass back to campus before first period. Either way my eyes are sliding closed, it's freezing outside, and I can sleep with the memory of Jade blowing her hair out from her eyes still hot in my mind. So that's clearly my best bet. By the time I get the bag zipped around me, I'm floating on a jade-green sea.

CHAPTER 13

It's the morning sunlight that crashes over me hours later. It takes me a couple of seconds to realize where I am and then to understand that if that attic is full of light, then I'm in some deep shit. It's going to look a little strange for me to simply trot downstairs and stop off at the front desk for some waffles or something.

My cell says it's ten after six, which gives me a slim glimmer of hope. How many people get to work that early? So I slither out of the sleeping bag, get my shoes tied around my feet. Each time my foot hits the floor, I picture someone sitting in one of the offices, glancing up at the ceiling. Holy crap — I honestly don't know how I'm going to do this. It's going to take me lowering the ladder into the administrative hallway to get out of here.

Pacing means more noise and so I won't let myself. Instead, I straighten out my bed and get my coat on. If someone catches me, I'll claim a janitor let me in early to get a book and I decided to use the chance to check out the attic for the Wells Farm ghost. It's lame, but something. At the last minute, right before I lower the ladder down, it occurs to me to take the chain with the master key off my neck and shove it down into my left sock under my shoe.

I get the ladder swinging about halfway down before I panic and just drop onto the floor. Somersault across the hall like I'm landing into gunfire or something. This doesn't really count as playing it cool. But I can't stop myself from freaking out — from leaping and batting the attic door shut and then tearing down the hallway and stairs like Cecil van Gunder's Young Spirit on the Staircase is chasing me out the door. If anyone was in the building, they'd see a prepped-out blur with a blue backpack hauling ass out of Ainsley House.

The field house parking lot has three cars in it already, so it's lucky I didn't fall asleep on the bench press or something. This is good, though, because then the building's already open. I don't have to risk using the key in the rising daylight. Get in and get out. That's the protocol for both the building and the shower. Put on the same clothes as yesterday, shellac my pits with deodorant, and hope for the best.

I'm spanking clean and dressed to go by six thirty. Get a pack of cookies out of the vending machine by the cafeteria for breakfast and then head back to the main buildings, ready for the day before most of campus is. The faculty straggles in from the staff lots and I get a lot of raised eyebrows. I haven't really been a regular at the library lately and now I'm sitting on the floor outside, like I've been waiting for Dylan tickets or something. And noticing a couple things about the teachers. 1) They're generally not morning people. They must get into school and work themselves into a frenzy of enthusiasm, because right now, they're an army of zombies shuffling through the hallways with coffee mugs. 2) They all carry canvas tote bags around with them — NPR giveaway ones, ones with animals parading across them, even ones with the Caramoor school crest printed on the sides. Like our faculty is solely responsible for keeping the tote bag industry in business.

The librarian apologizes to me when she opens the door, without knowing that there's no place on campus that I'm actually locked out of. She whispers the apology even though we're not actually in the room yet. Maybe that's how she talks all the time? Like she's so used to whispering all day at work, her voice has faded from lack of practice? I feel bad. She's got two tote bags and a laptop and she's struggling to get the door unlocked quickly for me, and here I am picturing her always getting the wrong sandwich in the drive-thru. Whispering over and over into the intercom.

I have enough time to knock off a few proofs for trig, and read half the chemistry chapter that was assigned last week. So that's something. Maybe I'd do better at boarding school, where I could wander into getting crap done.

If anyone notices I'm wearing the same clothes, no one says anything. There's a whole brigade of guys at Caramoor who wear the standard khakis and light-blue shirt every day any-how — the unofficial uniform. You'd have to be Soma in one of his flight suits to cause anyone to notice. There are probably a couple of extra ties at the bottom of my locker if I cared.

I don't care. That's what I keep repeating to myself, anyway. All through the pop quiz in English, which I tank. All through Euro and a chemistry lab that Soma and I would usually goof off through. Instead, Soma sidles up to Jake Stewart and I make a big show of setting up my table without looking for a partner at all. My feet itch and make me wish I had clean socks on. For the whole fifty minutes of lab, I only lift my eyes from the lab table to reread the instructions printed on the board. Follow them as carefully as if I were dissembling a bomb. Record all the data and check it. Write the intro to my lab report while most of the other pairs are madly sciencing.

On one hand, school sucks lately because it's so quiet around me. I hadn't realized how few people I actually spoke to, how more often I usually stood and nodded and laughed and let Soma be the ambassador between my brain and the world outside. He's not making those trips back and forth anymore. So I'm sort of ghostlike around here. I nod at guys and grin when some comment in class deserves it, but otherwise I've got other things to think about. It takes me most of lunch period to chase down Dad and make sure he hasn't tried the landline at home late at night or anything. He doesn't accuse me of losing my college fund at the pool hall down in East Hartford, so apparently he hasn't been checking up. The first thing he asks me is if I've run out of money, which means he must be feeling guilty.

"Is everything going okay, out there?"

"Out here? Sure is, Bear. Sure is." I wait for him to continue, but he doesn't ask how things are here.

"I'm getting to school okay. I ate at the diner last night."

"I knew as much. I knew you'd be just —"

"We haven't gotten any more postcards from Ethan." I don't know why I say it. Until the sentence came out, I hadn't even thought to check the mail.

"What?"

"I mean — well, maybe you'd been thinking that he got in touch again and he hasn't again so I figured you'd want to know that —"

"Well, we did just hear from him, Bear. Let's just focus on that."

"Right." I should make a list of things to talk about the next time I call my dad. I put making a list on my list of things to do and disgust myself. It takes effort not to hit myself in the forehead with the cell phone.

"So you just keep on calling when you need something."

"Right."

"How are those grades? I don't want to come home to phone calls from teachers."

"No, sir." Dad had his list all ready, apparently.

"And the house is still standing?"

"Yes, sir."

"No rats. No roaches. No heroin addicts squatting in the living room?"

"Dad," I tell him. "You said nothing about squatters in the living room."

"I'll speak to you in a couple of days, unless you need anything. Lori knows how to get in touch with me if you have trouble. Just call the office line."

"Yeah, thanks, Dad."

"Anytime." That's the note he hangs up on. So that wasn't a disaster. I take a few deep breaths and remind myself that I'm not the kind of kid that needs to come home to a house with lights on and something in the oven smelling up the house. That no one I know is that kind of kid anymore.

Soma breaks before I do. He's waiting at my locker at the end of eighth period, and for a second, neither of us says anything. I spin the numbers to my combination and start loading up my backpack. He watches me like it's the most fascinating thing he's seen since that time we saw a stomach stapling on the surgery channel.

"I would have driven you this morning."

"It was fine." That sounds cold when I say it, so I add, "But thanks."

"Yeah, well, I came to pick your ass up. The least you could do is be there." I panic for a minute before I remember that I don't answer to Soma Sancio. It's not like he's my dad and he's going to make me drop and do push-ups until I own up to lying.

"I had to leave early so I didn't miss part of first period again." Bingo. A perfectly reasonable explanation thrown back with a shot of guilt. "It's a long walk."

"Yeah, well, I'm not your driver —"

"I know." That I'll cop to. That was lousy of me. "Sorry, man. I've just had a lot on my mind." That's all I can come up with. It sounds false to me but both of us are looking for a way back now. Zip up my bag and stand there, shifting from one foot to the other. Step toward my best friend the slightest bit. "It's pretty cold out."

"Yeah. It's going to suck to walk home, huh?"

"Asshole."

"Go home and smoke a bowl?"

This is probably how caveman kids made up. One of them would accidentally kill the mammoth the other had his eye on or something and they'd avoid each other through the hunts and crap all week. Until it was Friday and time to gather around the fire and invent language, then it would be all about brotherhood again. When we pull into the driveway of my dwelling, Soma puts the car in park but keeps it running. He looks straight ahead toward the garage door and sort of blurts out, "This morning you weren't here and the whole time, up until I saw you first period, I thought you'd just booked. Left town like Ethan." Soma turns the key and takes it out of the ignition.

"Yeah, well. That would be stupid," I say. "Now I'm the favorite."

"Nah, *I'm* your dad's favorite." Now we're back to our old selves, sauntering up toward the side door. "You know your dad wishes I was the third son."

"That's right — he could will you all his army gear. You could have a whole new wardrobe." We go inside and the first thing I notice is how cold it is. Frost on the inside of the windows kind of cold.

"What the hell, dude?" Soma is standing in his army-navy-store parka, breathing out into his hand like he's trying to see the fog of his own breath.

"I must have left the heat off." Switch the thermostat up to seventy and then put on a pot of coffee in the kitchen.

"What's up, Starbucks? I thought we were going to do some calming down?"

"Yeah, but this'll warm us up."

"So will smoking." Soma opens the fridge and then the freezer, throws a frozen pizza into the oven.

"You need a cookie sheet for that." I dig one out from the cupboard beside the stove and slide it between the pizza and the rack. Set the timer for twenty minutes.

"You're like a housewife."

"Yeah, well. We're short one around here." Misfire. Soma slinks back to the living room, feeling guilty for reminding me of my orphan status. This is why I shouldn't be allowed to have friends. Every time I open my mouth, it feels like crap like this happens. Someone ends up feeling shitty.

Toss the TV remote to Soma in an effort to make up for it. "Be right back." I come back downstairs with a Ziploc baggie from Ethan's room and Soma has *Oprah* on. "What are you doing?"

"Oprah should run for office." He's still sitting in his winter jacket on the edge of the sofa. "Really. She's our culture's personification of wisdom."

"You are a twisted kid."

"Nah, I just appreciate a cultural icon when she's gazing out from the television in front of me. This one is about miracles. It's like she has her own religion now. Oprah says that miracles exist and so suddenly millions of previous cynics believe."

"I don't think that cynics watch *Oprah*." Soma nods slightly in agreement, but then points out the obvious.

"*We're* watching *Oprah*." He pulls a metal bong out of his backpack and starts packing it carefully, sees me staring at him, and asks, "What?"

"You brought that to school?"

"I kept it in my backpack."

"That's the size of a roll of paper towels."

"Lighter?" I toss him one and for about the thousandth time, open my mouth to tell him about the key. We have the whole weekend to put together the kind of key prank that guys would tell their sons about. It's Soma Sancio, the kid who managed to get school canceled for three days our freshman year just by flushing a T-shirt into the toilet. It wrecked the plumbing completely. All I have to do is let him loose on the school and just watch what happens. The bong gurgles in agreement beside me.

The minute I tell him, though, it's not mine anymore. Not really. In the first few days after Ethan left, all I could think about was that he knew he was leaving. That he could have been sitting next to me on the sofa, watching the TV, and the whole time he was choosing not to look over and say, "I'm taking off for a few months." I remember the night before, we had to empty the stupid dishwasher before putting in the dirty plates from dinner. I could drive myself nuts trying to remember, Did he wash more dishes that night because he was leaving? Or did he just hang back? I mean, why should he wash plates he wasn't going to eat off of again? I could make it mean something if I could remember.

Sitting next to Soma, though, with the key on a chain around my neck, I also understand how Ethan couldn't have told me. 1) There's the obvious fact that I would have stopped him. Pussy move on my part, but I would have. 2) And if I didn't, then he would have had to find a way to say good-bye. 3) And he'd have to give up the secret of leaving.

The truth is, for whatever reason, the months after Mom died were harder on Ethan. Before, he seemed unsettled in his own skin, testing the boundaries of everything. After, it was like all limits evaporated. He didn't even bother to sneak in late at night; he'd come crashing through at two or three in the morning, sleep all day, and show up to the dinner table with red eyes. He'd just push food around his plate, drink beer from the bottle right in front of my dad like it was nothing. And I'd sit there bracing myself for the inevitable explosion, but nothing happened. Just a tense silence. Ethan would sit down late and Dad would get up early, finish the last bites of his dinner standing over the kitchen sink. They spent the few minutes in the day that they actually shared a room staring grimly at each other — Ethan with his chin pitched defiantly up and Dad with his eyes bearing down on the table like he was trying to pin Ethan to his chair.

When did that start? Dad acting as if someone had to force him to look at Ethan? Back then, I wasn't paying attention. I figured Ethan just veered too far out of line and Dad was too tired from losing Mom to find a way to understand him.

"Dude, your house looks bizarre." Soma's voice gets lower when he smokes, so he croaks this from his seat on the low sofa. I can't help but laugh at him. He's sitting in the center square where most of the springs are shot. He's just about six inches from the carpet with the rest of the couch rising up around him. He's a head in the middle of a pile of crooked cushions. And when he talks, it sounds like his voice is traveling out of a deep well of pillows.

"You look bizarre." I bend to breathe in, and cough a little.

"It's dry."

"It's old. It's from Ethan's stash." Saying his name makes me want to check the mail, but that's another thing to save for later. Something else to keep quiet.

"Well, then . . ." Soma doesn't finish, but we're both thinking it. I must not expect him back. It's just a second of stiff silence and then he goes back to his critique of our housekeeping skills. "No, I'm serious. It looks weird in here."

"We have a cleaning lady." The same lady since Mom was sick.

"I'm not saying it's dirty. You just need some *Better Homes and Gardens* shit around here."

"You've been watching too much *Oprah*."

"I'm serious. You've got newspapers stacked up in the corner as high as the bookcase. You have all those ducks of your mom's piled onto one shelf." I blink and try to see it with Soma's eyes. He's actually being generous. "Is that garbage can from the bathroom?"

"It's peach plastic."

"Yeah?"

"Yeah, it's from the bathroom." The garbage can in question is full of empty bottles and cans. It's sitting next to the recliner. "We recycle."

Soma snorts into the metal tube and ends up choking. Smoke billows from his mouth and nostrils. "Your dad dating?"

"Shut the fuck up, dude."

"I'm just saying — this place needs a woman's touch."

"Yeah, well, then you should move in."

"Yeah, I'd do it, too. Tell your dad. I'll clean this place in a skirt if he lets me move in here." Soma's only half-joking on this one. Soma's the only son, caught between four girls. Two older, two younger. All of them full-fledged lunatics, except maybe the youngest, Cammie, who's four. Cammie always wears a raincoat and wants to be a hot air balloon when she grows up, though, so eventually she's going to be just as insane as the rest of them. Meredith is the oldest. She's a senior at Mount Saint Mary's, but it's her sixth year of high school. She's bipolar or something and she keeps having to take time off and then start over. His whole house is nuts because of it.

I mean, his house doesn't look that way. It's all coordinated tweed and corduroy and crap with family portraits climbing up the walls next to the staircase, but then Meredith and Jill, the second one, come barreling down the steps, tearing at each other's hair and ripping at each other's clothes. Sounds hot, but it's just crazy.

Soma's parents are okay. They're just all about Meredith. It's like they're on constant damage control. His dad is actually his stepdad. He's a dentist and he always talks in this slow, calm tone, like he knows he's about to inflict excruciating pain. I guess he's a standup guy. The two youngest girls are his and he adopted the older three kids. Soma didn't want to give up his real dad's name so his parents made a deal that he could change his first name, too, if he changed his last. His first name was Francis so that was a no-brainer. Plus he would have been Francis Sancio. He says that sounds like a brand of spaghetti sauce.

At Caramoor, you can't shut Soma up, but at his house, it's an entirely different story. He's the ghost of masculinity, slinking through the halls. If he had normal sisters, that would at least be helpful, then maybe he'd understand women the slightest bit. But instead he has the insane brigade. Which means he's equipped to work at a mental institution or something. Whatever ideas I might have about asking him for advice about Jade are dumb ones. He wouldn't really know how to talk to a girl who didn't burn her sister with a curling iron. And I'd have to tell him how I met her, which means telling him about the key. So there's one more subject I can't stop thinking about that I can't mention to him.

Soma's too stoned to pick up on any of this. I'm not much more clearheaded, sinking back into the recliner. He's lost in the couch and we have *Ultimate Fighting* on. He's probably just glad to have something besides girl shit on the TV and I'm just happy to sit in a room with someone else. Glad that we're not fighting anymore. It's Friday night, anyway, stupid to think that Jade would be alone by herself in her mother's classroom instead of out to dinner with an Arab sheik or something. On the television in front of us, men throw each other down on the mats, crack each other's spines over their knees. Somebody takes an elbow in an eye socket and Soma jerks like he's the one who's been hit.

"Do you smell something burning?" By the time we get it out of the oven, the pizza is a round, black husk. I turn on the fan and pour myself a cup of coffee to try to wake myself a little. Less than an hour and we've already almost burned the house down.

"Chinese food?" Soma asks brightly. Because it's on my dad's card, we order like we're feeding the entire weight-lifting crew. We order forty dollars' worth of food and when the guy on the other end of the phone gives me the total, we both just about fall over laughing. He asks, "No joking? No joking?" probably thinking we're a bunch of lame-ass brats ordering food to our algebra teacher's house.

"No joking," I try to reassure him, giving him my address as solemnly as possible. He asks for my phone number and as soon as I hang up, the phone rings again. By this time, Soma is clutching his side and wheezing.

"Chinese food?" the voice on the line asks.

"Yes. Please bring us some Chinese food." It takes half an hour for the doorbell to ring and even the kid making the delivery is dubious. It makes me wonder how often they get fake orders. That sort of sucks so I tip the guy a ten. Then he seems to doubt me a little less.

We spread all the food out on the coffee table and go to work on the egg rolls first. I look at Soma sprawled on a sofa cushion that he's pulled onto the floor and realize that he's here for the night. Logically, I know that I should just sit tight and enjoy the fact that I didn't manage to lose my best friend this week. But it's getting dark and rolling toward my usual witching hour. I can feel myself getting restless.

So I dig around the fridge and come back with three beers. Pack more weed into the bowl. And sit there and feel as jerkish as usual while Soma eats and drinks and lolls around on the floor. "You're not drinking?" he asks.

"Nah . . . one of us has to stay sober so we don't burn the place down."

"Yeah, you're just trying to ply me with booze. If I wake up pregnant, I'll know what happened." Can't get much past the stoned kid on the sofa cushions. Soma passes out before he even gets halfway through his lo mein.

I unfold the quilt from on top of the sofa and tuck it around him. Put another pillow under his head. For a while, at least an hour, I stay there and watch TV. Soma turns to his side and covers his eyes with one arm, but doesn't wake up. I put the cartons of food that we didn't even open in the refrigerator and leave a note on the brown paper bag all of it came in: *Got a little drunk, went out for fresh air*.

Then I open three more beers from the fridge and pour them down the sink. I am diabolical. Pour myself coffee from the pot and zap it in the microwave. Check to make sure the beeping hasn't woken up Soma. He's still out. It's tough bypassing his jeep to make the long trek up the hill to Caramoor, but I can't justify getting Soma drunk and then stealing his car. I tell myself I'm just going up to check a few things out and that I don't expect Jade to be there, but as soon as I get through the gate, I head straight to the Arts Studio.

CHAPTER 14

It's dark and my own disappointment surprises me a little.

"Shake it off, Simon." My own voice in the dark spooks me a little, and I unlock the building more so I can turn on a light than anything else. And then because I miss her, in my loser, stalker boy kind of way, I walk around the studio a little, looking for traces of her. Nothing at the pottery wheel. Nothing on the drying racks. In the center of the building, the art faculty has a little office with a desk for each of them. I can tell which one is Mrs. Larson's, because of the pictures of Jade pinned to the wall in front of it. In one she's a little kid, missing teeth but the smile is still unmistakable. And then another is a graduation picture. She's in one of those goofy board hats. So Jade's not in college, but she's not in high school anymore, either.

That's the big clue I come up with, playing detective. Mrs. Larson loves her daughter. Her daughter graduated high school. And then I hear her daughter's voice tentatively calling from the doorway. "Hello?" Jade doesn't even sound afraid now. More freaked out. "Hola, Andres?" Andres is our head janitor — and Jade seems disappointed that I'm not him.

"No, no, it's me . . . Jason." I fucking hate the name Jason.

"Oh." Now she's confused. "Is Andres here? Sometimes when I get here, he's still finishing up."

"No, I haven't seen him. It's just me." There's an apology in my voice that I didn't mean to put there.

"How did you get in the building?" Good question. She's no dummy, this hot chick in front of me.

"It was open."

"Really? Andres is usually really careful about that. I hope everything's okay."

"Yeah, everything's okay."

"I mean with Andres." I really wish I were passed out on my living room floor next to Soma right about now.

"Of course."

"Well, do me a favor — don't say anything to anyone about finding the building open. I don't want any of the cleaning crew to get in trouble. They're supersweet about letting me stay here and work."

I am never going to figure out this girl.

"Yeah, sure. But then you need to be aware of your surroundings. Anyone could have walked into the building." The genius bounces back.

And Jade looks as skeeved out as you might expect a young girl to look when you speak to her like you're a suspect on the sex-crimes *Law & Order*. "I just mean you should be careful." There's just no way to avoid sounding like a serial killer here. So I bail and go for the mercy appeal. "You scared me when you came in."

Nothing works better than the truth sometimes. "Yeah, you looked like you'd seen a ghost. Sorry if I startled you."

"I shouldn't have come in." Another truth. I'm two for two now. "But the lights were on." Two for three at least. "And I wanted to see you." Three for four.

"Yeah? Well, here I am."

"I figured it was a long shot, that you'd be out on a Friday night."

"I am." Jade gestures around the studio. "Out on a Friday night."

"Right." I'm stuck now, standing here wondering if it's just that it's always this nerve-wracking to talk to women. If this is how it's going to be for the rest of my life. But because I apparently hate myself, I keep going. "I just figured you'd be out with Prince Bandar or something."

"Who?"

"You know — some Saudi prince. You're the kind of girl who a man would trade many camels for." This, of all things, gets a laugh — the idea of being traded for livestock.

"Tell me you've gone home since school let out." Jade tosses this one over her shoulder, while she's setting up a workstation with a tub of clay and a bowl of water. Laying sheets of newspaper down.

"Is that concern I detect in your voice?"

She waves me off. "It's just that you seem to live here." Hopefully, Jade does not notice that I have ceased breathing. She laughs a little self-consciously. "I just don't want to find out that you don't exist and I've been talking to the ghost of Wells Farm or something."

"You've heard of the Wells Farm ghost?"

"Yeah, Preppy. My mom's been teaching here for fifteen years. I grew up on those stories. And then the *Unsolved Mysteries* thing —"

"Right. I just started reading a lot about it." God, I really *am* a complete moron. "I mean just for something extra." Not at all better. Who reads crap like that for no reason? Freaks, that's who. So I try to fix it. "You know, for extra credit." Oh, God. Just kill me. Even just a coma. God, just put me in a coma. One little, short coma.

"Well, I'd really like to hear about it sometime. When we're both not so busy." I wonder what it would be like to be able to talk to people like Jade does, how it would be to actually be able to express myself with some kind of grace and intelligence. It must be so nice to not be moronic.

"Yeah. Maybe sometime this week." That's reasonably adept. Not too eager, but sure of myself. The judges at the table in my head score me at seven out of ten. Not so shabby. "So, I'll let you get started."

"Yeah, well, you've got to go compose your genius music, right?" Jade has unwound the scarf from her neck and she's shaking out her hair as she says this. When she looks up at me, she's smiling so wide that I forget she shouldn't believe me as much as she does.

The truth comes out because I don't want to end the night on a lie. "Nah, I'm not such a genius. And really I just want to walk around campus a little. It's cold, but not freezing."

"You want some company?" I don't remember the word *yes* ever coming out of my mouth that quickly before. And I can't imagine ever saying it faster. I mean, maybe if there is a God someday some girl will ask me, "Do you want my mouth there?" But so far this holds the record.

So Jade winds her scarf back around her neck, zips her ski jacket up, and puts on earmuffs. She's wearing fuzzy earmuffs. I don't even think girls know half the ways they drive me nuts. I tug my hat farther around my ears just because I want to feel like I have my own adjustments to make. "You don't have a scarf?" Jade looks at me like I'm missing a leg or something. It took her awhile to get her scarf on, mostly because it's like eight feet long, striped in about twenty kinds of blue. You know those African ladies in *National Geographic* magazine, who wear metal rings coiled around their necks to stretch them? Jade's scarf looks like those metal rings, but you know, significantly less painful.

"We could both wear your scarf." I mean it as a joke, to make fun of how long the thing is, but it comes out like, "We could both climb in your pants." I must blush because Jade just laughs and sort of shoves me out of the door. "Don't they issue you official Caramoor blue-and-white scarves? You poor, unfortunate prep-school boys — how are you going to lead the future with cold necks?"

"Hey — where'd you go to high school?"

"Not here."

"Well, yeah, I would have noticed that." But the mood has shifted again. It's not just colder outside. She's even stepped away slightly. So no more personal questions. And no more comments about wearing her clothes. This means that I can think of absolutely nothing to say.

And that turns out to be nice. At first I don't speak because I'm scared to. I just crossed a line I hadn't even realized was there, into territory that Jade wasn't about to give me access to. But as we walk, the quiet turns from being painful to something better than that — companionable. The kind of quiet that feels like a choice more than an accident of stiffness.

Maybe I'm going to grow up to be one of those guys who ends up having very little to say. Like the old men who eat alone at the diner. Or like my dad. Maybe it's the same thing as the librarian speaking in a whisper even when she's not in the book stacks. But walking around out here, it just feels reassuring to have another set of footsteps echoing mine. Someone to talk to if I wanted that. If we came face-to-face with that buck again in the woods right now, Jade and I wouldn't even have to say anything immediately. It would be something we could describe to each other when we were ready to.

I don't know who decides on the rule, but neither of us speaks at all. Even when the cobbled sidewalk splits, Jade points to the left and we go that way, around the bend by the chapel. I sit on the chapel steps and she joins me, close enough that our shoulders brush and our jackets make a whooshing sound like when you're a little kid running around in snow pants. For whatever lame-ass reason, maybe because we're looking up and that's the direction people look when they're thinking about heaven . . . maybe it's because no one has worried about whether or not I was wearing a scarf in a long time . . . but for whatever reason I want to tell Jade about my mom. Not even really that she's dead. More like just that she existed. That she sang along to the radio while she made pancakes. And bought greeting cards compulsively and kept them all in a cupboard, organized by color and holiday. That if she had too much to drink, she'd piss off my dad by telling dirty jokes. And I'm sitting here in the dark next to a girl who doesn't even know that she's gone.

If I were a dirtbag, I would have told Jade and then tried for some sympathy ass. That's all I'm saying. But she doesn't even know my real name. Which shouldn't mean anything but for some reason right at that moment feels like the most tragic fact in the world. Swear to God, if I start to cry like some kind of emo pussy, I'm going home and closing myself in my room until I'm forty. Or I'll shut myself in Ethan's room because it's bigger and has better drugs.

It kills me sometimes that I can't ever do the thing that matters. Any other dumb-ass would have kissed Jade by now. But picturing how it would go, how I'd lean into her and have to duck around the hair blowing across her face, I just know I'd fuck it up. I can feel her shoulder pressed into mine, though, through both our jackets, and next to me she keeps exhaling like she's waiting for a ride that hasn't shown up yet.

Ethan would say I was just making sensitive-guy excuses to avoid doing the balls-out thing. The balls-out thing would be to turn around to face her and reach up to tilt her face from the sky to my own. And then kiss her until . . . I don't know . . . until I learned to do it right, I guess. But by the time my legs feel like they could support my weight and my arms give an indication that they're listening to the synapses in my brain firing off, *Reach for her. Reach for even just her wrist*, Jade stands up quickly. Maybe she's read my mind and understands how close to the edge we were treading. Or how far away. Maybe she's just not excited at the prospect of being grabbed on her . . . wrist.

She kicks at a small hill of old snow. "Will you walk me back?"

We can see the Arts Studio from the steps of the chapel so the look on my face most likely says, "The fuck?" Maybe that's Jade's own personal superpower. The ability to take a step back without making someone realize she's stepping away.

She's the one who tries again, though. "I mean — you never know who could be there when I open the door."

I get the game now, so I try to play it. "Yeah, it could be this weird Caramoor kid, who's pretending to be a musical genius."

"Yeah? Just pretending?" She doesn't sound like she'll totally write me off for it, so I try to fix the part of the lie that I can.

"Maybe just really, really exaggerating. Could you live with that?"

"Well, I'd have to stop calling you Bowie Boy in my head."

"You call me Bowie Boy in your head?"

"Yeah." Jade pauses, presses her lips together. "What do you call me in your head?" I wonder if anyone has exploded a lung just because a girl made him forget to breathe.

"Let's get you back to the Arts Studio, little lady." Jade pelts me with a lump of snow that hurts more than snow should.

"Oh, Jesus. I'm sorry." It sounds like she's scared and horrified but I can't tell at first because my face is buried in my hands. "Jason? Jason? Are you okay? Oh, my God — I'm so sorry." My right eye is all wet and won't stop blinking. I pull my hand away to see that there's blood on it, too. Hell of a snowball. It's dark and now I have to look at her with one eye winking. And not because I'm being slick. Look down and there's a pinecone, half-covered with snow at my feet.

"Nice."

"Jason, I'm so sorry."

"Yeah. My name is actually Emil." I guess I just figure that if my eye's going to hurt so much, I want to be called by my given name.

"What? Why would you lie about your name?"

"Just call me Bowie Boy."

"Why would you lie about your name?" She's mad now and I can't tell how much because I'm in too much pain. I can't even tell how far away she is because I can only see out of the one eye. "Jason, why would you lie about your name?"

And at least that gets us both laughing. I weigh it all in my mind pretty quickly. I can risk her mentioning me to her mom. Or lie again. She'll probably be able to tell and I don't want to lie again. And my eye stings. I don't want to sit there and pick another fake name.

"Jade, I met you right after calling your mom a lesbian. The last thing I wanted was for you to go home and tell Mrs. Larson about the jackass you met after-hours on campus." Then I go in for guilt points. "I don't know a whole lot about you."

There's a few beats of silence. "What did you think I'd do? Go home and sit at the kitchen table with the Caramoor yearbook, showing her mug shots of kids who thought she was gay?"

It's kind of uncanny. That's exactly what I pictured.

"I just can't believe you've had me calling you the wrong name. Is that it? I mean, are there other things? Do you really stay late here working in the electronic music lab? Or are you doing extra credit in taxidermy? Serial killer? Junkie?"

I can't let her think everything's a lie. "I put in a lot of extra hours in the music lab." Search for details to back myself up. "We've got first-rate equipment here. But I've been coming around more than I need to, probably. Just to see who's around on campus." I wrap up with a look that's aiming for charming but probably gets hung up at stalky.

But I am rewarded with Jade looking up and doing the thing where she blows wisps of her own hair out of her eyes. "You really *are* retarded. Come on, let's put ice on your eye." She turns toward the Arts Studio. "They keep ice packs in the freezer in the photo lab."

"You just nailed my eye with a snowball and now you're going to put ice on it?" If there's ever a contest in my life for who's been most whipped by some random hot girl he barely knows, I've already got it aced. Because I bend down and feel around and pick up the freaking pinecone she hit me with. Pocket it and follow her inside.

Dozens of black-and-white prints hang from clothesline criss-crossing the photo lab. "It's cool that you guys still do film prints." Jade's found a frozen Ziploc bag in the freezer and she's wrapping it in paper towels. "At Bard, things are moving toward mostly digital."

"You go to Bard?" I don't think she gave up that information by accident. It's more like my guilt jab outside hit hard.

Jade is still folding the paper towel deliberately into a perfect square, though, and when she speaks, her voice comes out careful and measured. So I definitely think it's deliberate, this tiny piece of history she's letting rise to the surface. "I went there for a while."

Now she has the freaking Scotch tape out, like she's wrapping me up a present. "They have a program for high school, too, called Simon's Rock. You can basically go to college early, and if you want to matriculate in later, you can."

"So what year are you?"

"Hard to tell."

I nod like it makes perfect sense that Jade doesn't know what year of school she's in and reach out for the pack. "You don't have to tie-dye it or anything, you know," I say. "It's just going on the eye I can't see out of." I neglect to say that it probably will indeed be saved and installed with the freakin' pinecone in the Jade Larson Museum of Guys Who Should Grow Some Balls.

"I'm really sorry . . . umm . . ."

"Emil."

"Emil. Honestly, I'm really sorry. Is it still killing you? Lemme see if anything's stuck in your eye." And so that's how we end up with me on an Arts Studio stool, forcing myself to look up into the fluorescent light, even though that feels like a laser melting my retina. This doesn't count as crying in front of Jade. I get that. But I don't particularly feel like the standard of manhood, either.

And then Jade licks the tip of her pinkie finger and presses it to the corner of my wet eye. Seriously. Like how when I was a little kid and my mom would wipe lunch off my face with her own spit. Except it's hot when Jade does it. I know. There's something wrong with me.

She is just as weird, though. Holding her little finger up triumphantly — "I got it." And showing me the tiny speck caught under her nail. "You should make a wish."

"That's not an eyelash."

"Why be picky? You don't even care if someone calls you the wrong name."

"I was thinking of changing mine, anyway."

Jade rolls her eyes. "Tell me about it."

"Yeah? What would you change it to?" I sort of expect her to say "Rainbow" or "Wisdom" or "Flexibility" or something. I don't know a lot about Bard, but I know it's a lot of hippie kids. Vegans who grow organic weed and only snort fair-trade blow.

"I don't know — Frances, maybe?"

"Frances?"

"Yeah, she was this famous actress who was involuntarily committed to a sanitarium. She first got arrested for drunk driving or something and then the court declared her insane and her mother committed her. And then she was basically tortured. They lobotomized her. Do you know what a lobotomy is?"

"Nope." Of course I'm praying it's not a sex thing.

"It's how they used to treat the mentally ill. They'd drill a hole in your brain, through your frontal lobe. It was supposed to calm people down, but really it just destroyed most elements of their personalities. Basically made them zombies. Rosemary Kennedy got one. They were usually performed on women."

"Huh." I nod as if this is a completely typical area to be an expert in. "So you'd want her name?"

"Yeah, well, she got out. And married and moved on with her life. She told everybody what happened."

"With half a brain?" It comes out like smart-ass, but really I'm trying to figure it out.

"She was a really amazing woman." Now Jade's playing defense.

"My best friend changed his name from Francis." Fuck. It sort of hurts me to remember Soma. He's probably awake on my sofa pissed at this very minute.

"Why?"

" 'Cause he's a guy and his name was Francis. He's not an actress with a hole in her head. And he hated being called Frankie." I think of Soma in one of his flight suits. Or in the head-to-toe camouflage. "He doesn't really look like a Frankie."

Jade just shrugs. "You should tell him that Kurt Cobain named his daughter Frances. It's a very distinguished name."

"I'm sure it's a perfectly lovely name for a crazy chick." Jade looks around the worktable, likes she's searching for something to throw at my other eye. Awesome. I've spent the past hour trying not to stare at her and now I'm going to end up blind.

"Hey, keep that ice pack on, dumb-ass."

If I were Ethan, I'd tell her that she should keep holding it there for me. I'd play it off like my eye might not open again unless she stood there, pressing a cool cloth to my face.

Instead I say, "Listen, I gotta go." Because I'm just the brother who, let's face it, is only going to torture himself with his inability to kiss her right now. And who has no depth perception and would probably knock skulls with her if he tried. And besides that, I can't get Soma out of my head right now. If he's awake, then I've totally screwed up whatever peace treaty that forty bucks' worth of Chinese food and open season on Ethan's weed might have earned me. I won't even be able to explain myself. I can't tell him about Jade without explaining all my after-hours scenic tours of Caramoor. And I can't explain those hours and keep my mouth shut about the key at the same time.

"I was supposed to meet my friend, that guy, awhile ago." It sounds like a lie. And Jade shrugs to let me know that she couldn't care less. "You know the one named Francis — I blanked and forgot." She's still standing there, cultivating this pristine indifference, so I just keep talking. "He changed his name to Soma, actually. Like the drug in *Brave New World*? He's a total jackass, but he's a really good guy. You'd like him. I mean you should meet him sometime. We should all hang out." I am just babbling now. Like full-on retard meltdown.

"Emil." It's nice to hear her say my name. "I don't want to meet your friends."

One time Ethan and I drove into town to pick up my mom's medication and accidentally backed over a broken bottle in the pharmacy parking lot. I feel like the sound the tire made when the shard of glass punctured it. I mean it sucks.

"Yeah. Of course not." That's all I can really make myself say. And then, "I'll see you around."

It's either good news or bad news that my cell phone registers a grand total of zero phone calls. Good because maybe that means Soma's still passed out in the living room and I can slip in and act like I've been snoring next to him in the living room all night. And that'll make it easier to pretend that the past ten minutes didn't happen, either. But maybe he didn't call because he woke up and wrote me off.

It's colder walking home than it was going. Partly because my eye feels like someone stabbed it with a fork and my gut feels like someone stabbed it with just about every other sharp thing on the planet. Jade's fucked up, that's what I'm going to keep telling myself. Throwing crap around like she's Courtney Love and lecturing me about the lack of equality in psychiatric treatment. Crazy girls are always doing that. Claiming it's the rest of the world that's actually nuts and they're stringing together some insane logic to go along with it. Don't they realize they're just revealing the madness? It's like they can't help themselves.

I was just being polite. Jade was the one who got all squir-relly when I had to get going, as if she expected me to hang around all night watching her do her arts and crafts and picking slivers of pinecones out of my eyes. Whatever. She's too much of a distraction, anyway. I have three days left, plus the weekend. There are still parts of Caramoor I haven't even looked at, let alone figured out if and how I could capitalize on them for a key prank. For christsake, my father is halfway across the country, I have a master key to the school, and I'm spending most of my time hovering around some girl in the Arts Studio.

It's almost one in the morning, pretty early by our standards lately. I hope she spends the whole rest of the night wondering if she caused permanent damage to my vision. For all she knows, I've dreamed of being a pilot since the age of six. I should walk back there in one of Soma's flight suits, ranting about my derailed career path. That would get to her. That would get me laid.

Soma doesn't even move when I forget and let the door slam behind me. First I'm relieved and then my heart skids to a stop. For a second I think he has to be dead. He must have found pills or something in one of the medicine cabinets or gone through Ethan's stuff. He must have woken up and kept drinking or just threw up lying on his back.

But I don't even have to lean in close to smell his breath. It hits me when I'm trying to decide whether or not his chest is rising and falling under the quilt I yanked over him hours ago before leaving. Corpses can't smell that much like beer and whiskey.

God. Right after Mom died, I got a little creepy about stuff like this. Like maybe Dad's car wouldn't pull into the driveway at the usual time and that would be enough to convince me he was wrecked somewhere along the highway. And it was worse with Ethan, because he was always doing such stupid shit, anyway. Stuff worth worrying over. I'd see these scenes in my head — Ethan drunk and passed out on the railroad tracks up by New Market Pond. Ethan stoned and stepping off the roof at some downtown loft party. Some days I'd feel my stomach clenching unlocking the front door and realize I'd spent the whole walk home convinced Ethan was going to be hanging from a beam in the attic. Sick shit.

It may not make any sense, but in some ways it's easier now that he's not around. It should be that there's more to worry about. A whole planet of peril and Ethan wandering around on it. Maybe because now at least I worry about the same things at the same pitch. The same level of unease without the rise and fall of thinking he's safe and then realizing he isn't. Now it's all in the same pit of not knowing.

Soma's not going to be going anywhere for quite some time, though. The thought of writing on his face with a Sharpie flits in and then out of my head. I could shave a stripe into his hair or even try to sew his mouth closed. I could superglue something onto his face. One of my mother's wooden ducks.

I don't do any of those things. Instead I push out the footrest of the recliner and turn on a rerun of *Saturday Night Live*. Shut my eyes and try not to think about the rigid line of Jade's lips. How she suddenly glossed over like she was a statue glazed with a thin veneer of bitch. Try to move backward instead and remember the weight of her shoulder leaning against mine. How our shoes looked lined up on one of the chapel steps — it's stupid to see the wooden ducks lined up in one tight flock on the living room shelf, to sit half-listening for Ethan's house key to turn in the lock, or look at the screen of my cell and wish my dad had sent a text or tried to call or anything. Those things make sense to miss and instead I'm sitting here wishing some girl I barely know would find her way to my doorstep. Like the daughter of one of our teachers is really going to show up and step out of her underwear in the middle of my living room. And ignore Soma on the floor long enough to do me.

She doesn't even want to meet my friends.

CHAPTER 15

I wake up to the television blaring about ten decibels higher than before and the footrest of the recliner folding in and out under my legs. Soma's standing over me and cackling, with his hand on the wooden lever on the side of the chair.

"Are you still drunk?" I ask.

He's not. He's just an ass. And this makes him laugh out loud and I can't get any leverage to knock some sense into him because my body keeps getting thrown off-kilter by the chair opening and closing beneath me.

"God," I say, "why are you still here?"

"There are two empty boxes of frozen waffles in your freezer."

"That's tragic, really. That's really the biggest problem my family is facing right now."

"Exactly. How could something like this happen in such a serene fortress of white-picket-fence prosperity? I almost feel obligated to call up Child Protection Services."

"Can't you just go back to sleep? Go on. Drink some more of my dad's beer."

"Waffles."

"You're insane."

"I'm this close to putting butter and syrup on the boxes and eating those."

I try to twist away from him, but he's still shifting the chair back and forth at five-second intervals. "Soma. Go home. There's carpet cleaner under the kitchen sink. Go sniff that." Turn to bury my face into the cushion and try to block out the light.

"Dude, what happened to your eye?" It starts throbbing as soon as he mentions it. I reach up to touch it and find it's all crusted over and sealed shut.

"Shit. You have the pinkeye." Soma says it like it's some venereal disease — like the clap or something. "Don't touch me, dude. Do not touch me with that eye."

"No, it's not that, it's —" What? I'm about to tell him that while I was just sitting in the chair all night, Mrs. Larson's hot daughter threw a snowball made out of a pinecone at me. I could have gone out for a walk and been looking up at the sky when it fell off the tree and nailed me. Or it could be the pinkeye and I could spend the day on my own at Caramoor, without feeling guilty about not sitting at the diner and seeing how many waffles we could cram down our throats.

"God. This sucks. I guess it *is* the pinkeye. Did you give me fucking pinkeye?" I rub at it and reach toward Soma.

"Do not come near me with your pinkeye hand. God. No, I didn't give you that crap — do you know how many times Cammie's brought that crap home from day care? It's, like, the most contagious disease that's not sexually transmitted."

"Let's just go get some waffles." I grab our jackets and hand Soma his.

"Emil! Stop touching my stuff. Go wash your hands." Honestly, I sort of wish we could do this all day. I'm on my way into the downstairs bathroom and Soma comes barreling up behind me. "Don't touch the doorknob. I'm going to have to go in there."

The best part of my morning is when I get to call out to Soma from the bathroom, "Should I not touch the flusher on the toilet?"

"No! Don't touch anything until I get out of here." So I get to stand there and watch Soma flush my piss down the toilet. Someday when Jade and I are married and have three kids or something and Soma and I are lounging poolside because she's off sculpting busts of the president or something, I'll laugh about the time she threw a pinecone in my eye and Soma will ask, "What?" and then I'll get to explain this moment. But that's a long way off. I mean she'd have to want to meet him first and all.

After the toilet flushes again, I hear the medicine cabinet open and shut a couple of times. "No prescriptions." Soma will steal anything if it's in pill form although I can't imagine there's anything left in there after Mom. "I'm looking for Scope."

"What?"

"I need mouthwash or something. I'm getting drunk again off my own spit, for christsake." Soma says this just as I'm burying his empties at the bottom of the kitchen trash so I know he's not exaggerating.

"That's shocking. Really."

"I'm serious. I bet I still wouldn't pass a Breathalyzer. I need some waffles."

"You need a toothbrush." I rummage around the junk drawer at the counter until I find the bunch of extras we keep for guests or trips. Take it out of the plastic packaging and even wrap the handle in a Kleenex before knocking on the bathroom door. When Soma opens the door, his head — face, hair, everything — is dripping wet. "Here." I offer it up proudly. "Look, I didn't even touch it with my pinkeye hand. Totally safe."

Soma gives me a dubious look. "I'm serious. No pinkeye." He still doesn't move to take it.

"What?" I said.

"I don't need it."

"What is your problem? It's a toothbrush, boozy." There's this weird silence.

"Where did it come from?" Soma's obviously embarrassed to ask and I still don't get it.

"My ass. But no pinkeye!"

"No, I mean —" It's like he's in physical pain. "Whose was it?" Soma finally gets out the question and then I realize that Soma thinks I ran to get him one of our toothbrushes from our bathroom upstairs. And I can't help fucking with him a little bit.

"It's Mom's." I try to say it as somberly as possible. His face looks even more pale and ill than it did from just the hangover. "Yep. I figured no one else is using it. So here you go, dude — my dead mother's toothbrush."

Now he's leaning against the door frame. It's like he's trying to figure out if he can run past me, if he can just elbow me out of the way and get to his car in the driveway. "Soma." I just hand him the plastic packaging from the counter. "You're a really sick kid, you know that?"

"Yeah, you're the one screwing around about it." But he says it sheepishly and his ears are pink as he turns back to the sink. "Thanks, though. Can I keep this?"

"Go for it."

"I'll keep it in the car. Just in case I need some freshening up on the go."

"Hey, I bet your sister keeps a toothbrush in the glove compartment, too." Meredith and Soma are always fighting over the car, but because she's usually grounded, it's pretty much a non-issue these days.

"Don't go there, man."

"Yep, because after all the blow jobs she gives curbside, Meredith's got to brush up those teeth."

"Dude, the only reason I'm not kicking your ass right now is because I don't want to catch pinkeye."

"Your slutty sister is not your fault, Soma." Now he's got his fist clenched at his side, but we both know he'd never hit me, anyway. Pinkeye or no pinkeye. "I cannot believe you thought I was giving you a used toothbrush."

"Just shut up."

"And what? Did you think you were going to catch cancer from the toothbrush?" The whole thing did make me wonder in some deviant-goth-kid way, whether or not her toothbrush was still in my parents' bathroom. And if it wasn't, who threw it out? I mean I can't picture my dad having to experience that moment. No wonder he's been working the hours he has. The past few months have probably been built out of those moments. Maybe that's the kind of job my aunts had. They had to walk around and get rid of stupid little things like that, the ones my mom didn't need anymore.

And then the thought seeps in that maybe she took care of those things herself. That's a moment I can't really think about with Soma standing right in front of me, though. And he is currently separating out a hunk of Ethan's weed into another Ziploc bag, as if that's just what people do when they leave each other's houses.

"Whoa. Make yourself at home."

"Sorry, but I have to. You're going to get your eye germs all over it, and then what am I going to smoke?"

"I don't know, maybe your own?"

"Nah. You don't want all of this. This much is just bad for you."

"Thanks for looking out for me. Go home. Now." Soma puts the baggie in a red metal pencil case that he keeps in the front pocket of his backpack. I don't think that case has ever seen a pencil.

"You should go to the doctor, get a prescription or an eye transplant or something." It really does hurt and I'm starting to worry that I might actually need a doctor.

"Yeah? You'll drive me?"

"Man, you can't ride in my car like that."

"I'll just get your sister to do it. She's not afraid of a few diseases."

"Fuck you, dude." But he stops before he gets into the car and calls from the driveway. "Wash your hands a lot. And don't touch the other eye." It's almost enough to make me feel guilty except I remember that he's walking away with about twenty-five bucks' worth of weed.

As soon as Soma pulls out of the drive, I head back to the bathroom to really look closely in the mirror and try to figure out just how bad the damage is. It's swollen shut, but what's worse is this wet crust that's sealing the two lids together. What the hell is that? For a second, I think maybe I should call the poison control hotline, but I can't really bring myself to call up and ask some old lady if pinecones are poisonous. So instead I get out my laptop and look it up.

It seems as if I will survive. Under possible eye injuries I find conjunctivitis, which is just the scientific word for *pinkeye*. There's cataracts and glaucoma, which I'm a little young for.

There's ulcers that come on gradually and are characterized by gradually increasing pain. Then there's ye olde detached retina or scratched cornea. Since a scratched cornea is a result of what happens when you get crap flying at your eye, it appears to be the most likely candidate. A detached retina sounds, and apparently is, worse. The robot doctor recommends flushing out the eye with water and using an ice pack. I don't want to talk smack about the medical expertise of internethospital.com, but the ice-pack method does not seem particularly cutting-edge or helpful.

What's worse than walking around like someone the bartender calls Winky is that every time my eye reminds me how sore it is, last night blinks by in snapshots of humiliation. Jade knows my real name. She knows I lied about being some kind of musical genius. She probably understands that half the time we're talking I'm only thinking about kissing her. And knows that half is an extremely conservative estimate on that front.

Not to mention the fact that she took the first available opportunity to shoot me down. It's about the two hundredth time I wished my parents hadn't sent me to Caramoor. Maybe that makes no sense. But it's been three years since I've sat in a class next to a girl or stood next to someone in a skirt in the lunch line. That has to be unhealthy. We're supposed to grow into steadfast chiefs of the tribe of men, but we're socially stunted by a lack of ladies.

Or I am at least. Ethan could talk to anyone. I don't know where he learned that. And Soma has a small online following. I have profiles on those sites and will basically write back to any girl in a tank top, but there's not a lot to say. It's not like junior high when you could stand around and bitch about gym class together. For all I know, Jade could have been acting the way you're supposed to act when you just keep running into each other accidentally late at night. It's not like I picked her up or anything. Had we met at a bar that I couldn't ever get into — well, that's what I mean. We wouldn't have. I could have been riding the train to New York and sat beside Jade on the train and it would have taken me the first six stops just to work up the nerve to speak to her. And then she probably would have moved her seat.

I mean guys must find ways to talk to Jade all the time. It's not like I was the one bright spot in a year of darkness for her or anything. We met because she was doing something she cared about and I kept showing up. She never wandered around campus looking for me. I didn't earn her.

So here it is, Saturday morning, and I have five more days to figure out about a decade's worth of stuff. At the very least I have to figure out how I am going to honor the time-tested, solemn tradition of wreaking hard-core havoc on the Caramoor campus. It has to be a plan that has the possibility of becoming legend. Just walking around and proving that the key actually works isn't accomplishing a whole lot. It just makes me feel cool for the ten seconds immediately after the key clicks into the lock.

So I sit down at the kitchen table with a three-ring binder and switch approaches. I'm just going to go at it like it was a school project. I know — I'm danger — I'm the freakin' key master. But the research phase is pretty much done. Now I have to sit down and come up with a plan that I can execute.

For a second, I catch myself wondering if Ethan would have trouble coming up with an inspired use for the key. But A) No, he wouldn't, and B) He didn't end up using it. I don't think. I mean, had Ethan used the key, we all would have heard about it. It would be an established folktale in American culture by now. Like Paul Bunyan. My best guess is that Ethan got the key last year and maybe he was excited about it. Maybe someone passed it on to him after the party we threw at our place. He would have pretended to be unfazed but probably it would have mattered a little to him — that his work was respected by the other bad-asses in the school. But then . . . well, we all had other things to worry about. So this one has to be for both of us.

So far I've got a list running of the places I've seen — the gym, headmaster's office, library, chapel, nurse's office, women's room. The faculty room and about a dozen classrooms. I've seen the therapeutic center, but it's probably worth spending more time looking around in there. Oh, and clearly I've been in the Arts Studio.

I've already decided not to do anything completely destructive. I think about those guys in the white pickup trucks and how wearily they climb in at the end of the night. No matter how kick-ass the key prank would be, it would only make me feel like crap if it just meant more scut work for the night crew. So that rules out pudding in the swimming pool or screwing around with the plumbing.

In a perfect world, I could orchestrate some kind of Jerry Bruckheimer project that could convince Jade I'm worth knowing at the same time. A valentine of epic proportions. Something requiring a helicopter. Caramoor has a pad installed on the roof of the field house. That's my favorite example of the ricockulous amount of money floating around that place. It's not like we have an aeronautics program or anything. But when Ethan was a freshman, one of his classmates' fathers paid to install it. The dad was some kind of newspaper mogul who had so many DWIs that his driver's license was suspended. So this was his solution. He flew his kid into school with a company helicopter. Awesome. That poor sucker had to explain why he couldn't just carpool like everyone else. Ethan said that the noise was insane and that they all called the kid Bruce Willis after that. So all I have to do is get my hands on a helicopter.

I could paint every brick of the Arts Studio green for Jade. But she never sees the building in the light. I'd have to write her name somewhere on it so that Mrs. Larson would notice but that would just make me seem like some pervy psycho. I could paint the inside walls, but Jade would probably walk in on me and throw a fit.

When the phone rings, at first I just let it go, thinking it's on the television. No one ever calls the landline anymore and, anyway, the ring sounds faint like it's far away. It's not until the machine picks up that I realize someone's calling us. It used to be my mom's voice on the machine, but now it's an electronic vocal recording. Another remnant of her that somebody gathered up and put away. The voice leaving the message isn't at all robotic, though. It's this high-pitched and shrieky whine that I've heard mimicked at least once a day for the past two and a half years.

"Emil? Emil Simon, this is Lou Anne Sancio calling." She doesn't muffle the phone with her hand so I can hear her hiss at Soma, "What's his cell phone number? Go get your cell phone and let me call on that." I find the kitchen phone under a paper plateful of chicken bones.

"Hello, Mrs. Sancio."

"I have a bone to pick with you, Emil." Of course I immediately think I'm in trouble and the most obvious reason is the weed that Soma left here with, but she goes on before my stomach fully crawls up my throat in fear. "Soma tells us that you've been staying for days in that big house all by yourself."

"Well, Dad's away on business and Ethan —"

"Yes, dear, but there's no reason for you to be there all alone. You should have been staying at our house. I know your father would have done the same thing for our brood." This is debatable.

"Thank you, Mrs. Sancio. Dad wanted me to stay and keep an eye on the house and whatnot." I do not tell her that my father thinks her son is going to grow up to be the next Unabomber and believes that she and her husband are directly responsible.

"Well, you know, our belongings are replaceable, but our children aren't." I have no idea what to say to this.

"Yes, ma'am. Really, I'm okay here. Dad's pretty much checking in on the hour."

"Soma tells us you have pinkeye. Pinkeye! You need to see a doctor, Emil. You need a prescription and some salve. I can be over there in two shakes of a lamb's tail and we'll take you to the doctor and then back here for a home-cooked meal. Fifteen minutes."

"No, Mrs. Sancio. I'm fine, really. I don't even think it's pinkeye. I think I scratched my cornea."

"What? How did you do that? Soma, did you scratch his cornea? Were you boys wrestling? You simply can't go to another person's house and tussle like, like a wilderness beast —"

"Mrs. Sancio, I really appreciate the offer, but I have a lot of homework to do and a list of chores to finish up before my dad gets back."

"Oh, you are such a darling thing. I just wish we'd known you were staying there alone and we would have made arrangements." Maybe they would have sent Meredith away and given me her room.

"Thank you, really. And please thank Soma again for the chemistry notes."

"What was that, dear?"

"Oh, I just spaced out the other day, but Soma lent me his notes — you know he always takes such thorough notes. Well, now I'm back up to speed."

"Well, then, that's wonderful. I'll tell him. That's just wonderful." Hopefully, Mrs. Sancio is glowing on the other end of the phone. I have to laugh at the idea that Soma's probably up in his room playing Halo and his mom's going to tear in there raving about how pleased she was to hear he'd been taking notes in chemistry. I don't think Soma even brings paper to school.

My face still hurts enough to propel me into the upstairs medicine cabinet for some pills. There's Advil and baby Tylenol, none of the serious stuff we used to stock in the house. I take some Advil with water I cup in my hands and slurp back. Then I realize that I'm starving and go into the kitchen to nuke some of the lo mein we didn't touch last night. If I could buy a horse, I could put a horse in one of the stalls of the old stables on campus. Even write something on its side with body paint. No one would have any clue where it came from. It's the best idea so far, but has some obvious problems. I mean, where do people buy horses in Hartford, Connecticut? And how much do those suckers cost? The horse thing can't be as big-budget as a freakin' helicopter, but it's still most likely out of my range.

I could do something with the vending machines. Fill them with really vile things. On Halloween, Ethan used to drive my mom apeshit by ordering fake severed fingers, hands, gooey rubber eyeballs, that kind of crap off the Internet. He'd hide them in her cupboards, in her shoes. At the end of the night, he'd toss them into the sacks of the last trick-or-treaters and she'd worry that the other neighborhood parents were going to call her up the next day to complain. I could fill the vending machines with crap like that.

Or beer. If I found a way to stock the Caramoor Academy vending machines with beer . . . I write down *Vending Machines* on the list. I can check out the locks on them tonight.

If Jade's around on campus, well, I won't know. That would mean checking in at the Arts Studio and only a douche bag completely without dignity would show up for another round with the crazy girl. I'd have to have a ball lobotomy.

It takes me an hour or so to clean up the kitchen and living room, but at least if Mrs. Sancio drives by to check on things, it won't look like I've turned the place into a frat house. The garbage strewn around the kitchen alone fills up three trash bags. It's not until I'm hauling those to the curb that I see the front stoop of our house. Jesus. Dad would kill me. The steps are covered with newspapers and rolled-up flyers. There are envelopes poking out of the door of the mailbox. It looks like our family moved away and didn't leave a forwarding address.

I fill another trash bag with last week's newspapers and supermarket ads. Take two trips into the house to bring in all the mail. I set most on the shelf in the hallway, but only after sorting through the whole pile for postcards. There's one from the vet reminding us that we needed to bring in Chauncey for a checkup. Chauncey was our dog that got hit by a FedEx truck three years ago. I put that in the pile with all the credit card offers and catalogs addressed to my mom. It's like there's this parallel universe of mail where no one acknowledges the reality of death. Ghost mail. Probably the ghosts of Wells Farm still get Pony Express deliveries and crap. There's nothing from Ethan. As soon as I realize that, at least I can exhale and start breathing again. Even if now it feels like I'm breathing glass.

I let myself read a chapter of Cecil's ghost book for every chapter of chemistry or French. This gives me a vague understanding of quantum numbers and the conjugation of verbs. It also means that I get to read an account of the Ainsley House's basement. Dear old Cecil claims it was used as a dungeon for captured British soldiers in the Revolutionary War and that the sound of rattling chains can be heard on particularly stormy nights. In the next chapter, Caramoor's own Encyclopedia Brown uses old ledgers and floor plans to prove that same basement is connected to a system of tunnels once used in the Underground Railroad. So Ainsley House has to qualify as one of the networking hub of restless spirits.

I haven't been in the basement. I don't even know if the key works in the basement. If it does work, there's no way to talk myself out of going after reading chapters seven and eight. And honestly what's so scary about the sound of rattling chains? Or the idea of a dungeon where men died off chained to a wall a whole ocean away from the place in which they grew up? Cake. So, yeah, I'm hoping the key doesn't fit the lock on that one.

Dad's away. I have tried to remedy a medical situation, cleaned most of the first floor of the house, sorted mail, and actually sat down and studied. Two different subjects. It's a little after two in the afternoon and already I am on such a roll, I almost steam myself some broccoli or something. Almost. Instead I try to maintain some semblance of childhood by eating Ring Dings for lunch. I move the mail from the shelf into Dad's office and sit down behind his desk. Everything in here looks the same as it's always looked — no tiny and strange unexpected changes. No small erase marks from where someone tried to make losing Mom easier. The same picture of her holding Ethan as a baby still sits framed on his desk. I've grown up looking at that picture. It's her cradling Ethan against her in a bed and the sunlight streaming in through the window and across her face. It looks like a halo.

And then there's Ethan's and my Little League roster photos in a double frame. We're both posed with our bats held back and I'm missing a lot of teeth. I never had a strong stance and you can practically see my bat wavering in the picture. You can tell about as much about my dad from his office as you can about Mr. Watkins from his. Meaning: nothing. There are those two photos and his diplomas on the wall and an old government poster that has a soldier on it and the phrase *Support Your Government — Buy Liberty Loans* bannered underneath. He has a bookshelf full of American history accounts and presidential biographies. If my mom had allowed it, Dad would have probably been one of those Civil War reenactors who drive out to old battle sites in antique uniform. But Mom had a thing about guns, even muskets. So instead he'd shut himself inside his office and read about Shiloh and the Union soldiers who had to wrap rags around their feet in the snow. Dad lapped that crap up. But that was mostly before my mother got sick. He didn't need to reenact anyone's battles after she got her diagnosis.

Whatever it is that I'm looking for, it's not hidden in my dad's office. There isn't a secret stash of letters from Ethan or doodles on the desk blotter about how much he loves me or anything like that. It smells like Old Spice in there, though, and Grey Flannel cologne. And because the whole west wall is windows, the little sofa in the corner is one of the warmest spots in the house. So that's where I doze off and let myself sleep for a few hours until it's dark enough to get back to Caramoor.

CHAPTER 16

When I wake up, my eye hurts a little less and I can open it slightly and even look at light. Ice it a little more and call and leave a message on Dad's voice mail and tell him that Soma's going to be over and that I hope he isn't blowing my college fund gambling or anything. Make sure my cell phone is charged, finish off the lo mein, and get in the shower.

I'm on campus by 7:30 PM and it's cold out — bitter Hartford kind of cold, but the whole night is stretched out in front of me and I'm too excited about it to think of the frost that has to be forming on the outside of the organs in my body. Because I can't feel my face, I can't feel my eye. So that helps. As soon as I get through the gate, I check around at each parking lot to make sure I'm alone on campus.

First thing I do is climb up to my little corner of the Ainsley House attic and just check on things up there. So far, it doesn't look like anyone has discovered my spot. No mice. No bats. No owls. Back downstairs, I raid the little kitchenette in the corner of the first floor and make myself hot cocoa in a Styrofoam cup. It's weird to drink the faculty's hot cocoa — even weirder than drinking my dad's beer out of the fridge.

I wander around the first floor looking for a door to the basement and find nothing. For some reason, there are three different bathrooms and four storage closets, but that's it. Go upstairs and let myself into Mr. Verlando's office. I don't even get so nervous anymore. This has to be an expellable offense, probably even more grievous than letting myself into Dr. Watkins's office, but my heart isn't even racing like usual. Guess I figure it's the weekend — who would show up to work or school on a weekend? Besides me. Verlando's desk is as messy as my locker. Papers, napkins — there are test scores just strewn out on electronically printed reports. Edwin Farnham III? Did extremely well on the SAT. That's not particularly useful, but it's interesting, anyway.

I don't know what I'm expecting to find. There's no map of the United States with tacks indicating where my brother has been. There are half a dozen coffee mugs clustered on the desk with various stages of mold growing on the bottoms. And there are drawers, all open. None of them lock and they're all crammed with files.

My file is under my graduating year and it's thick compared with the others. I hadn't been nervous before but now it's tough to breathe, it's like I have to wheeze through the lump in my throat. I don't want to open it. What does Verlando know, anyway?

He knows enough. When she wasn't flirting with our wilderness guide, Miss Gabaldon managed to observe that I seemed uncomfortable in a leadership position on the freshman camping trip. It's noted that Soma and I seemed to form a close bond, although Miss Gabaldon believed that might be to our detriment. "Two isolated students, furthering their marginalization by pairing off and away from their peers." Those are big words for our campus princess.

Progress reports from teachers all describe me as quiet and reserved in class. Mr. Von Kottwitz at least had the balls to write what he meant: "Emil seems sweeter than his older brother if not quite so dynamic. Intelligent, but no powerhouse." Nice. Someone apparently called Verlando when my mom was first diagnosed, because there's a notation dated May 20th and a directive to call me in. He put a note in the message window for me to come see him at the end of last year — I remember that. I didn't go.

There's a note from September that I seem emotional and withdrawn. Yeah, geniuses. My mom had cancer. Another note from October expresses concern that my grades are steadily declining. A whole page in November is reserved for dead-mom talk. Verlando made sure I came in that time and his notes describe me as "experiencing the psychologically traditional stages of grief and adjusting reasonably well to the profound changes in his family. Angry but appropriately so and expressing complexities of his emotions with introspection and intelligence." This makes me inexplicably proud. And then there's a part that's actually interesting: "Father has expressed concern about Emil's idealization of older brother, Ethan." What does that mean? Out of all the things we had to worry about in the fall, Dad would call the guidance counselor about me looking up to my big brother. That was the most normal thing going on.

Then there's a bunch of interim reports about how I have been generally screwing up academically. Apparently the faculty had a meeting and I was on a "list of concern" for the first time in my career at Caramoor Academy. There's a list of suggestions for involving me in the school community — one of which is the lacrosse team — proof that these people don't know me, don't know much. Sure, I am angry and resent the fact that I go to school with a bunch of douche bags. Let's give me a wooden stick and send me out on the athletic field with them. Another idea tabled is talking me into transferring into an art class, so that I have an outlet for my "obviously overwhelming emotions." I hope Jade's mom proposed that one. Clearly, I can't sign up for ceramics now if now Mrs. Larson has turned into *Jade's mom* in my head. The rest of the schemes are pretty much the same — *invite him to the multicultural dinner, offer spot on the debate team,* and then *cross-country?* complete with question mark. It's classic Caramoor — I can just picture the faculty meeting. Verlando mentions the screwups and all the faculty who need warm bodies to keep their programs running fight over who's going to get to enlist the new recruits. They're like extracurricular vultures or something.

My dad called about three weeks ago to see if my mood had picked up in school. Nope. And then there's a whole typed report about my meeting with Verlando last week. That's the one I'm most reluctant to read. Sit with it a minute, deciding. When we all used to go up to the lake house, Ethan had this thing about the closet in our bedroom. For whatever reason, it scared him in a way the ones at home didn't. When he cried about it, Dad made him sleep there for the night. Because the things you were afraid of only had power over you if you refused to face them.

The report says my preoccupation with Ethan continues to be "distracting and destructive." I am "unable to accept Ethan's culpability." That's a word I have to look up. And still I don't understand. What is Ethan guilty of? There are plenty of things I blame my brother for, mainly that he gave up and cut out. Just because I didn't think he was dumb enough to sign up for

Semester at Sea doesn't mean I'm petitioning him to win brother of the fucking year. Just because I think he's coming home doesn't mean I'm kidding myself about who he is.

The copier across the hall takes a few minutes to warm up. It hums in a creepy way that echoes through the empty office corridor. Make just one copy of that one page and put the original back in the folder. The last piece of the file is just a printed e-mail that Verlando sent to my teachers asking to give me extra consideration for exams and allow for makeups. That was pretty much the most helpful thing in the whole file. I stack it together and make sure everything is back in the order that I found it. Even shake the folder a little so it looks as disorganized as the rest of Verlando's files. Look through the rest of the desk drawers but none of them have files of alumni. So I don't get to see what enlightened observations he made about Ethan's character back in the day.

It's tempting to look at the rest of the files. For christsake, I have all the miserable secrets of every asshole I go to school with right there in front of me. And maybe last year, my key prank would have been to set up Caramoor's own smoking-gun Web site. I could have turned Verlando's halfhearted musings about the inner demons of our student body into a blog of daily revelations.

I just don't want to know any of it. I don't want to know that Edwin Farham might be acing the SATs but his dad's not going to be happy unless he gets into Stanford. Or who's getting high at lunch in a way that's worse than all the other guys getting high at lunch. I don't want to know who cuts himself with razors or who hates his dad for cheating on his mother. I couldn't care less who's gay and scared to come out. The crap that I'm keeping secret is enough for me right now. There just isn't any room to worry about the quiet turmoil of the kid sitting next to me.

If Verlando was at all useful, he'd keep files about the people who I actually want to understand. Faculty children, for instance. I'd cut off some crucial appendage for the chance to read why Jade shut down like she did when I asked her about college. If he had notes explaining how she could go from crouching over me with an ice pack to freezing me out five minutes later, then maybe he'd be worth listening to. I'd be fascinated.

Besides the ones in my fantasy file cabinet, the only actual folder I really want to read is Soma's, and that's only to see how widely Verlando misses the mark on him. But if it were Soma standing here and he thumbed through my personal file, I'd be pissed as all hell. So I leave it alone. There's nothing Verlando could tell me about him, anyway.

It probably just says he's performing below his potential — same as me. Same as most of us. Either they think you're buckling under all the pressure you put on yourself or they consider you a waste of a blue wool blazer. Either way, you're not enough. I bet I could sort through every single current file crammed in those drawers and find maybe six or seven kids in there that Verlando considered normal. And they'd all be the kids who do things like write newspaper articles about the thousands of community service hours they've logged in at the senior citizen center. The kids with the skinniest files have to be the most vacant bastards in the school. So it's tempting to take a look and read about the kind of kid they expect me to be.

Dude should keep his drawers locked. I almost leave him a note telling him so. Or just some signal on his desk to show him that someone besides the lady who cleans the offices has been here, rifling through all his confidential crap. I can't risk him knowing it was me who was here, though. Or worrying enough to snoop around Ainsley House and launch some campuswide investigation. I wonder if they'd blame it on Ruby if I did anything truly effective. I mean if you're going to haunt the grounds of a school those are the kind of paranormal activities you should take on: trashing administration's offices, spraying graffiti across the walls of the headmaster's office. And for a full five minutes, I consider using Ruby as a cover. It's just not worth being afraid again, every time I turn the key into a lock.

I do at least one weird thing before leaving Verlando's office, though. It doesn't really make sense, but I take a Sharpie out of this basket of Verlando's and crouch under the desk. I letter *Ethan Simon* carefully across the underside of the wood. Can't imagine that anyone will ever see it, so it doesn't count for much, but at least then Ethan has some kind of last word. If Verlando can sit around and just randomly decide what kind of person Ethan is or how much loyalty he deserves, then, I don't know — my brother gets his own say.

It feels even better than sipping faculty hot cocoa. I make myself another cup of that stuff, honestly just because I can and it feels cool to have the run of the faculty kitchen. And also I can take it with me to the field house. It's a good thing, too, because the walk over is as cold as I thought it might be. Feels like the temperature has dropped thirty degrees in two hours. So cold that it actually feels good to scald my throat a little, throwing gulps back from the big Styrofoam cup.

Hot cocoa outside tastes like football games. We used to go back to my dad's old town for homecoming every year. That's what kind of kid my dad was — you know, that guy who goes home twenty years later to watch his old team from the stands. My dad's that guy who still wears his varsity jacket around town and expects people he hasn't seen for twenty years to remember him. Back when we were little, Ethan and I ate it up, sitting in his lap and hearing how he ran for forty yards on the last play of every game that mattered.

And then we got older and knew enough to be embarrassed. Figured out that it actually wasn't the best deal to have the dad who hollered the loudest from the dugout on the Little League field.

The field house always smells like sweat and wet cotton. Good thinking on the part of the Caramoor founding fathers to put the rooms where we eat right next to the ones where we towel up each other's perspiration with our own shirts. And it's the strangest place to be quiet on the whole hushed campus. No basketballs dribbling across the wooden gymnasium floor or bleachers squeaking beneath spectators. It's almost completely dark except for the red glow of the exit signs above the doors and then the fluorescent lights in the downstairs corridors. And then the lit windows of the vending machines downstairs. Bingo. Possible scene of phase one of the Emil Simon key prank.

Sometimes, when I don't feel like sitting in the middle of the mayhem of the dining hall at lunch, I just get takeout here. Peanut butter cookies count as protein and then there's Raisinets and Goobers. Those are close enough to fruit. It's not the snack machine I'm so interested in, though, but the one beside it. The beverage machine is lined with rows of Snapple and bottled water. Really I'm just eyeing it, trying to gauge if beer would fit in the slots. It looks like cans wouldn't, but bottles just might.

I'd worry a little bit about the bottles breaking against the metal dispenser bin, but I could always rig up some kind of flannel lining to soften the fall. The most impressive part of the whole thing would be the visual image, anyway — rows of beer bottles ready to be exchanged for crisp dollars. So I feel around the edges of the machine for the latch and find the lock. There is no way my key is going to fit into there. It's like the size of the lock on a little girl's diary. It's a no go. Unless somewhere I come across a tiny key, but probably the guy who comes to restock the machines each week is the only one who has a copy. I could always hide behind the snack machine, wait for the delivery guy, ambush him, and steal the key. If I truly were a warrior for the cause of alcoholism on campus, that's what I'd do.

Their thirst is not my war. Upstairs I find the light box for the upper gym and turn on the overheads above the basketball court. They come on slowly, gradually, as if the bulbs have to wake up. I set the scoreboard up for myself and everything, wheel out the basket of balls, and shoot until my arms feel like jelly. I don't even have to start chasing down rebounds until getting twenty or so shots in. There's no one to see me toss up an air ball, and once I relax a little, I start sinking baskets like I'm some kind of blacktop god. Stand at half-court and throw Hail Mary after Hail Mary and listen to the echo of my shoes squeaking against the floors. Lie down at center court like I just collapsed after the winning three-pointer. Listen for a crowd that isn't there.

All the food lockers in the dining hall are locked except one freezer in the corner. It's honestly too cold for ice cream, but it's not very often you get the chance to walk around with a case of strawberry shortcake Popsicles under your arm. And that's what I do. I like this — being the new ghost of Wells Farm. Picture myself as another chapter in Cecil's book — the unidentified spirit enjoyed leaving gym equipment scattered on the floor and had a fondness for strawberry frozen desserts. He seemed to gravitate around the Arts Studio and was particularly active in the presence of young women who always had paint and clay on their clothes. Those seemed to really rattle his chains.

Trekking up the hill, I try to convince myself that I'm not slowing down just because the Arts Studio lights are on and Wilco is strumming from the speakers near the window. Talk myself out of stopping by to offer her a Popsicle because A) then I'd have to explain where they came from and B) who does that? Who tries to get in someone's pants by offering them a Popsicle? Then I try to convince myself that I'm not trying to get into Jade's pants.

But by this time, my feet are barely moving up the hill. I'm pretty much standing still and just leaning forward. "Hey, Jason!" It takes every effort to keep facing forward. I will maintain some dignity. At least she will have to call me by my own name. And then she breaks out this sweet, cooing voice, saying, "Come on, Emil — you'll always be Jason to me."

And that undoes me.

CHAPTER 17

The first thing I do is offer Jade a Popsicle because truly I am an idiot. She just looks at me a little quizzically and takes one carefully from the box. "Are these for your eye?" She pats the hurt eye with the ice pop, and for a few bizarre seconds I get hung up on the fact that now she's going to put something that was against my skin in her mouth.

"No, just a snack." I want a voice that doesn't sound like that of an extremely dumb person.

"That's a big box of snacks."

"I thought there might be starving artists around." Excellent. Now I'm back to banter. I can handle banter.

"So you're not working on some magnum opus in the electronic music lab."

"Your college words are hurting me."

"You're not remixing, Baby Bowie."

"Nope. I'm stealing Popsicles." And that's all the explanation I offer. It's pretty much all Jade seems to need. She's going to let me have my secrets as long as I don't tread on hers. This would work out perfectly, if I weren't such an ass, but I can't just let it be. Have to press her. "What about you? Shouldn't you be heading back to college soon?"

She's like one of those flowers that closes when you accidentally brush it with your hand. "Thanks for stopping by. I'm glad your eye is feeling better." She is a surgeon, cuts me loose with ruthless precision.

"Jade." It's all I can think to say. "Listen, it's really cold." What I mean is "You're really cold." We both know that.

She finally says, "It's not much warmer inside." But she turns toward the door and says it over her shoulder and I exhale a little, relieved that it looks like she wants me to follow. She's right. It's just as cold inside, but without the windchill.

"You should turn on the heat." Move toward the thermostat until she stops me with her voice.

"No. No." Jade's all alarmed at this. "You can't put that on." I don't say anything. I'm learning her rules. If I ask the question, she gets to refuse to answer it, but if I wait and it's important enough, she'll get around to telling me. "I'm not really supposed to be in here after hours. I have the key from my mom, but she could get in trouble for giving it to me. It's an insurance thing. I'm not a student or staff . . ." Jade trails off as if she's really afraid of what I think about all this.

"Yeah, well, it's not like they can tell who turned on the heat. It's not a phone bill or something with times."

"I know that." She says it like she totally didn't know that. "I still don't want to risk it. It's just easier to keep a coat on than to sit around and worry about it."

"Yeah, but sometimes it's been warm."

"Sometimes Felix leaves it on. I think he thinks I'm homeless."

"I think he thinks you're pretty. You're nuts. The Guatemalan janitor gets to decide whether or not you freeze your ass off."

"For one thing, he's from Argentina." I say a silent prayer of thanks that Jade pronounces it like an American and not Ar-HEN-tina, like our Spanish teacher would do. Because then I'd have to walk away from her and never look back. Or just dream about her fifteen minutes less each night. She continues, though, with her hippie bullshit. "He's a man who works with dignity. Just because it's not the job on the top of your and your prep school buddies' list of top ten careers doesn't mean he doesn't deserve your respect."

"Okay." There's no way I'm going to win this. "He is down-right noble. And so he wouldn't want you to freeze. That's why he leaves the heat on during the week for you." She seemed to be considering this. "You're just a masochist." I'm pushing my luck again. "You want to suffer a little." This gets a sheepish grin, though. And she does the thing where she blows her hair out of her eyes.

"Maybe. Where did you get the Popsicles?"

"Dining hall." I say it like it's the most natural thing in the world. Saturday night and I'm hanging out in the Caramoor cafeteria.

"Yeah? So Felix leaves that open for you?" She's asking lightly but she's watching me carefully. There's actually something about me that Jade wants to know.

"Yep." Sit down on a stool and say, "I'm the ghost of Wells Farm." She laughs but doesn't let me skate by that easily.

"No, I'm serious."

And so I answer her with total honesty. "Jade. I'm working hard to manufacture an air of mystery. So I can't tell you now." The hell? It's like I channeled Ethan's balls or something. I sit there, sort of amazed with myself. And thrilled. There is something about me that this girl wants to know. If this were a super-hero cartoon, the key around my neck would throb and glow.

"Well, if you could mysteriously get us into Ainsley House, there's a fireplace in there." She's right. It's huge, in the center of the reception area. It's like one of those pioneer hearths that whole families used to sit around.

Women amaze me. "You're incredible. You're paranoid that the school bursar will notice the heating bill or something, but lighting an actual fire in the center of campus seems like a perfectly reasonable idea."

"Well, it's free. And who's going to see it?"

I can think of about a dozen reasons why this is a terrible idea. It's going to leave ashes, proof that we were there. Someone could drive by and see smoke rising out of the chimney. And also, it's fire. We will be actually lighting a fire on campus. None of those seem particularly brilliant to me. Out of all of them, though, my main, immediate concern is the key. I need to figure out a way to get the door unlocked without Jade actually seeing it. She can think that I'm magic and just have to wave my hand across the heavy wood for it to open for us. That's fine. As long as she doesn't see me use the master key.

So I nod and head to the door and she tears out in front of me, like this is the most exciting thing that's happened all weekend. I mean, it is, for me. But she can't even slow down to less than a trot up the hill and she's already rubbing her hands together like she's standing in front of the hot metal screen.

I call after her, "Okay, then, but we have to make a deal about this." Jade turns around, with her hands on her hips. Juts her chin out and looks at me almost suspiciously.

"What kind of deal?"

"We go into the main building, but we also look through the basement. And you have to come."

"What's in the basement?"

"My love dungeon."

"That's what I figured." She still keeps walking, though, so that's a promising sign. "No, really — why would you want to go into the basement?"

"I've just never seen it, so I want to look." That's pretty much the truth. Keep on explaining. "There's supposedly tunnels and crap from when the farm was a part of the Underground Railroad. I just want to check it out. I was in there earlier, but I couldn't find the door."

"You're not much of an explorer, are you?"

"We should check out the basement first." That way the ghosts of Revolutionary War soldiers can kill me, before the fire department comes and my dad gets involved.

"Did you check around outside?" I look at Jade, but she's so wrapped up in a scarf and hat and crap that eye contact doesn't help clear anything up. But then she explains, "For the basement. Lots of old houses have cellars you can only get to from doors outside the house."

And of course, that's what we find. Two steel doors with steps leading into the darkness. It's beyond spooky. It's like we're staring down that stone well in *The Silence of the Lambs*. "Okay, wait here, and let me go get some flashlights." Cross-country would have been boring, but maybe I should run track — I get the front door unlocked in record time, take two flights of stairs up about three at a time, drag down the ladder to the attic, get up, grab my bag of camping gear, and sprint all the way back down to the ground floor where I can make sure that the front door stays unlocked for when Jade and I want to come back inside. Run back around to the rear of the building with two flashlights and a pair of collapsed lungs.

She is impressed. "Wow, you've even got your own gear here. You've been holding out on me." She grabs the Maglite and then heads down the steps first without any hesitation.

"Hey! I can go down first." But Jade's already downstairs and swinging her flashlight beam around the cellar's white walls. I'm easing my way down more slowly and looking furtively at the walls and corners, like there's going to be shackles nailed into the cement or smears of centuries-old blood seeped into the floor. It's just a lot of white-and-gray stone with really low doorways and narrow corridors. Like a maze running under Ainsley House.

In the corner, there's a sink. And we both end up standing next to that. Jade turns on the faucet and points to the clear water and says, "It's not brown or coppery." Like that means something. I move forward through one of the hallways and have to crouch down a little to walk through. Rooms stem from the sides of that hallway and look like tiny cells. You could lay down a mattress in each of them and maybe a tiny desk. A small suitcase or trunk. The cellar at Ainsley House would make a terrific monastery if Caramoor ever wanted to add that to its program.

Jade has already skipped ahead and found the boiler room. At least that scares her. Honestly, it's like something out of a horror movie. There's a huge generator humming and clanking in this pit dug into the middle of the room. It's hot and loud and there are nails driven into the wall with tools hanging from them. It looks like the torture chamber where a robot hibernates between killing human beings.

Spots of something dapple the floor beside the boiler. "Is that blood?" I ask about as casually as it's possible to ask that question.

Jade backs farther into the doorway. "I don't think so." But she's examining it pretty suspiciously. For a second, she crouches down, and I have this panicked moment where it looks like she's going to touch her fingers to it and lick them. Instead she just sniffs at it. "It doesn't smell coppery."

"What is it with you and copper?"

"Well, it's not blood." She's done with it then. If it's not blood, Jade's moving on to something else. "So what's supposed to be down here?"

I tell her about the chapters about the basement in Cecil's book. We feel around the walls and when we finally work up the nerve to cut through the boiler room, we find another hallway that narrows into a tunnel about the width of my shoulders that's walled in at the end with bricks.

"Maybe that was the Underground Railroad?" I try to picture a line of frightened slaves inching their way to freedom.

"I think you're taking it a little bit literally."

"What?"

"You know it wasn't a train, right? The Underground Railroad?" Jade's looking at me like she's my exasperated baby-sitter and I just microwaved the cat or something.

"I know that."

"It wasn't even actually beneath ground level. They mean underground like down low? Like hidden? You understand that, right?"

"Of course I do. But the tunnels were in the basement."

"Yeah, but they wouldn't have necessarily even gone through a tunnel. Wells Farm just would have been one stop in a long, secretive journey. They might have just put on costumes or something."

"What kind of costumes? White-farmer costumes?" I don't want to let go of the idea yet — Wells Farm as this safe stop on some treacherous trip. I want to know that people moved through here on the way to what they hoped was a much better life. That's the kind of foundation a school should be built on, right? That would be a good omen for guys like me and Ethan and Soma. Probably even for Jade.

"I could see it as a dungeon," she says. We both make a big show of feeling around the walls for shackles or bolts, but neither of us is actually trying — we don't want to find anything.

"Let's make a fire." Jade brushes the dust from her hands to the knees of her jeans. "Come on. I'm cold."

"Go stand near the boiler, then."

"Jason, you promised me a fire." Whip around to look at Jade, but she seems completely serious.

"Ummmm . . . my name is not Jason."

"Yeah, well, Emil would never break a promise to me." She wins with that one — she's sort of singing it at me and pouting at the same time. If I didn't know she was smart, I'd think she was dumb, but because I know . . . well, then, it's just cute.

"You're sure you don't want to check around the pipes, see if there's any deposits of copper or something?"

Jade shoves me a little and leaves her arm draped over mine as we climb back up the steps from the cellar.

"You have to have a kid sister," she says. I try to figure out if that's a compliment. She's still got her hands on me, so it can't be bad.

"Nope." And then I don't know what to say. Do I tell her about Ethan? And what do I say? *I have an older, much more attractive brother who would have been able to seduce you within about a half hour of meeting you. Actually a half hour is a generous estimate. He would have had you horizontal before he knew your name.*

I don't say the very last part. But I do say the rest. And Jade goes still for a second and I worry we've hit the deep freeze again. But she moves her hand over to clasp my arm. "Not every girl wants that guy." She kind of shrugs while she says it.

My lungs stop working, but in a good way. Jade and I walk around the building and up the porch of the farmhouse. I hold the door open for her and let myself enjoy the feeling. "Yeah? What other kind of guy do girls want?"

Hit the light switch just in time to get to see Jade say, "The kind of guy who takes more than half an hour." It's funny that you wait so long trying to get the guts to touch someone and then you finally do more because you can't stop yourself. I reach out and grab Jade's wrist before coming up with any kind of plan about what to do with this. So I just stand there, with my thumb on her pulse for a few seconds, before I let her hand drop down again.

The fireplace in the front room of Ainsley House really is more of a hearth than anything. I mean, it takes over the whole left side of the room. Wide stones wind their way around the vent, but in all that fireplace there's no wood. We both kind of stand there for a minute until Jade asks, "What are you looking at? Are you waiting for Santa?"

"Firewood." And that's all I have to say. Follow her to the side door marked *fire exit* and nearly choke on my own tongue when she opens it. But no alarms, and stacked near the wooden stairs outside is a pile of logs, neatly cut. "How —"

"I used to wait here for my mom to get through with class. Mrs. Schecter watched me from the front desk, but I got to play around the fireplace. I used to pretend that my Barbies were at a ski lodge in Tahoe." Of course she did. "Anyway, this door has never had a working alarm. It's just labeled that way for the fire marshal." I pick up two logs and then Jade piles a few more into my arms, asking, "Is that too heavy?" every time she adds another bunch. It's either really sweet or kind of insulting. I can't tell which.

We get a decent pile and I arrange three of them into a sort of pyramid in the middle of the hearth, then crumble up a newspaper from the reception desk and tuck pages beneath the logs. "You're good at this, Bowie." Out of everything my dad's taught me, who knew it would be my fire-building skills that would impress girls? I guess women don't really go for gutting fish.

"We used to go up to this cabin in upstate New York and Dad would put Ethan and me in charge of the fire. We had a big fireplace, like this, and that's basically what kept the whole place warm."

"Ethan's your brother?" Now we're on dangerous ground. Quicksand and I feel myself sinking. "The hot one? Who'd love me and leave?"

"Yeah. He's like that."

"How old is he? Hey, Emil — how old are you, really?" I consider telling the truth. I really, really consider it.

"Seventeen." I almost tell the truth.

"So how old is your brother?" Maybe if I tell her thirty, she'll stop asking. I will tell her he's thirty and in prison. For killing a baby. With another baby or something.

"He's nineteen."

"In college?"

I'm not sure what to say to that. For all I know, Ethan could be in college. Maybe he just walked away from here and caught a bus to Dartmouth or something. Ethan's somewhere in a library, behind a stack of leather, dusty books. Ethan's doing keg stands in some frat house, walking around with his collar up.

"Yeah, he's away at school."

"Where does he go?"

"It's just a little school — you probably haven't heard of it. Why? Are you going to go look him up?" I should just name one of the schools Dad was thinking about for him, but I don't want to lie to Jade again. Lying about my age is one thing because it accomplishes something.

"Settle down there, cowboy. I was just wondering." The firewood and paper are all set — they're a masterpiece of flammable construction. And then I realize that my lighter is upstairs in the attic. Much as I'd love to show Jade my sexy little sleeping bag, probably that would just freak her out.

"I don't have a lighter on me," is all I say. And Jade unzips a pocket of her jacket and tosses one at me.

"You don't smoke?" Jade asks like she's surprised, and for some stupid reason that gives me a thrill, like it means she thinks I'm some kind of rebel.

"Not cigarettes." Jade arches her eyebrows a little. "I don't have any weed on me —" but she cuts me off and even holds up her hand like she's warding me off.

"I don't do any of that stuff anymore. Just nicotine. Nicotine's my last vice."

"Yeah? Don't you go to Bard?"

"I used to go to Bard."

She pressed me about Ethan so I feel like it's allowed now. To push a little bit. But I'm careful.

"You're really not going back to school? Or just not there?"

"I don't know." So far, so good. "It's not really something I want to talk about." Now the glacier's floating back into her voice.

"It might help you figure it out."

"Probably not." We are both momentarily distracted by the lighter and how the flames catch the edge of the newspaper and the pages curl up, on fire. They eat through a whole ball of paper and then die out. Jade stands up and grabs some Caramoor Academy promotional pencils out of a Caramoor Academy promotional mug. "Here — we can use these as kindling."

"We can't use those!"

"Ah, so you *are* a die-hard Academy kid. You can't let yourself burn the school crest." She's teasing me a little, shaking the bunch of pencils at me like she's scolding me.

I accidentally snort. "That's not it. It's just . . . well, we just shouldn't do it, that's all." I'm not even sure why I'm worried — it just doesn't seem like the best idea. When I'm here by myself I'm usually so careful about leaving any trace behind me. I don't take stuff and I don't leave ashes in the fireplace. And now here I've taken a case of Popsicles and a bunch of firewood and now pencils.

"Where did we leave the Popsicles?" That would be just perfect, if someone comes on to campus and finds a random box of Popsicles. And that's how I get caught. Over a box of Popsicles.

"Probably near the cellar doors." I move to go get them and Jade puts her hand on my arm. It's like she's using any excuse to touch me or something.

"Leave 'em out there. At least they'll stay frozen." She smiles up at me and presses a bunch of pencils into my hand. Literally. Like, she closes my fingers around them. Oh. Holy crap, I get it now. She *is* using any excuse to touch me.

"We could probably get lead poisoning or something."

"You know there's not lead in pencils anymore, right?" She uses the same tone as she did with the great Underground Railroad debate and I don't like that tone. That's the you're-so-much-younger-and-dumber-than-me-and-it's-vaguely-cute-but-also-I'd-never-ever-take-you-seriously tone. So of course I handle it in the most mature way possible.

"Yeah. I know that."

"You know they're made of graphite, right?"

"I meant the paint. On the pencils." She was just touching me. I can't believe I'm ruining this by arguing over what pencils are made of. I kneel down on the stone and shove bunches of them under the newspapers, light the pencils, and then the paper. And even try to light some of the bark on the logs.

As much as it freaks me out to imagine someone driving by and seeing smoke tufting out the chimney, it was a really good idea to come here. There's a sofa and a couple of stodgy-looking armchairs. It's warm and the fire is awesome. And then the smell hits us. Jade says it first. "It's like burning rubber."

"Is there still rubber in erasers?" We hear a metallic sound, which is probably the erasers pinging off, but the fire has caught all of it — the newspaper's almost gone and the fire is licking the logs. We're in business. I get up to turn off the light, thinking we don't want anyone to walk by and see the first floor all lit up and then realize that it looks like I'm trying to set some sexy mood. I mean, all I need now is a freaking violin player or something.

"Look how awesome it looks," is all Jade says, though, and then it's not such a big, awkward deal. Sometimes I think she can feel me panic and that's when she says something deliberate like that, just to set me at ease. Like the way Ethan used to be able to tell when Mom went from being uncomfortable to being in excruciating pain. We'd all be sitting around the living room, watching old episodes of *Jeopardy!,* and Ethan would get up wordlessly and go get some pain pills out of that bathroom cabinet. It wasn't just that he was watching a clock and timing things, and I swear it wasn't that he just noticed her grimacing more often. It wasn't that he was looking harder. She never let it show. The only way you knew Ethan was right was how grateful Mom would look when she reached out to take the meds.

Jade's like that for me. She seems to get when I am flailing, no matter how cool I'm trying to play it off. And then she gives me exactly what I need to get myself back together. When I sit down on the couch, she sits next to me, but with her knees turned to face my whole body. We each have a square and then there's another cushion that's like a neutral territory between us. Our backs are to the corners so that we can face each other.

When Jade gets excited about an idea, she sort of slaps at things for emphasis. She could never work in the room where the government keeps the buttons that launch nuclear bombs. Right now, she's pounding her fist into the cushion between us, saying, "You know what we should make?"

I almost scream out, "Love!" Just to see what would happen.

I almost feel like if I said it enthusiastically enough, Jade would go with it. I'd just have to show enough spirit or something. All this is running through my head so my face probably stays blank, trying valiantly not to give anything away.

"S'mores!" She shrieks it. And because I don't react right away, because in my head, we are at least dry humping on the couch, she thinks she has to explain what a s'more is. "It's a sandwich but the bread is graham crackers and the meat is chocolate and the cheese is marshmallow." If aliens ever landed on Earth, Jade would make the perfect interpreter.

"I know what a s'more is."

"Oh yeah? Well — you know they served them on the Underground Railroad. It's true. It's because they were so portable."

"You're such a jerk."

"Gimme some marshmallows."

But there are just some things a man can't make happen, no matter how much he needs the extra boost of ladies believing he has magical powers.

"I can't just conjure up the ingredients for s'mores." For a second, I remember the Pop-Tarts upstairs, but the only thing I can think of to do is go to the bathroom and then come back with them and there's really no way to do that smoothly. "And I have heard of them. I have made them. You're looking at an expert in fireside cooking."

This gets a laugh. And she even swings a pillow toward me and settles into the middle square of the couch. That counts as progress. "Yeah, where did you acquire such skills?"

"Up at the lake house."

"Why don't you guys go up there anymore?"

Outside the window of Ainsley House, the moon looks blue through the clouds. Jade is inching closer to me on the sofa and there's an actual fire crackling in front of us. It's like a Pocono resort advertisement or something. Or a commercial for aftershave. I just don't want to be the kid with the dead mom right now. I imagine saying it and it just sounds hollow at best and at worst it sounds like I'm looking for some pity play. I don't want to see Jade's eyes get soft and her head to tilt to the side, like she's trying to measure how hurt and lost I am. I don't want to watch her look at me like I was the last puppy at the shelter.

"We don't go up so much after my parents split up. I think the memories really bother . . . us." That's not a lie. My parents are apart. Forever, too.

"Wow. That sucks. I'm really sorry." But she's the right amount of sorry, the kind of sorry where you can still make out after. "I never know what to say when people tell me that." Good thing I stopped there. "My parents have been together forever."

"Yeah, and they're happy?" I know plenty of people whose parents are still together, but that doesn't necessarily mean so much.

"Yeah." She actually takes some time to think about it. "I used to think it was bullshit, but I don't think so now. They met in high school. Stayed together three years and then college and then my mom went away to art school and my dad went into the army and that's it. Then they had me. They're really best friends — like sometimes I don't even feel like I belong. And I'm their kid." Jade pauses and shrugs. "If that's the worst thing, though, well, then . . ."

"That would still be weird. Feeling like you were intruding in your own life —"

"That's exactly what it feels like." Jade slaps the cushion between us, she's that excited. I try to think about times I've felt like that and it's not that my parents weren't happy together, but my mom was always a mom first. I never felt like Ethan and I were interrupting anything between her and my dad.

Toward the end, it felt more like it was Ethan and my mom who had some secret society in the house. Like they understood each other in a way that Dad and I just didn't get. Right before I started school again in September, she sat us down and told us she wasn't going to get any better. Dad was there, too. She sat with us at the kitchen table and Dad stood at the sink. Anyway, I didn't know what to say. All I could think was *Oh, God — I'm not going to have a mom — she's not going to be there to cheer me on or fix my tie around my neck or set me up in the family room with soup and crackers and magazines when I'm home sick from school.*

All I kept thinking about was how my life would fit around the hole in it. It was Ethan who put his hands on hers and said, "I'm really sorry, Mom." He was the first to understand that it was about what *she* was going to lose. Later on in my room, we got smoked up together and he went on to talk about it — all the things she wouldn't have now. Weeks in the mountains or walking on the boardwalk at the beach or her twenty-fifth high school reunion and holding grandkids. How she might even miss that Christmas with us. That was the first moment I really understood it, but Ethan got it all along.

"You still seem really upset about it." Jade means the divorce. "Was it recent?"

I take a deep breath, gulp down the raw spot in my throat. "November."

"Wow." She sighs a little. And I feel like an ass because she really does feel bad and she has no idea. She thinks that she's unlocked some kind of code to me, that she's uncovered some essential secret. It's like I'm Jason all over again. "Who do you live with now?" I almost tell her I live here and show her upstairs and take her hand and help her up the attic ladder. By almost, I mean it runs through my mind. That would be the most accurate answer this minute.

What I actually say is, "My dad."

"What about your brother? When he's not in school?"

"He's more loyal to our mother." It feels like my mouth is lined with cold ash. "He left to be closer to her." When I say it, I recognize it as what's true. And because I can't swallow anymore and the corners of my eyes are burning, I lunge at Jade. That's how my first kiss goes. I do it just so the girl doesn't see me cry.

CHAPTER 18

It doesn't seem like I'm so bad with the kissing thing. Probably not as adept as Jade's used to, and she might think I have some kind of drooling problem because my face is all wet from crying, but she does things that make me think that she's not just suffering through my dopey gropings. She moans. She has her hand on the back of my head, and when I kiss her a certain way I can feel her fingers tighten there.

When I lower my lips to the hollow at the base of her throat, she arches her back and presses herself against me. So I'm not terrible. It's weird to be able to lose yourself in all the different ways someone feels — how her hair is soft, but gets softer near her temples — it's like feathers there. Or how smooth and slick her mouth is. How warm she is. Even the undersides of her wrists are warm.

I come up for air and look down at Jade and now honestly understand how people talk about the earth stopping and their hearts swelling. Realize that it goes the same way when life has suddenly gotten better, just like when something's soured the world a little. Everything stops and when it starts again it's just the slightest bit different.

I look down at Jade and start to feel anxious, overwhelmed. I'm not sure what to do next, where to touch. She kind of tugs me back toward her and keeps kissing me. She shifts a little while she's doing it so that we're both on our side facing each other. She's good at it. Moving around and showing me where she wants me without anything feeling forced or awkward. She stops kissing and tugs my head back a little with her hand at the nape of my neck, makes me look her in the eye.

She asks me, "How old are you really?" Which is a little unnerving, because maybe I kiss like a twelve-year-old.

"Sixteen."

She tips her head like she's considering this. "Okay."

"Why did you leave school?"

"I was just really tired." She says it plainly, not like she's being smart-ass Jade, but like it's the closest thing to the truth she can come up with.

"How old are you?"

"Eighteen."

"You're eighteen and you're that tired?" I don't mean to be a smart-ass, either. I mean it. I want to know.

"Yeah, that's why I figured I should just come home. It wasn't like something happened there. Some trauma. I just got tired."

"Of what, though?" I don't mean it to sound like "What could possibly be so tiring?" and thankfully she doesn't seem to take it that way. I mean what was it about living on her own she couldn't handle? "You're so fierce," is what I say.

That makes her laugh a little, but it's a shallow, half laugh. "Because I'm not afraid to be here alone at night?" Yes. That's what I mean at first. I think of the long hours she spends in the Arts Studio, shaping and reshaping clay. Sitting in front of the wheel with her foot on the pedal. Realize I picture her doing that the same way I imagine Ethan on a train, on a bus. At peace. By themselves.

So I amend it a little. "Because you're not afraid to be alone." I sit there and look at her and try to picture her moving through a packed dining hall with a plastic tray. Sliding into a chair to sit at a table with a dozen or so other people with weird hair and paint on their clothes. "What was so tiring?"

Jade looks off to the side, at the fire, and I can see its reflection in her eyes. "All of it." Blows her hair out of her eyes. "Getting up, getting dressed. Sitting through class. Papers. Parties. Dinners with people I hardly knew, who talked about philosophy and sociology and The Future of the Arts. I couldn't make myself care."

"So that's it. You just came home?"

"Home was better."

"Is it, though?" Everything is coming out dicky, but I just want to understand. Jade sits up a little now, narrows her eyes. I better explain myself quickly. "You're here every night. I know — I'm here every night. And that's pitiful, because I go here — I'm here all day. But it seems like if you're here, well, then, it's because you don't want to be home."

"Is that why you come here?"

Yes. "Sometimes."

"Things are that weird now that your mom and brother aren't around?"

Bingo. "They're a little different."

"So how do you get in everywhere on campus?" I think about telling her. Just because then we could do this all over the place. Eventually, Jade's going to go back to school and probably she's not going to wait two years to do it, but maybe if I can make things around here a little interesting.... That's the kind of thinking that turns people into stalkers, gets men to cut off their ears.

"They leave a lot of the buildings open. No one's really worried about security around here."

Jade sits up more, tucks her hair back. She knows I'm lying.

"Yeah, that's why you jumped at the chance to light a fire tonight."

"Well, I did it, didn't I?" It's not until I see her rearranging herself that I realize how disheveled Jade is. Her hair's all tangled and her collar's stretched out a little where I was kissing her. It's hard to play all this cool. I want to strut around or something. Consider making up some flyers in the copy room and plastering them around campus.

It doesn't look like Jade's going to give me a picture of herself for an illustration. She shoves me off her a little, so that she can sit up fully and swing her legs to the floor. Looks out the window.

"You're mad," I observe.

"No. I'm fine." The furnace starts clanking a little and we both turn to look at the door, as if we both think someone's about to barrel through it. At least that makes things a little less tense. "I'm really not mad." The furnace sounds like it's banging against another furnace or something. I picture Ruby in a little ghostly smocked dress attacking the boiler with a hammer. Like she's trying to get my attention — *fix it, fix it, quick*. Maybe I'll just tell Jade that I've started imagining that the ghosts on campus talk to me and give me girl advice. Maybe that would give me some kind of mental default pass or something. Jade tells me, "I don't expect you to tell me everything. That wouldn't be fair."

"Because you haven't told me everything?" I feel a little lost, like something's slipping away as soon as it felt comfortable. I want to tell her to stop. Or just start kissing her again. Anything to make her look at me like she's seeing me again. But Jade's not having it. It looks like she's done with me, maybe for the night, maybe for longer.

"I've told you the important stuff. We should make sure that no one can tell we were here." She gets a plastic watering can from the receptionist's desk and fills it in the bathroom between the reception area and the business office. When the water hits the smoldering fire, it sizzles. Makes me want a plate of eggs.

"I don't know that we can just leave it in there like that." The ash and water look like gray mud on the stone hearth. It almost blends in, but if someone looked closely, they'd notice. "We've got to take care of it."

"Yeah, you have to take care of it." At least she laughs at my *who me?* face. "Yep. That's definitely a boy job."

"A boy job? Didn't they teach you feminism at your hippie college?" Another laugh. It can't be a lost cause if she's still laughing at my lame-ass jokes.

Jade says, "I found feminism to be very tiring." But she's fluffing the pillows and then crouching down to the stones to pick up bits of bark and twigs from the hearth. So it's just the gray sludgy stuff she objects to. I can deal with that. That's the girl who just let me kiss her and paw at her for the past hour or so. She could take a dump on the heating vent and I'd clean it up. Oh, my God. I'm disgusting.

The gray sludge is also sort of gross. I take care of it with a wet paper towel and sort of fold it away. I put it in the trash bin in the kitchen and then throw a bunch of clean paper towels over that. "You're not going to take it with you?" Jade asks me wryly. "As a souvenir?"

"Well, no. I figured maybe you wanted it for your scrapbook, but then —"

"Scrapbook?"

"Yeah, girls keep scrapbooks and stuff."

"No. *Moms* keep scrapbooks." See, that's the kind of comment Jade could never make if I'd told her the truth about this past year. There are very good and sensible reasons to keep those circumstances to myself. It's really not until I try to make excuses for it that I realize how awful of a lie it is. She already got over me telling her the wrong name and age. Now I'm hiding my orphan status.

So the fireplace is clean and the stones around it are cleared. Jade has straightened her clothes and the rest of the room looks the same as it does right now. It's sort of reassuring to think that this is a historically protected building. Decades from now I can walk in here and I bet it will look the same as it does right now.

"We ready?" Jade asks. She's looking around, too, although I'm pretty sure she's not memorizing the floor plan for future fantasies. Just when I think she sees the last hour as a mistake, some aberration she just wants to forget happened, she steps closer to me and snakes her hand around my waist. Rests her head sideways against my shoulder.

I sort of decide that I will never be ready to leave. Jade and I can live here and come out only at night.

When Jade leads me out, I make sure the door closes tightly behind us. I figure I'll come back later on to lock up. It's not so bitter cold out when we step outside, but I shiver and pull Jade closer to me, anyway. "Are you going to go back and get work done?" I ask. The Arts Studio is still all lit up, which was probably not the smartest move, to leave it like that.

Jade stops and looks at the building. She says, "I think I just want to go home."

"Are you going to get tired of me, too?" That comes out before I can stop it. At least my voice stays even. It just sounds like any other kind of question. Like "Can I call you later?" or "How about Chinese for dinner?"

Jade turns to face me. I could take the pause as an insult, I guess. But instead it's just reassuring that she's thinking it through. "No," she says. Who knew I'd ever be this thrilled to hear a girl say no. "I can't imagine getting tired of you."

Wow. "That's the best thing anyone's ever said to me."

"Well, it's really because you lie so much. You keep switching things up." She's laughing when she says it. My mouth now tastes like gasoline, but it's fine. Really, it's fine.

"Where are you going, then?" We're moving to the Arts Studio. Without answering, Jade ducks in and hits the light switch.

"I'm going to my car and you're going to walk me there. Do you need a ride home?" Of course this means I panic because I have to make a decision about kissing her good night way before I'd expected. In the next thirty seconds or something. Don't know if I'm supposed to wait or if it's presumptuous to kiss her, if she'll think I'm lame if I don't. Jade's looking at me so expectantly and for a second I think that means that I should lean on in and then she says, "Well?"

"I don't need a ride home." I sound demented. "Is this your car?" It's the only one in the lot. So probably, yeah. "It's a Honda." Can't keep the surprise out of my voice. "I figured you'd drive a VW van or something."

"Oh yeah? Did you think there'd be flowers painted along the side?"

"Sunsets, actually."

Jade laughs at that, says, "I think my mom drove one of those." She's at the driver's side now, with her keys in her hand.

"I'm going to walk." Everything I say sounds like it's in a foreign language.

"It smells like snow." I don't know if that's code or something, if Jade actually means, *Press me against my Civic and shove your tongue down my throat.* But she keeps talking weather. "I bet it looks beautiful here when the snow's really coming down." Jade stomps her feet against the pavement, kicks the tire of her car. "Oh, right — you've probably seen it already. Being that you live here."

"Well, I'll send you a postcard or something. No, really, I'm going to walk home."

"Okay. Be careful." She goes to move away. "Wait —why don't I just drive you down the hill?"

So I get in the car because at that point I sort of have to. Otherwise it just looks like fear of women drivers or something. Or like I'm lying again and have another girl waiting to entertain me in the field house. We get through the gate and down the hill and when I see the lights of town it's a little disappointing. I sort of prefer the planet when it's just me and Jade on it.

"Why can't I just drive you all the way home? I don't want to let you out on the side of the road like some kind of hooker." It's the first time a girl has ever called me a hooker.

"It's not that far," I tell her.

"Emil, it's okay — I offered." We get to the house and Jade pulls the car into the driveway. I wish I'd left a light on or something. It's the only completely dark house on the block. "No one's home?" Jade asks.

"Dad's away on business." I don't know why it's embarrassing to say. Years ago, when Mom was doing the whole career-woman thing, she really kept it together, but there were a couple times when I was the last kid picked up at day care. That's how I feel now. And that's probably what makes me hurtle myself out of the car so quickly.

But then the car door slams and I remember how Jade sounds when she gasps. How her hair feels in my hands. Run around to her side of the car and she's already got it rolled down. It's not the easiest thing to kiss a girl through a car window. Especially when she still has her seat belt on. I clunk my head twice, bite her lip once, and call out, "It'll get better, I promise," behind me on my way to the side door. I'm lit up in her headlights and because of them I can't see if she's smiling behind the wheel. But then she leans out and yells at me, "It's already good."

So probably we're both smiling while she backs down the drive.

CHAPTER 19

Okay, so I do this weird thing when I go in the house. I sit in every chair in the living room. Like now the cushions are going to feel different against my ass because I've kissed Jade. Go to the fridge and eat some sliced turkey right out of the package. Put a whole slice in my mouth and then follow that with a squirt of mustard. I'm gross. I'm insane. I'm a man.

Go from the kitchen to the front door to bring in the mail. More grocery store flyers and bills and then. A postcard. From my brother. From Ethan. The picture on the front is a photograph of a little boy in a red sweater standing in a field. It's eerie. The kid looks lost, but happy to be lost. Or maybe I'm just making that up since it's from Ethan. On the back, it says:

> *So long adrift, so fast aground,*
> *What foam and ruin have we found —*
> *We, the Wise Brothers?*

That's all it says. This one is addressed to me, though. The last postcard just had our address written on it. I try to imagine Ethan sitting at a desk and making the letters of my name. He had to think of me for the seconds it took to write them. And he thought of me when he came across that poem. Still, this is the kind of night that I really wish he'd just use the damn phone. He could call and I could ask, "Where are you?" and he wouldn't answer. And I'd say, "I made out with a girl tonight." And he would ask, "Is she hot?" And I'd answer, "Of course she's hot." And then I wouldn't be able to help it — I'd ask, "When are you coming home?" And then he'd probably hang up the phone.

So maybe the postcards are not such a bad way of handling communication after all.

I miss him. Take the stairs two at a time and grab one of his hoodies out of his closet. Shed my jacket and put that on, then this zippered sweater thing that I can't believe he left behind. He loves that sweater. Put that on, too, and then my jacket again. Go down to the hall closet and dig through until I find a scarf that doesn't smell like feet. It's tied around the snow shovel. I remember Ethan doing that because every time we had to shovel we could never find our wool stuff. Wrap that around my neck and check myself out in the hall window. And then I realize that I was the one who did that. It was me who thought to tie the scarf around the shovel. Weird that just because it was smart I figured it was Ethan.

I fold the postcard in half and put it in my jacket pocket. Have to get back to campus to lock up, and if it's going to snow, I'd rather be in the attic or the archives. Jade's right. If we do get a real snow, Wells Farm will be beautiful. And besides that, I still have to come up with my key prank. Once Dad gets home, it's not going be so easy to sneak out and spend nights there.

So that's the plan. This time, now that it doesn't matter so much, I remember to leave lights on in the living room. Step out into the cold and breathe in through my nose. When people say it smells like snow, I guess they mean the air smells clean and cold. Like toothpaste. It really doesn't feel so cold. The diner's lights are on, but there aren't any people sitting at tables. Just a couple of old men at the counter. If I go in there, the waitresses will fuss over me and I'll be the only guy younger than seventy slurping soup and feeding the table-side jukebox. It's good soup, but not amazing.

The hill feels like more of a trek tonight, probably because there's no chance of running into Jade at the end of it. I take time out from thinking about kissing her in order to think about listening to her. Her explanation. The things she finally told me. It's hard to picture the girl who bops all over the Arts Studio and goes apeshit at the prospect of s'mores having trouble getting out of bed in the morning. I can't imagine Jade just giving up. Sitting staring at the walls in a tiny, sterile dorm room. Pushing food around her plate or keeping a pillow over her face in the day. I can't see Jade ever being that weary.

It was different with my mom. It made sense that she got tired of fighting. It's not like we had some vast mystery on our hands. She had cancer. They found it in the spring. But it had metastasized, which meant it went into her bones. By the time September rolled in, she couldn't really walk. She was in pain all the time. I'd get home from school and she'd be sitting on the sofa and it looked like she'd spent most of the day trying not to scream. Ethan burned her CDs of relaxation music. One day I came home and found them smoking pot in the living room. Both of them. I remember how pissed I was. I never really confronted my brother about crap, but that day I followed him into the kitchen. "Why don't you bring out your Bob Marley albums, Ethan?" Asked him something smart-assed like that. He was an asshole about it. Asked me why I should be the only family member that got to raid his stash. I remember telling him he was turning our mother into one of his druggie buddies. I remember how furious he got. He wouldn't say anything at first, just glared at me. We just stood there staring at each other. Until Ethan finally asked me if Mom seemed better.

"What do you mean better?"

"Does she seem more comfortable? Maybe in less excruciating pain?"

"She seems stoned."

And then Ethan looked at me coldly and said, completely matter-of-factly, "Emil, Mom is going to die."

"I know that."

"No, I don't mean like hypothetically, she's going to die, we're all going to die. Just like the dog died. How everything eventually dies. She's going to die soon. Like, maybe she has weeks. Maybe a month."

"Paging Dr. Simon? So it's better to just keep her doped up, so that we can't even recognize her in the last weeks?" I remember saying it and realizing that was really what made me angry the most. That Mom had cancer, and that was going to take her away soon enough. And here Ethan was, turning her into someone else, taking her away sooner.

"It's not about you, Emil." That was pretty much the last important conversation Ethan and I had. "She's more than just our mom. She's a human being and she's dying and she's in an incredible amount of pain." After that he stopped really talking to me. Like he had decided that he wasn't going to waste any more time trying to explain himself. So I didn't say anything else about it. If Dad noticed that the living room smelled like weed all the time, he didn't say anything, either.

My mom held on as long as she could, and then she let go. She planned everything out for us. Wrote out shopping lists, ordered Hanukkah presents online. She even called a caterer and set the menu for our Christmas dinner. She organized her own memorial service. Scheduled dentist and doctor appointments for us. Had our good suits dry-cleaned, for christsakes.

Dad and I sat at the dining room table and wrote her obituary together. Like he was helping me with some project for school. We put that she'd died after a long illness. And that was true. We wrote that she was a loving wife and a caring mother and a rabid Beatles fan. And that was true, too.

We didn't describe how painstakingly my mom prepared for our first few days without her. And afterward we didn't really talk about her last day, not even to each other. How she waited until Dad took off for work and I left for school and Ethan was out on an errand. How she very carefully took enough painkillers to fall asleep and not wake up again. Ethan found her when he came home from the supermarket.

After all those hours waiting in Dr. Watkins's office, when I finally looked up at the knock, it was my dad who stepped through the door. Ethan stayed home. And Dr. Watkins shook Dad's hand and told him what a fine young man I was. He offered us one of the conference rooms to talk, but instead we just sat in the parked car.

Dad kept taking these deep breaths, and at first I thought that he was crying, which would have freaked me out even right then. He had been crying, I could see that. The corners of his eyes were swollen and red. He was trying to speak, but kept getting tripped up. I think I spoke first just to help him out.

"I knew this was coming, but I didn't know — I mean did you know? That it was so close?"

Dad let out his breath and stared out the windshield. "No. I didn't know."

"I mean just last week you guys were talking about another round of radiation."

"We were discussing that, Bear. But ultimately that's not what your mother wanted. She felt that it would only postpone the inevitable and she wanted to spend as much time as possible at home with you boys. Last time — it was just too much for her. There were no guarantees, and she didn't want to risk her last weeks with us being that miserable."

"She didn't seem so bad this morning. I mean, she was up making breakfast. She was working the waffle maker. I don't understand how —"

"Emil." Then he stopped speaking for what seemed like forever. And then the bell rang and about a hundred guys came tumbling out of each of the buildings around us. It was weird to see everyone through the lens of the car window. Like in police shows on TV, how the detectives watch the interview through the fake mirror. Everyone was so normal — their faces twisted with laughing, shouting so that, in the silent car, they looked like monsters. I remember seeing them and wishing I was any one of them. Just not me in the car hearing my dad talk about my dead mom.

We just sat there for a while with the car surrounded by teenage boys. The way a safari jeep might stop in the middle of a pride of lions. He waited until people had mostly wandered off. Buses pulled out before my dad started speaking again.

"Emil. Your mother was in a lot of pain."

"I know that." Jesus Christ. How could I not know that?

"Well, she was in physical pain, but also — it also hurt her terribly that you boys had to see her and worry. She knew she was deteriorating, things were only going to get worse."

"Well, they can't anymore, right?"

"Exactly." Another series of deep breaths and long exhales from Dad's side of the car. "Your mother made a choice this morning to end things while she was still lucid and able to do so."

"What does lucid mean?"

My father looked straight at me then, almost glared at me. He was annoyed. "It means aware." But I still wasn't getting it.

"What does the rest of all that mean?"

"Emil." He almost shouted my name. I mean he was stern about it. And then his voice goes quiet and soft. "Your mother took pills this morning. That's why — that's how — she made a decision."

"She killed herself?" I remember sitting there, imagining all four of us in the car, how usually I'd be in the back, behind the passenger seat, next to Ethan. It would be Mom sitting next to my dad in the car. I wondered if I could smell her perfume on the headrest, but she hadn't actually come out with us in the car for a while.

Dad only said, "I think it's a mistake to think of it that way." And we didn't think about it that way. It seemed as if Dad had been prepared — he knew what to do, exactly how she had wanted things handled. I guess they'd discussed it. At one point, in the days right after, I asked Ethan if he thought they'd planned it out together. Told him my vote was no, because Dad couldn't have just driven off to work like it was just another day at the office. I mean, wouldn't he have stayed home and spent that last morning with her? But Ethan just sort of stared off and left the room.

By the time I get up to the main gate on campus, I'm done remembering for the night. I'd rather hear chains rattling in the basement and a little girl running around upstairs. A little too late I realize that it's more eerie to go inside when that heavy front door's already unlocked. Reassure myself with the idea that we don't get many drifters passing through Caramoor. I'm the only vagrant in the area. Still, the steps seem to creak more loudly beneath my feet and it's colder inside, like somehow I let a wind get inside that's curling around the corners. It smells a little like burning leaves in Ainsley because of the fire. I hope that floats off before Monday.

It's strange the crap that feels real to me now, and what feels less so. Example: I can hardly believe that I kissed Jade, that she's a real girl, not just an imaginary friend I made up wandering around this place late at night. She's not just marijuana smoke formed into the shape of a woman. But then it seems perfectly natural to stand at the first-floor landing and call out, "It's just me this time, Ruby. I hope you didn't mind that I brought over a friend."

It's warm upstairs in the attic. I look around and try to envision what my little alcove would look like to Jade. Tiny and well-kept, hopefully. Maybe a little bit depressing. I'll have to get a vase of flowers in here or something. A disco ball. When I finally lie down, I close my eyes against the flannel lining of the sleeping bag and pretend I'm resting my face against Jade's soft neck. The sore eye feels a lot better that way. I fall asleep fast and I don't even have nightmares of soldiers shackled in the cellar.

It feels sort of luxurious to just let myself wake up when the sun slivers in through the space between the headboard and the window. I don't have to worry about the building filling up with faculty or ducking out along with the dump trucks. Get up and grab a Pop-Tart and pad downstairs. If I were Jacob Wells, then maybe I'd get up and dine on some porridge in the main hall before going quail hunting or something.

Instead I zip up my jacket and tie my shoes so that I can go down the hill and shower at the field house. I shoot some hoops first without wearing a shirt. Because A) I can and B) I don't want to get my shirt all sweaty. Figure this is what it's like to be some insane billionaire with a court somewhere on the premises of my vast estate. Except probably then it wouldn't take so long for the hot water to get going. And then I realize that I either have to dry my hair with paper towels or risk catching pneumonia on the way back up to Ainsley House. So I do a little of both.

Caramoor is a wash of light blues and grays. I had half-expected to wake up to see the entire campus blanketed in snow. Instead the sky looks heavy with hazy clouds and the air smells sort of antiseptic. Basically it's like the sky is an aspirin. I swing by the Arts Studio and make sure the heat's on in case Jade stops by to work. Then I kind of half-jog back up the hill to Ainsley. Get Cecil's book out of my backpack and camp out on the couch in the reception area. Right before noon, I call Dad's cell and tell his voice mail that things are fine and that I'm eating a lot of Chinese food. It's tempting to tell him something, anything, about Jade. He'd probably be relieved that I'm talking to a girl and not letting Soma dress me up in a skirt or something.

But it'll be more embarrassing to hear how happy he is about it. And how would I explain meeting her, anyway? *Hey, Dad, I've been hanging out after-hours at school using a key that my runaway brother gave me? And then I met the daughter of one of my former teachers? And spent last night grinding against her on a school sofa?* He'd still be pleased, I think, but secretly, and he'd have to make a big show of disapproving for the sake of the status quo. Instead I tell him that I hope his trip is going well and that he shouldn't worry about the house. That if it snows I'll leave the sidewalk and the driveway for him to shovel when he gets home.

In the faculty commons, I find some TV dinners in the freezer. They're Lean Cuisines, so I eat three of them. Some poor sucker's not going to have lunch next week. Hopefully, it's Verlando. After lunch I let myself back into the archives and start sifting through the thin pages of old yearbooks and literary magazines. Figure there might be some mention of the key in one of those, but there's nothing.

I do find a framed black-and-white photograph of the Caramoor Ghost-Hunting Society, 1953. Bunch of guys in three-piece suits sitting on the steps of Ainsley House. I bet one of them must be my old friend Cecil van Gunder and my money's on the guy who's already bald or the one who is actually wearing a monocle. They all look a little cartoonish, like they're playing dress-up as antique ghostbusters. Supergeeks fading into the yellowed corners of an overexposed photograph. If we all went to school together, these guys would probably be even more invisible than me. But if the key had been passed around back then, I guarantee one of these chuckleheads would have been holding it.

I put the picture aside, behind me. Wednesday is Valentine's Day and it's the kind of thing Jade would get a kick out of. I mean, if I'm going to give her anything. I don't know what people do, what chicks expect. What Jade would want. The last time I gave a girl a valentine was in the sixth grade and that's when you bought those superhero ones at CVS and handed them out to the whole class. There weren't so many limbs to crawl onto back then. In eighth grade, I bought this bracelet of black beads with a gold clasp and left it in Martinique Delmonico's mailbox. I wrote her name across the red wrapping paper, rode my bike to her house, early, before school. She wasn't even really someone I talked to, but I played trombone in band and she played clarinet. I spent most of the time emptying my spit valve on the shoes of the kid next to me and staring at Martinique. That can't count, though. I never even saw her wear the bracelet, and even if she loved it, she didn't have any reason to think it was from me.

Anyway, I can see myself giving Jade the photograph. Telling her that she could be in this year's Ghost-Hunting Society with me. Kind of funny, but it's not a cop-out. Giving her one of those stuffed apes that fart or sing Michael Bolton songs would be a cop-out.

She'd know it means something. But I'm getting ahead of myself. Planning out a present for a girl whose phone number I don't even know.

I spend a couple hours in the archives, just reading. Thumb through old issues of the *Daily Falcon* and get decades-old newspaper ink on my palms. Find a bunch of trophies cloaked in the dust in a cardboard box. Like a good two dozen of them. One has some brass guy standing at a lectern and the plaque says, NATIONAL ORATORY COMPETITION 1941. Another is just a wooden gavel with a plaque that says, CONNECTICUT STATE CONGRESS DEBATE, 1955. Guess these didn't make the cut for the trophy cabinet in the athletic building. Caramoor doesn't want the spotlight on their dominance at pansy-ass verbal sports. So I drag that box out and figure I can do something interesting with them.

I take one of the flannel shirts I've got packed and polish off each of the trophies until they are shining examples of the standards of Caramoor. Then I walk around campus and set one on a urinal in each boys' room in every academic building. It's not the ultimate key prank, but it's a worthwhile use of a Sunday afternoon. I think about going to town for dinner, but instead just grab some iced tea and chips from the field house vending machines. Walk by the Arts Studio, but I can see it's dark from the top of the hill.

For a second, I panic that maybe Jade's just not going to show up again — this will just be her way of disappearing from me. But it's not so tough to talk myself down from that. It still looks like snow and when I check my e-mail in the computer lab, weather.com is trumpeting a nor'easter that's about to pummel the East Coast. I can't decide if that's exciting or just a real pain in the ass. On the one hand, maybe I won't have school tomorrow. On the other hand, unless Jade shows up, I'm not sure I really want to be snowed in at Caramoor.

It'll be scenic. But cold as hell and I can just see Mrs. Sancio trudging over to Dad's and my house in snowshoes and then flipping out completely when I'm not home. She'll call my dad and announce that I have pinkeye and am now on the lam. Or she'll tell him I've been blinded and therefore might have syphilis. So those are some possible complications. Also it's cold here and getting a little bit lonesome. I'm worn out enough from the whole week that I decide to doze off up in the attic for a few hours, just to regroup.

I wake up to the creepiest howl since our dog got hit by the FedEx truck. It's just the wind this time, though, whistling through the slates in the attic walls. I can tell it's snowing even before pushing aside the headboard to check outside the window. Lie faceup in my sleeping bag for a little bit listening to the heaviness creak and settle on the house's eaves. I'm never going to get tired of how snow transforms everything. I mean, it's impressive anywhere. But at Caramoor, where it's just open fields and staggering pines and old brick houses with columns bracing the front porches — well, it's the kind of beautiful that silences everything. My heart feels like it's beating more quietly in my chest. Outside the window, the snow doesn't even look like it's falling — instead it's sort of blowing around. As if Ainsley House sits on a hill that's just a stop in the sky that the flakes are falling through and past.

Right after Mom died, I caught myself looking up at the sky a lot. But that's just retarded. We've got two strands of religion in our family, but together, they don't strengthen the rope that binds us to God or anything. My mom didn't believe in heaven. She didn't want to be buried in a Jewish cemetery. When she explained to us how the memorial service would be, I remember getting angry at how calm she was about it. Then I got scared, like maybe the cancer had gone to her brain or something. Looked at Dad, as if I could ask, "The hell? You're just going to go ahead with a funeral after she's dead and can't stop you, right?" Honestly, I sort of figured that would happen.

I did ask her if she was angry at God. And yes, upon reflection that's a hell of a personal question to inflict on someone, even if she did give birth to you. Ethan rolled his eyes and snorted and said, "Jesus Christ. You have no idea." I couldn't tell what he meant. No idea how much she hated God? No idea what she was going through? The last one wouldn't have been fair, because what the hell did he know? Just because he smoked up with her didn't mean he understood what she was feeling. It's like Ethan decided he had become a cancer-patient wrangler. He thought he spoke the language.

My mother didn't react like I'd asked some out-of-bounds, toss-the-kid-some-chemotherapy-and-see-how-he-likes-God question. She just said simply, "Lately, I think the closest thing to God is science." And then she went on to explain that she'd begun to think about medicine as God's reach toward us. That she wanted her death to contribute to that relationship. It seemed like she'd been thinking a lot about it, not like it was some crazy germ infecting her head. And even Ethan looked a little relieved after hearing her talk about it.

My mom's not up there, so I made myself stop looking at the sky like she was in it. Months ago, she was on a gurney somewhere and now she is not. I don't know what med schools do with cadavers after they're done with them and I don't want to.

Fredericka Wells is buried on campus. That's what Cecil's book says, anyway. Not in the Revolutionary War cemetery by the river, but in a little plot closer to the western edge of the old Wells property, so that her first house, the old Cornell homestead, was within sight. Apparently, her husband relented and gave her that piece of mercy after she died. Or maybe one of her kids did it. I bet we're the only school in the United States that has not one, but two graveyards on campus. I bet they advertise that crap in the brochures.

By the time I force myself out of the nylon cocoon of the sleeping bag, the snowflakes are floating fatly down and it looks deep out there. Snowdrifts surround the statue of General Ambrose Bronson, one of our more illustrious founding fathers. There's snow up to Bronson's bronzed horse, so that's like maybe two feet or something. Insane.

I start to panic a little bit that I'm snowed in, bundled up in a haunted house, having broken in and set a sleeping bag down like I'm some squatter come in from the cold to roost in the dusty slats of Ainsley's attic. If it were a horror movie, the chain saws would start churning now. It's also gotten really cold, so much so that I weigh the risks of starting another fire in the downstairs reception area. If there's no chance of getting any, though, it seems kind of stupidly crazy, instead of admirably crazy. I crack a pack of hand warmers instead and marvel at the fact that circumstances have actually evolved so that I am now a person who even has the slightest chance of getting some.

So it's hand warmers and hot cocoa from the faculty kitchen. I find a thermostat in a hallway on the second floor and sneak it up a little, but nothing happens. Find another one downstairs next to the business office and this one is actually connected to something. As soon as I boost the lever up to seventy degrees, I hear the furnace kick in. It makes the floorboards thrum.

When Ethan and I were little, the most agonizing thing about the snow was waiting for it to stop falling. That was the rule, for whatever reason — you didn't get to go out and play until the flakes had finally stopped and our mother knew exactly how much snow was on the ground. Maybe that meant there was a limit — we couldn't go out in snow that stood higher than our waists or something. Maybe she thought it was like the ocean, that eventually a tide of it might come in and sweep us away if the snow was still falling and she wasn't watching us.

It's weird when there stops being so many rules and yet you still follow the old ones. Like Dad and me sitting through dinnertime without TV. And how part of me still feels like on campus, I should be wearing dress code, that I should take off my iPod. Downstairs, I'm skulking around and nervous to touch the thermostat, but keep forgetting that it's actually trespassing, just being here. Every once in a while, I startle myself with my own face in the mirror above the fireplace — looking bizarre, with the sleeping bag shrouding my shoulders.

I spend most of the next hour wandering around the first floor, stopping by all the windows to see the snow piling up outside. It makes me a little stir-crazy, as if Ainsley House is a box in the ground and someone keeps shoveling down the snow, sealing me in. By the time I go upstairs and deck myself out in every single piece of clothing stashed in the attic, I'm done waiting. The snow has slowed to almost nothing, anyway. Just a few stray flecks occasionally streaking down and those could just be from the wind shaking the trees, anyway.

Okay, so it's like I'm one of those kids who grew up in Brazil or something and has never seen snow before. It isn't just beautiful. That's like saying Jade with her neck arched up and her face lifted toward me was "pretty." It was more like how maybe the coast of America first looked to Christopher Columbus or whatever poor bastard actually first arrived — not just beautiful, but totally undiscovered. Except by me.

As far out as I can see, it's just a pure, unbroken cover, even past the gates, to the road. Icicles hang off the trim of Ainsley and McCaffrey houses and the trees circling campus stand with their branches lowered with snow. It's amazing. Without even thinking about the fact that maybe the maintenance crew has to clock in some overtime to clear out campus, I unleash this cave-man yell, like just shouting across the campus can claim all of it as mine.

And then I spend the next hour or two running around like a little kid in snow pants and mittens. Fall down, eat snow, burrow into one of the huge drifts that have filled up the dugout on the baseball diamond. For a while, I just let myself play. It's like I can move backward in time through some kind of snow tundra tunnels. It's not until I'm tired enough to just fall down and lie there looking back out across campus that I see the problem inherent in my little jaunt back to childhood.

There are footprints all over the field. Mine. Meaning: I'm sort of fucked. There goes all of my painstaking attempts to leave no trace on campus. Ghosts don't leave footprints and I've sunk mine over Caramoor's main quad and across half the athletic fields. Whoever keeps track of those things will most likely notice. I don't know. Maybe they'll just pass it off as kids screwing around. Or some crazy homeless guy who got all excited at the chance to make snow angels.

Whatever gets into me translates into defiance. I look out at the pristine field and it looks like a blank sheet of paper. Every single step has to fall exactly, with no slips. On some of the letters I just drag my foot in the closest I can get to a straight line. It takes me until sweat is pretty much freezing on my brow to spell out I DON'T CARE in the snow. And seriously, I don't. Worst possibility is that it's just too risky to break back into campus and then what? I didn't launch the key prank of the century. I missed possible legendary status. It sucks, yeah. But there are worse things.

From ground level, my own little postcard probably reads as

nothing more than a bunch of lines in the snow. No more information than the ones Ethan sends from whatever city post office he stops by. But maybe it'll be visible from the second or third story of the building. Or if someone just randomly floats by in a hot air balloon. Thinking of it that way, I wonder if the message I want to leave to the world is, indeed, *I don't care*. A whole list of reasons for that one. A) It's a lie. Sometimes I care about everything so much my throat aches. I care about that stupid deer in the woods, how Soma might feel lately that everything he does is wrong to me. I care about the fact that our house has deteriorated to the point where we're throwing empty cans into the bathroom wastepaper basket. I care where Ethan's sleeping at night and what my dad sees when he closes his eyes and thinks about the word *family*. I care about Jade so much that I want to put her on a train to the future so that a future me, one who isn't going to fuck up everything he tries to get close to, can pick her up at a better station.

If I'm going to leave some kind of grand message for the world, it at least has to be honest. And besides that, there's another way that writing *I don't care* fails on all points. There's B) Apathy — what's the point? It seems kind of misguided to spend an hour tramping down snow just to say that I could give a cat's ass. So I get back to work and revise things a little bit. After another hour, I'm soaking wet, my legs are shaking with muscles spasms, but I've pounded the snow down to say SOMETIMES right next to the rest of it. Now my own personal canvas reads: SOMETIMES I DON'T CARE. Okay, so it's not the most brilliant Mayday call, but I'm freezing and the warmest thing in me is a tiny idea the whole exercise has ignited in my mind.

I just might have a key prank after all.

CHAPTER 20

Back at Ainsley, I've got to figure out if this is one of the times I care or not. My boots are soaking. It's like the rubber treads sponged up three inches of snow. I can leave them outside and risk someone walking by and noticing or I can wear them and track snow all through the building. The whole thing requires considerable acrobatics. I've got to unlock the door and then throw my shoulder against it because the old hinges have pretty much frozen into stubborn creaks.

When the door gives, I push through and land on my heavily padded ass. So many layers and they're all wet — you can actually hear a squishing sound upon impact. So the acrobatic angle does not work out so well. I get the boots off and then my jacket and use the first two layers I shed to sop up the small flood that came through the door with me.

My slick idea of putting on every single piece of clothing so that I could go outside and play in the snow like an eight-year-old? Was not so slick. The first three layers of my clothes are soaked through with sweat. It's pretty grim. Everything else is wet with snow. My skin is vibrating — I'm shivering that much.

So I lose everything. It takes me less than a minute and I'm sitting naked on the first floor of the main administrative building of Caramoor Academy. In front of windows. Curtainless windows. If there are ghosts in that building, I give them something to rattle their chains about. Hopefully, little Ruby gets a good giggle watching me trot my bare ass upstairs and up the attic ladder just to grab a sleeping bag to dress myself in. It feels warmer but not really much more comfortable. I don't mean in terms of texture. Flannel on balls is fairly pleasing. But my nerves kick in and the rest of my skin prickles, I feel so edgy.

All anyone has to do is track my footprints right to the house, come on in, and then I'll get my legendary status — I'll be the naked kid on campus. It takes me until the sun sinks down into the white blankets outside to finish drying my clothes under the electric hand dryers in the bathroom. At one point, I have three dryers going at once, and have to run from bathroom to bathroom, restarting the buttons for optimum drying ability. Just because no one has discovered my genius yet doesn't mean it's not staggering.

By now I'm Donner Party hungry. Shackleton expedition hungry. As ricockulous as it might be to put on half the clothes I just spent the afternoon getting dry, that's what happens. Once I'm halfway warm, I trot everything that's mine back up to the attic, just in case the place gets raided in my absence. Pack my wallet into my backpack and toss in Cecil's book, thinking I'll eat at the diner. It's just after eight and pitch-dark out. The snow glows like some kind of exotic beach, but this is the kind of weather that severs testicles. When I step out, I try to fit my steps in the footprints that I left earlier. There's a layer of icy frost over everything so that every time I lower a boot, it crunches through and then settles down. So the ground feels like that dessert my mom used to fire up the kitchen torch on — it's like I'm trekking across a crème brûlée.

It's strange to look down the hill without seeing the street crowded with headlights. New Market Avenue looks plowed, but the side streets don't seem to be. I walk down the entire hill without a single car passing me. Once I get to the main road, the only cars that inch past me are trucks and they've got plows rigged up to their fenders. The only lights in town are the neon ones and the only places that look open are the Sit 'n' Bull tavern, the gas station, and the diner.

My ass is cold and sore. It probably looks like I wet myself and there's nothing I want more than to sit down at the bar and order up a drink. To be old enough to do that. Walk past and I can hear hooting, but the laughing kind of hooting, the kind of noise my dad used to make when he'd laugh so hard he'd slap his thighs. Not the bird kind. Man sounds. When I first started Caramoor, back when Ethan and I were going to the same school each day, we had some dinners like that. He'd get Dad started on what some jackass said to Coach at practice or do his impression of Dr. Watkins's inspirational speech of the week and we'd all be trying to stop ourselves from snarfing seltzer water through our noses. We were jovial men around the table, comparing battle tales. Back then, before Mom got sick, if he came home in a good mood, Ethan and I rushed Dad like he was the star pitcher on the mound. We only looked up when Mom set full platters on the supper table. I guess because she was always there, usually beaming. It sucks that the thing less certain becomes most valuable.

The diner's about as full as the rest of the street is empty. Nowhere near as rowdy as the Sit 'n' Bull, but it does have its charms, mostly that no one here is going to check my ID. I order up a special of tuna casserole, mostly because it means I get free pudding for dessert. And tuna casserole used to be one of Ethan's and my favorite dinners, even though Mom would have to make a whole separate supper for Dad. He'd say that he didn't work his ass off to eat a dinner with potato chips crumbled on the top. "Dad won't eat off the white trash menu," Ethan would chant, his mouth crammed with egg noodles. And Mom would hush him, but softly snicker into her napkin.

The waitress is older, like in her forties, and looking at me apologetically when she lowers my plate to the place mat in front of me. Never a good sign. Clearly, she knows the kind of cheesy paradise I'd been expecting. No crushed potato chips, no big floppy noodles on the diner's version. It's pretty much just a can of tuna dumped on a plateful of boxed macaroni and cheese. If I were half six-year-old, half cat, this would knock my socks off.

It's awful. I try to mash the tuna into the noodles, but some of the can-shaped lump is crispy around the edges from the oven. I pour on salt and even add pepper, but that just makes me remember it more as it goes down. It's so stupid. After everything, this is what's going to make me cry.

"Honey, how is everything?" I can't tell if the waitress has been watching or if she doesn't know what she's opening herself up for with that question. So for a second I just look up at her. There's food in my mouth but I haven't steeled myself to swallow it yet. The tag pinned to her shirt reads *Maggie*. "Folks don't usually order that one. If I'd known, I would've warned you off it."

And now I don't know what I'm supposed to say to this. okay? No problem? Maggie's having that same old middle-aged-waitress effect on me, though. I want her to read me a story. I want to tell her that I miss my dad and wish I'd packed more thermal underwear. I want to whimper that my mom used to make hot chocolate. Not even the powdered kind, but the cocoa on the stove, warmed with milk.

"Sugar? You okay, sugar? How about a cheeseburger? On the house?" She must see my wet eyes. Yeah, I would have fit right in at the Sit 'n' Bull tavern. I'm a regular old bad-ass. I let myself nod and she reaches for the plate. "Let me take this concoction away, so that you still have an appetite."

"Thank you." I finally get out the words. And force out a smile so that the poor lady can at least walk away. Get out Cecil's ghost book from my backpack, but I can't concentrate enough to find some interesting tidbit about a poltergeist in the dining hall.

I don't get why I'm so sad. Still. Dad's been away for little more than a week. One lame-ass key prank is set up — the trophies in the bathrooms — but I've got a better one brewing that just needs some time for the snow to melt. There's an actual girl in my life. And not some blind girl in a wheelchair who's just happy to have someone push her up and down ramps or something. Soma would see her and say, "I'd hit that," in that sleazy mumble he uses when he reviews girls.

And there's a postcard from Ethan in my backpack. When Dad gets home, there will be some shit to eat — I should have found a way to straighten out the exam thing and probably Soma and I have been a little greedy with the beverage supplies. But the house is still standing. I don't suddenly have tattoos.

According to the Scientific Formula of Diner Waitresses and Motherless Children, my affection for Maggie is less than or equal to her pity and demonstrative maternal feelings toward me. Meaning: The lady delivers a colossal cheeseburger. With pickles. And fries. And onion rings. I feel like a rescued puppy. She sets down a refilled soda and I want to lick her hand.

Snow or no snow, every happy family in the Connecticut area seems to have voted on the diner for supper, I guess because it's the only place to walk to. I slouch down a little in case someone recognizes me. It's weird — we've lived in the same house my whole life, but as soon as I switched to private school, I fell off the radar. In sixth grade, this kid Gary Camp moved to Dallas, Texas, and I bet more kids remember that guy. He came back up for eighth-grade graduation and wore a cowboy hat to the semi-formal dance.

The last time I saw any of the kids from my old grammar school was Mom's memorial service. They came with all their mothers and pretended we still had crap in common. We all mostly sat stiffly in the den while I explained about ninety times that we didn't wear uniforms at Caramoor. This one girl, Jenny Hasburn, kept tugging at my tie, giggling about how us preps were so formal. Until finally Ethan stood in the doorway and coldly told her, "We're wearing ties because our mother died. It has nothing to do with our high SAT scores or pedigreed educa-tion." And then he sent her off to help her mom with the Jell-O salad. Ethan never reeled in girls for me, but he was awesome about getting rid of ones that sucked.

In the booth behind me, the two kids argue about who's going to shovel in the morning. They're brothers and the older kid keeps calling the younger one Dick Breath. "I'll tell you what, Dick Breath. You get up and start early and then I'll finish up after breakfast." And the other kid's all confused about it, trying to sniff out the scam.

"I'm not doing more than half of it," he whines. It makes me cringe a little and wonder if that's what my voice sounded like to Ethan. "Seriously. No more than half. Half is fair and I'm smaller, anyway."

"Yeah, yeah. You can do your Dick Breath half and when you're done, wake me up and I'll finish up." The older kid sounds smug, so he has to have some strategy. "How many shovels do we have, Dick Breath?"

Dick Breath mutters, "One."

"Well, there you go, then. We can't both shovel at the same time, so we'll take turns." Maybe he's hoping that by the time he wakes up, the sun will have thawed what's left. Or maybe he's got some dentist appointment. But there's no way Big Guy's going to pick up that shovel. And Dick Breath knows it.

"Mom —" His voice climbs about three octaves in one word.

"It sounds perfectly fair to me, Andrew. Look at this — they have Taco Bake as one of their specials." I bet Taco Bake is a bunch of Doritos in tomato soup. When Maggie brings my pudding, I ask her for the check, too.

"Sure thing, sugar." And she pats me lightly on the shoulder. At the register, I sign over a twenty-dollar tip and hope that doesn't freak her out.

When I step back into the cold, it really does feel like I'm leaving the warm and well-lit planet of the normal families for the land of the lost boys trudging along the side of the road. It takes me a few minutes to figure out where I want to go. I want to be in my house. I don't care how empty it is.

Our street is sort of plowed, which would matter to me if I could drive. When I get to our house, it's pretty easy to spot. Except for one set of footprints trailing up the front stoop, it looks pretty much untouched. Like no one has lived there for a long time and the mailman's just stopped by once in a while. I have to kick aside snowbanks just to get the side door opened. Come inside and check the answering machine. There's another message from Mrs. Sancio asking if I want to "weather out the weather" at their place. When she repeats the word *weather,* she lets out peals of laughter, as if it's the most hysterical pun she's ever heard. Women are nuts.

I check the school Web site and find a statement in bold, red font: Caramoor Academy has cancelled all classes and school functions in the interest of safety. No shocker there. At least Dad isn't here to rant about school closings. He takes that crap personally and feels financially cheated each time they shut down school. Says if you're going to run an all-boys school in the northeast, you better be ready to educate them in the snow.

I call Soma on the landline so that I can charge up my cell. When he picks up, he answers with a question as if he's not certain who might be calling him from my house.

"Hello?"

"Soma. Where are you at?"

"Dude." He almost yells it. "Dude — where are *you* at?" He pronounces the words deliberately. Like he's naming a band or something.

"I'm home. The cell phone's charging, that's all."

"My MOM called you."

"Yeah, I got it." Soma sounds entirely too hopped up. Like he's spent the past few days running experiments in a home meth lab. "Weathering the weather. Tell her I'm fine here. I think you should come over."

"Dude, you don't UNDERSTAND. She's worried. She called your dad."

"She did what?" I make the mad dash to the cell phone and turn it on. And there it is — I've missed six calls. I try to remember the last time I heard the phone beeping out its low battery. No idea. "Holy crap — why would you let her do that? What the hell, man? Did she get him on the phone? Tell me she did not get my father on the phone."

The line is silent. Apparently, Mrs. Sancio got my dad on the phone.

"What did she tell him, Soma? What did he say?"

"Why wouldn't you pick up your cell, man? We called you like eighty times on your cell phone."

"Soma." I close my eyes and open them again, but I'm still here.

"Well, the good news is that he couldn't get a flight to come home. Because of the snow. And then the —"

"That's the good news? How did she get his number? When was the last time she spoke to him? God — I gotta hang up. I gotta call my dad. If he ended up getting a flight — what were you thinking?"

"You didn't pick up the phone." I hear him shout at someone in the background. "Where's the number? The one for Mr. Simon's hotel? Yeah — he's fine. I TOLD you he was probably fine." Soma gets back to the line with me, says breathlessly, "I told her you were probably fine."

"Well, that's awesome, dude. Really. I cannot fucking thank you enough." Soma rattles off a series of numbers. "How does she even have this number? I don't have the hotel number."

"I don't know. He gave her a whole itinerary. With all the numbers." I will never understand the freakin' underground of surveillance that parents rig up with one another. All week long,

I've been leaving messages with his secretary, voice mails on his cell phone. Why wouldn't Dad leave me the itinerary? How does that make any sense?

"What am I gonna say?"

"I don't know, dude. Where the hell have you been?" Soma's right. There's not a lot of ways to explain this. To him. To my dad.

"I've been right here. I was up in my room." We lie to our parents all the time, Soma and me. But we don't lie to each other.

When he answers, his voice has a cold edge to it. I could open a can on it. "I don't know what's going on with you. But before you tell your dad that — he left a key with my mom. We went over there." So it wasn't the mailman on the front stoop. Now I'm looking around the kitchen, imagining Soma and Mrs. Sancio snooping around. Checking for me in the upstairs bedrooms. Goddamn it.

"I've been spending a lot of time at the diner. You know, just drinking coffee and working on my drawings." But Soma's voice doesn't ease up.

"Well, then, that's what you should tell him."

"Yeah." I go quiet because I'm busy choking on my own dread. "Hey, I was calling because you should come over. No school and all."

"I don't know, man. My mom's all freaked. You've won bad influence status. She's ready to send you and Meredith to the same teenage boot camp."

"Whatever. Get over here. Tell her I miss my mom." No one is immune to my charms.

Except my dad.

CHAPTER 21

When I call him, he picks up on the first ring. His voice booms. "Emil." There's a silence, and my throat feels scratchy. I can't work up enough spit in my mouth to swallow.

"You're not on a plane, are you?" Except when I say it, it comes out all rushed, like a balloon I blew up and then let go — *you'renotonaplane?*

"Do I need to be on a plane?" His voice is weird. Sounds like he's been yelling for a while. Like maybe he's just been screaming into the phone waiting for me to finally be on the other end. "Emil?"

"No, sir. I'm sorry that you got that call, sir. Mrs. Sancio must have stopped by while I'd gone to the diner for something to eat. I stayed there for a while. Catching up on homework and stuff."

"Right." He lets the silence hang just long enough for me to make myself a noose with it.

"Well, we had discussed the need to pull up my grades, sir —"

"Enough. Listen to me very carefully because I want an honest answer. A thoughtful, honest answer. Do I need to get an early plane home?" Part of me actually wants him to come. But what am I supposed to say? *Yes, please. I miss you?* That's not how the Simon men operate.

"Everything's okay here, sir. I'm sorry to have caused you concern."

"Concern?" My father sounds incredulous. "Emil, we have a lot of things to discuss when I get home."

Scratch that missing-him part and reinstate the previous mood of constant dread. "Yes, sir."

"Very serious things. You and I have a lot of ground to cover." For a second, I wonder if Dad knows what he's getting himself into with that one. Because I've been working on my list of topics for months now.

"Yes, sir."

"Okay, then. I will see you in three days. Mrs. Sancio will be keeping close tabs on you. If she telephones, I expect you to answer. Because otherwise, she has strict instructions to call and worry me. And frankly, I've had enough worry."

So that went as well as could be expected, really. I call back Soma and ask to speak to his mother.

"What?" he asks.

"Come on, I have to talk to her. Are you going to head over here or not? You might as well, because after Wednesday, I'm going to be chained in the basement."

"Do you still have pinkeye?"

"Yes. And you have to lick it. Lemme talk to your mom." He makes me call back on the landline. And by the time I wrap things up and am finally easing her off the phone, Soma's let himself in the side door. It's Sancios in stereo.

"Let me tell you, Emil — you need to call us if you need anything. If you want to get away from that big empty house, well, then, you come to ours, do you hear me? You gave your father and me quite a scare." I hold the phone away from my ear, just in case Soma missed the sound of his mother's voice.

"Yes, Mrs. Sancio," I say. "Soma just got here safe and sound. Have a great night!" And I set down the receiver while she's still squawking out of it. "Man, now I know why your sister's so crazy."

"My sister's not crazy." Soma says it automatically now, like it's the phrase *excuse me* after a burp.

"Okay, then. Now I know why your sister's so slutty."

"Asshole, where were you?" There are a couple different ways of deflecting this one. I go for stalling first.

"When? Most of the snowstorm had me stuck here. Where were you?" Best defense and all that crap. Really, we're just going through the motions. Soma knows I'm lying about something. We both know that I'll find a way to tell him about it eventually. He's just feeling me out, seeing if I'm ready to give it up yet.

I'm not. "Seriously. Besides breaking into my house with your mom, what've you been doing?" The world's officially gone off-kilter — I'm breaking into school, Soma's breaking into here, and there's actually no breaking going on at all. It's all keys and locks and sneaking through doors that we're not supposed to open. Ethan would eat this crap up like a stack of pancakes.

Soma says, "Look out at the truck." I go to the front window and sift through the lace curtains to see his jeep in the driveway. He's got a plow rigged up to it.

"Holy crap — where'd you get that?"

"Mr. Dad hooked it up, said it would give me a chance to earn some spending money." Which sounds a whole lot more dicky than it is really, like Soma's stepdad had recruited him for manual labor. But Mr. Sancio has to know how much Soma's going to love any kind of job that requires him to sit behind a wheel and move huge mounds of crap around. With five kids in the family, it's not like the guy could just roll bills out of his wallet for all of them. This way, Soma gets to run his own little demented business.

And apparently that's what he's done. Now I get why he was so desperate to talk to me. "You weren't online. You didn't answer texts or pick up the phone." When Soma gets a new project started, he's irrepressible. And talkative. "I needed a wingman."

"What would you need a wingman for? You were pushing snow around."

"You were supposed to ride shotgun and hop out and get the coffee." Of course. The awesome thing is — he means it. He really had this whole perfectly formed vision of how his little business venture would debut. And he got all bent because I wasn't there for it.

"So I'll ride shotgun now. You can show me how quickly you can clear my driveway. Come on, I'll even give you a truck-driver name. You can be Bucky or Red. No, wait." I snap my fingers. "You can go back to being Frank."

Soma grabs a beer out of the fridge before I can stop him. "Don't call me Frank. And what makes you think I'm going to clear out your driveway? You know what I've been charging for driveways all day? Forty bucks."

Forty bucks is not so shabby for about ten minutes of labor. "I don't know, dude. How about we trade the next few months of my life? Because those have evaporated thanks to your inability to rein in your mother."

"Yeah, yeah. Fine. We'll do your driveway. But later. Why don't you make yourself useful and get out a frying pan so I can warm up my testicles?" I close a frozen pizza in the oven for him instead, because by now all the Chinese food is questionable. "We are wasteful young men." Tossing out the lo mein really seems to wound him. I send him into the living room with a Ziploc bag and a wooden pipe.

I check the phone book but I don't find a Larson listed. I call information and then stutter through the electronic voice response so I can talk to an actual operator. The bored voice on the phone has no idea how much this matters to me. "Name and city."

"Larson." That part I say with certainty. And then, "I'm not so sure about the city." This does not thrill the lady on the other end of the line.

"I need a city, please."

"If I say Hartford, will that take care of the entire metro area?"

"Are you saying Hartford, sir?" I figure I might as well play fast and loose.

"Yes."

"I have Larson, W. and Larson, P., both in the Hartford area." At first I spaz out thinking I have to pick one. Sit there on the phone, remembering the photo of Jade with her dad — did he look like a Walter? A William? Peter? Preston? — "Sir?" she asks — Percy? Ward? "Sir, would you like both numbers?"

"I can take two of them? Really?" The silence at the other end of the phone says something. It says that if the operator could reach through the cord and strangle me, then my face would be currently turning blue. At least I have pen and paper prepared.

So now I have two phone numbers, one of which may or may not be Jade's. Just in case, at some point, in the future, I decide that calling her would be a natural progression of things and not just a breach into Stalking Country.

"Something's burning." Soma is going to make an annoying client to some nursing home attendant someday.

"You're smoking weed. That means it's on fire."

"Yeah, I mean in the kitchen." I use Soma's wool glove as a pot holder and grab the pizza. Hear Soma mumble, "Asshole," after the oven door slams shut.

"Hey — you really are a curmudgeonly bastard, you know that? You're going to make one ornery old man." I hear the whistle of Soma inhaling.

"What I meant to say was: Please may I have some pizza?" We sit in the same kind of companionable silence that we've always sat in. Things are going to be tense when my dad gets back. But at least they've settled down a little between me and Soma.

I'm not even hungry after the diner, but end up eating two slices because it's nice to chew next to someone. I keep touching the paper with the two Larson residence numbers in the same way that just days ago I kept touching the key around my neck. I wonder what she's doing now, if she's going nuts cooped up in the house with her mom and dad and the Great American Romance. Or maybe she's relieved that the snow means a reprieve from my moony face in the Arts Studio window.

"Hey. I got a postcard from Ethan."

"No shit." Soma stops chewing. "Where from?"

"Don't know. It's just a kid in a red sweater. Like an art photograph." Soma sits up in the blue leather recliner with a thwump. He turns to look at me. In disbelief.

"No, dumb-ass. The postmark. Where is it from?" In my head, I can hear crickets chirping. Water rushing. Pterodactyls screeching. I cannot believe how moronic I am. Move slowly toward my backpack and take the shiny card from the front zippered pocket. My hands are unsteady and for a second I can't look down. Maybe part of me didn't really want to know where Ethan was. "Didn't you check the other one?" Soma asks. He's squinting at me, like he's trying to see me through the haze of smoke. Or through my own stupidity. I leave the postcard on the coffee table and go upstairs to get the other one off my desk. Turn them both over like they're a hand in a poker game.

Boston. Both postcards are from Boston. At least it doesn't say Hartford. Because that would have been serial-killer crazy. This is borderline. "Dude, are you okay?" Soma looks worried again. But I'm still too stunned to sort it out. I had analyzed his handwriting, for christsake. Why wouldn't I have looked at the postmark? Why wouldn't Dad have seen it? And gone up there? "It's not like you could find him in Boston, you know. That's a big-ass city. It wouldn't have changed anything." Soma's saying all of this really slowly like it's something important that I take in.

"Do you think it's weird that my dad hasn't gone to find Ethan?" And now Soma looks away. It's just this slight shift or maybe I'm just paranoid from the pot. I watch him swallow, see the Adam's apple roll down his skinny neck.

"Ethan's a grown guy, you know? Maybe your dad just wants to give him some time to sort out shit on his own."

"He's only three years older than us." But Soma lowers his face back toward the pipe, inhales, and then raises his eyes to meet mine.

"Nah — Ethan's always been much older than us." And he's right.

"So what's in Boston? What do you think he's doing?"

"He's playing for the Red Sox, Emil, I don't know. There's a dozen different colleges in Boston — maybe he's at one of those. Or working construction. Maybe he's a bike messenger."

"Why a bike messenger?" I hear myself leap on that. It's such a detail. Maybe Soma knows something. Maybe somehow Ethan got in touch with him or something.

But all he says is, "What? You couldn't see Ethan working as a bike messenger?" And he's right, it's the kind of employment my brother would bust a nut over. Crisscrossing the city, dodging trucks — someone always waiting for him to arrive.

"You don't know —" I feel like an asshole even asking. And Soma's insulted. He doesn't even look straight at me.

"That's retarded." His voice shuts me down. "How would I know?" We sit there for a while watching the channels flip by until Soma finds a Georgetown game against Pitt. I take a couple hits and let myself get lulled by the back-and-forth of the game. It's almost half a quarter before Soma speaks up again. "You know, I'm sure he's going to come back. If you could have just split after this fall, wouldn't you have done it?"

"No." I mean it, too. I wouldn't have left him or Dad. God, I wouldn't have left my mother's sweaters in the closet. It takes awhile before I'm ready to speak out loud again. "Hey, Soma — where do I buy spray paint? Can I just go in some place and get it?"

"Whoa there, Basquiat — you're going to go write Ethan's name all over Boston?" That's something I hadn't even thought of. Maybe I really do have special needs and Soma's some guy my dad pays to take care of me or something. He's my attendant.

"I just want to be able to buy some. That's all. Not sure yet of the exact plan." And Soma doesn't question that. It's the kind of item he'd put on his shopping list, just in case. Right there along with nunchakus or smoke bombs. Just another contribution into the Frankie Sancio bag of tricks.

"Well, you're supposed to be eighteen. And they make you show ID."

"Really? So kids don't huff it?"

"Um . . . mostly because they don't want you to spray it. On walls and stuff. In our society, we call that graffiti. And we frown on it."

"Yeah. Wow, dude. What's wrong with me? I'm not making any sense, am I? It's like I'm all fogged up."

"You're just stoned." Yeah. I know Soma is right. It doesn't make me feel like less of an idiot, but it's something to hold on to. "And most small hardware stores will sell it to you, if you say it's for a school project. Not a megastore like Home Depot, but Archer's in town would do it." It takes me a minute to realize that we're back on spray paint and not discussing buying weed at Home Depot. I really feel caught in my head, am breathing heavily. There's sweat on my face or maybe tears.

"Just try to calm down a little. Watch the game. Hey, if they were playing BC we'd could search the stands for Ethan." Soma starts to laugh and then stops. He looks straight at me. "We could do that, you know."

He means this to be reassuring. "Yeah, I know." I nod and let my head fall back against the sofa and watch the ball travel through one set of hands after another. And when I finally doze off, the game's still on and I dream about rows of faces in a stadium. They all look a little bit like Ethan, but not quite. And I can't tell if they're yelling at me or cheering me on.

First thing in the morning, we plow my driveway. Soma's pretty good. He scrapes against the hedges a few times, but no major disasters. We keep busy. Shovel off the walk and stoop and drive into town for breakfast. We don't mention last night or my dad or the Commonwealth of Massachusetts. Soma wants IHOP instead of the diner and that's probably better, anyway — I feel weird about strolling in after leaving a twenty as tip. Looking back, that's the kind of tip you'd leave for a hooker or something, not a waitress. As far as I know, anyway. It's not like I'm too familiar with the going rate for hookers.

"What's on the agenda?" Soma's got about six silver-dollar pancakes stuffed in his mouth. Lately, my instincts have veered to CIA-level security, but I try to fight that. Last night hangs between us like a rope bridge between platforms on the freshman campout. I mean we got somewhere. And I don't want to be completely stranded with secrets again.

"Buying some spray paint. Calling a girl."

"Calling a girl? What girl? Are you going to spray-paint her?"

"Uh-uh. The spray paint and the girl are two separate projects."

"What girl?" This gets a gulp out of me. It's a toss-up, just how much to tell him. But if I don't tell someone eventually, Jade's going to stop being real to me.

"Mrs. Larson's daughter." Try to say it with a shrug, as if I don't expect it to be interesting.

"How the fuck did you meet Mrs. Larson's daughter?" The pair of senior citizens on the other side of the plastic partition peer through a fake fern at us. Soma lowers his voice to a hiss. "I thought she was a lesbian."

Thank God that wasn't just some dream I had. "I know. But no. She's not."

"How did you meet her? Wait. Have you actually met her? Tell me you're not just stalking her on the Internet. Dude — you can't do that with faculty kids." He says it like I've made some kind of habit of that.

"No. I met her. She's amazing." I don't know what's okay to say. Gentlemanly and crap. "We . . . she and I —"

"You banged her?" Soma shrieks it. The fern rustles again and the woman on the other side starts bitching to her husband how it takes a village to raise a child.

"No! No, that's not what I said. Jesus — can you lower your voice?" Clearly, this was a mistake. "Forget it." In my head, I hear Jade's cold voice. *I don't want to meet your friends.* "Just forget it. I shouldn't have mentioned it. Just my own fantasy world."

"Are you kidding? You and Mrs. Larson — that's now imprinted on my eyelids." Soma's got that gleam in his eye, like he's already planning out how to turn this into a comic book.

"Not Mrs. Larson — her daughter. *Her daughter!*" I'm trying to explain myself to a kid who smears butter on his pancakes with a sausage link.

"Yeah, well, how much does she look like Mrs. Larson? She's her daughter, right? That's genetics." Soma says the word like he invented the concept.

"Jade's her daughter. Not her miniature clone."

"That's her name? Only an art teacher would name her kid something like Jade."

"Whatever, SOMA." My plate's cleared so all I can do is stare at it and wish I could rewind back to silence.

"Soma is a chosen name. And it has great literary significance. Maybe when I'm older, I'll go back to Francis. So, okay, where did you meet her?" But this is the part of the story I wanted to keep for myself, anyway. There's just no explanation that's not going to cost every other secret along with it. So I go the only way I can — a fake rage that at least lets me escape answering.

"No. Forget it. I should never have mentioned it."

"What? Because I made a little fun of her name? Come on, Emil. Where'd you see her? Had to be at school, right? Because otherwise how would you know she was Mrs. Larson's kid?"

I argue because otherwise he's on to me. "Um . . . her last name is Larson? And that's not so common, so then I asked her if her mom taught at Caramoor." It sounds plausible to me. Except for the rarity of the name Larson part. But still, it's all probably more believable than what really happened, with Jade and me both using campus as some kind of refugee camp. "She's really —" I can't figure out the right word. Everything I think of sounds like one of Dad's old Beach Boys records. "I was really scared to talk to her. And she made it worth it and then she made it easy." That's honest, anyway.

It gets a sage nod from Soma. "That's why you've been spending so much time at the diner." He's so sure of everything. Even the crap that he makes up in his own head. "She's a waitress." I don't have to lie or even bother nodding really. Just make eye contact and let him run with it. So by the time we settle up the bill, Jade is a waitress at the diner who has to work part-time to help pay for tuition at Saint Helen's Academy, because her mom wanted her in private school and everyone knows that teachers don't really make big salaries. And probably her dad's involved in the visual arts, also, and just hasn't really broken through the small gallery scene yet. He decides that she's our age, but a few months younger, and I've been walking her home from work at night, since neither of us has our license yet.

"You're amazing," I tell him, and mean it. Except Soma thinks I'm talking about accuracy. It's the same with the spray paint. Taking Amtrak to Boston and spelling out a postcard for Ethan on park asphalt makes sense, but that's Soma's plan, not mine. It's like he imagines some unbelievable scenario and then convinces himself that just thinking it made it come true. "So after this, let's go to the hardware store and you can teach me how to buy spray paint," I say.

"I cannot fathom how you managed to skip that necessary educational milestone. It's un-American. That's what you should tell your dad about when he gets home. Ask him why he went to Vietnam just to raise his kid as some kind of commie bastard."

"Yep. Vandalism is the American way."

"Nah, that's not it. More like brotherhood is a noble cause." Soma figures out the check and puts down his money. I pay mine and triple the tip. He leaves the tip on the table and picks up the rest to pay at the register. "See — you're more concerned with tipping now because you've got some waitress tangled in your jock."

In the hardware store, Soma gets the old coot behind the counter jawing on about model rocketry. We spend about half an hour at the counter and end up buying cardboard tubing and plastic parachute material just to convince him, but the man's actually kind of a sweet old guy. He gives us a twenty percent discount on everything — including the three cans each of black and red spray paint.

We're on our way out the door when Soma spins on his heel and heads back to the counter. "On behalf of the Caramoor Model Rocketry Society, sir, I just want to thank you for your generosity and understanding." God. He always has to press this crap. It can't just be normal life — Soma has to turn it into theater. He thinks I'm going all the way to Boston, though, so it's not all his fault that now the store guy knows a student affiliated with Caramoor Academy just bought a six-pack of spray paint.

"Man, Francis — why do you gotta lie to this guy?" Both their eyes swing to me. Give the man my best *aw, shucks* smile and say, "I'm sorry, sir — Frankie's just afraid of school rivalry trouble — we go to the Solebury School. We compete against Caramoor, though, and they always beat us in tournaments."

We're outside less than a minute and Soma's at my heels asking, "What the hell? You are one paranoid asswipe. You think that guy's about to call up Dr. Watkins and announce that we stopped in there for some spray paint? You think dude's going to remember us in five minutes?"

He's right, of course. But it sort of sucks that when he lies, it's an exercise in slickness. When I do it, it's a symptom of early onset schizophrenia. "I just didn't want to worry about it later." Soma nods at that. He knows how I'll latch on to some tiny trouble and then stay with it. It's like I get on this weird, anxious loop and then can't shake myself free.

"Yeah, I hear that." Soma unlocks the door with the remote on his key chain. "You turned me into a liar, though. That old guy was ready to adopt me. Speaking of foster parenting, you should come to my house for dinner."

"No way." Lots of reasons for that: 1) I have to get back up to campus, 2) Soma's family freaks me out, and 3) Mrs. Sancio's going to just try and stuff me full of weirdo organic food and then interrogate me about where I've been for the past few days. None of these count as alluring. "Your sister scares me."

"Yeah, yeah. We keep her in restraints at the dinner table now." It says something about Soma's family that I'm not entirely sure that he's joking. "You just want to eat dinner at the diner."

"It's like you're psychic or something."

"Are you going to call her?"

"So have a good night. I'll be online later."

"Are you? Because you should probably think through what you're going to say. Maybe even practice. Call me later if you want to practice."

"Thanks for plowing the driveway."

"Are you going to ask her over? Dude, your dad's away. You should totally ask her over."

"And thanks for the ride to the hardware store."

Soma's just about frothing at the mouth now, leaning out the window, shouting after me, "Maybe we should go get some condoms?" Now he's playing it up for the neighbors. "If you end up killing her, call me. I love you like a brother, man. I will ALWAYS help you get rid of the bodies."

CHAPTER 22

I pick up the phone to dial Jade and end up calling my dad's cell instead. A little twisted, but his voice mail is exactly what I'd hoped for. My dad's voice sounds reassuring. It's meant to calm down clients, I think. *This is Philip Simon and I'm waiting for your message. Please leave your name and telephone number so that I can return your call.* I doubt Dad's waiting for my message, and honestly, I don't have anything new to say. "It's Emil — I just wanted to check in and, um, let you know I was home, in case Mrs. Sancio said I wasn't or something." That's probably a mistake. Too early to joke around about it. "I mean, I'm sorry about yesterday. Hope your trip is going well and all that."

So there's my second scariest call of the day. The other one can wait until I'm up at Caramoor. The sidewalks to town are mostly clear. It's like the whole neighborhood has been shoveling. In town, the walkways are salted and sanded, but climbing up the hill to school is pretty much an experiment in the absence of traction. I should have put on skis or something. It feels like I land on my ass about every fifth step or so.

It surprises me a little that the school isn't plowed. The road outside looks fine, but once I'm through the gates, it's a whole different story. There are veins of footprints running out from Ainsley House, with one thick artery back and forth to the main gated entrance. Check the treads of my boots and figure they all have to be mine. I don't know — it just seems like they would have wanted to get the paths and the parking lots cleared for school tomorrow. It'll be dark soon and I'm no groundskeeping expert but it seems like that would only complicate the job.

And it means that there's no place for Jade to park, should she just randomly stop by. It's a lame excuse, but it's what propels me up the hill to the front door of Ainsley. The whole time I shake the snow out of my boots and shed about three layers of clothing — while I push up the thermostat and dig the number out of my pocket it seems like a perfectly reasonable excuse to call someone. Considerate even.

The first number yields nothing but a cranky, older lady who sort of wheezes out every time she speaks. "Jade? No, why would Jade be here? No Jade here." It's not broken English, it's more like uncertain English. Like she's so old there's actually nothing in the world she's sure about.

"I'm terribly sorry to interrupt your afternoon, ma'am. I must have misdialed." I should open a nursing home or something. Between the shaky-voice lady and the hardware store owner, I'm a regular old folks charmer today. She's kind of squawking a little, so I just say, "Thank you for your time," and set the phone down gently, like that stops it from counting as hanging up on her.

So the second number has to be Jade's. Actually, that's not really true. If I were a teacher, I wouldn't list my number — even if I were a ceramics teacher.

I stall for a little bit by running upstairs and checking on the attic. Then make myself a cup of hot cocoa and microwave some popcorn. Then I take a piss. Then I sit back down at the receptionist's desk to dial again.

She picks up on the second ring. At first, though, I think it's the wrong number again, because she sounds like she's thirty-five and I know it's not her mom, because Mrs. Larson always talks in this hippie, happy singsong voice. "Is Jade there?" My voice sounds as shaky as the elderly lady's.

"Yes? Is this Emil?"

She sounds confused and sort of annoyed so it's tempting at first to just say no. I could try and sell her a magazine subscription or something. A calendar. Or I could tell her it's Jason on the phone. I've finished my electronic music symphony and named it after the silky place behind her ear. "Emil? Is that you?"

Now she sounds a little frightened and panicked. Jesus. I'm a moron. "It's me. Hey. How are you? It's Emil."

"What are you doing?" So already this isn't really going so well. I vaguely remember calling girls in middle school. You could pretend you needed the homework and then get started talking about how the class sucked and then hope the girl came up with something more interesting than her love of roller skating or unicorns.

"I was just checking in." I really didn't expect her to be annoyed that I called. Then again, it's not like she's going to win the easygoing-girl pageant or anything.

"Did you call my grandmother?" Oh. Crap. Don't know why that's so embarrassing, but the back of my neck goes hot all of a sudden. If I look up and check myself out in the mirror above the fireplace, I know I'm going to be bright red.

"I didn't really hang up on her."

"What? You hung up on her?"

"What did she say?" Trust some old bat to skip over the whole nuance of setting the phone down gently and run and tattle to her gorgeous granddaughter that I hung up on her nattering ass.

"Emil — she said someone from Mom's work called looking for me. She was totally confused and hysterical. She thought it meant my mother was in some kind of kiln accident or something."

I have this image of Grandma Larson in a gypsy shawl, answering the phone and gazing into a crystal ball attached to the phone jack or something. "Well, how did she know where I was calling from?" Just one thing. One part of this, God could make easy.

"Well, we gave Grandma this crazy futuristic gadget called caller ID. And it surprised her a little when Caramoor Academy flashed across the digital screen."

"Really? That's what it says?"

"Yeah. And I know that," Jade says pointedly, "because that's what it says on the one over here." Okay. So her attitude is a little earned. My heart skids around a little in my chest. Picture how I would have handled it if Mrs. Larson answered and saw that I was calling from inside the closed school. Probably I would not have handled that at all. I'd be buying a train ticket to Boston.

"I'm really glad it's you, then. Who picked up." Who now lives in my head. "And I hope it was okay to call information. The first one was a wrong number. I mean, I didn't mean to call your grandmother." I gulp back some hot cocoa for my dry mouth and end up scalding my tongue. It's like God hates me.

"Yeah. I figured that out." Silence. "I'm glad you called."

"Well, it's not plowed here. And so I figured I should call and tell you not to drive up. For some reason they haven't plowed yet. I didn't want you to get stuck."

"So you're calling from Caramoor to tell me that you're there but you don't think I should be?" She's using the babysitter voice again. But at least it's the hot babysitter voice. And not the elderly nanny or her grandmother.

"Yeah, is that weird?" I figure from now on, I should just ask. After all, I'm going to agonize about it for hours, anyway. Might as well get her feedback first.

"Yeah, but also sweet. You should take my number. And next time you want to tell me to stay home, call me on the cell phone." Jade gives me her number and I write it down in two places. Keep both sheets of paper even after I feed it into my phone under the name HER. "What are you doing there, anyway?"

I don't really know how to answer that. Probably it's still not okay that half the time I'm here just in case she is. "Just checking up on the place. Making sure it's still standing and all."

"Emil — did you WALK up there? In the snow? From where I dropped you?" It feels different when Jade acts all concerned about me than, say, the school secretary. I guess that's not particularly shocking. "I can't believe you. You're crazy." Her voice is soft like, if she were in front of me, this would be one of those times when she'd reach out to touch my arm or something.

"If it was plowed — do you think you'd come out — I mean, I'd totally understand if the other night was some weird kind of aberration for you or something." God, I'm a pansy. But I can't make myself stop. "I wouldn't expect there to be any — I mean, it would be great to see you either way, no matter what."

When Jade laughs, at least it doesn't sound like when girls laugh at me in my dreams before they turn into jackals. It's sort of sweet. "I would definitely come out. My parents are lunatics. My dad rented all these *Star Trek* movies and he's making me sit through them." Okay. So I'm more alluring than William Shatner. I don't know why I'm so disappointed. Maybe nothing

Jade says would be enough for me. But then she keeps going. "And if I were there, you could keep me warm."

That's pretty much enough. "Yeah." That's all I have to offer back on that one. "So I'm going to go." And go up to my attic bed and replay that in my head for a while. Stop myself from saying that part, but something in Jade's laugh tells me she knows exactly what I'm thinking.

"Okay, then, Emil — careful who you call from that phone. And if you get stuck and need a ride, you could call me from town, you know." I did not know that.

"So many perks to chasing older women."

"I'll talk to you later."

"Unless I decide to call your grandma instead."

After we hang up I feel wild-eyed, like I have an extra pint of blood coursing through me. Run around and check to make sure all the trophies are still on top of the urinals. Go upstairs and lounge around the attic for a little bit. It's strange to stride by all the closed doors to the offices and not want to unlock them. But there's not a whole lot that I want to know anymore. Not here, anyway.

I doze off a little upstairs and wake up to the growl and thrum of machinery outside. See that it's night and it looks like every white maintenance truck has been outfitted with its own plow. It's like a brigade of steel blades carving their way through campus. For a second, I wonder if anyone found my little message to the world stamped into the snow. And then I remember that these guys are cold and working hard and probably not so fascinated by my self-indulgent footprints. I sit with my elbows on the sill and watch like I'm little again, staring out into the snow on Christmas Eve.

It's ten thirty by the time it's quiet enough for me to risk turning on a flashlight. I wander around Ainsley, making sure to gather up empty packets of hot cocoa and Styrofoam cups. Lower the thermostat. And make sure that I lock the door behind me. Right before leaving campus for the night, I let myself into Miss Gabaldon's room and write, *Ben Hendrikson doesn't deserve you* across the chalkboard. Which is, admittedly, fairly childish, but I tell myself that it's a gesture on behalf of Soma and so I let it slide.

I trudge home and waver a little bit in front of the diner, considering hot soup and buttered bread. I could even call Jade and get a ride back to the house. But then I picture pulling up into the drive and having to figure out if I'm supposed to invite her inside. And then what room do I lead her toward? Where do I have her sit?

I let myself off the hook with the thought that it isn't my last chance to have her over. Even before Dad comes back and chains me to the radiator for last night's debacle, I still have Tuesday night. So I wuss out. Tell myself that the phone call went well and that it's probably better to just revel in that for a night. That she'll be in the Arts Studio tomorrow night. I can meet her there, maybe ask her to get something to eat with me. That's a plan.

By the time I've let myself into the house, I have myself convinced that I am a lady-killing genius who's going to be getting some all night long tomorrow. No one's on the answering machine and it doesn't look like we had any mail delivered at all. So much for the neither-rain-nor-snow-nor-sleet crap. I stand in the living room and look around, trying to see how the house might look to Jade. It doesn't have the historical grandeur of Ainsley House, but it's not so bad.

I already straightened up a lot for Mrs. Sancio, so it's not really a matter of the place being clean. More like woman-friendly. It means hiding the framed school picture of me with silver braces splitting open my face. And making sure there aren't any sweaty socks stuffed between the sofa cushions. Beer cans beside the recliner. That kind of stuff. Check around for a bottle of wine that I could open if I needed to. Change the sheets on my bed, just in case.

I tell myself that it makes sense to sleep in Ethan's room because of the fresh sheets on my bed. For the sake of preservation or whatever. In the back of my mind, maybe I just figure that I can soak up some of Ethan's masculine superpowers by sleeping in his room. This is supposed to be the silver lining of having a big brother. All the times he tickled me until I pissed my pants, the kidney punches and embarrassing nicknames, all the wedgies were supposed to at least pay off for some brotherly wisdom later on in life. *Later on* meaning now. And the brotherly wisdom meaning sex stuff. Not how to do it. I've seen pornos. It's more that I want to ask him what not to do. Rules and courtesies and that kind of crap. Really, I just miss him. By now, the cleaning lady's probably changed his linens a bunch of times since he took off, anyway. But it calms me a little bit, to lie down in bed and stare at my brother's ceiling instead of my own. Like maybe there are answers there before that only he got to see.

I fall asleep to one of Ethan's old French rock records playing and wake up to my alarm clock sounding distantly across the hall. Today I dress out of his closet — put on one of his long T-shirts under a short-sleeved shirt. Take his black tie that has silver kung fu guys all over it. I don't look bad. I'd do me.

For no other reason than boredom with my own reflection, I

take a pair of scissors to my hair and snip away at the shaggier parts. Mostly on the top and sides. It's hard to make it even, so I go shorter than I meant to trying to fix it. It looks . . . ungood. I tell myself that I needed some raw edges and at least now it appears to be a choice. And then go to get a wool beanie out of Ethan's top drawer, put it in my back pocket.

"Man — what did you do to your hair?" Apparently, it's noticeable. When Soma comes over, he immediately grabs my head with his hand and pulls it down to examine the top and sides.

"I cut it. A little bit is all. Needed a change." And Soma sort of ruffles it up top some.

"It's not terrible." This is either high praise or just Soma's version of extraordinary kindness. "You got a hat?" So the beanie goes on my head pretty quickly.

"Seriously, Emil. It doesn't look so bad. Just different. You ready for the lit quiz?" The world has really turned over on its side if Soma's checking up on my study habits. All of a sudden he's the responsible one.

"I read the book."

"Dude, you're on smack. It's on both books — two of them." And that's how the whole day goes. The snow's almost melted down, but it still bothers me to see everyone else trampling all over campus like they own the place. All my carefully measured footprints are pretty much just an enormous smear in the snow. The trophies make a minor stir, but are pretty much forgotten by sixth period. So much for my key mastermind skills. By the time the last bell rings, I'm beat. Not tired, just sort of beaten down. I'd planned to stay at school and lift weights or something in case I managed to get Jade to touch my arms, but campus feels too hot. It's making me itch.

In town, I go into the diner for coffee and wander around the shops along the main drag. Get some wrapping paper at the card store — a kid's pattern with ice-cream cones instead of some pink valentine kind that will only torment me about how Jade might interpret that. In the drugstore, I buy some smelly body wash. According to the plastic bottles, it looks like the choice is between smelling like a new car or an over-muscled sailor. I go with the sailor because I figure girls like the ocean.

There's a little gourmet shop that sells cheese and sausage and weird kinds of ravioli with fillings like squash or goose or whatever. I choose a bunch of different kinds of chocolates that I can put in the back of the refrigerator and pretend to have just found them lying around. No hearts.

At home, all the purchases set down on the counter spell out one thing: I'm whipped. And damaged in some crucial part of my brain. I spent money on soap that's going to make me smell like the old man and the sea. Candy for a girl who I don't even have set plans to see tonight. My hair looks weird and I'm wearing someone else's clothes.

But I get in the shower, anyway, and suds up with the crazy sailor soap. Put back on the same clothes and work some shiny stuff into my hair. I look well-scrubbed and smell less like stale coffee and Taco Bell. So I'm ready. Wrap up the Ghost-Hunting Society photograph and think about writing something on the paper, but I can't think of anything besides crap like *For Jade, my partner in crime* or *Jade, my favorite hunting partner*. And from there it goes straight to sexual partner and that makes me choke on my own tongue.

CHAPTER 23

Turns out that I didn't have to write anything. Jade totally gets it. I've never made anyone squeal about a present before, and she does. Even though I totally screw up the actual handoff, because by the time I get back to school and pace around the campus for a while until the Arts Studio lights go on, my mouth is so dry, it feels like I smoked three bowls and ate a block of salt for dinner. Can't really talk so instead I just hand over the wrapped frame. At first Jade kind of steps back and I think I've blown it, but she shakes more of her hair loose and says sort of uncertainly, "I didn't get you anything. . . ."

And then I have to find a way to speak because she looks so embarrassed and tentative. "No — it's just that I found it and just thought you'd like it. Like it already belonged to you or something." God. I suck at this stuff. "Just open it, will you?" It comes off like I'm pissed off. I lack all charm. But then she does tear it open and lets loose a squeal like a little kid getting a cone of cotton candy and if I had enough guts or upper body strength I'd swoop her up into my arms.

"So this is a valentine?" Jade steps toward me and presses one of her hands against my chest, right on my collarbone. I don't know what the right answer is.

"I didn't see any hearts on the wrapping paper." Or balls on myself.

"Right. Well, I really love it. Where did you get it? God, you just own this place, don't you? You just haven't wanted to tell me because that means you sort of own my mom." Jade says this and bites her lip a little, kind of laughing. And I make myself take the risk of reaching for her. Catch her wrist and at first I worry that it comes off as too rough, but she tilts her head up. Bend to kiss her and feel her hand press harder against me, like she's pushing me away and tugging me toward her at the same time.

"Are you ready to take a break?" Ask her like that's a completely casual question.

"Well — I just got here so — I guess I could just not settle down to work tonight?"

"Oh — you just got here?"

"Yeah — I figured you had been stalking around outside, waiting for the lights to go on." Jade's on to me.

"No way — I just came straight from working out."

"Dressed like that? In a tie?"

"Yep."

"Emil?" I'm preparing myself to hear her tell me I'm just too creepy. That she tried to make herself see past the awkward pauses and my inability to tell her the truth about basic informational tidbits, like my name. But that I'm too young and, honestly, she's just too hot — she's going to go back to Bard and major in fellating sculptors.

"Yeah?" Brace myself. Brace myself.

"Happy Valentine's Day." And she kisses me again. So, yeah, happy Valentine's Day, indeed.

She makes things easy, the way she always seems to make things easy. Asks me where we should go get something to eat. When I tell her that most nights I stop by the diner, Jade rushes to get her jacket on as if I just mentioned reservations to some hotshot after-party. She wins over our waitress and orders spaghetti and meatballs and tells me that we should eat like the dogs do in *Lady and the Tramp*. We talk to each other. If it were a real restaurant and not an all-night diner, we could have closed the place down. She lets me pay and that's officially the first time I've bought a girl dinner. Because Soma doesn't count.

We get back in her car and Jade drives to my place like it's the most natural thing in the world, like this happens all the time. There's a minute in the driveway that's tense because she puts the car in park, but doesn't kill the engine. "We have wine in the house. I know you said you're not so into that anymore, but if you wanted to smoke a bowl . . ."

"Why, Emil, I'd just figured you'd put a roofie in my root beer." Jade looks over at me and squints in the dark. "You're aiming to get me into some kind of altered state, aren't you?"

"That was the idea, yes."

"Okay." And she keeps saying that. Okay to the candy I find in the fridge, to a glass of wine, okay to checking out the milk crate of the records that I pretend are mine. Okay to putting on a record from some dude whose name I can't pronounce and believing me when I say it's my favorite. And then okay to sitting on my bed and lying back and letting me unbutton and unwrap and unfasten things. When she tugs my tie and both the shirts over my head and reaches to touch the key dangling from my neck, I shake my head instead of explaining. And even then Jade says, "Okay." And when I can't stop shaking and one of my legs trembles so much that I think it's some kind of seizure, that's okay, too. And she lets me fumble around and find the way to move and then she shows me how to make it okay for her, too. And maybe even better than that. Once in a while she sounds a little like it's better than okay.

We sleep together. I mean we do the other stuff, too, and that's unbelievable. I understand how people write songs about sex and manuals on it. I get why people buy it. And why people tell you not to have it. Because, I mean, there doesn't seem to be any point to doing anything else afterward. But later when I let myself calm down and stop staring at her and shocking myself, I wake up with my limbs tangled up with Jade's and her loosened braid wrapped around my fingers. And her eyes flicker under their lids and when I shift a little bit, Jade closes her hand around one of the sheets and bunches it in her fist.

The next time my eyes open, the naked girl in my bed is sifting through the sheets. "This is the shameful part — looking for the rest of my clothes." She's got on her shirt and one sock. I see her getting ready to leave and am flattened by grief. So weird that this feels like the biggest loss of this year. Try to pull her back down toward me, but Jade's wide-awake. "I can't just stay out. You want me to tell my mom you were earning some extra art credits or something?"

I can tell by her face that when I speak, nothing coherent comes out, but what I mean is between something shabby like "Thank you" and "I worship you." Probably telling a girl you worship her is a mistake, though. Even in bed.

"Go back to sleep. You have school."

"I thought that *was* school." And that gets a laugh from Jade — the kind I like, the one that ends with a snort. "My dad comes home today." I say it and pretty much freak when I hear it out loud. Sit straight up in bed and move to find my clothes like his plane is due to land at dawn in the living room. Jade just shoves me back down and tousles my hair a little.

"Well, go back to sleep for now. And call me when you can see me." She looks at me steadily, like maybe she's memorizing me, too. "Emil, it's going to be okay. Close your eyes now." And I do, and fall asleep without seeing her back in my doorway. Barely hear the front door close or Jade's car start up and pull away.

When the alarm goes off, I have to spend a whole snooze session convincing myself that it happened just like it did. Get in the shower and feel a little insane thinking about the fact that the last person to touch my body wasn't me. When Soma pulls up, I sprint out before he can even hit the horn. I fully expect him to see something on my face, but he just looks at me a little strangely. "The hair's not really that bad, you know." And that's it, pretty much. Either he's forgotten that last night was Valentine's Day or he thinks I made up Jade, too.

All day, it feels like the last of something. Sitting there at the different desks, shuffling through the school day, but my body's all charged weird with stray volts of Jade, and in my head, I'm practicing my side of a never-ending argument with my father. In each class, I listen to the taps of chalk against the blackboard, but my head is already swarming with too much. I spend the entire seven hours bristling, the hair on my arms rising and settling, alternating between feeling high from last night's thrill and dulled by this morning's dread.

If growing up in our house gave Ethan and me one superpower, it's the eerie sonic ability both of us have to hear my father's car turn into our street and pull into the drive. We can both hear it, the way that bats hear avalanches stirring up or whatever. But it turns out that kind of power doesn't translate to campus. When the bell rings and I join the river of guys flooding down the steps and into the quad, I float along with Soma toward his car until he's the one who stops short.

"Tell him about the girl," he says somberly as if he's enlightening me spiritually or providing me with an option I haven't already considered and discarded about twenty times since my dad's last chilly phone call two days ago. Soma brushes off my shoulders and slaps my back like I'm a fighter he's letting loose in the ring. "Don't let him smell fear. But also — avoid outright defiance. Try to reason with him." Dad's sedan is parked first in the circle, which probably means he got here early and has been waiting in the car. Stewing. He waves at us. The passenger side window eases down and Dad nods and says, "Soma," in the way he must greet people at sales conferences.

"Welcome back, Mr. Simon. I bet you're glad you missed the snow." Soma is a kiss-ass, but right now he's working it on my behalf. "I'll talk to you later, Emil. Gonna need your help on that chem lab." A little over the top there, bucko. My father's been gone nine days; it's not like he's woken up from a five-month coma. Even if he had been in a coma, he still wouldn't buy that anyone would ask me for chemistry help.

We do the thing where I say, "Hey, Dad," and he nods and asks how school was. If I'd prepared myself more, I would have some epic story to launch into. Something he'd find funny or at least interesting enough for a distraction. But all I come up with is "Fine." A regular showstopper. Look around the car and say, "Your luggage is back there — you must have come straight from the airport."

"I had a car drop me off at the office, and then picked up mine at the garage." Fascinating. I'm in the middle of nodding furiously when he continues with the kicker — "I would have just waited for Soma to drop you off at home, but I wasn't sure if you'd actually arrive." One gauntlet. Thrown down.

I guess that there's a point where you've screwed up enough that you just have to sit there and take it. I mean, it's not like there's a whole lot for me to say. He wants me to ask, "What?" and let him keep going. So that's what I do.

"'What?'" he repeats. "Well, we can start with the idea that when you assured me that you could stay at home alone, I assumed it was understood that you would actually be staying at home. I didn't consider that you might just be checking in once in a while, like someone hired to water the plants. That's certainly not what you led me to believe. Not beforehand. Not in the many voice mails you left or messages with Lori. Am I wrong here, Emil? Am I mistaken?"

"No, sir." Outside, the snowbanks blur past. I've never wished so hard to be walking through the freezing wind before.

"You have some explaining to do." It's probably poor form to ask how much explaining. I don't know how much my dad knows, how he knows I wasn't at the house in the first place. We pull onto our street and his face doesn't register. He's like chiseled stone, immovable, beside me.

"I don't know where to begin, sir." That's as honest as I can afford to be right now. The row of square windows across the garage door look like lenses. For one bizarre second, I picture Dad setting up webcams around the house, keeping tabs on me from his laptop. That wouldn't hold with all his talk about privacy and personal liberty. I almost try to face him down with that crap, but decide that launching an offense is a lost cause at this point. When he gets out of the car, he heads to the side door of the house without looking back at me. I could run if I wanted to. He doesn't take his luggage out of the car so maybe he's the one planning to desert.

Dad lurches around the first floor of the house as if he's looking for someone. Probably it's too much to expect him to be pleased that I cleaned the place up. He sits down at the kitchen table and kicks out the chair across from him. This sucks balls. He's going to make me sit across from him and look him in the eye, while we both know I'm going to be trying to tell him as little as possible.

"You can begin by telling me where you were in the middle of the night. On Wednesday. Thursday. Saturday. Sunday. And by Sunday, I mean last Sunday. In the middle of a blizzard."

"In the middle of the night." Now I'm back to thinking, *webcam?* Looking around the kitchen for blinking red lights. And freaking out.

"I realize that you left messages. And seem to have checked the answering machine. But when I first called late at night, Emil, I didn't see the need to leave messages. I figured you'd spent the night at Soma's. It wasn't until Mrs. Sancio was kind enough to call me when she couldn't get in touch with you that I realized those assumptions were in error and perhaps my trust was misplaced."

"Oh." It's something I honestly never thought of. That he'd call the landline so often. He and I never call each other on the landline. Pretty much the only reason would be to check up on me. Which is, apparently, exactly what he was doing.

"Where were you? Emil, are you in some kind of trouble?" I don't know what he expects me to say to that — what counts as trouble. I can't just come clean. He wouldn't buy it at first and I'd have to show him the key. And when I did, it's not like he would simply nod and watch me tuck it back under my shirt. He would take it. I'd be the asstard who not only never managed to pull off any kind of real key prank, but ended up getting the key confiscated. Lost it for good and killed off the whole tradition along with it. "Is there a girl?"

"Yeah, there is." It's not a lie. "I snuck off to spend time with her." Again, technically accurate. "I'm sorry if I misled you. It didn't seem like — I just didn't think it would turn out to be such a big deal."

"How could it not be a big deal? You are sixteen years old. And I've got poor Mrs. Sancio on the phone, apologizing for whatever rift there must be between you and her kid. Because why else would you hole yourself up in that big empty house instead of spending the nights at their house —"

"I'm sorry if I offended Mrs. Sancio." Dad's fist slams down on the table and the saltshaker clinks to its side. Bad luck all around.

"This is not about Mrs. Sancio. Do you realize I was calling home in the middle of the night? And getting the answering machine? And was halfway across the country?" Now he's reached a roar. "And that I did not know where you were?"

"Why is that such a big deal?" When my voice erupts, it does so with more force than either of us expected. Dad and I both look sort of startled at each other. Toward the end, my voice cracks a little, so it's not like I've maintained any kind of dignity. I figure I might as well go all out at this point. "You don't know where Ethan is. It's been months, it's like he doesn't even exist. So why should it matter where I'm at? And it didn't really.

You said it yourself — you were across the country — it's not like you came running home."

"So that's what this is about? Some brainless bid for attention. You wanted to see that you mattered. Never mind my business, never mind that you're sixteen years old. God forbid that I expect you to pull some weight around here. You don't need to tell me how hard this year has been. Do you think that when I thought about raising a family, when I thought about raising children, that this is what I imagined? What your mother and I imagined? Get your head out of your ass, Emil. You are not the only one who's lost your mother."

"Well, I'm the only one who's seemed to notice." It's as if the whole room goes cold or something frozen settles over the house. Like outside, a huge cloud just passed in front of the sun. Dad goes completely still, except for the red vein at his temple that begins to pulse. I don't know how to turn things back. It's like the moment right before I turned the key at the front gate of Caramoor. Everything is about to shift and change a little. Except there's nothing here that I actually want to unlock and know about. I don't want my father to unleash all the fury that's flushing his face so red. I keep talking, try to explain myself. "And you keep saying that I'm sixteen. What about Ethan? How old do you think nineteen is? What if he's hurt somewhere or strung out or just hit his head and doesn't know who he is or how to call? What about money — what's he living on? He's in Boston. Did you know he was in Boston? Did you check with the police there —"

"Did you speak to your brother?" That's what he finally interrupts me to ask. Of everything, that's what my dad is so weirdly angry about. "Did he call here? Emil, you have to tell me the truth now. Have you been in contact with Ethan?" I don't get it. It's like he's angrier at the idea that Ethan might have talked to me than the fact that he hasn't talked to either of us. "Has he called here?"

"No, Dad. If he called here, I would have told you. We would have gone and gotten him, right? But what if he does call? Why don't we have a trace on the phone or something? How come we haven't hired a private investigator or put up signs? Or called in the cavalry? He just takes off and we don't even try to track him down?"

"Yes. That's exactly right. A trace on the phone — what do you think this is — some kind of cop show? Your brother wants to be a man, then fine, he gets to be a man. You don't get to make that choice yet." This has him on his feet now. Dad's opening and shutting the kitchen cupboards and ranting along like what he's really enraged about is that dinner isn't on the table. He's got a jar of pasta sauce on the table and taco shells and a can of cranberry sauce. Like he's going to punish me with the worst Mexican food ever. "And bear in mind that we live with the decisions we make, Emil. Ethan's living with his choices now. We are not abandoning him. He's not lost or impoverished. He's working for a living and learning what it means to be a man and to contribute something to the world. And to this family."

"You know where he is." All the fluorescent lights seem to flicker and brighten in the kitchen at once. I'm so stupid. This whole time. I think about the last days before Ethan left. How the two of them would just glare at each other. How my dad's gaze at the table was relentless, staring Ethan down. Staring him gone.

"I know that he's all right. And he knows to call here, to call me, if he isn't."

"You sent him away," I say. But really I don't actually believe that. I only mean for him to thunder on about Ethan's choices or whatever. I say it so he can argue. But he doesn't, really.

He clarifies. "Ethan and I came to a mutual understanding." Meaning: He sent Ethan away. I didn't know I could still cry like when Ethan and I used to fight and something was just so unfair that I literally couldn't swallow it. And my throat burned like it was where the hot tears began. I cried angrily and helplessly. And I cry now, angrily and helplessly. "How could you do that — didn't enough happen this year? Look at what it's like now." I want him to see the living room with what looks like a year's worth of newspapers stacked around his recliner and the recycling spilling all around the kitchen. How we're still eating off the same stupid Fourth of July place mats from back before Mom really got sick.

Dad's slumped over the counter. Before it looked like he was reading the back of the box of taco shells and now he sets them down and strides over so fast that I think he's about to hit me. But instead he sits down and sort of shakes himself out a little. Takes a deep breath. And stares at me for a second. Not like he's trying to win, but like he's trying to see something. Measuring me somehow. "There are ways that I expect you to be a man, Emil. To take responsibility for your mistakes. I expect you to hold yourself to the standards with which your mother and I raised you. To step up and be a man without dwelling on his losses. At the same time, I lost my mother when I was thirty-five. And that was hard. I can't imagine what last year was like for you. There are ways in which I want you to still have the chance to be a kid. Your mom would have wanted that, too."

"I think it's a little late for that." We're never the same temperature, my father and me. As soon he warms up, my voice goes cold.

He nods then and splays his fingers out on the table. "Your brother was home that day, Emil." He looks at me and I look at him. I don't get it. When I start to get it, I hear it coming the way you hear something approach from far away. The way you feel a train under your feet way before you actually hear the whistle or the engine. "Ethan was home, that morning, with your mother."

"Ethan went to the store." But it doesn't sound like me when I say it. It sounds like a song playing, on a radio in a room down the hall. "She made up a long grocery list because she didn't want Ethan to come home until —"

"No. That's not how it happened." In some corner, my dad's explaining it — my mom was just in too much pain. And she and Ethan were home alone together through some of the worst of it — long, dark afternoons that tunneled toward the same conclusion for both of them. And he started hoarding her pain meds. That he'd researched options. The two of them — Ethan and Mom — had discussed them and decided. And my father didn't know until Ethan called him at work and told him she was gone.

My dad's still talking but I'm remembering Ethan with rolling papers on his lap, licking and sealing a joint for our mom. Or standing beside her on the sofa with pills in his hand and the dutiful glass of water. I keep catching glimpses of my father trying to make it make sense. Tune in to hear him say, "Ethan made a decision he still stands by. Unfortunately, it was not his decision to make. And I don't want to sleep with him under this roof." I wonder how long my dad's been practicing all the parts of this speech, how many golf balls he's launched onto the driving range figuring out the words.

I get bits and pieces. Ethan's in Boston and he's not allowed to contact me. Dad keeps track of him by credit card charges. He's taking classes at some arts league. Renting a room in a four-bedroom share. I don't know that I care anymore. It's not that I'm angry. It's February. My mom would be dead by now no matter what. Maybe what I feel is sort of robbed. And untrusted. It's like no one's said anything to me that's counted for months. I wish I'd told Jade that my mom died and that I'd never mentioned to her that I had a brother.

It registers that Dad's stopped talking only because his mouth stays shut for a couple of straight minutes. I tell him I'm going to go to bed now. And he tells me that it's not even five thirty, but he doesn't stop me from standing up and moving toward the stairs. I've got my hand on the banister, on the dark, shiny spot where all of us have held on to the wood.

"Emil." My dad's voice is commanding. It stops me right there and for a minute I think he's remembered that he wants to know where I've been sleeping. After everything, he's going to make me tell him that. But he says, "We're going to get through this, you know. All of us. We just need some time."

He says it like he's sure of it, but when I turn back up the steps he's still nodding to himself, standing by the front door like he's waiting for a car to pull in the drive.

CHAPTER 24

I wake up panicking because the alarm hasn't rung and at first I figure that I'm in the attic at Ainsley House. That's how screwed up everything is lately. I just assume I'm hidden in the attic at school. But it's my bed with my blankets, and my alarm clock on the bookcase reads 1:30 AM. For a second I can even see Jade's hair curling against the pillow and then I'm up, moving around in my room without remembering the heart-to-heart from hell with Dad.

It's when I'm tying up my boots that it hits me that he's home now and I probably shouldn't thump all the way down the steps. And then I remember that my brother helped my mom kill herself. So probably I can sneak out tonight without any major ramifications. I grab the plastic bag of spray paints out from under the bed and stuff that into my backpack. And clunk downstairs and out the door.

If I were a real bad-ass, I wouldn't look back, but I stop for a moment and wait to see if my mom and dad's bedroom window lights up. The whole house stays dark, though. So I keep walking.

I thought I'd feel better once I got on campus, that it would help to be back on my own terrain, where I decide on the secrets. But it just feels empty. And when I unlock the front door of Ainsley, the key sticks, and for a second I think it's going to break off in the lock. There's a plan finally shifting and forming in my mind and now I'm going to lose the key in the front door.

I'll be the first key master in the history of the school to have managed to get the locks changed.

The roar that rises out of my throat sounds like the kind of frustrated bellow let loose by some animal in a trap. If I were a bear in the forest, with my leg in a set of iron teeth, I'd make that noise and a bunch of birds would flood up into the sky. Instead the key turns. Thank you, Ruby. I consider opening up the offices and going through Verlando's files again, rereading them to see how much he knew. But then I remember how Verlando never seemed particularly concerned about Ethan's heading off into the sunset. It was more a question of which academic program he might apply to. Semester at Sea, for christsake. I think about waiting for hours across from Dr. Watkins because Dad had to pick up Ethan. And then how it was just Dad and me closed up in the stuffy car. Neither of those guys have any answers for me. I mean, they probably had answers months ago. It's just that no one bothered to let me in on them.

So I just grab a flashlight from the attic and head back down to the grounds. The Arts Studio's dark and quiet. Jade's either been here and left or she's home getting ready to meet some guy who actually knows how to have sex. She's decided to track down my older, more practiced brother. Hell, apparently they can charge the hotel room to my dad's credit card. I'm not being fair, anywhere even close to the vicinity of fair. I know this. But I want a dollar or something for every time I worry about someone who was keeping some huge truth from me.

And I'm pissed off because I can't even get all self-righteous about it. Now that I know how it feels to be so blindsided I'm going to have to sit down with Jade and tell her all the things I lied about. At least it makes things blurrier that everyone had lied to me, too. I'm going to have to lead her through the whole laby-rinth. Here I was agonizing about telling Jade the truth about the past year and I wouldn't have even been telling the accurate truth. So, yeah, I was already a liar, but Dad and Ethan made a bigger liar of me. And Mom, too.

It's weird and hard to hate her, but for a second, right now, I do. It's not like she got some rosy end of the deal — I know that. She didn't have Ethan fake her death so that she could run away to Vegas or something. I mean, I think. Who the fuck knows at this point? And my mom probably didn't know how all the pieces would settle afterward, but she could have guessed. My dad wouldn't even let Ethan or me control the living room remote. I don't know how she convinced herself that he'd get over not controlling that. It shames me a little that I'm partly just pissed she didn't come to me. And then it shames me even more to feel this glimmer of gratitude for that. Ethan and I used to fake fight about who she loved more. We'd measure who got the bigger mound of macaroni and cheese on our plates. I don't know who comes out as the favorite — the kid who's willing to collect the pills or the one who would never let you take them.

That's the kind of question I'd like to toss toward a grave-stone. Like they do in the movies when the guy in the black suit shows up and tears at the granite marker with his fingernails and sobs, "Why? Why?" That's the kind of crap I want to pull right now. Except we don't have one of those. Maybe to prevent exactly that kind of scene.

So it's cracktard crazy, but I decide right then that I want my grieving-son moment. I want to claw at a gravestone, for christ-sakes. I march down through the lower fields like I'm going off hunting or to war — with purpose. There's the Revolutionary

War graveyard right near the quad, but now I've got it in my head that it has to be Ruby's or Fredericka's. A woman's grave. I have to find it to yell at it. Get to where I can see Cornell House and start kicking at dead leaves, stamping down the remnants of last weekend's snow. Beaming the flashlight toward the ground until it bounces across something pale against the dark trees.

It's pink, like maybe they carved it out of sandstone and it faded in the sun. I had sort of hoped that I'd find something profound written on it, like EMIL SIMON, FORGIVE YOUR MOTHER. But the engraving is mostly worn down. I figure it's Fredericka's because A) I can trace an *F* and an *R* in the top left corner, and B) it's not like there's a lot of other candidates. Closer to the ground, you can see an *H* and an *M* in there so maybe they chose to write something about Fredericka finally going home. I hope they did, anyway.

I'm kneeling on the ground for a few minutes, examining the scratches in the stone, before it sinks in that there are bones in the ground below me. Yes, that's a basic concept, but it still creeps me out. I wait it out and see if it gets to be comforting. But it doesn't. Maybe if it were actually my mom. Or maybe whatever my mother had against graves, she passed on to me.

Still, I sit there and ask a bunch of questions out loud. Just to have voiced them. Mostly about what I'm supposed to do now. My mom doesn't settle on a low tree branch in the form of an owl or anything. And Fredericka's hand bones don't scrape through the icy ground to pet me. But it helps me sort some of it out. I know Dad's going to have to let me go see Ethan. Maybe he doesn't want him to come back, but I need to talk to him.

I also figure out that I'm not really cut out for the key. I mean, plans are in place, but not for anything that will impress the jackholes at school. The truth is that someone else deserves the key, someone who's not going to break in just to borrow books from the library.

So I swear on the grave that's not my mother's that I'm giving myself two more nights with the key. And that's it. If I'm sneaking out after that, it'll be to practice my skills in the back of Jade's car. And if all else fails, we can drag a freakin' air mattress into the Arts Studio.

It takes me a little bit to figure out how to get up onto the roof of the field house. Clearly, there has to be a way because otherwise that kid Rajiv would have been stranded up there after his dad dropped him off in the family helicopter. It turns out I make the same dumb-ass mistake I did with the Ainsley House basement — spend a good half hour looking for some magic door in the ceiling of the gymnasium before it dawns on me that there's probably a ladder or something on the outside of the building.

They must have built something safer for Rajiv's landings. Because the rungs that I find bolted into the back of the building look about as safe as the ladders going up water towers. Except without the usual protective metal cage. They're also set fairly far apart, so that I kind of have to do a pull-up to get my legs up to the next rung. At least I thought to bring the backpack, so everything I need is on my back. Including the flashlight, so I pretty much have to feel my way to each bar and then strain to pull myself up.

About a quarter of the way there, I realize how far up it is. I mean, essentially I'm scaling a building. We're talking superhero antics here. There's nothing below me but sidewalk and that weird brush thing they make us scrape our cleats on. By the time I'm halfway up, my arms feel like jelly. Epileptic jelly. I try to decide if I could hold on with one arm in order to grab my cell phone out of my pocket. That would be an awesome call. *Please come quickly. Somehow I've ended up on the side of a building and am feeling a little peaked. Bring a giant net.* My dad would hang up and put me on a train to a major metropolitan area.

Soma would just pull up in the jeep and say, "Wow, man. Sucks that you ended up on the side of that building." He'd be completely unfazed and probably have a pulley system or something in the car. I keep going because it's less effort to keep punishing my arms than to wrestle my cell out of my pocket. And I'm just too afraid to throw in a complicated maneuver like dialing the phone. Some dude on campus has to come up here once in a while for his job and for his sake I hope he's seven feet tall.

When I finally reach the cement ledge of the building, I almost back up and hurl myself off it. At first it looks like the entire roof, the ground in front of me, is covered with ice and snow. Almost every other corner of campus has thawed, I think, but the one place I need to be relatively even and dry looks like there's a perfect blanket of snow. Luckily, my legs are still too rubbery to jump. Because it's just this thick tarp. Maybe a landing pad? It's weird to think a helicopter pad would actually be padded, but I guess they came up with the name somehow. It's not like there's a lot of common ground between aviation and linguistics.

At first I think I'm going to have to roll up the tarp. Which would be problematic considering my arms are so tired that I'm currently having trouble holding up the flashlight. But it doesn't come loose when I tug at it. In reality, it makes a pretty good canvas. There are a few stubborn patches of snow and I kick at those a little and then roll around across them to try to soak up the puddles. I sort of wish someone could see me now. Emil Simon: suspended for climbing up onto the field house roof, pretending to be a roll of paper towels.

I get the flashlight set up on the ledge winding around the roof, but the light's still flimsy. It's risky to wait until the sun comes up a little, but there it is. I'm just a wild beast of high stakes and dumb gambles. And that gives me a chance to think about what I'm actually going to put down there on the blank square in front of me. On the way over, I'd planned to write something brutal. Something that would make pilots flying over the school look down and cry.

The truth is, after climbing that ladder, I don't think anyone's going to see that roof for months. If not years. It just isn't that kind of key prank. More proof that I'm not cut out to serve as the king rebel of Caramoor. Which is fine. I know who should get my discarded crown. But first I'm going to pull my own key prank, one that's up here and is all mine, just for me.

Before you can see any edges of the sun rising, the sky over the river lightens. Directly above me, the night sky looks almost black and then blue around the edges. Right over the river, it goes golden and the bare branches of the trees look lit from behind. It's pretty incredible. And now at least I can see what I'm doing. I'm not exactly a graffiti god — but I want the letters to come out straight and even. Basically, the aim is a postcard, only written on the roof.

I write it out first in black and then outline it in red. Measure out the letters with my feet to make sure they all stretch to a similar height. It's mostly hard to space out the line, but I get it and straighten out some of the unevenness with the red paint in the second round. When I'm done, the Caramoor helicopter pad reads COME HOME in giant block letters.

It's not that I've huffed half the paint or anything. I don't expect my mom to come floating down from heaven. We Simons don't believe in that kind of crap. And I'm not thinking, *Wow — I hope you can see that from Boston,* either. It's more that out of everything I want said, that I would want them to hear, this's it. I just want to say that out loud somehow, to know there's a message out there that they can see from far away.

And after I pass along the key, when I go back to being just another asstard that's here from eight until three, I'll still have a piece of campus that only I'll know about. Someone might find it, some bearded giant of a roofing guy, or some ballsy kid who decides to rappel off the top of the field house or something, but he won't know how it got there. Or what exactly it means or who it's written to.

Descending the ladder, I ease my way along carefully, reminding myself that if I didn't fall off climbing up I probably won't manage to kill myself easing my way down. But the whole time I expect to step back into air. I can see it so clearly. One of the coaches will find me on my back, probably only paralyzed so that I have to die a slow death knowing that everyone thinks I tried to off myself by taking a header off the top of the field house. Some jackhole will come and give an assembly about it. And it'll take me too long to argue when I have to type my answers out with a straw.

I have maybe eight rungs left when the gray face of the wall in front of me is lit up. All of a sudden I can see my own shadow against the building. Drop down to the ground and throw my arms over my face. I can hear the spray cans in my backpack rattle. "Holy shit, Emil — what are you doing?" It's not some burly maintenance guy or Dr. Watkins or my dad. It's Jade standing beside the glaring headlights of her Honda Civic, her hands on her hips. She's in sweats and sneakers and it looks like even her ponytail is twitching.

Or she's shimmering. The headlights are like strobes bouncing off my eyes. "Maybe you could kill the brights?" I ask, still crouched down on the wet ground, squinting, trying to stand up like some prisoner dumped in front of a firing squad. And Jade's peppering me with questions.

"What are you doing? Were you up there? I saw you climbing down when I pulled up. From the top? Were you on the top of that building? Do you know how dangerous that is? Are you crazy? Do you know what time it is?" It's as if someone wound her up and she just had to yammer out all the phrases, like a programmed doll. I wait for her to wind down and my heart to stop sliding around my chest.

Finally, I get the breath to say, "It's great to see you." And is. It always is, but this time it's mostly because she's not a cop.

"What are you doing?" It's the refrain of the Jade song. I go for a good, strong offense.

"It's not like these are your regular hours, either —"

"I went for a drive. I didn't climb up a building."

"I don't have a car."

Jade turns away then and I see her shoulders roll back like she's made some kind of decision. The way people do to get through something, to get it over with. And of course, I can't exactly blame her. A lot of the crap I told her is a lie and a lot of the crap I would have told her if I were actually trying to tell her the truth would have been lies. It's like a seven-layer crap cake. It's so stupid. She saw me naked, for christsake. I just want her to know me.

"Emil —" I can't afford to make or let her say it. In my head, I start listing the things I'd miss about Jade if she just walked away from me. And sex is only at number three or something. The whole collection at least makes me try to stall her.

"There's a lot I have to explain to you. I think. I mean, if you're wondering. But it's really actually late — early, but late."

"I can take you home." It doesn't sound like she means for good, at least. Jade lets out a snort — not the adorable preliminary giggle kind, but the I-can't-believe-I-showed-this-jackass-how-to-put-on-a-condom kind of snort. I get in the car and we sit there for a minute, staring out at the field house looming in front of us. *It's really big* is all I keep thinking. Meaning: I can't believe I just climbed up that. And then I say that out loud. And tap at the windshield to show Jade a cluster of deer making its way across the north field.

"And now he conjures animals." She says it all sarcastic, but it feels like that right now. My arms are all weak and shaky, like I just flew around the planet. Twice.

"It's getting lighter, you know. We better go soon." But that sounds too much like she's a taxi I've hailed so I add on, "The maintenance crew gets here pretty soon and my dad'll be waking up."

"You do this every day, don't you?" She's not accusing me. It's more like she's just trying to get her head around it.

"You knew that."

"I didn't know it was like this. All night." And she says it like that changes something.

"It's not really a big deal. I walk around, sometimes I read in the library."

"And you never sleep."

"Early on in the night. Like at dinnertime." That's all either of us says for a while, turning the corners of all the streets. It numbs me to remember the last time Jade drove me home, how we were silent and tense for a different reason. She's smart, knows enough to park a couple houses before my own. "There's a lot I have to tell you," I begin again.

"You keep saying that." And she's right. But that doesn't mean it's ever stopped being true. And maybe I can tell her like this. Next to her, in the car. Her eyes on the road and the radio playing low.

"Wanna take a road trip?" I ask. "With me? Today?"

"No. Not with you."

"Maybe you want to take a drive on your own and then just happen to pick up some stranger on the side of the road or something?"

"That's kind of dangerous, I think." I see her mouth working, though, chewing the inside of her cheek. So I know she's considering it. "I don't really deal well with strangers." She says this like the word *strangers* is some code for douche bags or something. But I just climbed a building. With spray paint. I figure I can maybe also stop Jade from dropping me off by the Rothbergs' stupid duck-shaped mailbox and writing me off forever.

"I think we should drive up to Boston." I hear myself saying it before I even know it's a real decision. "I want you to meet my brother."

CHAPTER 25

I haul ass inside, knowing that Dad's probably already noticed my empty bed. I'm in the shower before he wakes up, though. He knocks while I'm still standing under the hot water and opens the bathroom door. He hasn't done that for years. Welcome to the world of total suspicion and no boundaries.

"Did you go out last night?" he asks.

"Yeah — I woke up and couldn't go back to sleep so I went for a walk. To clear my head." I don't say *to clear my head of last night's traumatic disclosures,* but that's what he's supposed to understand that I mean.

He doesn't say he's sorry. He says, "Did you ever get anything to eat?" Which is close. "We can stop by McDonald's on the way to school."

Hot dog. I want to say, *Maybe because my brother killed my mom, I get to have an extra hash brown.* "Thanks, Dad." I try to use the hearty voice, the kind that the good son would use, but it comes out sounding sarcastic, anyway. Still, I tried.

We're in the drive-thru when he comes out with the real concerned parent card. "Maybe you should stop by the counselor's office today? Just to hash out some of the circumstances we discussed last night."

"Verlando just handles the ADD kids."

"I know that. I mean the other lady. The one who wears the big earrings."

"The trauma counselor?" I want to tell him that the only guys who see the trauma counselor are the ones who cut themselves and then roll up their shirtsleeves so that a teacher notices and sends them to the counselor's. And those guys are really not the guys who are cutting themselves. They're the ones who are fucked up enough to cut themselves just to get out of class. Which is fucked up, but in more of a manipulative way. I guess maybe gay guys who are considering coming out might work through that in the therapeutic center. And we have a couple OCD kids, who include the office as part of their rituals. But for the most part, Caramoor is an all-boys school. We work through our shit by doing push-ups or listening to old Get Up Kids records.

The truth is that without a bunch of teenage girls running around eating or not eating or getting beat up by their college boyfriends or being date-raped or whatever, our counselor lady's probably sort of bored. Soma wore a flight suit over his clothes for a year and he never stopped by the office. He did go to Verlando's office, though, to see about getting extra time on tests.

"I don't want to go to the trauma counselor."

"Well, maybe we should look into someone outside of school. Do you think that would be a good idea? Just someone to talk to." He's really trying. You can tell he's read a book about it or something — he's trying to keep his voice all light and casual. He's being "understanding but persistent." And I don't know why I can't make myself cut my dad some slack. He and I drew the same sucktastic cards for this whole thing. It's not like he's the one I should be angry at.

But I can't stop myself from punishing him a little bit more. "I want to talk to Ethan." Silence. "That would help me." And as soon as I say it, I know it's a misfire. Because if he says no, then it means Jade and me driving up there is a choice piece of outright defiance. And if he says yes, it means that I'm about to cut an afternoon of classes to ride up to Boston for nothing, really. So that later my dad can get pissed and pleat his brow with furrows and say, "I said you could talk to Ethan." And then ground my ass. No way to win here.

My father exhales a little, switches on his blinker, and makes the turn. He does everything so deliberately. He never would have backed himself into that kind of shitbox.

"Okay — I'll tell you what — you start seeing someone. You know — to talk things out. And I'll set up some phone calls with you and your brother. I'm sure he'd like that, too." I swing to face him and he looks steadily at me. So now I feel like a real jackass.

"All right." I guess later on, I can argue some resentment for the fact that I have to haggle. Claim that I wanted to see Ethan face-to-face, not just pace through the house's ground floor with the cordless phone. So I nod a little at my dad and sink some more inside.

"Yeah? Good. All right, get out. Have a good day at school. If you need anything, call my cell." It's like my dad woke up as a different guy. I'm expecting to find a Ziploc bag full of oatmeal cookies in my backpack. And I almost don't want to leave the car in case this version of him disappears on the way to work.

In homeroom, Miss Gabaldon has us fill out these charts that map out the courses we'll take next year and our plans for the summer. I sign up for ceramics and write down that I'll be visiting my brother in Boston for the month of July. Hope that raises Verlando's unibrow. The whole time, I'm making lists in my head. Maps to Boston. Items to shove into a backpack. Questions I'm going to want to ask. Questions I'd better be ready to answer.

By the time we've finished our forms, Soma's asked me about last night six times. And at first I don't answer, so he just launches into a list of possible scenarios. "Why are you choosing courses for next year? You *know* you're going to CMA." He means Commonwealth Military Academy and he seems convinced of it. And then two minutes later, "If he kicks you out, you can move into my sister's room." And then when I still don't answer, "So, was he *that* glad you got laid?" This one gets a look from me. So he says, "I apologize — He was *that* glad you met a fine young lady of upstanding morals and lovely disposition?"

"You're an ass," I say. Soma just stands there, nodding. He must really want to know what happened. "It's fine. We had a good talk." It sounds unbelievable to me, but Soma keeps nodding, like that's the best news he's heard in weeks.

"That's great, dude. Really." And he kind of pats me a little, so that part of me wonders how much he's known all this time. I can't believe I'm going to get on a highway and pay tolls up to Boston and not even tell him about it. For a second, I feel like a traitor, one of those jackholes who finally gets in some girl's pants and then forgets the cardinal law of male solidarity — bros before hos. But then Brother Soma goes on to say, "Do you think they'll let me take both History of Genocide and Medieval History? Because that would be mayhem." Lately we're not even in the same century. Soma would want to stop off at a renaissance fair or something.

The day's insane — I have to run outside into the quad between all my morning classes because we don't get cell phone reception inside the fortress of old Caramoor. Text Jade back and forth, finally get her to say she'll drive up to the bottom of the hill and wait with the car running. At eleven thirty. It's dumb but I'm all jittery — not even from thinking about all the crap I have to say to Ethan. But because I've never cut class before. It's like my conscience can't catch up with who I am now — not so much the forgettable normal kid anymore. Now I warrant a thick folder in Verlando's desk. Now I have issues.

So there's all that crap to take care of and then on top of it, there's pretending like today's not anything unusual. As if all I'm worried about are classes and makeup exams. But then every time I duck outside to check messages, I see the field house and remind myself that earlier today, before the sun had even crawled up to its top rung, I stood on top of that building. That's kind of a rush.

So I get through English, chemistry, and Modern European History. At 11:15, when I'm supposed to be changing into stale sweats for gym class, I head down the hill and shoulder my way through the thick hedges with my arms wrapped around my face. Break through the thicket, and it's like some kind of bank heist — Jade's sitting in her idling car and guns the engine as soon as my ass hits the seat. She's got the windows rolled down and I look at her and shout over the wind, "It's like the Underground Railroad!"

And Jade buzzes up the windows and says, "Settle down there, white boy. Where are we going?"

"Boston." And she just looks back and forth from the road to me, finally slows down when we get to the main road.

"Did you print out directions?" And this is where I see my plan falter. Not just falter — collapse. Dissolve into dust under the impact of my stupidity. This is my screwup. It's like somehow not ever looking at the postmarks on his postcards. I must have this blank spot on my brain when it comes to actually tracking down Ethan. You could X-ray my head and you'd find one of those shadows, a dark spot blanketing one whole side.

Jade's pretty calm about the whole thing, which could either mean that she expected me to be this inept, which sucks, or that she's just that serene, which doesn't. She reminds me of my mom a little. I know that sounds sick, but I don't mean it like that. Just that all women seem to have this superpower, this composure when crap goes haywire. When we were little, we could be in the car and I'd be choking on a chicken nugget and Ethan's nose would be randomly spurting blood and Mom would pull into a gas station and nonchalantly give me the Heimlich and stop Ethan's nosebleed up with a couple of French fries or something. Without ever even raising her voice or dissolving into sweat or something. That's how Jade looks with her knee propped against her steering wheel, guiding the car down my street — utterly unflappable.

"Do you have a plan?" That's what I manage to ask while she's pulling up the drive.

"Well, you have the address at home, right?" Jade's looking at me as if I'm a map she's holding upside down. "Emil? Let's go get the address." There's a pause where the only noises in the car are the shifting gears. She's pulled up in front of the house and looks at me like she's just going to sit in the car. Because that's how it would work, I guess. If I were a normal kid who knew where my brother lived. I mean, the house where he lived and not just the general metropolitan area.

At first I get out of the car. Running through options, I'm honestly considering just ducking inside the house, maybe taking a piss or something, and then coming out with a random address that I'll pretend is Ethan's. Once we're in Boston, he can have moved. I can trot back out with directions written on a scrap of paper that can conveniently blow out a window on the turnpike. I get halfway up the driveway before realizing that's lying, too. Turn around, get back into the car. And say it before Jade even has a chance to ask me what the hell is going on.

"So he ran away?" she asks after I tell her the first part of it.

"Yeah." Pause. Pause. Pause. "Well — sort of."

"Because of your mom."

"Well, sort of." I remember the smell of wood burning in the fireplace at Ainsley House and bending my head toward Jade's. The whole sad divorce story. House splintered in two and all that crap. "My parents didn't split up."

Jade stays silent.

"I mean they split up, but not like — they didn't get a divorce."

"You mean your mom died of cancer last year." She pulls the keys out of the ignition and closes her fingers tightly around them. Then she gets out of the car and leans against it, looking toward the road.

"What the hell?" I want to dive across the roof of the car and tackle her. Knock out a few of her teeth. I will save them so she's not marred for life for anything, but right now I want to hit her.

"How could you know that? And not say anything?" And then say it so casually. In the same way she might say, "One summer you went to space camp." Or "You have a fondness for Chinese food." Like it was a small detail. And not the single detail.

It doesn't make me less angry that Jade looks back at me so steadily. Her lips purse a little. And she looks up and off to the side, like she's trying to remember something. Maybe the rest of the details of my life. "You're the one who lied."

"Yeah, well, you let me."

"I didn't. I didn't know then." It's funny how the same thing that drives me nuts for Jade is driving me nuts now. But not the good kind. She's so calm. I want to shake her up a little. When my fist comes up, she doesn't flinch. Not when it's in the air, not when I hit the hood of her car hard.

She just keeps studying me. "What are you waiting for?" My voice is the kind of cold usually reserved for my dad. "I'm not going to flip out like some sad actress. You really get off on tragedy, don't you?"

But Jade doesn't strike back. She just talks. "Tamara was over for dinner last night and she mentioned you to my mom. They discussed their concerns, told me about a kid whose mother died. How his older brother had left town. And I thought, that's so sad — I wonder if he's a friend of Emil's."

"Who's Tamara?"

"Your homeroom teacher, dumb-ass."

"Tamara —"

"Gabaldon. My mom is her teaching mentor. She eats dinner at our house twice a week. She's like my mom's much better daughter. You know, they're very concerned about you." Jade's voice rises to an even more feminine trill. "'It's all such a shame. He's such a sweet boy and so bright.'"

She sidles around the car. "I didn't tell them you were also stellar in the sack." The idea of Miss Gabaldon eating dinner at Jade's house is more than I can bend my brain around right now. Her mom's second daughter. I can't not picture Jade and Miss Gabaldon jumping around in lace stuff, swatting each other with pillows. Painting each other's fingernails and crap like that. That's probably not how it actually is. But I'm not going to ruin it by getting clarification.

"So she told you." It doesn't help a whole lot. They were sitting around talking about us, my family, even if they were talking kindly.

"No — she didn't tell me. She and my mom were talking. They didn't know — they don't know I know you. And you know what, Emil? I sort of don't. Why would you lie about that? You keep lying to me."

By this time classes are probably filing in to sixth period classes. Any minute now, one of the sweet secretaries is going to get a notice that I've skipped class. "I don't have Ethan's address." That's what I end up blurting out. "I know he's in Boston. My dad's been paying his credit card bills. But I can't call him for the address. Unless maybe if we get all the way up there. But he still might say no. I don't know what I was thinking, dragging you into this."

"Does your dad pay his rent with his credit card?"

"I don't know."

"Well — think about it. Where does your dad keep bills, financial records, that kind of thing? At the very least we can take it with us. And figure out stuff on the way." It amazes me that she still wants to sit in a car with me.

Jade is much less reverent about Dad's personal space. Given that she doesn't know him, I guess this makes sense. I go into his office and feel like he's somewhere watching me on a closed-circuit TV. She just tears in, though, opening desk drawers, shuffling through files. She's thumbing through three volumes of his leather-bound appointment books at the same time and I'm still barely through the doorway, just sort of gaping at her. "What?" she asks. "You need to help. You'll recognize this stuff much sooner than I will." We find the cell phone bill. He still gets three of them, which means my dad has known Ethan's cell phone number all this time.

"I can't believe he sat there watching me call the old number. He just sat there."

"Where?"

"Nothing."

"You have his cell phone bill. Come on. We'll totally be able to find him with those numbers. Take that — take all of them." Jade's gone all bounty hunter on me. I half-expect to see her start tipping over file cabinets or loading up a tranquilizer gun. She's crouched down over the file drawer in my father's desk, yanking out a battered folder. "I got the credit card bills. Wow — your dad's so organized. We would have been lost at my house. My parents just stuff all the mail in this huge soup tureen."

"What's a soup tureen?"

"You know — a soup tureen. The big covered bowl you serve soup in. It has its own ladle."

"God — our families are different."

"My mom makes crap like that." Somehow I've managed to offend Jade, now after the whole scene outside the house. "Sometimes we eat soup." She's all indignant about it, as if I've implied that they eat soup in some kind of squatter's camp. Or soup from shoes or something.

"What I meant was that your family probably has more ceramic stuff." I say it as seriously as I can muster, and for a few seconds, we just face off against each other. Jade laughs first and it's the snorting kind that probably means we're headed back toward normal.

And then we're headed out of Connecticut. Breeze out of the house after shutting all the drawers and doors we just opened. Before I even start sifting through the paperwork on my lap, I make myself call my dad at work. He must have put the secretaries on family emergency alert because instead of getting the usual bland "I can transfer you to his voice mail," I get, "Is everything okay, Emil?"

"Everything's fine, but I should talk to my dad right away, I think." My dad's mercy pretty much hinges on my calling before Caramoor does. And he's right there. Clearly, he's taking this new dedication to fatherhood seriously.

"Emil. Is there a problem at school?" I briefly consider hanging up and working at one of those Alaskan fishing canneries.

"Well, that's the thing."

"What is the thing, Emil?" New Version of Dad loses a little patience, sounds more like Old Version.

Deep breath. Deep, cleansing breath. "The thing is, I'm not at school."

"I find that strange because I dropped you off there. Were you feeling ill? Are you at home? Where are you now?" I look across at Jade, like that's going to help. Shockingly enough, though, it does.

"I'm in a car with my girlfriend." And then, because that sounded too weird: "My friend. And we're going to go, I mean, we're on our way to Boston." Silence on the other end of the phone. "We're going to go to Boston and see Ethan."

"Really? You weren't just hoping to take in a Red Sox game?" Yep. Old Dad's back.

"Listen — I know you're mad and I'm in a shitload of trouble, but I have to do this. Because of . . . because of everything you told me last night." This gets a sidelong glance from Jade. "I have to see him." More silence. "I'm going to have a hard time finding him. But I will find him. So I was wondering if you could just give me the address." Catch myself gesturing at the papers in front of me like my dad can see them piled up. "And I was also hoping you could call school. And let them know that I had your permission to leave early."

It feels like we drive forty miles before my father speaks. "I will call school and tell them that you are on a family errand, but I will not say you left with my permission. I will not let you make a liar out of me." There is an opening for me to state the obvious there — it's like he's daring me. But I don't say it and so he keeps going. "I am sorely disappointed in you. When we spoke this morning, I'd been optimistic, but this is a whole new kind of trouble you've gotten yourself in." I'm not totally sure what he means by that, like cutting class is somehow worse because I crossed state lines, but it's time to pull out the pity stops.

"Dad — I'm sorry — but everything we talked about — I just need to figure it all out." It's weird because that shouldn't feel hollow. It's the truth, after all. I'm not making this crap up. Last night I found out my brother helped my mom check herself out early. I should be appropriately lashing out at figures of authority and traditional values. But it feels like a scam. I guess because you're not supposed to plan out emotional meltdowns. Otherwise that makes them emotional campfires or something.

And he knows it's horseshit. He and I — we just don't talk like this. But I've got him. I now have an issue I can flex. A pity muscle. "I need to do this." That's honest, at least.

"You do what you need to do, but there are always consequences for your actions. We will talk about the issue of trust when you get home, and you will schedule a meeting with Mr. Rollins to discuss the fact you left the academy this afternoon without my permission. In the meantime, I'll call the Upper School office so that they know you are accounted for."

"What about Ethan?"

"Let me call back with Ethan's phone number and address and leave it on your voice mail. Let me say this: You should call your brother. Let him know that you're on your way up there."

"Because he wouldn't want to see me, right?" I say it sarcastically and it sounds like a little kid. Like I'm stamping my foot with my voice. It amazes me how I can flip from being thankful that Jade's driving to completely embarrassed. She's getting front-row seats to my cracked-out family. But I can't stop myself from plowing through the conversation. I can stop myself from crying, but that's about it. And that's pretty much miraculous. I choke out, "He's my brother. And it's not like I'm going to move in or anything — I just want to talk."

I have to concentrate harder on the not crying thing when my dad's voice goes gentle. "I know. I understand. In my experience, though, talking with Ethan lately — it's just not always that easy. Maybe if you give him a chance to prepare himself. It's been a long time since you two spent any real time together."

"You don't have to tell me that."

"Of course not." And then because the line's drawn between us again, my dad gathers up all his sternness and issues the following statement: "You've been through a great deal this year, and I've seen you grow up a whole lot. You don't need your older brother in order to keep doing that." My father, a fortune cookie in khakis.

"I'll make sure to call him first. Thank you for getting me the information." I sound like a robot, programmed to lie.

"How would you have even known where you were going otherwise? I'd just like to know that — what were you thinking?"

"I would have figured it out —"

"You don't just sniff that kind of thing out —"

"Dad." I stop him to say it. "I have your bank statements here. I brought the cell phone bills and some credit card stuff."

"I see."

"I figured you'd rather I be honest."

"Certainly. Go through my personal files. Steal financial records. As long as you're honest about it." There's a long sigh on the other end of the phone. It sounds like when you release air out of a bike tire. Dad's kind of flattened, I guess. "I expect you home tomorrow afternoon. I'm sure Ethan can put you and your friend up for the night. There's no sense in driving up there and back in one day. How long has your friend had her license? Are her parents aware that you've embarked on a road trip during school hours?" There's no pause for me to fill with answers, though. It's just my dad rattling off some list of questions he thinks he's supposed to ask. "Tomorrow afternoon, we're going to sit down together. I'll try to arrange for some sort of counselor to be there. Because you and I have a great deal to talk about, young man. I don't even know where to begin. I don't know where to go from here."

"Yes, sir." I mean, what else am I supposed to say?

I snap the phone closed and drop it in the bin built into the door.

CHAPTER 26

Sometime during the conversation, Jade turns the radio from low to off. For a few minutes, everything is silent except for the sound of the highway passing under the car.

"I can't believe Miss Gabaldon eats dinner at your house."

"Yeah, that's the earth-shattering revelation of the day."

"Is she normal, like to talk to and stuff? Do you talk about movies or bands or Ben Hendrikson?"

"Yeah, I mean she's normal and all, now. For a while, she used to dry hump all the furniture and stuff, but my mom kept squirting her with the water bottle until she calmed down. Jesus, Emil. She's a person, you know. She's not a whole lot older than I am."

"Yeah, I know." And I can't stop myself from grinning.

"Pervert."

"My mom died." Once again I am the king of the shift in conversation.

"Yeah. I'm sorry. When they were talking, I heard my mom say cancer."

"But that's not how she died." Silence. Silence. More road under the car. "She took a lot of pills. She was hurting really bad and she took a lot of pills."

"Oh." Yeah, oh.

"Ethan gave them to her. That part I just found out. My dad just told me. Last night. I thought Ethan ran away, but he didn't. The two of them decided on it, I guess. But I think my dad pretty

304

much kicked him out." This is, arguably, the most important, most mature conversation I've ever had, but I can't stop myself from talking like this. Like a ten-year-old writing a letter to a friend from summer camp. A camp for smackheads, but whatever. Now she knows.

"So we're going to go see Ethan now."

"Yeah." It helps that Jade said *we*.

"So you can talk to him."

"Yeah."

"What are you going to say?"

And at first I don't answer, turn up the radio and stay quiet for three songs. Look out the window. She's got her Bob Dylan playlist on and it's mostly the divorce songs from *Blood on the Tracks* and I keep thinking that I hope there's never a point when Jade listens to these songs and thinks of me.

"I haven't decided yet. I'll know when I see him." We slow down to pay a toll and Jade apologizes for not having E-Z Pass, like that's going to be the thing that undoes me at this point. That'll be the point where I break down.

"I don't think I've actually ever been out of state with this thing," she says, tapping the steering wheel. "We should go on road trips this summer. We could buy a tent. I mean, if you don't have stuff planned." And this is the best yet because she says *we* again, references the future, and expresses nervousness. I'm a god. I'm a young, virile god.

"I figured this went through your wild, crazy college days with you."

"Uh-uh — the Civic was a gift from my parents to make me feel better when I came home." There goes Soma's waitress theory. The daughter of the starving artist. "It was supposed to help make my transition easier. To stop me from isolating myself." Jade drops her voice for the last part, mocking someone. It sounds like her parents are shopping at the same bookstore as my dad lately.

"Well, that plan was ass."

"Hey — settle down there," she says.

"Yeah, well, you've been sort of isolated. You drive out to an empty high school campus in the middle of the night. Without me, you'd still be isolating yourself."

"My mom was trying to talk me into volunteering at an old folks' home. Or walking dogs or something. But then I met you."

"Your mom knows about me? Does she know it's me? So I'm like community service or something?"

"God." Jade speeds up, switches lanes like she's trying to drive away from me. "That's not what I meant. She knows I met a friend. Jesus, Emil. I'm really sorry about everything your dad just told you. Really, I am. But give me a break here. It's not like this is all I've ever done, you know. Hanging out at a school, making the same stupid pot over and over again. And I'm not saying I'm not glad I met you." By this time, Jade is pretty much yelling. "But this isn't what I planned for this year, you know."

"Are you going to go back to school?"

"God!" I'm just waiting for her to start honking her horn on me. It's like she's gone demonic. "You're just like my parents. I don't know. I don't know if I want to go back there or go somewhere else or stay at home and take classes. Or walk across Europe or rebuild schools in Indonesia or any of those other big-time, life-changing experiences."

"You could go to Semester at Sea."

"What?"

anent just because you've learned them so quickly. The
t, it was really stupid. It was almost the end of the semes-
way. I should have finished up. And I'd been seeing
and I liked him — I wasn't really unhappy. It was
nd I was there with these two girls who lived on my
knew me. If one of them had asked me if I was sad, I
said no. And I wouldn't have been lying. But then
get a bowl of cereal. In our dining hall, they have a
on. Rows of plastic dispensers and you go there and
stic scoops to serve yourself. And then by the bever-
was this thing we called the cow. It was this metal
thing with three different nozzles and you waited
hen got whatever kind of milk you needed."
e those at hotels and stuff. And camps."
so you know what I'm talking about." I want to
e I asked why she quit college and Jade is talking
e breakfast cereal system at Bard. But she's driv-
n and so I'm trying to be polite. And counting on
phor.
t milk on my cereal. Skim. And this guy next to
the whole milk in his coffee and I looked across
his hands. Looked up and it was this guy
been my boyfriend from the first week of school
winter break. Half a year. And we looked at
en he turned and I turned and we each went
ate tables. But you know — we spent months
tty much lived together and then there we
n't even muster a 'good morning' at the milk
h a stupid, tiny moment. But it totally undid
le quiet and then says, "I don't want you to

"Nothing — it's a bad joke, I mean, just with myself.
Nothing."

And so that's all we have to offer each other for a good long
time. We drive awhile with quiet between us. Bob Dylan goes
through his Christian phase and Jade switches the radio to NPR,
like she's trying to prove she's the grown-up or something. We
start seeing signs for Boston. Boston 80 miles. Boston 64 miles.
And the closer we get, the more I feel my heart shrivel up, the
more my stomach feels like it's been forced into a blender.

"I'm sorry I yelled at you." When Jade speaks, her voice
sounds all rough. It sort of sucks that we've both been sitting
next to each other, separately trying not to cry. "I just wish
you'd get it."

"I can't get it if you don't tell me why you left."

"I told you why I quit."

"No. You said you were tired."

"Well, that's why."

"That's not why. Nobody quits school because they're tired.
They have a coffee, they do some blow. They take naps."

"This was like an extended nap."

"What am I supposed to say to that?"

"This doesn't have anything to do with you."

"But it does, the same way it matters that you didn't know
my mom died. Or that I didn't know what Ethan did or that my
dad had sent him away. That kind of thing matters. It doesn't
make sense to be near each other and not know if something's
eating the other person up inside."

"Nothing's eating me up inside." Now she's the one who
sounds like a little kid.

"Fine, then. I want to know what made you so tired."

Jade reaches out and at first I think she's going to grab me, but instead she switches off the radio. Roughly, like she'd just as soon tear off the knob and throw it out the window. "You're not the first person I've slept with, you know."

Great, this is what I deserve. She's going to tell me she was so tired from banging hundreds of guys at college or something. And they're all going to be stupid hippie guys, the kind that think they're really good at pool or spend their summers tagging owls or something.

And then I realize she said *person* and not *guy* and I think, *Jesus, she's actually a lesbian*. Here I thought I was so damn manly and I ended up sleeping with a lesbian. And her mom's probably a lesbian. I'm running through all of these with this perfectly blank look fixed onto my face, because whatever it is, I can't freak out. I know that much.

"What are you thinking?" Jesus Christ. Jade's pretty much the only girl I've actually talked to for years but I know this much about girls — they always have to know what you're thinking. What the hell is that? If it was worth mentioning or if I didn't think it was going to get me slapped, I'd say it. Now I have to sit here, coming up with some profound thought so that Captain Confession over there can think she coaxed it out of me.

"I'm just listening." At least that's honest.

"There were a lot of guys at college." Crap. God, why couldn't she have just been a lesbian? She has to see some flicker on my face because her voice lurches up. "I'm not a slut, Emil. It's not like that. It's different — I mean you can't even understand, you've never lived away from home or in a dorm. It's just different."

"That's right. I'm practically an infant over here."

"That's not what I meant."

"That's kind of what you meant. I'm

"Stop. This doesn't have anything to Just listen. It's different, because it's n to know someone. It's so small there. every day and so then there's some don't know, you do what we did — to each other and then finally you'r

"That's how amoebas have sex.'

"It's not about sex, even. That's mostly because it's really hard to a that happens. Because everythi fast-forward. It's not the date-o at-night kind of couple you wer in the same bed all the time, and Your CDs get all mixed up an like all of a sudden, you hav

"Well, what's so bad al don't want that?"

"I don't want it if it's that stuff. Everyone's tr figured it would be like those guys — I meant t close to someone, like and then all of a sudc fit and that's it. That thought it was even careless with each (playing by the rul

"What were th

"That you let

so perm
day I lef
ter, any
someone
brunch a
hall, who
would've
I went to
cereal stati
use the pla
ages, there
refrigerator
on line and
"They ha
"Okay —
say No becau
to me about t
ing me to Bost
it being a meta
"I went to p
me was pouring
and recognized
Andrew, who'd
until right after
each other and t
back to our separ
together. We pre
were — we could
machine. It was su
me." Jade gets a lit

think I'm this weird stalker chick who's going to flip out when we stop seeing each other. I understand how most things like that aren't permanent. But I'm never going to get how you can be that close to someone and then not. How you can end up total strangers. Does that make sense? Does that sound crazy?"

"No. It doesn't sound crazy." At first I think I should stay quiet, leave it at that. But then we're trying this new honesty thing. So I tell her, "It's a little weird that you came home because of it."

"Well, it *was* weird. The whole thing was weird. I went back and sat down and I felt like the whole room was folding up. Like I couldn't breathe. And then I walked back up the hill to my dorm and started packing."

"What did you tell your mom and dad?"

"That I needed to come home. That kids in my dorm were shooting heroin and maybe I should just live at home and take classes at Trinity or U. of Hartford."

"And that was it? That was enough?" My dad would have signed me up for the army or something.

"Yeah. They drove up and got me that night."

"Are you sorry you came home?" And I really don't mean it like she might regret meeting me. I mean making a decision like that on a whim, basically because of one cold bastard.

"No. I couldn't stay there. There were all these people and I knew them or thought I did and it didn't matter. I still felt like I could disappear and it wouldn't make a difference. None of us really mattered to each other."

"Yeah? It sounds like Caramoor."

"Tamara says that's just part of making your own way in the world." It takes me a minute to realize that she means Miss Gabaldon, and that fries my brain a little.

"Tamara's dating a douche bag."

"Yeah. You know when you and I first met, I told her I'd met Ben's little brother."

"Why the hell would you do that?"

Jade laughs then, like a little kid. "Because that's the name you gave me, Jason. She'd told me that Ben had a little brother. I thought you were too sweet to be a Hendrikson, though."

"THANK YOU." Roll down the window and yell. "THANK YOU!" It feels right to ride next to Jade in the car, like we're on this adventure together. Along the highway the trees blur and shimmer and the more north we drive, they change a little. Like there's a whole different kind of forest in Massachusetts. Foreign trees. Boston trees.

"We're close, you know. Maybe you should call Ethan?" Jade says it softly, the way that you tell someone bad news.

"Yeah, I'm not going to call him." I concentrate on the trees outside.

"If we get lost, you're going to call him to find out how to get to his place."

"Yeah, says who?"

"Says the girl who's been chauffeuring your ass all over the Northeast today." I don't know how to tell her that Ethan probably wouldn't give us the right directions. That I don't want to call him and give him a chance to disappear before I get there.

"Probably it would be better to just show up and go from there, I mean if we can swing it that way."

"What's he like, your legendary brother?"

"I don't know. He's sort of a stranger."

CHAPTER 27

We end up stopping three times for directions to find the address Dad left on my voice mail, but Jade doesn't mention calling Ethan again. His neighborhood doesn't look like a city, so much. It's more like a stretch of row houses with brick faces and front stoops. The church on the corner of his street is the biggest building on the block. His little house doesn't have a number, but we figure it out by counting from the house three doors down that does.

By the time Jade gets the car into a space across the street, I'm feeling a whole lot like I did this morning — shaky after climbing up the side of the field house. I'm wishing there was a bed around. Or some weed. Jade doesn't even ask why we're just sitting in the car still. She unflips the visor and puts lip stuff on, packs up the iPod, and puts it into the armrest compartment. I keep imagining the door opening and Ethan's face when he sees me standing there. Every time I picture it, he's not smiling.

I finally force myself out of the car and up the steps. The first time I knock, we stand there for a while, shifting our weight and listening to the floorboards creak beneath our feet. "I don't think you really knocked." Jade looks sideways at me.

"I did knock. You saw me knock."

"Usually when you knock on a door, there's a noise involved."

"All right, then you knock."

"I think it's somehow psychologically necessary for you to knock."

"Yeah, that's crap."

Jade ends up knocking. Otherwise we'd have just stood there for hours, I think, with my knuckles pressed slightly against the chipped blue paint of Ethan's front door. A girl who isn't Ethan opens the door and squints out at us as if we're selling something she can't possibly want. She's hot in a sour kind of way. Black, sleek hair cut like a helmet close to her head. She's wearing a dress that looks like some fifties' waitress uniform and ugly, clunky shoes.

"Can I help you?" If she were from my neighborhood, this girl would probably think I was a disabled kid selling calendars. It takes my mouth a long minute to work itself into something that pronounces words. And even then they come out stumbling.

"Yeah. Hi. Yeah. I'm not sure if we have the right address — we're here to see Ethan Simon." I don't say he's my brother. Or give my name. And I put a weird accent on my own last name, like suddenly I'm French Canadian.

"Yeah? Ethan's at work." The queen of charm steps outside with us and pulls the door closed behind her. She concentrates on Jade then, looks her up and down like she's trying to guess the size of her clothes or something. Jade takes over then.

She tells the girl who we are, but says we're on a college tour and my dad wanted me to drop off some cash with Ethan. I don't totally get the plan, but as long as Jade's the one talking, I can just nod and stand there with my hands in my pockets. "Are you guys roommates? Oh, wow — are you involved? Ethan didn't mention a girlfriend. Right? These guys haven't seen each other in months, isn't that crazy? God, I have to pee — it's okay to come in, right? Just to wait until Ethan gets in? I'm sorry — what's your name?" Michelle isn't thrilled to let us in, but she seems as steamrolled by Jade as I feel.

The two of us find pretty much nothing to say to each other while Jade's in the bathroom. "Ethan didn't mention —" she says.

"Yeah, I figured. We've had kind of a rough year in our family. Are you an art student? My dad mentioned Ethan was all set up living with artists." I'm pretty much continuing Jade's tradition of vague chattiness. Michelle's not an artist. She does roller derby. "Wow. Yeah. That's great." Apparently, roller derby is the most empowering sport for women. I don't know what to say to any of this. Ethan's working at a video store and his shift ends at seven. Which gives Jade and me an hour to stand around and torment Michelle with cheerful small talk. There are three other roommates, but one's at work waiting tables, another usually spends weeknights at his boyfriend's place, and the other's in the hospital with cat scratch fever. Which is a real thing, Michelle tells me. It's an infection caused by an untreated cat scratch, shockingly enough. None of the housemates owns a cat; that girl just liked feeding strays.

At first, I think Jade's taking a crazy long time in the bathroom, like maybe she's developed dysentery or something, but then I catch sight of her jacket through the kitchen doorway. She's just hanging back, letting me flounder. Amusing herself. She doesn't even come back into the front hall, but plants herself in a sunken sofa the color of cranberry juice. Or bloodstains. "This place is really fantastic," she calls to us from the deep valley of the middle sofa cushion so that Michelle pretty much has to motion me to follow her into the living room so that we can join her. The two of them talk about rent and roommates and I get a little lost looking around for anything in the room I might recognize as Ethan's.

At home, back in the old days, you could have walked into our living room and found our sneakers kicked off under the coffee table. Ethan's always had this habit of peeling off his sweaty socks and leaving them tucked into weird corners — balled up on a windowsill, tucked under the base of a standing lamp. It drove Mom nuts.

But there are no socks on this floor. There's a lot of big pillows scattered around and a pile of blankets and bedding in the corner. Michelle sees me looking and says, "Just in case anyone needs to crash." I can't stop watching the front door, listening for quick steps outside, a key in the lock.

Michelle and Jade make a few more lame stabs at conversation until Michelle surrenders the living room, announcing she's got some calls to make, and disappears behind this weird beaded curtain at the top of the stairs. And so that's it. It's just Jade and me sitting in the middle of the dingy living room, waiting to ambush my brother. Jade pats the seat beside her, but I don't want to be stuck in the springless sofa when Ethan strides through the door.

So instead I slap down one of the floor cushions in front of her and sit there, with my spine lined up to the sofa's frame. It hits me how tired I am, how much has happened since I woke up before it even got light that morning. There's a TV with a remote — easily the most expensive thing in the room, but neither of us makes a move to turn it on. I'm just watching the blank door as if a story's about to be played across it.

Half of me wants to go home. Maybe it's enough that Ethan will come home from work and some sullen girl will tell him his little brother stopped by. He'll know I know then, maybe. And honestly, I don't know what else I'd say, anyway. "Maybe we should just leave and stay at a hotel —" is what I end up suggesting to Jade. "We could do more of that sex stuff. Sleep in an actual bed and order a big plate of bacon up to the room."

"Yeah, that's not really going to solve anything."

"It would, though. I really think it would."

"Yeah? You cut class, pissed off your dad, and drove three hours, all for some sex and a plate of bacon."

"Totally reasonable." I doze a little bit or else just zone out. Jade and I sit in the same kind of companionable silence that we did in the sitting room at Ainsley House. Jade flips on the TV with the volume down low and we sit listening to the creaks of the settling house around us. Outside it's dark and every once in a while Michelle passes through to the kitchen and comes out with a cup of tea, a bowl of cereal. Each time, she says, "You guys want anything?" in the way that makes it clear we had better not. We see a couple episodes of *Law & Order* before we hear footsteps on the other side of the front door. Jade reaches for my shoulder. And then the front door opens up so that Ethan's framed in the blank space.

All this time, when I've pictured him, he's looked like I feel — worn down, tattered. But really it ends up being just the same old Ethan who strides into the living room. I guess I figured he would have stopped eating or bathing or would have at least set his arm hair on fire with a cigarette lighter or something. That he'd look guilty.

He's wearing clothes I recognize and his hair's just a little longer — shaggy curls that just brush the collar of his shirt. It's just Ethan, really. Except he stops striding as soon as he catches sight of us. And I might be making it up, but he might even go just a little bit pale. Now he looks like my memory of him. The ghost of my brother.

But when he speaks, his voice doesn't sound shaky or stressed at all. It's kind of frat-boy hearty: "Hey, hey — look who's here!" Like he's been expecting me all this time. "How long have you been waiting? Did you drive up?" He keeps lurching toward me and then stepping back near the door. "Where's Michelle at?" and then, "What is this? Does Dad know you're here?" And that's the first time Ethan seems at all tense. And I'm not doing any better. It takes me a couple of tries to even talk back to him. And by the time I'm ready, Ethan's moved on to Jade. It's not like how I figured he'd talk to her. He steps back a little. He doesn't try to work her the way I usually see him talk to girls.

He crosses in front of us to the kitchen and goes to the fridge. We follow. "Hey, beer? Anyone want a beer?" Ethan starts taking a bunch of bottles out. "Either of you guys ever heard of a Texas beer?"

"Um . . . no," I say. Jade wanders back into the living room. I hear the volume on the television rise up in staggered notches.

"Yeah? A Texas beer — it works best with cheap beer — it's half beer, half tomato juice." It's weird that my first thought is that Ethan's coked up. Once I rule that out, I get to the idea that maybe he's nervous. Because probably I've seen my brother coked up more often. Our family is screwed. "And so then you throw in a shot of Tabasco." He's stirring the stuff with the flat end of a plastic knife. "You want one? You want a Texas beer?"

318

"No, that's okay."

"Are you guys staying the night? We're all set up in the living room."

"Yeah — we saw that."

"Because there's no sense you turning around and going back tonight."

"Thanks."

"So Dad knows you're here — I mean, he must have sent you, right?"

"That's the best you can come up with? That's why you think I came?" That one comes out before I mean it to. None of this feels real. It's like I walked into the middle of a sitcom about two brothers hanging out in Boston, neither of whom killed their mom. We're not those people anymore.

But it's like Ethan didn't even hear me. "What? Dad wants me to come home now? Exile's over? Let me guess — my room is just like how I left it." There's the hard corner on Ethan's voice that I remember from right after Mom died. Back then, though, I just figured he was bitter that she died all of a sudden, after everything. That no one had a chance to say good-bye, crap like that. But that's not Ethan — it's me who's angry about that.

"No. He didn't want me to come here. Dad doesn't want you to come home." Right before saying it, I realize that I'm a little scared of Ethan. Not that he'd hit me or break a bottle or my head or something. But that he doesn't like us, really. My dad and me. We're not useful to him.

"Well, as long as he keeps paying the bills — I'm not going to fight him on that. Why would I fight him on that? This is a great city, Emil. I'm taking classes, living with artists. We've got a real community going."

"Yeah, Michelle was telling me all about roller derby."

"It's a whole lifestyle — I mean there is a whole world outside of Caramoor Academy." I almost tell him about the key, how I took it from his room. All the stuff I found. Everything. But Ethan wouldn't get it. And then he'd have to find a way to ruin it.

My brother's braced against his shabby kitchen counter with a big glass of tomato juice and beer in front of him. He's wired and waiting and keeps taking swigs and then tapping out more Tabasco into his glass. He looks older from behind.

"Why did you do it?" I ask him in the exact way I didn't want to ask him. Vague and sudden so that it gives him room to misunderstand the question. So I keep going: "Dad told me, and I had to see you face-to-face. To know why you did it." Ethan's always skated by, gotten away with everything. But he doesn't miss this one. When he turns around, he looks straight at me. His eyes have narrowed and he looks a little mean, like a caught dog.

"Because she was in pain." And that's what I knew he'd say. "She was in pain and that didn't seem to matter to either of you. For you, it was all about how long we could keep her around."

"I'm sorry." And Ethan nods, because of course he thinks that's all I meant to say. That's all Ethan can imagine that I'd say. And right then, I could leave it and drink whatever asstastic concoction he pours into my glass and let him tell me how hot Jade is and how he's so happy to be out from under Dad's thumb. I could let it stand. And I'd have my brother back in some way. I mean it could be about a million times worse. He could be nodding off on dope at some train station. He could have been on a bike and gotten hit by a car. He could have taken a hard punch to the head and then forgotten us. I could just let him be right on this one thing.

But I keep going. "I'm sorry I said 'why.' I guess what I meant was 'how.'" And that's it. Something settles over Ethan then that makes him look hard and gone. He looks at me like I'm a stranger, like he wouldn't even say good morning to me if we were both on line for milk. He looks at me like he looked at our dad right before he left. He empties the drink in front of him and grabs another bottle of beer from the refrigerator.

"It's really great of you to stop by. Feel free to bed down in the living room for the night. It's late. I guess I'll head up and see Michelle now." When Ethan shuffles off, I watch him climb up the first four steps before the staircase turns and I can't see him from the kitchen at all. Someplace in my head, I hear what we'd sound like screaming at each other. I can even picture myself tackling him, how our elbows and knees would bang against the edge of each step. I want us to wrestle until we're worn out from wrestling, so that we can do that thing that boxers do when they're worn out from hitting each other — how they kind of rock back and forth in the middle of the ring, arms all tangled. Sweating and crying and bleeding on each other.

I close my eyes and see myself pulling Ethan down the steps, with my fingers curled inside his mouth, slamming his head against a wooden step over and over. It feels like a balloon's expanding in my chest, filling with hot, hollow air. I want to hit my brother until blood seeps out of his ears. I know that's sick. But what's sicker is that I want him to hit me. I want him to care enough to lash out at me. I've come all this way. And all I get all over again is Ethan's back. Turning it isn't even hard for him.

In the living room, Jade's conked out in the sinking sofa. She's pitched to the side with her jacket rolled up under her head. I lift her feet up and cover her with one of the blankets from the pile on the floor. Try to switch out the jacket with a pillow but Jade slaps my hands away. "Those things have diseases." I can't tell if she's kidding or dreaming or totally serious.

Ethan's living room doesn't have curtains. Even when I turn off the lamp by the sofa, there's still light on Jade's face. Outside on the street is a row of lamps and beneath one of them I can see the Civic. Part of me wants to swing her over my shoulder and carry her out. We can sleep in the car until she's awake enough to drive. It's a weird feeling to be sitting up late in Ethan's new house — like kneeling in the chapel at school late at night or trying to make out the words on the back of books in the darkened library. I know where I am. I even sort of recognize it, but also I know I don't belong.

When Jade wakes up, she sits straight up like she's having a nightmare.

"We're still here," she says.

"Yeah."

"What did he say? When are we going?"

"Nothing. Soon."

"Nothing?"

"I mean, what could he say?"

Jade starts to get herself together. She shakes out her hair, reaches for her boots on the floor. I tell her, "We don't have to go right this minute."

"You want to stay?" No. No way. "You think you can talk him into coming back with us? Maybe sitting down with your dad?" Nope. Not that, either.

"It's the middle of the night."

"Yeah — so no traffic."

"Really? You don't mind?"

"Emil," she says, and I finally get that she's been waiting all night. "Let's go. I'll stop in at their bathroom again, before we get back on the road." She zips up her boots and hops up then. "Maybe you should go up and say good-bye?"

It's a bad idea and I'm clear on that the whole trip up the steps. I wouldn't have woken Ethan up when he lived in the bedroom across the hall from mine. It's not like I'm going to go in and shake him off Roller Girl or anything. They've got some kind of plastic covering up the steps. So far it's the only carpet I've seen in the place and it's laminated. There are four doors along the upstairs hall, but only one is closed. There's a bathroom, a closet crammed with clothes, and an empty bedroom. And then the closed door.

There's never a moment when I think I'm going to open it. Or even knock. I have this key around my neck, though — it's like I forgot what it's like to stand in front of a locked door. So I stand there remembering, that's all.

The whole time I back up and stumble down the steps, I'm remembering. Making sure I notice the scratched wood of the banister beneath my hand, the number of steps winding down to the first floor. In the kitchen, I memorize the dishes piled in the sink and the canister of iced-tea mix on the counter. The pile of pillows. The way the streetlights outside cause the window-panes to crisscross the wooden slats of the floor in shadows. When I picture Ethan now, I'll know what he looks like standing in his kitchen, his living room, on his front porch. It won't be something I worry about anymore.

CHAPTER 28

Jade's right — without traffic, we pretty much rocket home. Once we're on the highway, the road's empty. The tollbooth takers are friendly from loneliness. Jade keeps asking if I'm okay until I tell her she's not allowed to ask again. I sleep on and off. When we start to see signs for Hartford, I put in my stop request and Jade looks over at me, amazed.

"You just can't get enough, can you?" she says.

She pulls up through the gates so that I can hop out of the car and grab my bag from the floor.

"You have about an hour and a half to daylight," Jade tells me while I'm grabbing my bag from the backseat. "But I guess you know that."

I nod and close the back door, then open it again: "Thank you," I tell her in a way I hope shows how much I mean it. And then because that still doesn't seem good enough, I tell her, "You know he was probably faking it." Jade leans back, looks over the headrest.

"What?" She's tired. She doesn't have time to guess at what I'm aiming at.

"That guy getting milk — I bet he was faking it. I can't imagine you not mattering." And she looks away, like I said the wrong thing, but when she turns back, she's got the sweet smile on. And then I shut the door and let her drive away.

I use the minute it takes to see Jade's taillights descend back down the hill to tick through some kind of plan. By the time the school's drive goes totally dark again, I'm turning the key in the front door of Ainsley House. So now it's just the ghosts and me again at Caramoor. Walk down the halls and find myself saying good-bye to the place, which is ricockulous because I'll be back here in a little more than three hours. But I know it's about to feel less like mine.

I decide to start from the top and work my way down, so I head up to the attic first. Clear out anything personal, but leave the bed in there, even some cans of food and bottled water. Someone's going to find it eventually and they won't know how long it's been since someone has slept under the eaves of the old farmhouse. They can think Ruby lives there, or one of the Revolutionary War guys has set up camp upstairs.

I hit the library next and type up a letter on one of the school computers and then sit in the corner couches for a little while and look over Cecil van Gunder's book. I've thought about keeping it or even passing it along to Jade, but that isn't exactly fair to good old Cecil. I can't imagine that *The Ghost of Wells Farm* has ever hit the best-seller list. And besides that, this way some other kid can find it and think he's the first one to notice its green-gray spine in the stacks. I reshelve it and make sure I lock the library door behind me.

This morning, the tile floor of the locker area is still streaky with ammonia, and I feel embarrassed walking across it. The cleaning crew must see us as rich punks making their job even harder. But this is the last time I'm going to cause them any trouble. Instead I'm unleashing a whole tornado of trouble onto campus. *Sancio* is only three lockers down from *Simon*. I can stand between them and reach both Soma's and my lockers at the same time.

I unclasp the chain around my neck and surprise myself with how different my bare neck feels after wearing the key for a week or two. It makes me wonder how long my dad kept wearing his dog tags after he came home from the service. The key slides down off the chain into the palm of my hand. I set the chain down and put the key in an envelope I snagged from Ethan's kitchen table — one of those small manila kinds that's used to pack drugs in. I wonder for a second if that's a giveaway — if Soma will recognize it. But it's the type of envelope you can buy by the hundreds at Staples, and it doesn't smell like weed or anything.

I fold the note I typed in the library and tuck it inside the envelope. Once I seal it, I hold it up to the light to see if the key's outline is visible through the thick paper. It just looks like a plain old envelope that the orthodontist sends those tiny rubber bands home in. I picture Soma's face when he swings open his locker and sees it taped inside the metal door. He'll tear it off and weigh it in his hand for a second, guessing at what's inside. It feels like a regular old key, but maybe at first he'll think it's a bunch of coins or some kind of medallion. It'll remind him of when he was a little kid and wanted to grow up to be a pirate. For a second, he'll think he's found a treasure. And he won't be wrong.

So that's done. My mother's silver chain winks on the blue tiled floor and it takes me a little bit to get it fastened again. It's sort of delicate and looks more like a necklace without the heavy key straining the silver links. I don't care. I'll keep it on for a little while longer.

Soma keeps his locker rigged just like I do — with a pencil so he doesn't really need to work the combination to open it. And that makes delivery simple enough. At first it's even a little disappointing because it means I don't have to stand there with my ear to the door listening for the click of the correct numbers. I step toward it and open the locker — nothing particularly covert or Navy SEAL about that. I take the Scotch tape from my backpack and the SOMA SANCIO tag that I printed out. Stick the label across the envelope and tape it up so that it's eye level.

It looks professional. That's what I'll tell Verlando when he asks me my career goals. *Sir, lately my experiences have led me to believe that I'd make a top-notch assassin.* Probably there's a summer program he'll have me apply to or something. Even the note is a work of genius: *The Caramoor Academy Secret Order of the Key has chosen you as this year's Ambassador to the Ghosts of the Old Homestead. Only you may hold the key. Only you may use the key and you alone shall decide when and on whom the key shall be next bestowed. Your reputation for mischief and imagination precedes you. We expect to see you honor our benevolence with timely acts of chaos and rebellion on the Caramoor campus. Prove everything. Tell no one.*

Soma's going to eat that crap up. And he'll consider telling me. I know he will. He'll creak open each door in Ainsley House and see the dark corridors yawning on either side and he'll want to call me, just like I wanted to call him. He'll weigh having the whole place open up only for him against sharing each newly accessed room with me. Or he'll balance there being two of us in the middle of the night against hurting me with the fact I wasn't the one chosen.

Just like Ethan probably heard me run out the door and down the porch steps the morning my mom died, and I'm going to have to believe that his first instinct was to stop me and make sure I told her good-bye. That as distant and cold as he might have seemed, Ethan was only following some rules he found and felt he had to hold on to. And that's how it still is with him. I have to make myself believe that when he heard us leave earlier tonight, even then he wanted to stop me. That he'll feel something when he sees the blankets folded up neatly on his shabby couch. I take out the pencil from the bottom and slam Soma's locker shut. That way, there's no chance of changing my mind.

I grab my backpack and head out the front door of Ainsley. I leave it unlocked, but not open.

Later on today, Soma's going to open up his locker and find a slim yellow envelope with his name printed across it. Inside will be a set of rules and the key. I know that, for the next year or so, he'll think about calling me every night he spends on the dark grounds of Caramoor. Maybe he'll lean toward telling me, but he won't. The key will be a secret that Soma keeps for himself. I'll never tell him that I know he's keeping it.

I guess it'll be like those arching red letters scrawled across the roof of the field house. *Come home.* Unless Caramoor goes back onto someone's flight plan, no one's going to know they're up there. Like the parenting books I know my father's reading late at night when the light's still bright under his door. Or the shabby steps of Ethan's new, unnumbered address. All those secrets I stop myself from saying out loud. But I'll know. And that will be enough for now.